■ 国家级一流本科课程"英国文学史及作品选读"建设成果
■ 上海高校市级一流本科课程"英国文学史及作品选读"、"美国文学史及作品选读"建设成果
■ 上海海事大学规划教材项目

英美文学赏析与思辨

BRITISH AND AMERICAN LITERATURE: APPRECIATION AND CRITICAL THINKING

郭海霞 / 编著

东南大学出版社
SOUTHEAST UNIVERSITY PRESS
·南京·

内容提要

本教材分为英国文学和美国文学两部分，较为全面且扼要地介绍了各时期主要英美文学知识、社会背景、文学流派及其特点，各时期代表作家的创作思想、人物刻画和写作风格，以及不同文学体裁的语言特点及代表作品的主题思想等。

本教材注重课程思政元素的提炼及呈现，通过主题探究，以时代性素材激发学习者的学习兴趣，最终达到价值塑造、知识传授和能力培养的目的。

本教材积极实践新文科融合创新的理念，注重历史、哲学、政治、经济、社会、伦理及理、工、农、医等跨学科知识的融入，以全面拓展学习者的综合素质。

图书在版编目（CIP）数据

英美文学赏析与思辨 / 郭海霞编著. --南京：东南大学出版社，2025. 3. --ISBN 978-7-5766-1692-7

Ⅰ. I561.06; I712.06

中国国家版本馆 CIP 数据核字第 2024ZV7332 号

责任编辑：刘　坚（635353748@qq.com）　　责任校对：张万莹
封面设计：王　玥　　责任印制：周荣虎

British and American Literature: Appreciation and Critical Thinking

英美文学赏析与思辨　Yingmei Wenxue Shangxi Yu Sibian

编　　著	郭海霞
出版发行	东南大学出版社
出 版 人	白云飞
社　　址	南京市四牌楼2号（邮编：210096　电话：025-83793330）
经　　销	全国各地新华书店
印　　刷	广东虎彩云印刷有限公司
开　　本	787 mm×1092 mm　1/16
印　　张	22.25
字　　数	560千字
版　　次	2025年3月第1版
印　　次	2025年3月第1次印刷
书　　号	ISBN 978-7-5766-1692-7
定　　价	59.00元

本社图书若有印装质量问题，请直接与营销部调换。电话（传真）：025-83791830

前言
PREFACE

科学越来越进步,科技越来越发达,而人们是否感觉越来越幸福?生活里无法言说的感触与情绪,或许在文学的世界里才能够得以释放。摇摇欲坠的自我和空虚的生活如何去应对?如何摆脱自己身上的噩梦?在压抑的世界里如何生存?文学能够触及这些问题,它提供了一个广阔的精神空间,也许它无法提供鲜明的答案,但是它会促使你去思考和辨别。

英美文学是世界文学宝库中的一颗璀璨明珠,承担着文明的传承与交流,世界文明体系的解读与构建,在帮助英语类专业学生了解英美文化,提升外语水平和跨文化交际能力,培养学习者正确的世界观、人生观、价值观、中国情怀和国际视野等方面起着重要的作用。亚里士多德说文学比历史更真实。阅读外国文学名著是不同国家和民族相互了解和沟通的最好方式。研习外国文学是一次次精神上的往返之旅,我们在本土文化与外族文化之间穿梭,不知不觉完成了一次次旅程。

《英美文学赏析与思辨》的主要内容分为英国文学和美国文学两个部分,将英国文学和美国文学按文学史的时间顺序编排,浓缩性地涵盖了基本文学常识、文学术语、概念、思潮、流派、代表作家及其经典作品等。

教材内容全面,凸显经典。通过对本教材的学习,学习者可以比较全面地了解各时期的主要英美文学知识、社会背景、文学流派及其特点;通晓各时期的代表作家的创作思想、人物刻画和写作风格;欣赏并体会经典诗歌、小说和戏剧等的语言特点以及主要代表作品的主题思想。

教材注重课程思政元素的提炼与呈现,以中国特色、中国文学和中国文化等元素增强文化自信,以时代性素材激发学习者学习兴趣,最终达到价值塑造、知识传授和能力培养三位一体的教学目的。教材还结合当今我国的海洋强国、航运强国和海洋命运共同体战略和意识,特别选取英美海洋文学的代表性小说,如《鲁滨逊漂流记》《老人与海》和《白鲸》等作为其中的重要内容。

教材积极实践新文科融合创新的理念,注重历史、哲学、政治、经济、社会、伦理、心理以及理、工、农、医等跨学科知识的融入,提高学习者的思辨能力和跨文化交际能力。教材的编写体例和板块包括：作者简介、作品简介、作品选文、注释、主题探究、价值引领、文化延展、中西比较、问题讨论等。

　　为了方便学生和教师的使用，本教材配有电子版和视频版教学参考资料。只需扫描章节中所附的二维码便可获得。

　　本书的编写和出版得到了上海海事大学2022年本科教学建设项目"规划教材"的资助，特此致谢。在本教材编写的过程中还得到了许多老师和研究生们的支持和帮助，在此对刘春芳、穆从军、冯延群、夏晓柳、金冰雪、刘家琪、章芝妍、陈天慧、刘庭秀、蔡书夏、张骋力、王彩伦、崔正国等老师和同学表示诚挚的感谢！东南大学出版社的刘坚老师为本教材的出版提供了大量的建议和帮助，若无他的专业眼光、学术功力，以及事无巨细的安排，教材的出版绝无可能，在这里对他表示深深的感谢！

　　希望通过英美文学的学习，我们每个人能够做到"不以区分中西为心魔，不以新旧贴标签，养世界之眼光，涵广阔之态度"。

　　让我们开始英美文学的旅程吧！

目录

CONTENTS

Part Ⅰ British Literature

Unit 1 Early and Medieval English Literature / 003
Geoffery Chaucer: *The Canterbury Tales*

Unit 2 The English Renaissance / 007
William Shakespeare: "Sonnet 18"; *Othello*

Unit 3 The Period of the English Bourgeois Revolution / 012
John Donne: "Death, Be not Proud"; "Song"

Unit 4 The Eighteenth Century: the Enlightenment and Classicism / 018
Daniel Defoe: *Robinson Crusoe*

Unit 5 Sentimentalism and Pre-Romanticism in Poetry / 027
William Blake: "The Sick Rose"; "London"
Robert Burns: "A Red, Red Rose"

Unit 6 Romanticism / 036
William Wordsworth: "My Heart Leaps Up"
John Keats: "To Autumn"

Unit 7 Victorian Age (Ⅰ): English Critical Realism / 043
Charles Dickens: *Oliver Twist*

Unit 8 Victorian Age (Ⅱ): Poets of the Mid and Late 19th Century / 052
Robert Browning: "My Last Duchess"

Unit 9 Victorian Age (Ⅲ): Thomas Hardy & Bernard Shaw / 058
Thomas Hardy: *Tess of the D'Urbervilles*
Bernard Shaw: *Mrs. Warren's Profession*

Unit 10 Some Women Novelists / 072
Jane Austen: *Pride and Prejudice*
Charlotte Brontë: *Jane Eyre*

Unit 11 Modernism in Poetry / 085
W. B. Yeats: "When You Are Old"

Unit 12   T. S. Eliot: "The Love Song of J. Alfred Prufrock"
Unit 12   Modernism in Fiction (Ⅰ): Katherine Mansfield & Virginia Woolf / 097
         Katherine Mansfield: "The Garden Party"
         Virginia Woolf: "The Mark on the Wall"; *Mrs. Dalloway*
Unit 13   Modernism in Fiction (Ⅱ): James Joyce & D. H. Lawrence / 121
         James Joyce: "A Little Cloud"
         D. H. Lawrence: *Sons & Lovers*
Unit 14   Poets after the Second World War (Contemporary Poets) / 136
         W. H. Auden: "As I Walked Out One Evening"
         Philip Larkin: "Toads"
Unit 15   Novelists after the Second World War (Contemporary Novelists) / 145
         Doris Lessing: *The Golden Notebook*
         Kazuo Ishiguro: *An Artist of the Floating World*
Unit 16   Despair and Absurdity in Contemporary English Drama / 155
         Samuel Beckett: *Waiting for Godot*

Part Ⅱ   American Literature

Unit 17   Colonial America / 159
         Anne Bradstreet: "To My Dear and Loving Husband"
Unit 18   American Romanticism: / 163
         Washington Irving: "Rip Van Winkle"
Unit 19   New England Transcendentalism / 181
         Ralph Waldo Emerson: *Nature*
Unit 20   Nathaniel Hawthorne & Herman Melville / 186
         Nathaniel Hawthorne: "The Minister's Black Veil"; *The Scarlet Letter*
         Herman Melville: *Moby Dick*
Unit 21   Edgar Allan Poe / 202
         Edgar Allan Poe: "The Raven"; "The Fall of the House of Usher"
Unit 22   Walt Whitman & Emily Dickinson / 209
         Walt Whitman: "Song of Myself"
         Emily Dickinson: "Success"; "I'm Nobody! Who Are You?"
Unit 23   The Age of Realism / 218
         Mark Twain: *The Adventures of Tom Sawyer*
         Kate Chopin: "A Pair of Stockings"

Unit 24	American Naturalism / 233	

Unit 24 American Naturalism / 233
Stephen Crane: *The Red Badge of Courage*
Theodore Dreiser: *Sister Carrie*

Unit 25 Imagism / 252
E. E. Cummings: "r-p-o-p-h-e-s-s-a-g-r"; [in Just-]

Unit 26 Modern Fiction (Ⅰ) / 257
Sherwood Anderson: "Paper Pills";
F. Scott Fitzgerald: *The Great Gatsby*

Unit 27 Modern Fiction (Ⅱ) / 270
Ernest Hemingway: *A Farewell to Arms*; *The Old Man and the Sea*;
"A Clean, Well-Lighted Place"; "Hills like White Elephants"

Unit 28 Modern Fiction (Ⅲ) / 301
William Faulkner: "A Rose for Emily"

Unit 29 Contemporary Poets / 312
Wallace Stevens: "The Emperor of Ice-Cream"
Robert Frost: "The Road Not Taken"

Unit 30 American Drama / 318
Tennessee Williams: *A Streetcar Named Desire*

Unit 31 Black American Literature / 332
Toni Morrison: *Beloved*

Unit 32 Chinese American literature / 340
Amy Tan: *The Joy Luck Club*

Part I
British Literature

Unit 1
Early and Medieval English Literature

Geoffrey Chaucer: *The Canterbury Tales*
▽

作者简介 (Introduction to the Author)

Geoffrey Chaucer (about 1340—1400) is the founder of English poetry and wrote the unfinished work, *The Canterbury Tales*. It is considered one of the greatest poetic works in English. Geoffrey Chaucer was born circa 1340 in London, England. Chaucer's family was of the bourgeois class. They descended from an affluent family who made their money in the London wine trade. According to some sources, Chaucer's father, John, carried on the family wine business. In 1357 Chaucer became a public servant to Countess Elizabeth of Ulster. He continued to work as a public servant to the British court throughout his lifetime. *The Canterbury Tales* became his best known and most acclaimed work. In this professional life, Chaucer was able to travel from his home in England to France and Italy. There, he not only had the chance to read Italian and French literature, but possibly, even to meet Boccaccio, whose *Decameron*—a collection of tales told by Italian nobility holed up in a country house to escape the plague ravaging their city—may have inspired the frame story of *The Canterbury Tales*. He died on October 25, 1400 in London, England and was the first to be buried in Westminster Abbey's Poet's Corner. His contribution to English poetry lies chiefly in the fact that he introduced from France the rhymed stanza of various types, especially the rhymed couplet of 5 accents in iambic meter (the heroic couplet) to English poetry. Though drawing influence from French, Italian and Latin models, he is the first great poet who wrote almost exclusively in the English language.

作品简介 (Introduction to the Work)

The Canterbury Tales tells the story of a group of pilgrims (fancy word for travelers) on their way to Canterbury, who engage in a tale-telling contest to pass the time. Besides watching the interactions between the characters, we get to read 24 of the tales the pilgrims tell. Geoffrey Chaucer likely wrote *The Canterbury Tales* in the late 1380s and early 1390s, after his retirement from life as a civil servant. Chaucer's decision to write in his country's language, English, rather than in the Latin of so many of his educated colleagues, was a big break with learned tradition. But the risk paid off: we know *The Canterbury Tales* was enormously popular because so many more manuscripts of the tales survive than of almost any other work of this time period. *The Canterbury Tales* were still going strong when the first printers made their way to England, and William Caxton published the first printed version of *The Canterbury Tales* in 1476.

The General Prologue to *The Canterbury Tales* and the interactions between the pilgrims that occur in between the tales, then, form a story of their own. The General Prologue begins with a description of how April's showers cause flowers to bloom, crops to grow, birds to sing, and people to want to make pilgrimages—journeys to holy places. In England, people especially like to go to Canterbury to pray at the shrine of a holy saint who healed them when they were sick.

作品选文 (Selected Reading)

The Canterbury Tales

The General Prologue

(Excerpt)

When April with his showers sweet with fruit
The drought of March has pierced unto the root
And bathed each vein with liquor that has power
To generate therein and sire the flower;
When Zephyr[1] also has, with his sweet breath,
Quickened again, in every holt[2] and heath,
The tender shoots and buds, and the young sun
Into the Ram[3] one half his course has run,
And many little birds make melody
That sleep through all the night with open eye
(So Nature pricks them on to ramp and rage)—
Then do folk long to go on pilgrimage,
And palmers[4] to go seeking out strange strands[5],
To distant shrines well known in sundry lands.
And specially from every shire's end[6]
Of England they to Canterbury wend[7],
The holy blessed martyr[8] there to seek
Who helped them when they lay so ill and weak.

（Some spelling modernized.）

作品译文(扫码阅读)

注释（Notes）

1. Zephyrus：the west wind（西风）；在英国，春天从大西洋上吹来的西风是温暖和煦的。

2. holt：即 grove（林地）。

3. ram：one of the astrological signs in the Zodiac（白羊宫），古代用于解释天体运动的黄道带十二宫之一。太阳经过白羊宫时正值春天，所以前文称太阳为 the young sun。

4. palmers：手执棕榈叶的朝圣者；香客。

5. strange strands：异国他乡。

6. from every shire's end：从四面八方。

7. wend：古体，go。

8. martyr：殉道者。这里指坎特伯雷大主教托马斯·阿·贝克特。他竭力反对亨利二世国王削弱教会的权力，因而遭到暗杀。死后葬于坎特伯雷大教堂，被尊为圣徒，供人朝拜。

主题探究（Themes）

（扫码阅读）

文化延展（Cultural Extension）

2010 年诺贝尔文学奖得主马里奥·巴尔加斯·略萨说："若是没有了文学，人就丧失了人之为人的东西。"学习文学会使你成为一个有温度、有情趣、会思考的人。人与动物的区别就在于人性之中对形而上事物的追寻和探索，而动物则不具备这样的天资。人对精神性事物的迷恋不是出于任何目的和功利，只有人才具有这样的天

赋和渴望。愿我们每个人都成为"精神上的享乐主义者"(an intellectual epicure)①

同时,文学在民族与国家想象和构成中起着重要作用,而民族与国家影响着文学书写和叙事所采取的立场,国家、民族性嵌入文学之中,就如心脏深扎于人体之中。因此,它们之间如影随形,文学成为民族与国家的表征,民族和国家借文学"为自己建立骄傲与后盾,亦以此对抗具有敌意的环境"②,正如巴尔扎克所说,小说是一个民族的秘史。

问题讨论(Questions for Discussion)

1. Since *The Canterbury Tales* is a story about a storytelling competition, many of the questions it asks are about stories: What makes for a good story? Why do we tell stories? Why should we tell stories?

2. What are the different definitions of what makes a good story in *The Canterbury Tales*?

3. If you are asked to compare Chaucer with any other of the European authors you happen to be familiar with of more or less the same period, how does Geoffrey Chaucer differ from him or her?

4. What is the most outstanding feature in terms of the poetic style Chaucer has demonstrated in the General Prologue?

5. How is the setting of the tales described? With such a setting, could you predict the tone of the tales that are to follow?

6. Many of the characters, but especially the Host, try to draw morals from the stories they tell and hear. How do the morals they draw match up with your understanding of the story? What might this say about the characters as readers, or about stories more generally?

(请扫码观看视频 Feudal England & *The Canterbury Tales*)

---

① Charlotte Brontë. *Jane Eyre*[M]. Ware, Hertfordshire: Wordsworth Editions Limited, 1999: 277.
② 孙红卫. 民族[M]. 北京:外语教学与研究出版社,2019:72.

Unit 2
The English Renaissance

William Shakespeare: "Sonnet 18"; *Othello*
▽

作者简介 (Introduction to the Author)

William Shakespeare (1564—1616) is the greatest of all Elizabethan dramatists and poets. He remains the most influential writer in English language. Shakespeare was baptized on 23 April 1564 in Stratford-upon-Avon. Stratford was one of the most beautiful and historic places in rural England which had an impact on Shakespeare. His father was a successful glover and rose to be bailiff. Shakespeare was probably educated at the grammar school in Stratford. At about 14, he left school due to his father's bankruptcy. He married Anne at 18 and they raised three children. Shakespeare came to London around 1586 and in turn worked as a horsekeeper, stage-boy and actor. He also wrote plays at that time. His three parts of *Henry* VI were on the stage and made a big impression in London in 1592. One of the University Wits once attacked him as "upstart crow". According to the customs in 16th century England, he sought the Earl of Southampton's patronage and dedicated his poems to the young lord. Throughout his life, he wrote 37 plays and 154 sonnets. He borrowed his plots widely from legends, history and romances by his contemporaries. Shakespeare produced most of his known works between 1590 and 1613. He died in 1616. Shakespeare expanded the dramatic potential of characterisation, plot, language, and genre. His plays are the mirrors of his age, reflecting the contradictions of that time. And they break the rules of the classical unities of time, place and action. His use of language helps shape the standard English and his expressions are still recognizable in today's English speech. Considering his contributions to sonnet, it is also called Shakespearean sonnet.

Sonnet 18

作品简介 (Introduction to the Work)

"Shall I compare thee to a summer's day?" is one of William Shakespeare's most beautiful pieces of poetry. This sonnet is also referred to as "Sonnet 18". It was written in the 1590s and was published in his collection of sonnets in 1609. In this collection, there are a total of 154 sonnets. These themes of these sonnets are usually love, beauty, time, and jealousy to mortality and infidelity. As the number of this sonnet is eighteenth, it is clear that "Sonnet 18" discusses the themes of mortality, the value of poetry, and the attainment of immortality. Praising an anonymous person (usually believed to be a young man), the poem tries out a number of clichéd metaphors and similes, and finds each of them wanting. The speaker reflects on how every worldly entity is mortal. However, he is going to use his poetry against this enemy and win immortality for his beloved by canonizing him in his poetry. The rhyme scheme of the sonnet is ababcdcdefefgg and the words used in the sonnet are straightforward and ordinary. The tone of the sonnet is romantic and full of flattery. The speaker speaks of his beloved beauty as there is no match for it. In the end, it develops a highly original and unusual simile: the young man's beauty can be best expressed by comparing him to the poem itself.

作品选文 (Selected Reading)

Sonnet 18

Shall I compare thee[1] to a summer's day?
Thou[2] art[3] more lovely and more temperate:
Rough winds do shake the darling buds of May,
And summer's lease[4] hath[5] all too short a date;

Sometime too hot the eye of heaven[6] shines,
And often is his gold complexion[7] dimm'd;
And every fair from fair sometime declines,
By chance, or nature's changing course untrimm'd;

But thy[8] eternal summer shall not fade,
Nor lose possession of that fair thou ow'st;
Nor shall Death brag thou wander'st in his shade,
When in eternal lines[9] to time thou grow'st.

So long as men can breathe, or eyes can see,
So long lives this[10] and this gives life to thee.

作品译文(扫码阅读)

注释（Notes）

1. thee：古体，you 的宾格，此处常认为是一位年轻男子。
2. thou：古体，you 的主格。
3. art：古体，are 的第二人称，第二人称为主语时，谓语要加上-t、-st 或-est。
4. lease：租期，这里指夏天持续的时间。
5. hath：古体，have 的第三人称，第三人称要加-th 而不是-s。
6. the eye of heaven：这里指夏天通红的太阳。
7. gold complexion：(太阳)的金色容颜。
8. thy：古体，you 的形容词性物主代词。
9. eternal lines：这里指永恒的诗歌艺术。
10. this：指这首诗，这整句话赞扬了诗歌的永恒流传性，点明主旨。

主题探究（Themes）

（扫码阅读）

文化延展（Cultural Extension）

  人文主义是文艺复兴时期新兴资产阶级反封建反教会斗争中形成的思想体系、世界观或思想武器，也是这一时期资产阶级进步文学的中心思想。它主张一切以人为本，反对神的权威，把人从中世纪的神学枷锁下解放出来。宣扬个性解放，追求现实人生幸福；追求自由平等，反对等级观念；崇尚理性，反对蒙昧。

  人文主义是文艺复兴的核心思想，是新兴资产阶级反封建的社会思潮，也是资产阶级人道主义的最初形式。它肯定人性和人的价值，要求享受人世的欢乐，要求人的个性解放和自由平等，推崇人的感性经验和理性思维。而作为历史概念的人文主义，在欧洲历史和哲学史中则主要被用来描述 14 到 16 世纪间较中世纪比较先进的思想。历史学家一般将这段时间里文化和社会上的变化称为文艺复兴，而将教育上的变化运动称为人文主义。

  彼特拉克（Francesco Petrarca，1304—1374），意大利诗人。1304 年 7 月 20 日生于阿雷佐城，1374 年 7 月 19 日卒于阿尔夸。父亲是佛罗伦萨的望族、律师。他自幼随父亲流亡法国，后攻读法学。父亲逝世后专心从事文学活动，并周游欧洲各国。他还当过神甫，有机会出入教会、宫廷，观察生活，追求知识，最早提出以"人学"对抗

"神学",被称为"人文主义之父"。

问题讨论(Questions for Discussion)

1. Why "Sonnet 18" is probably the most famous and widely read of 154 sonnets of Shakespeare?

2. Who is "thee"?

3. When reading poetry, you may assume your role as an archaeologist and take some measurements, for example, what's the weather like?

4. What do you hear? How does the poem sound?

5. Who is the speaker, can she or he read minds, and, more importantly, can we trust her or him?

6. Does this poem necessarily keep living so long as humans keep breathing? Is the speaker right?

Othello

作品简介(Introduction to the Work)

Othello, in full *Othello, the Moor of Venice*, tragedy in five acts by William Shakespeare, written in 1603—1604 and published in 1622 in a quarto edition from a transcript of an authorial manuscript. The play is set in motion when Othello, a heroic black general in the service of Venice, appoints Cassio and not Iago as his chief lieutenant. Jealous of Othello's success and envious of Cassio, Iago plots Othello's downfall by falsely implicating Othello's wife, Desdemona, and Cassio in a love affair. With the unwitting aid of Emilia, his wife, and the willing help of Roderigo, a fellow malcontent, Iago carries out his plan. Iago manipulates Othello into believing his wife Desdemona is unfaithful, stirring Othello's jealousy. Othello allows jealousy to consume him, murders Desdemona, and then kills himself. In *Othello*, William Shakespeare creates a powerful drama from a marriage between the exotic Moor Othello and the Venetian lady Desdemona that begins with elopement and mutual devotion and ends with jealous rage and death. Shakespeare builds many differences into his hero and heroine, including race, age, and cultural background. Yet most readers and audiences believe the couple's strong love would overcome these differences were it not for Iago, who sets out to destroy Othello. Iago's false insinuations about Desdemona's infidelity draw Othello into his schemes, and Desdemona is subjected to Othello's horrifying verbal and physical assaults.

ACT Ⅰ. SCENE Ⅰ.: In the streets of Venice, Iago tells Roderigo of his hatred for

Othello, who has given Cassio the lieutenancy that Iago wanted and has made Iago a mere ensign. At Iago's suggestion, he and Roderigo, a former suitor to Desdemona, awake Desdemona's father Brabantio to tell him that Desdemona has eloped with Othello. This news enrages Brabantio, who organizes an armed band to search out Othello.

ACT V. SCENE Ⅱ.: Desdemona is asleep in bed when Othello enters. He kisses her and wakes her and once again charges her with infidelity. Over her protests of innocence, he smothers her. When Emilia comes to tell Othello about the violence in the streets, he acknowledges the killing, telling her that Iago had informed him of Desdemona's infidelity. Emilia's cries of "Murder" bring Iago, Montano, and Gratiano. Iago, under pressure, admits accusing Desdemona. When Emilia discloses the truth about the handkerchief, Othello tries, unsuccessfully, to kill Iago, and Iago kills Emilia. Othello, aware of his enormous error in regarding Desdemona as unfaithful, stabs himself, falling dead on the bed beside Emilia and Desdemona. Iago is taken away to be tortured and killed.

作品选文 (Selected Reading)

(扫码阅读)

Othello

(Excerpt)

(请扫码观看视频"Sonnet 18"和 *Othello*)

Unit 3
The Period of the English Bourgeois Revolution

John Donne: "Death, Be not Proud"; "Song"

作者简介 (Introduction to the Author)

John Donne (1572—1631) is the leading figure of the metaphysical school. He is also famous for his sermons. *The Songs and Sonnets* is usually seen as his best-known lyrics. Donne was born in a Catholic family circa 1572. When he was four years old, his father died and later his mother married a wealthy widower. He studied first at Oxford, and then at Cambridge and later studied law in London. On account of Queen Elizabeth's opposition to heretic, Donne gave up his Catholic faith and became an Anglican. He spent most of his money on women, pastimes and travel. In his spare time, he travelled to Europe and visited many countries. He also read a lot of books in different areas such as theology, medicine, law and classical literature. In 1601, Donne secretly married 17-year-old Anne More who was Egerton's niece, which ruined his career and put him in jail. In 1615, he became chaplain to the king. In 1621, he was appointed as Dean of St. Paul's. During that time, he wrote many great sermons and religious poems. Donne died in 1631 and was buried in old St. Paul's Cathedral. Donne made a bold attempt on imagery, rhythm and stanza of poems. One of the striking feature is his use of conceit. His works are witty, employing paradoxes, puns, and subtle analogies. In his poetry, sensuality is blended with philosophy, passion with intellect. Without doubt, his originality in poetry gained recognition. His works also influenced the late 20th century literature.

Death, Be not Proud

作品简介 (Introduction to the Work)

"Death, Be Not Proud", also called "Holy Sonnet 10", was written by the English poet and Christian cleric John Donne in 1609 and first published in 1633. The poem is a direct address to death, arguing that it is powerless because it acts merely as a "short sleep" between earthly living and the eternal afterlife—in essence, death is nothing to fear. The sonnet written mostly in iambic pentameter and is part of a series known as Donne's "Holy Sonnets" (or "Divine Meditations"/ "Divine Sonnets"). In keeping with these other poems, "Holy Sonnet 10" is a devotional lyric that looks at life's biggest questions in the context of Donne's religious beliefs.

In this sonnet, John Donne divests death of its powers and emphasize that man, though fated to die, is more powerful than death itself. The poem paints a picture of death as prideful—vain, even—and works to deflate death's importance by arguing firstly that death is nothing more than a rest, and secondly that following this rest comes the afterlife, which contradicts death's aim of bringing about a final end. With death's powerlessness proven by the end of the poem, it is death itself, not man, who is going to die.

作品选文 (Selected Reading)

Death, Be not Proud

Death[1], be not proud, though some have called thee
Mighty and dreadful, for thou art not so[2];
For those whom thou think'st thou dost overthrow[3]
Die not, poor Death, nor yet canst[4] thou kill me.
From rest and sleep, which but thy pictures[5] be,
Much pleasure; then from thee much more must flow,
And soonest our best men with thee do go,
Rest of their bones, and soul's delivery[6].

Thou art slave[7] to fate[8], chance[9], kings, and desperate men,
And dost with poison, war, and sickness dwell[10],
And poppy or charms can make us sleep as well
And better than thy stroke; why swell'st thou then?
One short sleep past, we wake eternally[11]
And death shall be no more; Death, thou shalt die.

作品译文(扫码阅读)

注释 (Notes)

1. Death：这里用了呼语(apostrophe)的修辞手法,直接和死亡对话。

2. so：指人们通常认为的 mighty and dreadful。
3. overthrow：kill
4. canst：can 的古体第二人称形式。
5. pictures：死亡给人留下的形象。
6. delivery：基督教认为好人死后会上伊甸园，这里指灵魂回归到伊甸园的过程。
7. slave：死亡并不能主动让人去死，而是只能服从于下述的情况。
8. fate：指人最终会老死。
9. chance：指人因为意外死亡。
10. with…dwell：死亡和毒药、战争、疾病这种邪恶的事物为伍。
11. One short sleep past, we wake eternally：人死后等耶稣召集善良的基督徒，他们就可以重返伊甸园，在那里永远快乐地生活下去。

主题探究（Themes）

（扫码阅读）

价值引领（Value Guidance）

死亡这个话题历来讳莫如深，传统的中国式"回避式死亡教育"中，家长们会说"去很远的地方旅行了"，对"死亡"的概念进行修饰和模糊，我们用"离开"和"沉睡"来形容"死亡"，只因它太过沉重，可如果过度美化或故意避而不谈，会导致我们认为，去世只是短暂的离开，因此我们学不会好好告别；又或许会造成死亡焦虑，让我们感觉孤独、悲伤。因为对于生命的终结，我们一无所知，也无计可施。我们在害怕些什么？带不走的人、工作、财产等等吗？没有人准备好了死亡，没有人希望生活会变成那样。但其实，既然有"生命"的开始，那就逻辑地意味着"死亡"的必然，我们每个人都终将归于泥土，就像《黑客帝国》里说的："Everything that has a beginning has an end."

试着从死亡的角度来看看我们的一生，回想一位临走的逝者，他们衣着整洁，面带微笑，安详而舒适地沉睡，仿佛做着这辈子最安宁的梦，那里生长着所有幸福的记忆。海德格尔说人是向死而生的存在。死亡是人活着的一部分，只有把死亡纳入活里面，人生才是一个整体。没有对死亡的意识，人也就不知道如何去积极地生活，因此，与其说"不知生，焉知死"，倒不如说"不知死，焉知生"。死亡让我们对生活的意义和价值在本质上有所思考,教会我们更好地"向死而生"。让我们活在当下,珍惜当下,就像印度诗人泰戈尔的诗中所写:生如夏花之绚烂,死如秋叶之静美(Born as the bright summer flowers / Died as the quiet beauty of autumn leaves)。

问题讨论(Questions for Discussion)

1. Does the speaker sound like a cocky trash-talker, or is he just trying to talk himself out of being afraid? Could it be both?

2. Does the poem seem to have any setting whatsoever? Is there any way to visualize what's going on?

3. What do you think of the form, the rhyme and the metre of the poem?

4. Does the comparison between death and sleep make sense outside of a theological context? Is the speaker justified in thinking that death will bring pleasure?

5. There are many symbols in the poem. Can you list some? And which is the most obvious one?

6. Do you think it's truly possible to welcome the experience of death in the way that the poem seems to suggest? Or, is everyone afraid of death, and some people just pretend not to be? Why are soldiers more willing to put their lives on the line?

Song

作品简介 (Introduction to the Work)

"Song", often known by its first line, "Go and catch a falling star", is an unusual poem among John Donne's work in several ways. It is a three-stanza poem that is separated into sets of nine lines. The lines follow a consistent rhyme scheme, conforming to the pattern of ababccddd. The lines also stick to a syllable pattern that changes within the different sets of rhyme. This is a very unusual pattern that works best if read aloud. The fact that Donne titled this piece "Song" makes it clear that it was meant to be read, or sung. It was published in 1633, is a fantastical take on a traditional and misogynistic theme: women's supposedly inevitable infidelity.

The speaker begins by commanding his listener to perform a series of impossible tasks, with the implication being that female honesty or faithfulness is in the same realm of impossibility. The other tasks the speaker commands are more abstract and wistful. Expanding on this idea, the speaker says that even if his listener spent an entire lifetime searching for a faithful woman, he wouldn't find her. To conclude, a speaker tells a listener that he can look the whole world over, but finding a woman who'll be faithful to him is about as unlikely as finding a mermaid or meeting the devil.

作品选文 (Selected Reading)

Song

Go and catch a falling star,
Get with child a mandrake root[1],
Tell me where all past years are,
Or who cleft the devil's foot[2],
Teach me to hear mermaids[3] singing,
Or to keep off envy's stinging,
　　And find
　　What wind
Serves to advance an honest mind.

If thou be'st born to strange sights,
Things invisible to see,
Ride ten thousand days and nights,
Till age snow white hairs on thee,
Thou, when thou return'st, wilt tell me,
All strange wonders that befell thee,
　　And swear,
　　No where
Lives a woman true, and fair.

If thou find'st one, let me know,
Such a pilgrimage[4] were sweet;
Yet do not, I would not go,
Though at next door we might meet;
Though she were true, when you met her,
And last, till you write your letter,
　　Yet she
　　Will be
False[5], ere[6] I come, to two, or three.

作品译文(扫码阅读)

注释(Notes)

1. mandrake root:曼德拉草的根须形似男人,据说女子服用可以怀孕。
2. cleft the devil's foot:传说中魔鬼的脚状如羊蹄分叉。诗人问是何人劈开魔鬼的脚,这是无法回答的问题。
3. mermaids:美人鱼,古希腊神话中的海妖塞壬(Siren)。美人鱼的歌声会让人沉醉,美人鱼会趁机把人拖入海底,只有《荷马史诗》中的奥德修斯幸免于难。
4. pilgrimage:朝圣之路,指去见这位忠贞又美丽的女子。
5. false:not faithful or loyal
6. ere:before

主题探究(Themes)

(扫码阅读)

问题讨论(Questions for Discussion)

1. How do you like the form, rhyme and metre of this poem? Does John Donne follow the traditional form of lyric poems and sonnets prevalent during the Elizabethan period?
2. According to John Donne, he has totally distinct attitudes toward women. In this poem, what does the poet think of women?
3. There are many images in "Song". Could you classify them and explain what they suggest respectively?
4. Who is "thou"?
5. Do you agree with poet's opinion of women? Why?

Unit 4
The Eighteenth Century: the Enlightenment and Classicism

Daniel Defoe: *Robinson Crusoe*
▽

作者简介 (Introduction to the Author)

Daniel Defoe (1660—1731) can be seen as a jack of all trades. He is a writer, trader, soldier, journalist, pamphleteer and politician. His masterpiece *Robinson Crusoe*, published in 1719, is the precursor of English realistic novel. Defoe is also considered as the founder of English novel. Defoe was born in a Nonconformist family in London. His father was a butcher and tallow chandler. He was educated at dissenting school. After graduation, he traveled to Spain, Italy, France, Germany and so on as a merchant. In 1684, Defoe married the daughter of a merchant, receiving a large dowry. In his business life, there are a lot of ups and downs. Besides, he was an active participant in political activities and wrote many political tracts, which caused him problems with the authorities. In 1703, he was sent to prison because of his satire on Church of England. He founded *The Review of the Affairs of France and of all Europe* in 1704, relating to British politics. It was the first journal to discuss British politics independent from the control of the government. Defoe was also a prolific writer and produced hundreds of works, covering various areas. He lived a miserable life in later years and died in 1731. Defoe invented the image of adventurous bourgeois in *Robinson Crusoe* and the name of the protagonist thus entered the language. His works employed the first person narrative, thus creating a new way of writing. He emphasized individual experience and authenticity in his works, aiming to show people's real life.

作品简介 (Introduction to the Work)

The novel *Robinson Crusoe* tells the story of a young and impulsive Englishman that defies his parents' wishes and takes to the seas seeking adventure. The young Robinson Crusoe is shipwrecked and castaway on a remote tropical island for 28 years. More specifically, Defoe was likely inspired or influenced by the real-life adventures of Alexander Selkirk. Selkirk was a Scottish man who survived for four years stranded on an island in the south Pacific. His amazing story of survival spread widely after he returned to

Europe in 1711 (not long before Defoe published *Robinson Crusoe*). This classic tale of adventure features cannibals, captives, and mutineers, which is both a gripping tale and a sober wide-ranging reflection on ambition, self-reliance, civilization, and power.

In the novel, Crusoe describes how, as a headstrong young man, he ignored his family's advice and left his comfortable middle-class home in England to go to sea. His first experience on a ship nearly kills him, but he perseveres. Now several hundred pounds richer, he sails again for Africa but is captured by pirates and sold into slavery. He escapes and ends up in Brazil, where he acquires a plantation and prospers. Ambitious for more wealth, Crusoe makes a deal with merchants and other plantation owners to sail to Guinea, buy slaves, and return with them to Brazil. But he encounters a storm in the Caribbean, and his ship is nearly destroyed. Crusoe is the only survivor, washed up onto a desolate shore. He salvages what he can from the wreck and establishes a life on the island that consists of spiritual reflection and practical measures to survive. He carefully documents in a journal everything he does and experiences.

The story begins with Crusoe describing his early life in York, England. He eagerly wanted to venture out to sea, although both his parents urged him not to and tried to persuade him to stay home and lead a comfortable life. Despite his parents' warnings, Robinson left home and joined a ship to London without telling his parents.

作品选文 (Selected Reading)

Robinson Crusoe
(Excerpt)
Chapter 1 Start in Life

I was born in the year 1632, in the city of York, of a good family, though not of that country, my father being a foreigner of Bremen, who settled first at Hull. He got a good estate by merchandise, and leaving off his trade, lived afterwards at York, from whence he had married my mother, whose relations were named Robinson, a very good family in that country, and from whom I was called Robinson Kreutznaer; but, by the usual corruption of words in England, we are now called—so we call ourselves and write our name—Crusoe; and so my companions always called me.

I had two elder brothers, one of whom was lieutenant-colonel to an English regiment of foot in Flanders, formerly commanded by the famous Colonel Lockhart, and was killed at the battle near Dunkirk against the Spaniards. What became of my second brother I never knew, any more than my father or mother knew what became of me.

Being the third son of the family and not bred to any trade, my head began to be filled very early with rambling thoughts. My father, who was very ancient, had given me a competent share of learning, as far as house-education and a country free school generally go, and designed me for the law; but I would be satisfied with nothing but[1] going to sea; and my inclination to this led me so strongly against the will, nay, the commands of my father, and against all the entreaties and persuasions of my mother and other friends, that there seemed to be something fatal in that propensity of nature, tending directly to the life of misery which was to befall me.

My father, a wise and grave man, gave me serious and excellent counsel against what he foresaw was my design. He called me one morning into his chamber, where he was confined by the gout, and expostulated[2] very warmly with me upon this subject. He asked me what reasons, more than a mere wandering inclination, I had for leaving father's house and my native country, where I might be well introduced, and had a prospect of raising my fortune[3] by application and industry, with a life of ease and pleasure. He told me it was men of desperate fortunes on one hand, or of aspiring, superior fortunes on the other, who went abroad upon adventures, to rise by enterprise, and make themselves famous in undertakings of a nature out of the common road; that these things were all either too far above me or too far below me; that mine was the middle state, or what might be called the upper station of low life, which he had found, by long experience, was the best state in the world, the most suited to human happiness, not exposed to the miseries and hardships, the labour and sufferings of the mechanic part of mankind, and not embarrassed with the pride, luxury, ambition, and envy of the upper part of mankind. He told me I might judge of the happiness of this state by this one thing—viz.[4] that this was the state of life which all other people envied; that kings have frequently lamented the miserable consequence of being born to great things, and wished they had been placed in the middle of the two extremes, between the mean and the great; that the wise man gave his testimony to this, as the standard of felicity, when he prayed to have neither poverty nor riches.

He bade me observe it, and I should always find that the calamities of life were shared among the upper and lower part of mankind, but that the middle station had the fewest disasters, and was not exposed to so many vicissitudes as the higher or lower part of mankind; nay, they were not subjected to so many distempers and uneasinesses, either of body or mind, as those were who, by vicious living, luxury, and extravagances on the one hand, or by hard labour, want of necessaries, and mean or insufficient diet on the other hand, bring distemper upon themselves by the natural consequences of their way of living; that the middle station of life was calculated for all kind of virtue and all kind of enjoyments; that peace and plenty were the handmaids of a middle fortune; that temperance, moderation, quietness, health, society, all agreeable diversions, and all desirable pleasures, were the blessings attending the middle station of life; that this way men went silently and smoothly through the world, and comfortably out of it, not embarrassed with the labours of the hands or of the head[5], not sold to a life of slavery for daily bread, nor harassed with perplexed circumstances, which rob the soul of peace and the body of rest, nor enraged with the passion of envy, or the secret burning lust of ambition for great things; but, in easy circumstances, sliding gently through the world, and sensibly tasting the sweets of living, without the bitter; feeling that they are happy, and learning by every day's experience to know it more sensibly.

After this he pressed me earnestly, and in the most affectionate manner, not to play the young man, nor to precipitate myself into miseries which nature, and the station of life I was born in, seemed to have provided against; that I was under no necessity of seeking my bread; that he would do well for me, and endeavour to enter me fairly into the station of life which he had just been recommending to me; and that if I was not very easy and happy in the world, it must be my mere fate or fault that must hinder it; and that he should have nothing to answer for, having thus discharged his duty in warning me against measures which he knew would be to my hurt; in a word, that as he would do very kind things for me if I would stay and settle at home as he directed, so he would not have so much hand in my misfortunes as to give me any encouragement to go away; and to close all, he told me I had my elder brother for an example, to whom he had used the same earnest persuasions to keep him from going into the Low Country wars, but could not prevail, his young desires prompting him to run into the army, where he was killed; and though he said he would not cease to pray for me, yet he would venture to say to me, that if I did take this foolish step, God would not bless me, and I should have leisure hereafter to reflect upon having neglected his counsel when there might be none to assist in my recovery.

I observed in this last part of his discourse, which was truly prophetic, though I suppose my father did not know it to be so himself—I say, I observed the tears run down his face very plentifully, especially when he spoke of my brother who was killed; and that when he spoke of my having leisure to repent, and none to assist me, he was so moved that he broke off the discourse, and told me his heart was so full he could say no more to me[6].

I was sincerely affected with this discourse, and, indeed, who could be otherwise; and I resolved not to think of going abroad any more, but to settle at home according to my father's desire. But alas! a few days wore it all off; and, in short, to prevent any of my father's further importunities, in a few weeks after I resolved to run quite away from him. However, I did not act quite so hastily as the first heat of my resolution prompted; but I took my mother at a time when I thought her a little more pleasant than ordinary, and told her that my thoughts were so entirely bent upon seeing the world that I should never settle to anything with resolution enough to go through with it, and my father had better give me his consent than force me to go without it; that I was now eighteen years old, which was too late to go apprentice to a trade or clerk to an attorney; that I was sure if I did I should never serve out my time, but I should certainly run away from my master before my time was out, and go to sea; and if she would speak to my father to let me go one voyage abroad, if I came home again, and did not like it, I would go no more; and I would promise, by a double diligence, to recover the time that I had lost.

This put my mother into a great passion; she told me she knew it would be to no purpose to speak to my father upon any such subject; that he knew too well what was my interest to give his consent to anything so much for my hurt; and that she wondered how I could think of any such thing after the discourse I had had with my father, and such kind and tender expressions as she knew my father had used to me; and that, in short, if I would ruin myself, there was no help for me; but I might depend I should never have their consent to it; that for her part she would not have so much hand in my destruction; and I should never have it to say that my mother was willing when my father was not.

Though my mother refused to move it to my father, yet I heard afterwards that she reported all the discourse to him, and that my father, after showing a great concern at it, said to her, with a sigh, "That boy might be happy if he would stay at home; but if he goes abroad, he will be the most miserable wretch that ever was born: I can give no consent to it."

It was not till almost a year after this that I broke loose, though, in the meantime, I continued obstinately deaf to all proposals of settling to business, and frequently expostulated with my father and mother about their being so positively determined against what they knew my inclinations prompted me to. But being one day at Hull, where I went casually, and without any purpose of making an elopement at that time; but, I say, being there, and one of my companions being about to sail to London in his father's ship, and prompting me to go with them with the common allurement of seafaring men, that it should cost me nothing for my passage, I consulted neither father nor mother any more, nor so much as sent them word of it; but leaving them to hear of it as they might, without asking God's blessing or my father's, without any consideration of circumstances or consequences, and in an ill hour, God knows, on the 1st of September 1651, I went on board a ship bound for London. Never any young adventurer's misfortunes, I believe, began sooner, or continued longer than mine. The ship was no sooner out of the Humber than the wind began to blow and the sea to rise in a most frightful manner; and, as I had never been at sea before, I was most inexpressibly sick in body and terrified in mind. I began now seriously to reflect upon what I had done, and how justly I was overtaken by the judgment of Heaven for my wicked leaving my father's house, and abandoning my duty. All the good counsels of my parents, my father's tears and my mother's entreaties, came now fresh into my mind; and my conscience, which was not yet come to the pitch of hardness to which it has since, reproached me with the contempt of advice, and the breach of my duty to God and my father.

All this while the storm increased, and the sea went very high, though nothing like what I have seen many times since; no, nor what I saw a few days after; but it was enough to affect me then, who was but a young sailor, and had never known anything of the matter. I expected every wave would have swallowed us up, and that every time the ship fell down, as I thought it did, in the trough or hollow of the sea, we should never rise more; in this agony of mind, I made many vows and resolutions that if it would please God to spare my life in this one voyage, if ever I got once my foot upon dry land again, I would go directly home to my father, and never set it into a ship again while I lived; that I would take his advice, and never run myself into such miseries as these any more. Now I saw plainly the goodness of his observations about the middle station of life, how easy, how comfortably he had lived all his days, and never had been exposed to tempests at sea or troubles on shore; and I resolved that I would, like a true repenting prodigal, go home to my father.

These wise and sober thoughts continued all the while the storm lasted, and indeed some time after; but the next day the wind was abated, and the sea calmer, and I began to be a little inured to it; however, I was very grave for all that day, being also a little seasick still; but towards night the weather cleared up, the wind was quite over, and a charming fine evening followed; the sun went down perfectly clear, and rose so the next morning; and having little or no wind, and a smooth sea, the sun shining upon it, the sight was, as I thought, the most delightful that ever I saw.

I had slept well in the night, and was now no more sea-sick, but very cheerful, looking with wonder upon the sea that was so rough and terrible the day before, and could be so calm and so pleasant in so little a time after. And now, lest my good resolutions should continue, my companion, who had enticed me away, comes to me; "Well, Bob," says he, clapping me upon the shoulder, "how do you do after it? I warrant you were frighted, wer'n't you[7], last night, when it blew but a capful of wind?" "A capful d'you[8] call it?" said I; "'twas a terrible storm." "A storm, you fool you," replies he; "do you call that a storm? why, it was nothing at all; give us but a good ship and sea-room, and we think nothing of such a squall of wind as that; but you're but a fresh-water sailor, Bob. Come, let us make a bowl of punch, and we'll forget all that; d'ye[9] see what charming weather 'tis now?" To make short this sad part of my story, we went the way of all sailors; the punch was made and I was made half drunk with it; and in that one night's wickedness I drowned all my repentance, all my reflections upon my past conduct, all my resolutions for the future. In a word, as the sea was returned to its smoothness of surface and settled calmness by the abatement of that storm, so the hurry of my thoughts being over, my fears and apprehensions of being swallowed up by the sea being forgotten, and the current of my former desires returned, I entirely forgot the vows and promises that I made in my distress. I found, indeed, some intervals of reflection; and the serious thoughts did, as it were, endeavour to return again sometimes; but I shook them off, and roused myself from them as it were from a distemper, and applying myself to drinking and company, soon mastered the return of those fits[10]—for so I called them; and I had in five or six days got as complete a victory over conscience as any young fellow that resolved not to be troubled with it could desire. But I was to have another trial for it still; and Providence[11], as in such cases generally it does, resolved to leave me entirely without excuse; for if I would not take this for a deliverance, the next was to be such a one as the worst and most hardened wretch among us would confess both the danger and the mercy of.

注释（Notes）

1. nothing but：only
2. expostulate：劝告，告诫。
3. fortune：这里指财富。
4. viz.：即，也就是。
5. labours of the hands or of the head：体力或脑力活动。
6. so full he could say no more to me：这里原本是 so full (that) he could say no more to me，so… that…结构里面 that 可以省略。
7. wer'n't you：weren't you
8. d'you：did you
9. d'ye：did ye, ye 是口语化的 you。
10. fits：一阵忽然的冲动,这里指想要回家的冲动。
11. Providence：大写时表示天意。

主题探究（Themes）

（扫码阅读）

文化延展(Cultural Extension)/ 价值引领(Value Guidance)

英国因其独特的地理环境,有着悠久的海洋文化与文学传统,英国古今一大批作家都有着割舍不去的海洋情结,因此,英国海洋小说是英国文学之林中的一大景观。它如同促使它生长与进化的社会土壤一样,在历史的洪流中不断地改弦易辙,急剧演变。英国海洋小说,如其他类型的小说一样,不可避免地经历了一个从原始到成熟的发展过程。从整体来看,英国海洋小说从无到有,经历了雏形(18 世纪以前) → 成型(18 世纪) → 成熟(19 世纪) → 繁荣(20 世纪)数百年的发展历史。事实上,它的每一个发展阶段都同英国当时的社会、历史、政治、文化和经济息息相关。英国海洋小说的发展不是一个孤立或自发的文学现象,而是与英国的社会变化以及异域(尤其是欧洲各国)文化的繁荣昌盛彼此交融的[①]。

作为岛屿国家,英国的历史和文学受到海洋的巨大影响。英国率先实现了工业革命,成为世界上最先进的国家之一,开创了世界的一种新文明。作为一个四面环海的岛国,英国孤悬于欧洲大陆之外,却能威慑世界。对于身居海岛的英国人而言,像《鲁滨逊漂流记》这样的英国海洋小说弘扬了英国的海洋传统和属性,充满了英帝国的骄傲和民族自豪感,增强了民族的整体认同感,正是他们文化记忆的媒介和集体记忆的表现形式。对于英国海洋小说中殖民英雄的崇拜情结和异域书写,即对异族形象的贬低和丑化以反衬"英格兰性"的叙事我们应保持清醒的认识。像鲁滨逊等这些早期的殖民者身上大胆冒险和孜孜进取的精神,他们遇到困难不怕艰险、保持乐观和积极应对的态度值得我们学习,但是他们的"白人至上论"和"西方中心主义"等文化优越感和文化偏见应受到批判。在凝聚英国人国家认同和文化自信的自由贸易中,鸦片贸易和奴隶贸易的罪恶不能被忽视。英国人离开不列颠岛,在全世界寻求商业利益,伴随着殖民、贸易和商业的繁荣与辉煌,不可否认,英国人的优越感和文化自信进一步强化,但是鸦片贸易和奴隶贸易给他国人民和其他民族带来的痛苦和灾难应被永远牢记。

道德修养(Moral Cultivation)

亚当·斯密(1723—1790)是苏格兰启蒙时代最杰出的思想家之一,他以著作《国富论》和《道德情操论》的贡献被誉为现代经济学之父。他的思想影响深远,不仅塑造了经济学领域的基本理念,也对道德哲学产生了深刻影响。斯密的道德情操论是其思想体系中重要的一部分,强调了个人的利己与社会的利他之间的平衡关系,为人们理解人性、道德形成和经济制度奠定了基础。斯密认为,人性的本质体现了自利和同情这两种基本情感的交织。个体天生具有自利的倾向,这种自利并不是消极的,而是驱使个体追求自身幸福和利益的动力。然而,同情也是人性不可或缺的一部分,它使得个体能够感同身受他人的痛苦和喜悦,从而形成社会的凝聚力。斯

---

① 郭海霞. 英国海洋小说的起源与发展[J]. 外国语文,2012,28(S1):44 – 45,84.

密认为,人们基于同情的情感,愿意帮助他人,追求社会和谐与共同的利益。

这种自利与同情之间的平衡关系体现了斯密对人性深刻的理解。他并不主张否定自利,而是强调自利与同情之间的互动与调和。在斯密看来,道德情操是在个体社会交往中逐步形成的。他强调,审美和道德是相互影响的。个体通过观察社会中不同行为的结果,逐渐形成了对这些行为的审美评价。随着时间的推移,这些审美评价演变成为道德准则,指导个体的行为。斯密将道德准则归纳为两个基本原则:利益原则和道德情感原则。亚当·斯密的道德情操论与他的经济思想有机融合,为自由市场经济提供了道德基础。他认为,自由市场的竞争机制可以促使个体追求自身利益,但同时也能通过市场的自发调节实现社会的整体效益。亚当·斯密的道德情操论深刻地揭示了人性的多种层面,强调了个人利己与社会利他之间的平衡关系。他的思想影响了经济学和道德哲学领域,为人们理解经济行为、道德准则以及社会组织提供了重要的理论基础。通过对人性的深刻洞察和社会行为的精确分析,斯密的道德情操论依然在今天的世界中发挥着重要的指导作用。他的思想提醒我们,在个体追求利己的同时,也需要考虑他人的需要,实现个体与社会、公正与效率的和谐统一。正是基于这种平衡,人类社会才能实现持续发展和共同繁荣。

问题讨论(Questions for Discussion)

1. What relationship between humans and the natural world does Robinson Crusoe propose?

2. What is Crusoe's attitude toward foreign cultures?

3. How would you characterize Crusoe's relationship to Xury? To Friday?

4. Are there women in *Robinson Crusoe*? What role do they play? Why, in the end, does Robinson Crusoe get married? Is it significant that his wife is only mentioned in one sentence?

5. How might some of the ideas we find in *Robinson Crusoe* be problematic for readers in the 21st century?

6. There are many symbols in the book, such as the sea, the Bible, the flu and so on. What are their symbolic meanings?

7. What might be the appeal of a book like *Robinson Crusoe* to 21st-century readers?

(请扫码观看视频 *Robinson Crusoe*)

Unit 5

Sentimentalism and Pre-Romanticism in Poetry

William Blake: "The Sick Rose"; "London"
Robert Burns: "A Red, Red Rose"
▽

作者简介 (Introduction to the Authors)

William Blake (1757—1827) is a painter, printmaker and poet in the late 18th century. He is one of the precursor of English Romanticism. He is famous for his two volumes of poems, that is, *Songs of Innocence* and *Songs of Experience*. He was born on 28 November 1757 in London. His father was a hosier. Though his parents were English dissenters, he was baptized at St James's Church. He cultivated a kind of fantastic character in such a strong atmosphere of religion. And throughout his whole life, the Bible remained a source of inspiration to him. He didn't receive any formal education but learned by himself. At the age of 14, he was apprenticed to an engraver. He once made illustrations for Dante's *The Divine Comedy*, Gray's poetry, Marry Wollstonecraft's works and Bible. In 1782, he married the illiterate Catherine and taught her to read and engrave. In his lifetime, Catherine helped him to print his works and comforted him throughout many misfortunes. His poems and illustrations were closely combined, waiting for reader's speculation. During the French Revolution, Blake made acquaintance of Paine and Godwin, by whom his poetry was influenced. However, both his poems and paintings were unacknowledged by people at that time and the Royal Academy. Unknown and poor, he died in 1827. He had a significant role in the poetry and art. It was during the modernist period that his works began to influence many writers and artists. He showed imagination, natural feelings and revolutionary spirits in his poems, opposing to the classical tradition of his age. Besides, his distinctive prints held a special place in British prints.

Robert Burns (1759—1796) is the greatest Scottish poet and lyricist in the late 18th century. He is regarded as the national poet of Scotland and the ploughman poet. Burns was born in a poor family in Alloway, Scotland. He worked on the land at a young age and became the family's chief labourer at 15. Receiving a little formal education, he always tried his best to make time to read books. His peasant origin was beneficial to capture the simplicity, directness and optimism of old songs. After his father's death, the family lived a harder life. In order to earn the passage to overseas, Burns sold the poems collected in *Poems, Chiefly in the Scottish Dialect*, which unexpectedly made a great success. So, he was invited to Edinburgh and then visited northern highlands. This travel offered a rich source of folk songs for him. Since then, Burns had been kept writing. He spent his spare time collecting, editing and imitating traditional Scottish folk songs. In 1789 Burns was appointed to duties in Customs and Excise. As a public supporter of French Revolution, he was unfortunately persecuted. Burns died in 1796, at the age of 37. And his poems can be divided into three types: political poems, satire and lyric. His contribution to the literature is that he collected, revised and drew his inspiration from Scottish folklore. He is the only one to glorify peasant in 18th English literature. His poetry is rich in such qualities as love, humor, pathos, musicality and love of nature, which suggests the coming of English Romanticism.

The Sick Rose

作品简介 (Introduction to the Work)

"The Sick Rose" was written by the British poet William Blake. First published in *Songs of Innocence and Experience* in 1794, it is one of Blake's best-known poems, while also remaining one of his most enigmatic works. It is a two stanza poem that is separated into two sets of four lines, or quatrains. These quatrains follow a consistent rhyme scheme that conforms to the pattern of abcb defe. This very even pattern contributes to the overall tone of the text. It helps foster a feeling of dread, as if something is going terribly wrong. In eight short lines, the speaker addresses the "Rose" of the title, telling it that an "invisible worm" has made it sick. This crafty worm has flown through a stormy night to satisfy its "dark secret love" in the rose's "bed"—an action that will "destroy" the rose's life. The poem is about a rose and a worm, but obviously there is some hidden meaning in the poem. Thus "rose" and "worm", "joy" and "destroy" are paired off. The first words in each pair suggest beauty and happiness, whereas the second words in each pair suggest evil and destruction. The poem is filled with symbolism, and both the world of innocence and the world of experience are presented.

Where the rose is the symbol of beauty and innocence, worm is the symbol of experience and spiritual death where innocence is destroyed by experience. All these are God's design. Innocence must show the path to the world of experience how much painful it may be for the sake of the world of better innocence, the Heaven.

Unit 5 Sentimentalism and Pre-Romanticism in Poetry

作品选文（Selected Reading）

The Sick Rose

O Rose thou art sick.
The invisible worm,
That flies in the night
In the howling[1] storm:

Has found out thy bed
Of crimson joy[2]:
And his dark secret love
Does thy life destroy.

作品译文（扫码阅读）

注释（Notes）

1. howling：怒号的，这里用来形容狂风的肆虐。
2. bed / Of crimson joy：这里有一个跨行。crimson 指深红色的，形容玫瑰花的颜色。

主题探究（Themes）

（扫码阅读）

问题讨论（Questions for Discussion）

1. "Rose" tends to symbolize beauty and love in traditional meaning. Why is the rose sick? How do you like the meaning of "the sick rose" in this poem?
2. There are many images in this poem, could you list some?
3. How do you interpret "dark secret love"? Is this referring to the rape or something else?

4. What do you think of the form and meter of "The Sick Rose"?

5. Sex in this poem seems to be dark, dangerous and even violent. Why do you think Blake presented it that way?

6. Could death just be a metaphor for something else?

7. Robert Burns has a poem titled "A Red, Red Rose". Could you make a comparative study between them?

London

作品简介 (Introduction to the Work)

"London" by William Blake is a dark and dreary poem in which the speaker describes the difficulties of life in London through the structure of a walk. It is a four stanza poem that is separated into sets of four lines, known as quatrains. These quatrains follow a rhyme scheme of abab throughout. The first stanza explores the sights around the city of London while the following three focus more on the sounds the speaker can hear. William Blake analyzed the horrors and sorrows of his city as he meandered through the streets. He was surrounded by dejected Londoners and, what he considered, evidence that his government had too much power and too little interest in helping those they were supposed to serve. The poem here suggests three evils—cruelty, war and lust. The cry of the little chimney sweeper, made to work, in the cold early morning stands for the first evil. The brutality of man-made war is represented by the hapless soldier's sigh, whereas human lust and immorality are marked in the harlot's cry, the new-born infant's tear and "the Marriage hearse".

The speaker of this poem makes it very clear that he believes the government to have too much control and society to be too stringent. To endure the 1800s in England was to know the most restrictive of worlds, where laws were broken only on penalty of death, and people followed a specific societal protocol. It is still universal and timeless, as every society has restrictions that it has placed on human lives.

作品选文 (Selected Reading)

London

I wander thro'[1] each charter'd[2] street,
Near where the charter'd Thames does flow.
And mark in every face I meet
Marks of weakness, marks of woe.

In every cry of every Man,
In every Infants cry of fear,
In every voice: in every ban,
The mind-forg'd manacles[3] I hear

How the Chimney-sweepers cry
Every blackning Church appalls[4],
And the hapless Soldiers sigh
Runs in blood down Palace walls

But most thro' midnight streets I hear
How the youthful Harlots curse
Blasts the new-born Infants tear
And blights with plagues the Marriage hearse[5]

作品译文(扫码阅读)

注释 (Notes)

1. thro': through
2. charter'd: 给予特许权的。charter'd street 和 charter'd Thames 指伦敦的街道和泰晤士河为商业资产阶级占有和专用。
3. mind-forg'd manacles: 精神枷锁。forg'd 即 forged。
4. appalls: 即 appals, 其宾语是 blackning Church。
5. Marriage hearse: 这里用到了矛盾修辞法(oxymoron),婚礼本应带来新生命,却用来修饰灵柩,造成一种诡语性的暗示。

主题探究 (Themes)

(扫码阅读)

文化延展(Cultural Extension)

工业革命为什么首先发生在英国？许多人提出不同解释。有些人说英国的农奴制瓦解较早，为工业准备了"自由"的劳动力。有些人强调圈地的后果，认为圈地运动把农民赶离土地，迫使他们到工业生产中寻找出路。有些人说英国的海外殖民掠夺提供了原始资金，让英国的工业得以发展。还有人认为地理位置也是重要因素，英国是岛国，海上交通便利，又处在世界贸易的有利位置上，易于开辟世界市场。当然，所有这些因素都是存在的，但根本的一个因素却是：光荣革命后英国建立了一个合适的政治制度，这个制度保证社会有宽松、平和的环境，让人们追求个人的目标，最大程度地发挥创造能力。同时，在经济理论方面，对这种模式的工业化发展道路，亚当·斯密和大卫·李嘉图从经济学的角度加以论证，杰里米·边沁则从伦理学的角度予以支持。亚当·斯密和大卫·李嘉图论证说，一个国家的经济只有在最"自由"的状态下才能最好地发展，一切国家干预都会对经济造成破坏，只有"一只看不见的手"即纯粹的经济规律不受节制地起作用，才能把这个国家引向富强。杰里米·边沁告诫说，良好的社会应追求"最大多数人的最大利益"，只有当每一个人都追求到他自己的最大利益时，全社会的最大利益才能够实现。斯密—李嘉图的"自由经济理论"和边沁的"功利主义"是英国工业化道路的指导思想，在这种思想指导下英国走上了自由资本主义道路，它一方面使英国顺利完成工业化，成为世界上第一个工业化国家，但同时也造成许多社会问题，给后来实行工业化的国家留下了许多深刻的教训。[①]

问题讨论(Questions for Discussion)

1. What do you hear in Blake's "London"? And what do these sounds symbolize?

2. The symbol of death and disease appeared frequently in the poem. Can you find some?

3. For the most part, "London" is written in iambic tetrameter. However, the shift from 8 beats to 7 is quite noticeable. What's the implication of them?

4. Repetition is one of the most noticeable features of the poem. What's the function of it?

5. Why are there so many children in this poem (chimney-sweepers, infants, etc.)? What do they symbolize, and why do you think so?

6. What do you make of the phrase "marriage hearse"? Why might marriage be associated with death in "London"?

7. Wordsworth has a poem, "London, 1802". Can you do a comparative study with

---

① 钱乘旦，许洁明. 英国通史：珍藏本[M]. 上海：上海社会科学院出版社，2017：221–222.

"London"?

A Red, Red Rose

作品简介 (Introduction to the Work)

"A Red, Red Rose" is a poem composed by Scotland's national poet, Robert Burns. It was first published in 1786 in a collection of traditional Scottish songs set to music. Burns's poem was inspired both by a simple Scots song he had heard in the country and by published ballads from the period. The poem has the form of a ballad and is meant to be sung aloud. Robert Burns played a key role in the popularization of "A Red, Red Rose", as his written version of it was published in *A Selection of Scots Songs*, *The Scots Musical Museum* and *A Select Collection of Original Scottish Airs for the Voice*. It is a poem of four-line stanzas with abba rhyme schemes, and that format automatically links the reader to concepts of love and emotion. It describes the speaker's deep love for his or her beloved and promises that this love will last longer than human life and even the planet itself, remaining fresh and constant forever. With the addition of metaphors and similes that describe the narrator's affection and the woman who holds that affection, the narrator attempts throughout the lines to express the depth of his "luve".

This could be a final reassurance to his "dear" since the ending stanza reveals that he has to leave her for "awhile", but regardless of the reason, the main element of this work remains the "luve" itself. Through repetition, simile, metaphor, and structure, Burns has created a work that dives into the heart of this narrator's affection.

作品选文 (Selected Reading)

A Red, Red Rose

O my Luve[1] is like a red, red rose
That's newly sprung in June;
O my Luve is like the melody
That's sweetly played in tune.

So fair art thou, my bonnie lass,
So deep in luve am I;
And I will luve thee still, my dear,
Till a' the seas gang dry[2].

Till a' the seas gang dry, my dear,

And the rocks melt wi'³ the sun;
I will love thee still, my dear,
While the sands o' life shall run⁴.

And fare thee weel⁵, my only luve!
And fare thee weel awhile!
And I will come again, my luve,
Though it were ten thousand mile.

作品译文(扫码阅读)

注释 (Notes)

1. Luve: love, 苏格兰方言。
2. Till a' the seas gang dry: Till all the seas go dry, 大海干涸。
3. wi': with
4. sands o' life shall run: 生命像沙漏一样流逝。
5. fare thee weel: farewell to you, 再见。

主题探究 (Themes)

(扫码阅读)

思维延展 (Mind Extension)

How to Write a Response to a Poem?
(By Colby Phillips, eHow Contributor)

For many young readers, the first classroom encounter with poetry is met with confusion, as unfamiliarity with the basics of meter, rhyme schemes, rhythm and verse structure make interpretation seem difficult. If you are a student with the assignment of interpreting a poem, you can proceed by analyzing the poem in terms of structure, language and meaning.

1. Analyze the poem's structure, which includes questions about the form of the poem, its genre, use of meter (rhythmic structure) and rhyme scheme. Notice whether the poet adopts a traditional form, such as the sonnet or haiku, or the modern convention of free verse. The number of syllables in each line is a clue to its structure, as is the arrangement of verses (stanzas). Rhyme schemes are typically analyzed using the shorthand of matching letters (for example, "abab abab.")

2. Comment on the poet's use of language. If the word choice seems unusual, ask why the poet chose these particular words. Notice the ways in which the language sounds like music, paying attention to such elements as tone, pitch, rhythm and melody. Take note of uses of metaphor, simile, metonymy, alliteration, symbolism and imagery.

3. Interpret the meaning of the poem. What is the main idea the poet is trying to communicate? What mood does the poem attempt to establish, and what kind of emotional response does it evoke in a reader? Note the use of literary techniques such as irony, foreshadowing, suspense, narrative voice and setting.

(Read more: How to Write a Response to a Poem | eHow. com http://www.ehow.com/how_8551160_write-response-poem.html#ixzz29z4kVeqF)

问题讨论(Questions for Discussion)

1. Why does the speaker compare his love to a red, red rose?
2. The speaker changes from comparing love to a red rose to comparing love to a melody, and why?
3. Do you ever doubt the speaker's love after reading the whole poem?
4. What do you think of the form and meter of this poem?
5. What's the function of the repeated use of "still" and "till"?
6. The poet applies several natural images. Why does the poet associate nature with love?
7. Could you imitate the first stanza to create a new one?

(请扫码观看视频 Sentimentalism and Pre-Romanticism in Poetry)

Unit 6
Romanticism

William Wordsworth: "My Heart Leaps Up"
John Keats: "To Autumn"
▽

作者简介 (Introduction to the Authors)

William Wordsworth (1770—1850) is the leading figure of the English Romantic poetry, and he is seen as a "worshipper of nature". His *Lyrical Ballads*, composed with Samuel Coleridge, marked the beginning of Romanticism in English poetry and started the modern poetry. Wordsworth was born on 7 April 1770 in Cockermouth, Cumberland, known as a part of the Lake District. Therefore, he developed a keen love of nature from his early years which characterizes all his works. His father was a lawyer and they lived well. When he was only eight years old, his mother died, and six years later, his father passed away. In his life, he constantly suffered from the deaths of his family members and his friends. Wordsworth was encouraged to read a lot of books when he was a child. In 1787, he was educated at St John's College, Cambridge and received his BA degree in 1791. After graduation, he made a series of tours in the Continent. During that time, he visited Revolutionary France, where he was inspired to some thoughts of "freedom, equality and fraternity". Besides, He fell in love with a French woman and had a daughter Caroline. His experience in France exerted great influence on his poetry. In his later years, he lived with his sister Dorothy who always provided spiritual support for him. In 1843, Wordsworth was named Poet Laureate and he died at home in 1850. After his death, his semi-autobiographical poem *Prelude* came out in print. Wordsworth's poetic philosophy reversed the rule of British classical poetics, which promoted the growing Romanticism. He changed the course of English poetry by using simple, colloquial language.

John Keats (1795—1821) is one of the representatives of positive Romanticism in 19th century. He wrote the best odes in English literature. Though Keats was closely associated with Shelley and Byron, his poetry with strong aesthetic tendency mainly showed the eternal beauty and truth rather than social duty. Keats was born in London in 1795. His father managed the stables and the family is not wealthy enough to afford the fees to elite schools. In 1803, he was sent to John Clarke's school where he developed his interests for literature. Keats showed special preference to ancient Greek mythology, Homer and Spencer. At the age of 14, he became an orphan. Then, he left school and became an apprentice to a surgeon. However, he resolved to be a poet rather a surgeon under the influence of Leigh Hunt and Shelley. With the help of Shelley, Keats published his first collection of poems in 1817. In 1818, Keats started on a walking tour through England and Scotland, which stimulated his concern for the miserable people. But his democratic ideas in his poetry offended the aristocratic bourgeois literary circles and get harshly attacked. Keats' short life was filled with rejection, sickness and poverty. He died of tuberculosis at 25 in Rome. His poems were indifferently received in his lifetime, but gained their reputation after his death. Keats is usually considered as a pioneer in aestheticism. Keats made a bold attempt on forms, meter, and language of poetry which enriched the expression of English poetry. And his idea of "Beauty is truth, truth beauty" influenced a lot of poets.

My Heart Leaps Up

作品简介 (Introduction to the Work)

"My Heart Leaps Up" is a short lyric poem by the Romantic poet William Wordsworth. It was written on March 26, 1802 and later published in 1807 as part of Wordsworth's *Poems, in Two Volumes*. Like many of his poems from this period, "My Heart Leaps Up" was inspired by nature, as the speakers describes the feeling of joy upon seeing a simple rainbow. The poem also appreciates the importance of carrying child-like enthusiasm and wonder throughout life, an idea that Wordsworth returns throughout much of his work. The poem's simplicity carries over into its use of rhyme scheme. There are a total of nine lines in this piece. Each line ends with one of 4 sounds, each sound is repeated twice, except "man", which ends two lines and is rhymed with "began". The rhyme scheme of this piece can be sketched as abccabcdd. Regarding the meter, the poem is written in iambic tetrameter. There are three variations: the second line is in iambic trimeter, the sixth line contains two iambs, and the last line is in iambic pentameter.

This poem begins with a reference to a rainbow. Whenever Wordsworth beholds it, his heart gets filled with enthusiasm and energy. It is the sensation of joy existed in his heart when he was a child. As an adult, he still enjoys the beauty of a rainbow. He wishes to retain this childish self even if he matures and grows old. If it does not happen, he will embrace death unquestionably. According to him, nature, symbolized by the rainbow, will always be divine, and he thinks it should be for everyone.

作品选文（Selected Reading）

My Heart Leaps Up

My heart leaps up when I behold[1]
A rainbow in the sky:
So was it when my life began;
So is it now I am a man;
So be it when I shall grow old,
Or let me die!
The Child is father of the Man;
And I could wish my days to be
Bound each to each by natural piety[2].

作品译文（扫码阅读）

注释（Notes）

1. behold：看，注视。
2. piety：虔诚，虔诚信念，natural piety 指对自然的崇拜和虔诚，相对《圣经》的宗教虔诚而言。

主题探究（Themes）

（扫码阅读）

价值引领（Value Guidance）/ 中英比较（A Comparison between Chinese and English Literature）

英国浪漫派诗人，特别是华兹华斯的诗歌在描写自然风光、平常事物之中寓有深意，寄托着自我反思和人生探索的哲理思维。大自然无疑是华兹华斯诗歌的核心、心灵最重要的给养，是他才华的源泉、无限歌颂的对象。他在自然中看到自然，更看到人的心灵与内在生命,他歌颂自然之美,即在歌颂人类具有崇高可能性的纯净心灵,正如此首诗歌中所说:"The Child is father of the Man"。《道德经》第五十五章告诉我们:"含德之厚,比于赤子。"儿童的知识和欲望都比成人少,他们离德不远。孩童的率性纯真是人人都应极力保持的,儿童的生活最接近人的原始自然状态。在欲望充斥的当今时代,只有简单、朴素的心灵才是符合道德的。

相比于华兹华斯诗歌中面对大自然的反思与自省,我们中国古代描写大自然的诗歌是以宁静、和谐和美丽的面貌来呈现自然,体现出一种闲适无为的心情,如王维的《鸟鸣涧》:人闲桂花落,/夜静春山空。/月出惊山鸟,/时鸣春涧中。

问题讨论(Questions for Discussion)

1. The image "rainbow" brings about the speaker's emotions. What do you think of the significance of it?

2. What's the attitude of William Wordsworth towards nature?

3. How do you understand the line "The Child is father of the Man"?

4. Could you analyze the rhythm of the poem "My Heart Leaps Up" of William Wordsworth?

5. According to Wordsworth, does he want his heart to leap up in the following days? Why?

6. Do you have the same state of mind as the speaker from child to man? If it changed, how do you like about it?

To Autumn

作品简介 (Introduction to the Work)

"To Autumn" is an ode by the English Romantic poet John Keats written in 1819. It is the last of his six odes (which include "Ode to a Nightingale" and "Ode on a Grecian Urn"), which are some of the most studied and celebrated poems in the English language. The poem praises autumn, describing its abundance, harvest, and transition into winter, and uses intense, sensuous imagery to elevate the fleeting beauty of the moment. "To Autumn" is the last major work that Keats completed before his death in Rome, in 1821, where the 25-year-old succumbed to tuberculosis. Scholars have unanimously decreed that "To Autumn" is one of the most perfect poems in the English language, despite being his last.

"To Autumn" is one of Keat's most sensual, image-laden poems. It is a sumptuous description of the season of autumn in a three-stanza structure, each of eleven lines, and of an abab rhyme scheme. The first stanza deals primarily with the atmosphere of autumn. Within the first stanza, autumn may be a friendly conspirator working with the sun to bring fruits to a state of perfect fullness and ripeness. Within the second stanza, autumn is personified and is perceived during a state of activity. Autumn may be a thresher sitting on a granary floor, a reaper asleep during a grain field, a gleaner crossing a brook, and, lastly, a cider maker. The third stanza goes back to the beauty of autumn, advising her not to mourn the loss of springtime, for there is ample life in autumn.

作品选文 (Selected Reading)

To Autumn

Season of mists and mellow fruitfulness,
Close bosom-friend of the maturing sun[1];
Conspiring with him how to load and bless
With fruit the vines that round the thatch-eves run;
To bend with apples the moss'd cottage-trees,
And fill all fruit with ripeness to the core;
To swell the gourd[2], and plump the hazel shells
With a sweet kernel; to set budding more,
And still more, later flowers for the bees,
Until they think warm days will never cease,
For summer has o'er-brimm'd[3] their clammy cells.

Who hath not seen thee oft amid thy store?
Sometimes whoever seeks abroad may find
Thee sitting careless on a granary[4] floor,
Thy hair soft-lifted by the winnowing wind[5];
Or on a half-reap'd furrow sound asleep,
Drows'd with the fume of poppies[6], while thy hook
Spares the next swath and all its twined flowers:
And sometimes like a gleaner thou dost keep
Steady thy laden head across a brook;
Or by a cyder-press[7], with patient look,
Thou watchest the last oozings hours by hours.

Where are the songs of spring? Ay, Where are they?
Think not of them, thou hast thy music too,—

While barred clouds bloom the soft-dying day,
And touch the stubble-plains[8] with rosy hue;
Then in a wailful choir[9] the small gnats mourn
Among the river sallows, borne aloft
Or sinking as the light wind lives or dies;
And full-grown lambs loud bleat from hilly bourn[10];
Hedge-crickets sing; and now with treble soft
The red-breast whistles from a garden-croft[11];
And gathering swallows twitter in the skies.

作品译文(扫码阅读)

注释 (Notes)

1. maturing sun：使万物成熟的太阳。
2. swell the gourd：使葫芦膨大,指葫芦成熟。
3. o'er-brimm'd：over-brimmed, 满得溢了出来。
4. granary：storehouse for grain
5. winnowing wind：the wind used to separate dry outer covering from grain
6. Drows'd with the fume of poppies：因罂粟花香而沉醉。
7. cyder-press：苹果榨汁机。
8. stubble-plains：收割后有残株的田地。
9. wailful choir：哀鸣。
10. hilly bourn：hill region
11. garden-croft：菜园地。

主题探究 (Themes)

(扫码阅读)

价值引领（Value Guidance）

　　济慈的《秋颂》被很多学者认为是他的颂歌里最完美的一首，它的主题是秋季的温暖和丰硕。人皆颂春天的美丽，而济慈则感到秋天的成熟更可爱。1819 年 9 月的一天，也许由于工业化的缘故，伦敦的上空正烟雾弥漫，而诗人漫游乡野，感到空气清爽，收割过的田地显得特别温暖。相比大多数描写秋天之萧瑟凋敝的诗歌，在这首诗中自然以宁静、和谐而美丽的形象呈现在人们面前，这也使人们更加坚信：要坚持人与自然和谐共生，"像保护眼睛一样保护生态环境"，像对待生命一样对待自然，做一个热爱自然、热爱生态环境的人。

问题讨论（Questions for Discussion）

　　1. What images are emphasized in each stanza? (visual /gustatory /tactile /olfactory / auditory)

　　2. Which parts of nature does Keats choose to represent in the poem? Does he devote any attention to the wilderness?

　　3. What do you think of the form, the rhyme and the meter of the poem?

　　4. How is autumn personified in the poem? Do you think we can know for sure that autumn is a woman in Keats's poem? Does it make a difference what gender he/she is?

　　5. What evidence can you find of time passing within the poem?

　　6. Why do we tend to automatically associate autumn with death? Does the poem make this association anywhere?

（请扫码观看视频 William Wordsworth & "The World Is Too Much with Us"）

Unit 7
Victorian Age (Ⅰ): English Critical Realism

Charles Dickens: *Oliver Twist*
▽

作者简介 (Introduction to the Author)

Charles Dickens (1812—1870) is best-known for his character portrayal and is usually regarded as the greatest novelist of the Victorian era. With a sense of social responsibility, he moralized people and criticized the society in his works. His works reflected all aspects of social life and exposed some social evils in Victorian era, showing the spirit of his age. Charles Dickens was born in 1812 at Portsmouth. His father was a clerk in the Navy Pay Office. When he was 12 years old, his family was imprisoned for debt. Dickens had to work in a blacking factory during the week and spent at the prison on Sundays. The lonely and miserable life left a deep influence on his thoughts and works. At 15, he became a lawyer's clerk. He also had worked as a reporter in parliament, which helped him get familiar with politics. And he always spent his spare time reading great works in British Museum Library. He had traveled to America and European several times, which provided the raw material for his works. *David Copperfield* is usually considered as his autobiographical novel. Dickens died suddenly from a stroke in June, 1870 and his death was mourned by thousands of people when he was buried at Westminster Abbey. Dickens deserves to be read slowly because of his powerful rhythms, supple patterns of alliteration, the hammer blows of anaphoric insistence. Most of his novels published in monthly or weekly installments, pioneered the serial publication of narrative fiction, which became the dominant Victorian mode for novel publication. The installment format allowed him to modify his plot and character development based on his audience's feedback.

作品简介 (Introduction to the Work)

Oliver Twist, or, *The Parish Boy's Progress*, a novel by Charles Dickens, published serially under the pseudonym "Boz" from 1837 to 1839 in Bentley's Miscellany and in a three-volume book in 1838. The novel was the first of the author's works to realistically depict the impoverished London underworld and to illustrate his belief that poverty leads to crime. Dealing with burglary, kidnapping, child abuse, prostitution and murder, *Oliver*

Twist is one of Charles Dickens' darkest works. The novel introduces famous and endurable characters in the form of the vile Fagin, hateful Bill Sykes, and the brooding Monk balanced on the brighter side by the hero Oliver Twist and The Artful Dodger. The tale also takes the corrupt and incompetent institutions of 19th-century England to task for making worse the very problems they set out to cure. *Oliver Twist* is classic Dickens with memorable characters, evocative descriptions, melodrama and a plot thick with coincidence.

At the beginning of the novel, the narrator introduces Oliver Twist, the novel's young protagonist, who is born in an unnamed town in 1830s England, in a workhouse for the poor. His mother, whose name no one knows, is found on the street and dies just after Oliver's birth. Oliver spends the first nine years of his life in a badly run home for young orphans and then is transferred to a workhouse for adults. The narrator comments that, if Oliver were aware of his poverty, he would be crying even louder. The narrator closes out the novel by detailing the fortunes of the characters. Rose and Harry marry, and they move to the country parsonage where Harry works; Mrs. Maylie comes as well. Oliver's inheritance is meted out, by Brownlow, half to Oliver and half to Monks. The narrator ends the novel by describing Oliver's happiness with his aunt Rose, his adopted father Brownlow, who educates him in the books he once promised Oliver would read, all in the beautiful country village.

作品选文 (Selected Reading)

Oliver Twist

(Excerpt)

Chapter 1

Treats of the Place Where Oliver Twist Was Born;
and of the Circumstances Attending His Birth

Among other public buildings in a certain town, which for many reasons it will be prudent to refrain from mentioning, and to which I will assign no fictitious name, there is one anciently common to most towns, great or small: to wit, a workhouse[1]; and in this workhouse was born; on a day and date which I need not trouble myself to repeat, inasmuch as it can be of no possible consequence to the reader, in this stage of the business at all events; the item of mortality whose name is prefixed to the head of this chapter.

For a long time after it was ushered into this world of sorrow and trouble, by the parish surgeon, it remained a matter of considerable doubt whether the child would survive to bear any name at all; in which case it is somewhat more than probable that these memoirs would never have appeared; or, if they had, that being comprised within a couple of pages, they would have possessed the inestimable merit of being the most concise and faithful specimen of biography, extant in the literature of any age or country.

Although I am not disposed to maintain that the being born in a workhouse, is in itself the most fortunate and enviable circumstance that can possibly befall a human being, I do mean to say that in this particular instance, it was the best thing for Oliver Twist that could by possibility have occurred. The fact is, that there was considerable difficulty in inducing Oliver to take upon himself the office of respiration,—a troublesome practice, but one which custom has rendered necessary to our easy existence; and for some time he lay gasping on a little flock mattress, rather unequally poised between this world and the next: the balance being decidedly in favour of the latter. Now, if, during this brief period, Oliver had been surrounded by careful grandmothers, anxious aunts, experienced nurses, and doctors of profound wisdom, he would most inevitably and indubitably have been killed in no time. There being nobody by, however, but a pauper old woman, who was rendered rather misty by an unwonted allowance of beer; and a parish surgeon[2] who did such matters by contract; Oliver and Nature fought out the point between them. The result was, that, after a few struggles, Oliver breathed, sneezed, and proceeded to advertise to the inmates of the workhouse the fact of a new burden having been imposed upon the parish, by setting up as loud a cry as could reasonably have been expected from a male infant who had not been possessed of that very useful appendage, a voice, for a much longer space of time than three minutes and a quarter.

As Oliver gave this first proof of the free and proper action of his lungs, the patchwork coverlet which was carelessly flung over the iron bedstead, rustled; the pale face of a young woman was raised feebly from the pillow; and a faint voice imperfectly articulated the words, "Let me see the child, and die."

The surgeon had been sitting with his face turned towards the fire: giving the palms of his hands a warm and a rub alternately. As the young woman spoke, he rose, and advancing to the bed's head, said, with more kindness than might have been expected of him:

"Oh, you must not talk about dying yet."

"Lor bless her dear heart[3], no!" interposed the nurse, hastily depositing in her pocket a green glass bottle, the contents of which she had been tasting in a corner with evident satisfaction.

"Lor bless her dear heart, when she has lived as long as I have, sir, and had thirteen children of her own, and all on 'em dead except two, and them in the wurkus[4] with me, she'll know better than to take on in that way, bless her dear heart! Think what it is to be a mother, there's a dear young lamb do."

Apparently this consolatory perspective of a mother's prospects failed in producing its due effect. The patient shook her head, and stretched out her hand towards the child.

The surgeon deposited it in her arms. She imprinted her cold white lips passionately on its forehead; passed her hands over her face; gazed wildly round; shuddered; fell back—and died. They chafed her breast, hands, and temples; but the blood had stopped forever. They talked of hope and comfort. They had been strangers too long.

"It's all over, Mrs. Thingummy!" said the surgeon at last.

"Ah, poor dear, so it is!" said the nurse, picking up the cork of the green bottle, which had fallen out on the pillow, as she stooped to take up the child. "Poor dear!"

"You needn't mind sending up to me, if the child cries, nurse," said the surgeon, putting on his gloves with great deliberation. "It's very likely it will be troublesome. Give it a little gruel if it is." He put on his hat, and, pausing by the bed-side on his way to the door, added, "She was a good-looking girl, too; where did she come from?"

"She was brought here last night," replied the old woman, "by the overseer's order. She was found lying in the street. She had walked some distance, for her shoes were worn to pieces; but where she came from, or where she was going to, nobody knows."

The surgeon leaned over the body, and raised the left hand. "The old story," he said, shaking his head: "no wedding-ring, I see. Ah! Good-night!"

The medical gentleman walked away to dinner; and the nurse, having once more applied herself to the green bottle, sat down on a low chair before the fire, and proceeded to dress the infant.

What an excellent example of the power of dress, young Oliver Twist was! Wrapped in the blanket which had hitherto formed his only covering, he might have been the child of a nobleman or a beggar; it would have been hard for the haughtiest stranger to have assigned him his proper station in society. But now that he was enveloped in the old calico robes which had grown yellow in the same service, he was badged and ticketed, and fell into his place at once—a parish child—the orphan of a workhouse—the humble, half-starved drudge—to be cuffed and buffeted through the world—despised by all, and pitied by none.

Oliver cried lustily. If he could have known that he was an orphan, left to the tender mercies of church-wardens and overseers, perhaps he would have cried the louder.

Chapter 53

And Last

The fortunes of those who have figured in this tale are nearly closed. The little that remains to their historian to relate, is told in few and simple words.

Before three months had passed, Rose Fleming and Harry Maylie were married in the village church which was henceforth to be the scene of the young clergyman's labours; on the same day they entered into possession of their new and happy home.

Mrs. Maylie took up her abode with her son and daughter-in-law, to enjoy, during the tranquil remainder of her days, the greatest felicity that age and worth can know—the contemplation of the happiness of those on whom the warmest affections and tenderest cares of a well-spent life, have been unceasingly bestowed.

It appeared, on full and careful investigation, that if the wreck of property remaining in the custody of Monks (which had never prospered either in his hands or in those of his mother) were equally divided between himself and Oliver, it would yield, to each, little more than three thousand pounds. By the provisions of his father's will, Oliver would have been entitled to the whole; but Mr. Brownlow, unwilling to deprive the elder son of the opportunity of retrieving his former vices and pursuing an honest career, proposed this mode of distribution, to which his young charge joyfully acceded.

Monks, still bearing that assumed name, retired with his portion to a distant part of the New World; where, having quickly squandered it, he once more fell into his old courses, and, after undergoing a long confinement for some fresh act of fraud and knavery[5], at length sunk under an attack of his old disorder, and died in prison. As far from home, died the chief remaining members of his friend Fagin's gang.

Mr. Brownlow adopted Oliver as his son. Removing with him and the old housekeeper to within a mile of the parsonage-house, where his dear friends resided, he gratified the only remaining wish of Oliver's warm and earnest heart, and thus linked together a little society, whose condition approached as nearly to one of perfect happiness as can ever be known in this changing world.

Soon after the marriage of the young people, the worthy doctor returned to Chertsey, where, bereft of the presence of his old friends, he would have been discontented if his temperament had admitted of such a feeling; and would have turned quite peevish if he had known how. For two or three months, he contented himself with hinting that he feared the air began to disagree with him; then, finding that the place really no longer was, to him, what it had been, he settled his business on his assistant, took a bachelor's cottage outside the village of which his young friend was pastor, and instantaneously recovered. Here he took to gardening, planting, fishing, carpentering, and various other pursuits of a similar kind: all undertaken with his characteristic impetuosity. In each and all he has since become famous throughout the neighborhood, as a most profound authority.

Before his removal, he had managed to contract a strong friendship for Mr. Grimwig, which that eccentric gentleman cordially reciprocated. He is accordingly visited by Mr. Grimwig a great many times in the course of the year. On all such occasions, Mr. Grimwig plants, fishes, and carpenters, with great ardour; doing everything in a very singular and unprecedented manner, but always maintaining with his favourite asseveration, that his mode is the right one. On Sundays, he never fails to criticise the sermon to the young clergyman's face: always informing Mr. Losberne, in strict confidence afterwards, that he considers it an excellent performance, but deems it as well not to say so. It is a standing and very favourite joke, for Mr. Brownlow to rally him on his old prophecy concerning Oliver, and to remind him of the night on which they sat with the watch between them, waiting his return; but Mr. Grimwig contends that he was right in the main, and, in proof thereof, remarks that Oliver did not come back after all; which always calls forth a laugh on his side, and increases his good humour.

Mr. Noah Claypole: receiving a free pardon from the Crown in consequence of being admitted approver against Fagin: and considering his profession not altogether as safe a one as he could wish: was, for some little time, at a loss for the means of a livelihood, not burdened with too much work. After some consideration, he went into business as an Informer, in which calling he realises a genteel subsistence. His plan is, to walk out once a week during church time attended by Charlotte in respectable attire. The lady faints away at the doors of charitable publicans, and the gentleman being accommodated with three-penny worth of brandy to restore her, lays an information next day, and pockets half the penalty. Sometimes Mr. Claypole faints himself, but the result is the same.

Mr. and Mrs. Bumble, deprived of their situations, were gradually reduced to great indigence and misery, and finally became paupers in that very same workhouse in which they had once lorded it over others. Mr. Bumble has been heard to say, that in this reverse and degradation, he has not even spirits to be thankful for being separated from his wife.

As to Mr. Giles and Brittles, they still remain in their old posts, although the former is bald, and the last-named boy quite grey. They sleep at the parsonage, but divide their attentions so equally among its inmates, and Oliver and Mr. Brownlow, and Mr. Losberne, that to this day the villagers have never been able to discover to which establishment they properly belong.

Master Charles Bates, appalled by Sikes's crime, fell into a train of reflection whether an honest life was not, after all, the best. Arriving at the conclusion that it certainly was, he turned his back upon the scenes of the past, resolved to amend it in some new sphere of action. He struggled hard, and suffered much, for some time; but, having a contented disposition, and a good purpose, succeeded in the end; and, from being a farmer's drudge, and a carrier's lad, he is now the merriest young grazier in all Northamptonshire[6].

And now, the hand that traces these words, falters, as it approaches the conclusion of its task; and would weave, for a little longer space, the thread of these adventures.

I would fain linger yet with a few of those among whom I have so long moved, and share their happiness by endeavouring to depict it. I would show Rose Maylie in all the bloom and grace of early womanhood, shedding on her secluded path in life soft and gentle light, that fell on all who trod it with her, and shone into their hearts. I would paint her the life and joy of the fire-side circle and the lively summer group; I would follow her through the sultry fields at noon, and hear the low tones of her sweet voice in the moonlit evening walk; I would watch her in all her goodness and charity abroad, and the smiling untiring discharge of domestic duties at home; I would paint her and her dead sister's child happy in their love for one another, and passing whole hours together in picturing the friends whom they had so sadly lost; I would summon before me, once again, those joyous little faces that clustered round her knee, and listen to their merry prattle; I would recall the tones of that clear laugh, and conjure up the sympathising tear that glistened in the soft blue eye. These, and a thousand looks and smiles, and turns of thought and speech—I would fain recall them every one.

How Mr. Brownlow went on, from day to day, filling the mind of his adopted child with stores of knowledge, and becoming attached to him, more and more, as his nature developed itself, and showed the thriving seeds of all he wished him to become—how he traced in him new traits of his early friend, that awakened in his own bosom old remembrances, melancholy and yet sweet and soothing—how the two orphans, tried by adversity, remembered its lessons in mercy to others, and mutual love, and fervent thanks to Him[7] who had protected and preserved them—these are all matters which need not to be told. I have said that they were truly happy; and without strong affection and humanity of heart, and gratitude to that Being[8] whose code is Mercy, and whose great attribute is Benevolence to all things that breathe, happiness can never be attained.

Within the altar of the old village church there stands a white marble tablet, which bears as yet but one word: "Agnes." There is no coffin in that tomb; and may it be many, many years, before another name is placed above it! But, if the spirits of the Dead ever come back to earth, to visit spots hallowed by the love—the love beyond the grave—of those whom they knew in life, I believe that the shade of Agnes sometimes hovers round that solemn nook. I believe it none the less because that nook is in a Church, and she was weak and erring.

注释 (Notes)

1. workhouse: an institution provided by the parish to house and feed the destitute, 即济贫院,给予非常低的工资,生活工作环境极其恶劣。

2. parish surgeon: local medical practitioner attending a workhouse, probably

awarded the contract after tendering the lowest bid for his services

   3. Lor bless her dear heart: Lord bless her dear heart.

   4. wurkus: workhouse

   5. knavery: 恶行。

   6. Northamptonshire: 北安普顿郡,位于英格兰中部。

   7. Him: 在句中时大写指代上帝。

   8. Being: 这里指上帝。

主题探究 (Themes)

（扫码阅读）

文化延展 (Cultural Extension) / 价值引领 (Value Guidance)

    维多利亚时代在经济上高速繁荣,在文化上光辉灿烂,它的确是英国历史上值得称颂的一个时代。维多利亚时代中期,英国达到强盛的顶峰,当时,它的工业生产能力比全世界的总和还要大,它的对外贸易额超过世界上其他任何一个国家。贵族是社会的上层,土地仍是最重要的财富。中等阶级在 19 世纪一直呈上升趋势,他们有独特的生活方式。维多利亚时代是英国历史上最为保守的时代,对性采取压抑的态度,在公开场合不可谈论它,性快乐被看成是邪恶的表现,女性尤其不能有性的要求。19 世纪也是妇女地位最低下的一个世纪。19 世纪是一个科学成果倍出的世纪,达尔文的进化论是其中最杰出的成就。19 世纪也是个文学和艺术作品倍出的时代,查尔斯·狄更斯是作家中的佼佼者。其他知名作家包括萨克雷、勃朗特姐妹、托玛斯·哈代等,他们的作品至今仍脍炙人口。

    在维多利亚时代,财富的分配始终不均,贫富对比十分明显。一方面,有贵族宫殿式的庄园公馆;另一方面,则是农人破败的茅屋草舍。一方面,是工厂主舒适的生活享受;另一方面,则是失业工人绝望的生存挣扎。狄更斯对弱势群体的关注以及童工问题的揭露在一定程度上影响了英国社会福利政策的形成。狄更斯揭露资本主义中上层社会的虚伪,叩问国家良心,不断促进社会公平正义。关于英国工人阶级,马克思和恩格斯有这样的描述:他们在自己的平静、刻板的生活中感到很舒服,如果没有工业革命,他们是永远不会脱离这种生活方式的。诚然,这种生活很惬意,很舒适,但到底不是人应该过的。他们确实也不算是人,而只是一部替一直主宰历史的少数贵族做工的机器。工业革命只是使这种情况发展到了极点,把工人完全变成了简单的机器,剥夺了他们独立活动的最后一点残余。但是,正因为如此,工业革命也就促使他们去思考,促使他们去争取人应有的地位。①

对于宪章运动,人们也许认为,它既然是工人的运动,就必然是反资本主义的,必然代表更先进的生产关系,代表着更高的社会阶段对资本主义的否定。宪章运动的确是工人的运动,而且是反资本主义的;但它不是由工业化所产生的工厂工人的运动,相反,它是被工厂制所消灭的手工工人的运动,代表着前工业社会的独立小生产者的愿望和理想,因此它站在前资本主义的立场上反资本主义,而不是企图对资本主义做出超越。在工业革命中,许多手工工人受机器排挤,丢失了他们的饭碗,他们因此对工业化十分不满,对工业革命造成的资本主义制度深恶痛绝,他们怀念过去,反对现实,从而成为工业革命时期最坚定的反体制力量。反资本主义有两种反法,一种是站在资本主义前的立场上反资本主义,一种是站在资本主义后的立场上反资本主义。有意思的是,英国的工厂工人融入了资本主义的体制之中,它们反对资本主义剥削,但只想限制这种剥削,并不想打碎这个体制②。

问题讨论(Questions for Discussion)

1. In the world of *Oliver Twist*, is the middle class always morally superior to the working class?

2. In the world of *Oliver Twist*, what causes an individual to turn to crime?

3. Do you agree that the Church of England is condemned in *Oliver Twist* for its cruel and inhuman policies towards the care of the poor, and there is little optimism in the novel for the implementation of a better system?

4. The final chapter describes all the "good" characters settled in a country village. After spending almost the whole novel depicting the grittiness of everyday life in London, why does Dickens have his main characters retreat to the countryside?

5. Why is Nancy unable to leave her old life?

6. If names are so important to identity, speculate on whether you think Oliver would change his last name from "Twist" to his father's name, "Leeford", after the close of the novel, and explain your opinion.

7. Who is the narrator, can she or he read minds, and, more importantly, can we trust her or him?

(请扫码观看视频 English Critical Realism)

---

① 中共中央马克思恩格斯列宁斯大林著作编译局. 马克思恩格斯选集:第一卷[M]. 北京:人民出版社,2012:89.
② 钱乘旦,许洁明. 英国通史:珍藏本[M]. 上海:上海社会科学出版社,2017:74.

Unit 8
Victorian Age (Ⅱ): Poets of the Mid and Late 19th Century

Robert Browning: "My Last Duchess"
▽

作者简介 (Introduction to the Author)

Robert Browning (1812—1889) is a playwright and is considered as the most original poet of the Victorian Age. He is seen as a sage and philosopher poet. He was born in Camberwell, a London suburb in 1812. His father was a well-paid clerk in the Bank of England, who was a literary collector. So, Browning read a lot when he was a child. And his mother was a talented musician who taught him music. Most of his education he had received was from his parents and a private tutor. He learned many languages and wrote some poems at a young age. Browning showed great admiration for Shelly and wrote *Pauline* in homage to Shelly. He also wrote some stage plays which help to sharpen his poetic skills. It is the frequent use of dialogues between characters in plays that he created "dramatic monologue". For Browning, Italy was his university where he was fascinated by the art and atmosphere. In 1846, he married the poet Elizabeth Barrett and from then on they had lived in Italy. In 1868, he finished *The Ring and the Book* which finally brought him the renown he had sought for. Browning died in 1889 and was buried in Poets' Corner in Westminster Abbey. His chief contribution to English poetry is his skillful use of the "dramatic monologue", allowing characters to speak for themselves without any judgment. It influenced countless poets for almost a century. Browning usually brought some social problems to light and expressed his concerns and attitudes towards them in his works.

作品简介 (Introduction to the Work)

"My Last Duchess" is a famous poem written by Robert Browning. It was published in a book of poems named *Dramatic Lyrics* in 1842. As the name *Dramatic Lyrics* suggests, Browning tried to produce new trends in poetry after some experiments. He tried to combine some features of stage plays with some Romantic verses to produce the new type of poetry in the Victorian era. Robert Browning alarmed his readers with his unique characteristic of adding psychological and psychopathic realism and use of harsh language in his poetry. These traits can also be observed in the poem "My Last Duchess". He got inspired to write this poem by the history of Alfonso II of Ferrara, who was a Renaissance duke, whose young wife died mysteriously in 1561 under suspicious circumstances. After her death, the duke got married to the niece of the Count of Tyrol. This poem is a dramatic monologue. In a dramatic monologue, the speaker addresses alone at the stage in the presence of a silent listener. In "My Last Duchess", the poet doesn't address the readers himself. The scene unfolds through the monologue of the speaker who is the Duke of Ferrara.

The Duke's monologue shows his psychological state and his treatment with his former Duchess. The Duke speaks about his former wife's perceived inadequacies to a representative of the family of his bride-to-be, revealing his obsession with controlling others in the process. Browning uses this compelling psychological portrait of a despicable character to critique the objectification of women and abuses of power.

作品选文 (Selected Reading)

My Last Duchess
FERRARA[1]

That's my last Duchess painted on the wall,
Looking as if she were alive. I call
That piece a wonder, now; Fra Pandolf's[2] hands
Worked busily a day, and there she stands.
Will't please you sit and look at her? I said
"Fra Pandolf" by design[3], for never read
Strangers like you that pictured countenance,
The depth and passion of its earnest glance,
But to myself they turned (since none puts by
The curtain I have drawn for you, but I)
And seemed as they would ask me, if they durst[4],
How such a glance came there; so, not the first
Are you to turn and ask thus. Sir,' twas not
Her husband's presence only, called that spot
Of joy into the Duchess' cheek; perhaps
Fra Pandolf chanced to say, "Her mantle laps
Over my lady's wrist too much," or "Paint
Must never hope to reproduce the faint
Half-flush that dies along her throat." Such stuff

Was courtesy, she thought, and cause enough
For calling up that spot of joy. She had
A heart—how shall I say? —too soon made glad,
Too easily impressed; she liked whate'er
She looked on, and her looks went everywhere.
Sir, 'twas all one[5]! My favour at her breast[6],
The dropping of the daylight in the West,
The bough of cherries some officious fool
Broke in the orchard for her, the white mule
She rode with round the terrace—all and each
Would draw from her alike the approving speech,
Or blush, at least. She thanked men—good! but thanked
Somehow—I know not how—as if she ranked
My gift of a nine-hundred-years-old name[7]
With anybody's gift. Who'd stoop to blame
This sort of trifling? Even had you skill
In speech—which I have not—to make your will
Quite clear to such an one, and say, "Just this
Or that in you disgusts me; here you miss,
Or there exceed the mark"—and if she let
Herself be lessoned so, nor plainly set
Her wits to yours, forsooth, and made excuse—
E'en then would be some stooping; and I choose
Never to stoop. Oh, sir, she smiled, no doubt,
Whene'er I passed her; but who passed without
Much the same smile? This grew[8]; I gave commands;
Then all smiles stopped together. There she stands
As if alive. Will't please you rise? We'll meet
The company below, then. I repeat,
The Count[9] your master's known munificence
Is ample warrant that no just pretense
Of mine for dowry will be disallowed;
Though his fair daughter's self, as I avowed
At starting, is my object. Nay, we'll go
Together down, sir. Notice Neptune[10], though,
Taming a sea-horse, thought a rarity,

Which Claus of Innsbruck[11] cast in bronze for me!

作品译文(扫码阅读)

注释 (Notes)

1. FERRARA：斐拉拉公国。
2. Fra Pandolf：潘道夫教兄。这是作者虚构的作家。Fra 是意大利教士姓名前的称号，译为"教兄"。当时不少的画家都是教士。
3. by design：on purpose，故意地。
4. durst：古语 dare 的过去式和过去分词形式。
5. all one：all the same
6. my favour at her breast：我送给她的胸针。
7. nine-hundred-years-old name：指公爵的家族延续了九百年，实际上没有这么久，大概有 650 年的历史。
8. This grew：这种情况愈演愈烈(意指公爵夫人变得越来越"不检点")。
9. Count：欧洲大陆用法中的伯爵，对应英国的 earl。
10. Neptune：罗马神话中的海神尼普顿，常常驾驶着海马拉的战车，相当于希腊神话中的海神波塞冬。
11. Claus of Innsbruck：Claus 是作者虚构的雕刻家；Innsbruck 在今天奥地利境内，当时以雕刻闻名，布朗宁于 1838 年曾到过那里。

主题探究 (Themes)

(扫码阅读)

文化延展 (Cultural Extension)

爵位是欧洲封建君主国内分封贵族的等级制度。它最早出现于中世纪，在近代的一些国家中仍然沿用。一般以占有土地的多少来确定分封爵位之高低，主要可分为公爵、侯爵、伯爵、子爵、男爵这五等。

公爵：在贵族中，公爵是第一等级，地位最高。这个爵名的由来有三：一是欧洲氏族社会解体时期，日耳曼部落的军事首长；二是古代罗马部落的军事首长；三是古罗马时代的边省将领，后指地方军政长官，其拉丁文原意为"统帅"。随着封建关系的发展，王权的日益强化，公爵成了统治阶级中的上层人物。在英国，公爵最初是由十四世纪的英王爱德华三世分封的，被封为公爵的全是王室成员。十五世纪后才打破这一惯例，少数非王室人员也被封为公爵。

侯爵：侯爵是贵族的第二等级。查理大帝在位时它是指具有特别全权的边区长官，相当于藩侯，查理曼帝国分裂后，变成了独立的大封建领主。封建王权加强后，侯爵成为公爵与伯爵之间的爵衔，其地位与其他伯爵相等，十到十四世纪后，才确认侯爵的地位在伯爵之上。

伯爵：在罗马帝国时，伯爵是皇帝的侍从，掌管军、民、财政大权，有时也出任地方官吏，封建制度强化后，伯爵可割据一方，成为世袭的大封建领主。后来，其地位渐次低落，介于侯爵与子爵之间，为贵族的第三等级。在英国，伯爵之衔历史最久，在1337年黑太子爱德华被封为公爵之前，它是英国最高的爵位。

子爵：子爵原系法兰克王国的国家官吏名，最早是由国王查理曼于八世纪时封的，后来传到欧洲其他大陆国家。起初，子爵是伯爵的副手，后来独立存在，也可世袭。子爵爵位到十五世纪才传入英国，博蒙德·约翰于1440年第一个被封为英国子爵，其地位在男爵之上。

男爵：男爵是贵族爵位中最低的一级。在十一至十二世纪时，它是欧洲君主国国王或大封建主的直接附庸。在英语中，男爵（Baron）一词，是诺曼人在征服欧洲大陆时引进来的，本义为"只不过是普通的人"，后来演变为"强有力的人"。当时，英国的那些直接从国王那儿得到土地的大地主，均可称为男爵，但这并非由国王分封。到了1387年理查二世封约翰·比彻姆为男爵后，男爵才成为英国贵族的正式爵位。

上述的这五个贵族爵位，又根据其能否传给后代，分为世袭贵族和终身贵族两类。世袭贵族死后可由长子继承，终身贵族仅限本人活着时担任，死后其子不能承袭。

英国的封号授予分成七级，分为贵族（peerage）与平民两大部分。而除了英国王室以外，贵族分为五等；因为中国周朝的诸侯亦分为五等，所以中文就直接对应翻译为公爵、侯爵、伯爵、子爵与男爵；另外还有两种封号：准男爵（Baronet）与骑士（Knight），他们属于平民，而非贵族。到20世纪末之前，英格兰、苏格兰、不列颠和联合王国的贵族拥有在上议院获得席位的权利。英国国会在1999年通过新法例以后，世袭贵族不再自动成为上议院成员。

问题讨论 (Questions for Discussion)

1. What do you think of the form and meter of the poem?
2. What do you think of the Duchess and the Duke?
3. How does the Duke want the people around him, such as his "last Duchess" and the servant of the Count who listens to her story, to respond to his power? How does he attempt to shape their reactions?
4. The Duke claims that he doesn't have "skill in speech" to make his "will clear" to the Duchess. Is he right? Does he display any evidence of rhetorical skill in the poem itself? If so, then why couldn't he communicate with the Duchess?
5. What is the Duke really hoping to communicate by telling the story of his "last Duchess" to the Count's servant? Who is meant to receive the message?
6. How do you understand the last three lines of the poem?

(请扫码观看视频 Poets of the Mid and Late 19th Century)

Unit 9
Victorian Age (Ⅲ): Thomas Hardy & Bernard Shaw

Thomas Hardy: *Tess of the D'Urbervilles*
Bernard Shaw: *Mrs. Warren's Profession*
▽

作者简介 (Introduction to the Authors)

Thomas Hardy (1840—1928) is an English novelist, poet and architect living at the turn of the century. He was born in Dorsetshire, son of a mason. His mother was well-read and educated Hardy from his early age. His formal education began at 8 and ended at 16. And then he was apprenticed to an architect following in the footsteps of his father. He once won the prizes from the Royal Institute of British Architects and the Architectural Association. However, he gradually realized that he preferred literature rather than architecture. So, he finally devoted himself to writing. In London, he made acquaintance with Horace Moule and exposed to Darwin's theory which impressed him a lot. His early years in the rural were also to have a profound influence on him. Hardy was intellectually advanced but emotionally traditional, cherishing the patriarchal way of life. And most of his novels are set in Wessex, a fictional primitive region. These novels revealed the miserable fate of peasants under the influence of industrial revolution, showing his pessimistic point of view. He died at the age of 87. His body was buried in Westminster Abbey, whereas his heart was buried in Stinsford churchyard. His poetry marks the transition from the Victorian Age to the modernist movement of the 20th century. Owing to his early experience, the architectural structure can be found in his works. Besides, nature in his novels was always personified and symbolic, like a character in the development of the plot. Hardy's novels exposed all sorts of social problems and attacked Victorian morals which helped to flourish the English Realism.

Bernard Shaw (1856—1950) is a prolific playwright, critic and political activist and he wrote more than 60 plays. He is considered to be the best-known English dramatist since Shakespeare. He was born in Dublin in 1856. The family lived a life of "shabby-genteel poverty". When he was young, he learned music from his neighborhood. Thus the strongly rhythmic and musical language can be found in his works. He received education until 14. In 1876, Shaw came to London and then became a member of Fabian Society. He believed in peaceful evolution of socialism and acted as a liberal humanitarian and reformist. During the First World War, he urged people against the imperialist war. Touched by Ibsen's plays and upset about 19th English theatre, Shaw insisted the moral teachings of his plays and rejected the idea of art for art's sake. The mission of his plays was not only to reveal the moral, political and economic truth, but to criticize the contemporary evils. Therefore, most of his plays can be termed as problem plays. Shaw was awarded the Nobel Prize in Literature in 1925. And in 1931, he visited China and was warmly received by Chinese people. Shaw died at the age of 94. Shaw's fame is worldwide. His sharp wit, eloquent dialogues, satires and instinct for theatrical effect had brought a new kind of energy and intelligence to drama. His plays enlightened people about social problems in disguise of witty dialogues. His music criticism and two plays which were adapted to musical comedies by others left a varied musical legacy.

Tess of the D'Urbervilles

作品简介 (Introduction to the Work)

Tess of the D'Urbervilles, novel by Thomas Hardy, first published serially in bowdlerized form in the *Graphic* (July—December 1891) and in its entirety in book form (three volumes) the same year. It was subtitled *A Pure Woman* because Hardy felt that its heroine was a virtuous victim of a rigid Victorian moral code. Now considered Hardy's masterwork, it departed from conventional Victorian fiction in its focus on the rural lower class and in its open treatment of sexuality and religion. *Tess of the D'Urbervilles* is as famous for its heroine as for its notoriously tragic plot. Originally shunned by critics upon its publication in 1891 because of "immorality", the novel traces the difficult life of Tess Durbeyfield, whose victimization at the hands of men eventually leads to her horrific downfall. Tess spares the reader none of the bitterness inherent in English country life, and Hardy's often romanticized love for the landscape of Wessex is balanced by the novel's grimly realistic depiction of social injustice. After her impoverished family learns of its noble lineage, naive Tess Durbeyfield is sent by her slothful father and ignorant mother to make an appeal to a nearby wealthy family who bear the ancestral name d'Urberville. Tess, attractive and innocent, is seduced by dissolute Alec d'Urberville and secretly bears a child, who dies in infancy. Later working as a dairymaid, she meets and marries Angel Clare, an idealistic gentleman who rejects Tess after learning of her past on their wedding night. Emotionally bereft and financially impoverished, Tess is trapped by necessity into giving in once again to d'Urberville, but she murders him when Angel returns. In the end, Tess is arrested and sent to jail. Angel watches as a black flag is raised over the prison, signaling Tess's execution.

作品选文 (Selected Reading)

Tess of the D'Urbervilles
(Exerpt)

Chapter 1

On an evening in the latter part of May a middle-aged man was walking homeward from Shaston to the village of Marlott, in the adjoining Vale of Blakemore or Blackmoor. The pair of legs that carried him were rickety, and there was a bias in his gait which inclined him somewhat to the left of a straight line. He occasionally gave a smart nod, as if in confirmation of some opinion, though he was not thinking of anything in particular. An empty egg-basket was slung upon his arm, the nap of his hat was ruffled, a patch being quite worn away at its brim where his thumb came in taking it off. Presently he was met by an elderly parson astride on a gray mare, who, as he rode, hummed a wandering tune.

"Good night t'ee[1]," said the man with the basket.

"Good night, Sir[2] John," said the parson.

The pedestrian, after another pace or two, halted, and turned round.

"Now, sir, begging your pardon; we met last market-day on this road about this time, and I said 'Good night,' and you made reply '*Good night, Sir John*', as now."

"I did," said the parson.

"And once before that—near a month ago."

"I may have."

"Then what might your meaning be in calling me 'Sir John' these different times, when I be plain Jack Durbeyfield, the haggler?"

The parson rode a step or two nearer.

"It was only my whim," he said; and, after a moment's hesitation: "It was on account of a discovery I made some little time ago, whilst[3] I was hunting up pedigrees for the new county history. I am Parson Tringham, the antiquary, of Stagfoot Lane. Don't you really know, Durbeyfield, that you are the lineal representative of the ancient and knightly family of the d'Urbervilles, who derive their descent from Sir Pagan d'Urberville, that renowned knight who came from Normandy with William the Conqueror[4], as appears by Battle Abbey Roll[5]?"

"Never heard it before, sir!"

"Well it's true. Throw up your chin a moment, so that I may catch the profile of your face better. Yes, that's the d'Urberville nose and chin—a little debased. Your ancestor was one of the twelve knights who assisted the Lord of Estremavilla in Normandy in his conquest of Glamorganshire. Branches of your family held manors over all this part of England; their names appear in the Pipe Rolls[6] in the time of King Stephen. In the reign of King John one of them was rich enough to give a manor to the Knights Hospitallers; and in Edward the Second's time your forefather Brian was summoned to Westminster to attend the great Council there. You declined a little in Oliver Cromwell[7]'s time, but to no serious extent, and in Charles the Second[8]'s reign you were made Knights of the Royal Oak for your loyalty. Aye, there have been generations of Sir Johns among you, and if knighthood were hereditary, like a baronetcy, as it practically was in old times, when men were knighted from father to son, you would be Sir John now."

"Ye don't say so!"

"In short," concluded the parson, decisively smacking his leg with his switch, "there's hardly such another family in England."

"Daze my eyes, and isn't there?" said Durbeyfield. "And here have I been knocking about, year after year, from pillar to post, as if I was no more than the commonest feller in the parish... And how long hev this news about me been knowed, Pa'son Tringham?"

The clergyman explained that, as far as he was aware, it had quite died out of knowledge, and could hardly be said to be known at all. His own investigations had begun on a day in the preceding spring when, having been engaged in tracing the vicissitudes of the d'Urberville family, he had observed Durbeyfield's name on his waggon, and had thereupon been led to make inquiries about his father and grandfather till he had no doubt on the subject.

"At first I resolved not to disturb you with such a useless piece of information," said he. "However, our impulses are too strong for our judgement sometimes. I thought you might perhaps know something of it all the while."

"Well, I have heard once or twice, 'tis true, that my family had seen better days afore they came to Blackmoor. But I took no notice o't, thinking it to mean that we had once kept two horses where we now keep only one. I've got a wold silver spoon, and a wold graven seal at home, too; but, Lord, what's a spoon and seal? ... And to think that I and these noble d'Urbervilles were one flesh all the time. 'Twas said that my gr't-grandfer had secrets, and didn't care to talk of where he came from... And where do we raise our smoke, now, parson, if I may make so bold; I mean, where do we d'Urbervilles live?"

"You don't live anywhere. You are extinct—as a county family."

"That's bad."

"Yes—what the mendacious family chronicles call extinct in the male line—that is, gone down—gone under."

"Then where do we lie?"

"At Kingsbere-sub-Greenhill: rows and rows of you in your vaults, with your effigies under Purbeck-marble canopies."

"And where be our family mansions and estates?"

"You haven't any."

"Oh? No lands neither?"

"None; though you once had 'em in abundance, as I said, for your family consisted of numerous branches. In this county there was a seat of yours at Kingsbere, and another at Sherton, and another at Millpond, and another at Lullstead, and another at Wellbridge."

"And shall we ever come into our own again?"

"Ah—that I can't tell!"

"And what had I better do about it, sir?" asked Durbeyfield, after a pause.

"Oh—nothing, nothing; except chasten yourself with the thought of 'how are the mighty fallen.' It is a fact of some interest to the local historian and genealogist, nothing more. There are several families among the cottagers of this county of almost equal lustre. Good night."

"But you'll turn back and have a quart of beer wi' me on the strength o't, Pa'son Tringham? There's a very pretty brew in tap at The Pure Drop—though, to be sure, not so good as at Rolliver's."

"No, thank you—not this evening, Durbeyfield. You've had enough already." Concluding thus the parson rode on his way, with doubts as to his discretion in retailing this curious bit of lore.

When he was gone Durbeyfield walked a few steps in a profound reverie, and then sat down upon the grassy bank by the roadside, depositing his basket before him. In a few minutes a youth appeared in the distance, walking in the same direction as that which had been pursued by Durbeyfield. The latter, on seeing him, held up his hand, and the lad quickened his pace and came near.

"Boy, take up that basket! I want 'ee to go on an errand for me."

The lath-like stripling frowned. "Who be you, then, John Durbeyfield, to order me about and call me 'boy'? You know my name as well as I know yours!"

"Do you, do you? That's the secret—that's the secret! Now obey my orders, and take the message I'm going to charge 'ee wi'... Well, Fred, I don't mind telling you that the secret is that I'm one of a noble race—it has been just found out by me this present afternoon, p. m." And as he made the announcement, Durbeyfield, declining from his sitting position, luxuriously stretched himself out upon the bank among the daisies.

The lad stood before Durbeyfield, and contemplated his length from crown to toe.

"Sir John d'Urberville—that's who I am," continued the prostrate man. "That is if knights were baronets—which they be. 'Tis recorded in history all about me. Dost know of such a place, lad, as Kingsbere-sub-Greenhill?"

"Ees. I've been there to Greenhill Fair."

"Well, under the church of that city there lie—"

"'Tisn't a city, the place I mean; leastwise' twaddn[9] when I was there—'twas a little one-eyed, blinking sort o' place."

"Never you mind the place, boy, that's not the question before us. Under the church of that there parish lie my ancestors—hundreds of 'em—in coats of mail and jewels, in gr't lead coffins weighing tons and tons. There's not a man in the county o' South-Wessex that's got grander and nobler skillentons[10] in his family than I."

"Oh?"

"Now take up that basket, and go on to Marlott, and when you've come to The Pure Drop Inn, tell 'em to send a horse and carriage to me immed'ately, to carry me hwome. And in the bottom o' the carriage they be to put a noggin o' rum in a small bottle, and chalk it up to my account. And when you've done that goo on to my house with the basket, and tell my wife to put away that washing, because she needn't finish it, and wait till I come hwome, as I've news to tell her."

As the lad stood in a dubious attitude, Durbeyfield put his hand in his pocket, and produced a shilling, one of the chronically few that he possessed.

"Here's for your labour, lad."

This made a difference in the young man's estimate of the position.

"Yes, Sir John. Thank'ee. Anything else I can do for 'ee, Sir John?"

"Tell 'em at hwome that I should like for supper,—well, lamb's fry if they can get it; and if they can't, black-pot; and if they can't get that, well, chitterlings will do."

"Yes, Sir John."

The boy took up the basket, and as he set out the notes of a brass band were heard from the direction of the village.

"What's that?" said Durbeyfield. "Not on account o' I?"

"'Tis the women's club-walking, Sir John. Why, your da'ter[11] is one o' the members."

"To be sure—I'd quite forgot it in my thoughts of greater things! Well, vamp on to Marlott, will ye, and order that carriage, and maybe I'll drive round and inspect the club."

The lad departed, and Durbeyfield lay waiting on the grass and daisies in the evening sun. Not a soul passed that way for a long while, and the faint notes of the band were the only human sounds audible within the rim of blue hills.

Chapter 2

The village of Marlott lay amid the north-eastern undulations of the beautiful Vale of

Blakemore or Blackmoor aforesaid, an engirdled and secluded region, for the most part untrodden as yet by tourist or landscape-painter, though within a four hours' journey from London.

It is a vale whose acquaintance is best made by viewing it from the summits of the hills that surround it—except perhaps during the droughts of summer. An unguided ramble into its recesses in bad weather is apt to engender dissatisfaction with its narrow, tortuous, and miry ways.

This fertile and sheltered tract of country, in which the fields are never brown and the springs never dry, is bounded on the south by the bold chalk ridge that embraces the prominences of Hambledon Hill, Bulbarrow, Nettlecombe-Tout, Dogbury, High Stoy, and Bubb Down. The traveller from the coast, who, after plodding northward for a score of miles over calcareous downs and corn-lands, suddenly reaches the verge of one of these escarpments, is surprised and delighted to behold, extended like a map beneath him, a country differing absolutely from that which he has passed through. Behind him the hills are open, the sun blazes down upon fields so large as to give an unenclosed character to the landscape, the lanes are white, the hedges low and plashed, the atmosphere colourless. Here, in the valley, the world seems to be constructed upon a smaller and more delicate scale; the fields are mere paddocks, so reduced that from this height their hedgerows appear a network of dark green threads overspreading the paler green of the grass. The atmosphere beneath is languorous, and is so tinged with azure that what artists call the middle distance partakes also of that hue, while the horizon beyond is of the deepest ultramarine. Arable lands are few and limited; with but slight exceptions the prospect is a broad rich mass of grass and trees, mantling minor hills and dales within the major. Such is the Vale of Blackmoor.

The district is of historic, no less than of topographical interest. The Vale was known in former times as the Forest of White Hart, from a curious legend of King Henry III's reign, in which the killing by a certain Thomas de la Lynd[12] of a beautiful white hart which the king had run down and spared, was made the occasion of a heavy fine. In those days, and till comparatively recent times, the country was densely wooded. Even now, traces of its earlier condition are to be found in the old oak copses and irregular belts of timber that yet survive upon its slopes, and the hollow-trunked trees that shade so many of its pastures.

The forests have departed, but some old customs of their shades remain. Many, however, linger only in a metamorphosed or disguised form. The May-Day dance[13], for instance, was to be discerned on the afternoon under notice, in the guise of the club revel, or "club-walking", as it was there called.

It was an interesting event to the younger inhabitants of Marlott, though its real interest was not observed by the participators in the ceremony. Its singularity lay less in the retention of a custom of walking in procession and dancing on each anniversary than in the members being solely women. In men's clubs such celebrations were, though expiring, less uncommon; but either the natural shyness of the softer sex, or a sarcastic attitude on the part of male relatives, had denuded such women's clubs as remained (if any other did) of this their glory and consummation. The club of Marlott alone lived to uphold the local Cerealia[14]. It had walked for hundreds of years, if not as benefit-club, as votive sisterhood of some sort; and it walked still.

The banded ones were all dressed in white gowns—a gay survival from Old Style days, when cheerfulness and May-time were synonyms—days before the habit of taking long views had reduced emotions to a monotonous average. Their first exhibition of themselves was in a processional march of two and two round the parish. Ideal and real clashed slightly as the sun lit up their figures against the green hedges and creeper-laced house-fronts; for, though the whole troop wore white garments, no two whites were alike among them. Some approached pure blanching; some had a bluish pallor; some worn by the older characters (which had possibly lain by folded for many a year) inclined to a cadaverous tint, and to a Georgian style[15].

In addition to the distinction of a white frock, every woman and girl carried in her right hand a peeled willow wand, and in her left a bunch of white flowers. The peeling of the former, and the selection of the latter, had been an operation of personal care.

There were a few middle-aged and even elderly women in the train, their silver-wiry hair and wrinkled faces, scourged by time and trouble, having almost a grotesque, certainly a pathetic, appearance in such a jaunty situation. In a true view, perhaps, there was more to be gathered and told of each anxious and experienced one, to whom the years were drawing nigh when she should say, "I have no pleasure in them," than of her juvenile comrades. But let the elder be passed over here for those under whose bodices the life throbbed quick and warm.

The young girls formed, indeed, the majority of the band, and their heads of luxuriant hair reflected in the sunshine every tone of gold, and black, and brown. Some had beautiful eyes, others a beautiful nose, others a beautiful mouth and figure; few, if any, had all. A difficulty of arranging their lips in this crude exposure to public scrutiny, an inability to balance their heads, and to dissociate self-consciousness from their features, was apparent in them, and showed that they were genuine country girls, unaccustomed to many eyes.

And as each and all of them were warmed without by the sun, so each had a private little sun for her soul to bask in; some dream, some affection, some hobby, at least some remote and distant hope which, though perhaps starving to nothing, still lived on, as hopes will. Thus they were all cheerful, and many of them merry.

They came round by The Pure Drop Inn, and were turning out of the high road to pass through a wicket-gate into the meadows, when one of the women said—

"The Lord-a-Lord! Why, Tess Durbeyfield, if there isn't thy father riding hwome in a carriage!"

A young member of the band turned her head at the exclamation. She was a fine and handsome girl—not handsomer than some others, possibly—but her mobile peony mouth and large innocent eyes added eloquence to colour and shape. She wore a red ribbon in her hair, and was the only one of the white company who could boast of such a pronounced adornment. As she looked round Durbeyfield was seen moving along the road in a chaise belonging to The Pure Drop, driven by a frizzle-headed brawny damsel with her gown-sleeves rolled above her elbows. This was the cheerful servant of that establishment, who, in her part of factotum, turned groom and ostler at times. Durbeyfield, leaning back, and with his eyes closed luxuriously, was waving his hand above his head, and singing in a slow recitative—

"I've-got-a-gr't-family-vault-at-Kingsbere and knighted-forefathers-in-lead-coffins-there!"

The clubbists tittered, except the girl called Tess—in whom a slow heat seemed to rise at the sense that her father was making himself foolish in their eyes.

"He's tired, that's all," she said hastily, "and he has got a lift home, because our own horse has to rest to-day."

"Bless thy simplicity, Tess," said her companions. "He's got his market-nitch. Haw-haw!"

"Look here; I won't walk another inch with you, if you say any jokes about him!" Tess cried, and the colour upon her cheeks spread over her face and neck. In a moment her eyes grew moist, and her glance drooped to the ground. Perceiving that they had really pained her they said no more, and order again prevailed. Tess's pride would not allow her to turn her head again, to learn what her father's meaning was, if he had any; and thus she moved on with the whole body to the enclosure where there was to be dancing on the green. By the time the spot was reached she had recovered her equanimity, and tapped her neighbour with her wand and talked as usual.

Tess Durbeyfield at this time of her life was a mere vessel of emotion untinctured by experience[16]. The dialect was on her tongue to some extent, despite the village school: the characteristic intonation of that dialect for this district being the voicing approximately rendered by the syllable UR, probably as rich an utterance as any to be found in human speech. The pouted-up deep red mouth to which this syllable was native had hardly as yet settled into its definite shape, and her lower lip had a way of thrusting the middle of her top one upward, when they closed together after a word.

Phases of her childhood lurked in her aspect still[17]. As she walked along to-day, for all her bouncing handsome womanliness, you could sometimes see her twelfth year in her cheeks, or her ninth sparkling from her eyes; and even her fifth would flit over the curves of her mouth now and then.

Yet few knew, and still fewer considered this. A small minority, mainly strangers, would look long at her in casually passing by, and grow momentarily fascinated by her freshness, and wonder if they would ever see her again: but to almost everybody she was a fine and picturesque country girl, and no more.

Nothing was seen or heard further of Durbeyfield in his triumphal chariot under the conduct of the ostleress, and the club having entered the allotted space, dancing began. As there were no men in the company the girls danced at first with each other, but when the hour for the close of labour drew on, the masculine inhabitants of the village, together with other idlers and pedestrians, gathered round the spot, and appeared inclined to negotiate for a partner.

Among these on-lookers were three young men of a superior class, carrying small knapsacks strapped to their shoulders, and stout sticks in their hands. Their general likeness to each other, and their consecutive ages, would almost have suggested that they might be, what in fact they were, brothers. The eldest wore the white tie, high waistcoat, and thin-brimmed hat of the regulation curate; the second was the normal undergraduate; the appearance of the third and youngest would hardly have been sufficient to characterize him; there was an uncribbed, uncabined aspect in his eyes and attire, implying that he had hardly as yet found the entrance to his professional groove. That he was a desultory tentative student of something and everything might only have been predicted of him.

These three brethren told casual acquaintance that they were spending their Whitsun holidays in a walking tour through the Vale of Blackmoor, their course being south-westerly from the town of Shaston on the north-east.

They leant over the gate by the highway, and inquired as to the meaning of the dance and the white-frocked maids. The two elder of the brothers were plainly not intending to linger more than a moment, but the spectacle of a bevy of girls dancing without male partners seemed to amuse the third, and make him in no hurry to move on. He unstrapped his knapsack, put it, with his stick, on the hedge-bank, and opened the gate.

"What are you going to do, Angel?" asked the eldest.

"I am inclined to go and have a fling with them. Why not all of us—just for a minute or two—it will not detain us long?"

"No—no; nonsense!" said the first. "Dancing in public with a troop of country hoydens—suppose we should be seen! Come along, or it will be dark before we get to Stourcastle, and there's no place we can sleep at nearer than that; besides, we must get through another chapter of A Counterblast to Agnosticism[18] before we turn in, now I have taken the trouble to bring the book."

"All right—I'll overtake you and Cuthbert in five minutes; don't stop; I give my word that I will, Felix."

The two elder reluctantly left him and walked on, taking their brother's knapsack to relieve him in following, and the youngest entered the field.

"This is a thousand pities," he said gallantly, to two or three girls nearest him, as soon as there was a pause in the dance. "Where are your partners, my dears?"

"They've not left off work yet," answered one of the boldest. "They'll be here by and by. Till then, will you be one, sir?"

"Certainly. But what's one among so many!"

"Better than none." Tis melancholy work facing and footing it to one of your own sort, and no clipsing and colling at all. Now, pick and choose."

"'Ssh—don't be so for'ard!" said a shyer girl.

The young man, thus invited, glanced them over, and attempted some discrimination; but, as the group were all so new to him, he could not very well exercise it. He took almost the first that came to hand, which was not the speaker, as she had expected; nor did it happen to be Tess Durbeyfield. Pedigree, ancestral skeletons, monumental record, the d'Urberville lineaments, did not help Tess in her life's battle as yet, even to the extent of attracting to her a dancing-partner over the heads of the commonest peasantry. So much for Norman blood unaided by Victorian lucre.

The name of the eclipsing girl, whatever it was, has not been handed down; but she was envied by all as the first who enjoyed the luxury of a masculine partner that evening. Yet such was the force of example that the village young men, who had not hastened to enter the gate while no intruder was in the way, now dropped in quickly, and soon the couples became leavened with rustic youth to a marked extent, till at length the plainest woman in the club was no longer compelled to foot it on the masculine side of the figure.

The church clock struck, when suddenly the student said that he must leave—he had been forgetting himself—he had to join his companions. As he fell out of the dance his eyes lighted on Tess Durbeyfield, whose own large orbs wore, to tell the truth, the faintest aspect of reproach that he had not chosen her. He, too, was sorry then that, owing to her backwardness, he had not observed her; and with that in his mind he left the pasture.

On account of his long delay he started in a flying-run down the lane westward, and had soon passed the hollow and mounted the next rise. He had not yet overtaken his brothers, but he paused to get breath, and looked back. He could see the white figures of the girls in the green enclosure whirling about as they had whirled when he was among them. They seemed to have quite forgotten him already.

All of them, except, perhaps, one. This white shape stood apart by the hedge alone. From her position he knew it to be the pretty maiden with whom he had not danced. Trifling as the matter was, he yet instinctively felt that she was hurt by his oversight. He wished that he had asked her; he wished that he had inquired her name. She was so modest, so expressive, she had looked so soft in her thin white gown that he felt he had acted stupidly.

However, it could not be helped, and turning, and bending himself to a rapid walk, he dismissed the subject from his mind.

注释（Notes）

1. t'ee: to thee, to you
2. Sir：大写的 Sir 不仅可以表示先生，还可以表示骑士或者准男爵的头衔。
3. whilst：古语 while。
4. William the Conqueror：征服者威廉，原为占领法国诺曼底的维京人后代，入侵英格兰后成为英国国王，给英国带来了欧洲大陆的文化和语言。
5. Battle Abbey Roll：纪功寺文档，记载跟随威廉王征战英国的诺曼贵族的一份名单，现保存于纪功寺。
6. Pipe Rolls：派普名册，记录皇家每年收支情况的文件，始于 1131 年，止于 1842 年。
7. Oliver Cromwell：奥利弗·克伦威尔。英国内战期间资产阶级革命中的革命派领袖，用强大的铁骑兵打败了国王查理一世的军队，并把查理一世砍头，后成为共和国的护国公，实行严峻的清教徒式政策。
8. Charles the Second：查理一世之子查理二世，人称"快活王"。因克伦威尔的统治不得人心，而且他成为护国公以后也与议会不和，克伦威尔死后议会实行了君主复辟，查理二世成为新的国王。
9. 'twaddn'：it wasn't
10. skillentons：skeletons
11. da'ter：daughter
12. Thomas de la Lynd：人名，托马斯·德·拉·林。
13. May-Day dance：在欧洲传统节日五朔节，英国人为了庆祝春天的来临，会围着五月花柱跳舞。
14. Cerealia：赛丽斯节，指庆祝罗马丰收女神赛丽斯（Ceres）的节日。

15. Georgian style：英国国王乔治一世到乔治四世统治时期(1714—1830年)流行的风格。

16. untinctured by experience：innocent，不谙世事。

17. Phases of her childhood lurked in her aspect still：她的童年的各个阶段的特征，现在仍然还留在她的身上。

18. *A Counterblast to Agnosticism*：《驳不可知论》，该书名疑为哈代杜撰，与英国科学家赫胥黎的"不可知论"有关。

主题探究 (Themes)

（扫码阅读）

问题讨论 (Questions for Discussion)

1. Which characters choose to live in the past, and what are the consequences?

2. Angel calls Tess "Demeter" and "Artemis" during their courtship. Why does he choose these two goddesses in particular? Why does Tess not like being called "Demeter" and "Artemis" (or any other goddess name)? Why does she insist, "Call me Tess"?

3. Why does Hardy not depict Tess's trial or execution?

4. Who is the narrator, can she or he read minds, and, more importantly, can we trust her or him?

5. What leads to the tragedy of Tess?

6. Is Alec a villain?

7. Is it possible to read this novel as a cautionary tale about the evils of refusing to educate young women about sex? Is it productive to read it in that way?

价值引领 (Value Guidance)

关于创伤记忆：现实生活中，我们往往缺少与过去的不幸和遭遇做告别的勇气和果断，我们常常会被过去所困，沉浸于往事，即使是废弃之物，都攥在手里不肯松手。一切顺其自然，放下过去，放过他人，也放过自己。忘掉过去的伤疤，不纠结于以往的生活，坦然面对新生活，踏踏实实地过好当下的每一天。调整好自己的心态，人生的快乐砝码掌握在自己的手里，无论他人说了什么话，做了什么事，亦或是有怎样的过往，都不能影响我们快乐的航道。

(请扫码观看视频 *Tess of the D'Urbervilles*)

Mrs. Warren's Profession

作品简介 (Introduction to the Work)

Mrs. Warren's Profession, a play in four acts by George Bernard Shaw, written in 1893 and published in 1898 but not performed until 1902 because of government censorship; the play's subject matter is organized prostitution. The play is about a former prostitute, now a madam, who attempts to come to terms with her disapproving daughter. It is a problem play, offering social commentary to illustrate Shaw's belief that the act of prostitution was not caused by moral failure but by economic necessity. Elements of the play were borrowed from Shaw's 1882 novel *Cashel Byron's Profession*, about a man who becomes a boxer due to limited employment opportunities. In *Mrs. Warren's Profession*, Vivie Warren, a well-educated young woman, discovers that her mother attained her present status and affluence by rising from poverty through prostitution and that she now has financial interests in several brothels throughout Europe. Vivie acknowledges her mother's courage in overcoming her past but rejects her continued involvement in prostitution. She severs her relationship with her mother, also rejecting Frank and the possibility of other suitors.

Act I takes place in the countryside town of Haslemere, where Vivie Warren is staying after having graduated from Cambridge University with honors. She is soon joined at the cottage where she is staying by Praed, an architect and artist friend of her mother's; her mother, Mrs. Warren, whom she has not seen in a long time; Sir George Crofts, her mother's friend and business partner; Frank, her friend who is interested in her romantically; and the Reverend Samuel Gardner, Frank's father, with whom he is staying since he has no money to support himself.

(扫码阅读)

Mrs. Warren's Profession
(excerpt)

Unit 10
Some Women Novelists

Jane Austen: *Pride and Prejudice*
Charlotte Brontë: *Jane Eyre*

▽

■ 作者简介 (Introduction to the Authors)

　　Jane Austen (1775—1817) is one of the most important English woman novelists. She is ranked among the greatest British novelists. Jane Austen was born in Hampshire where her father was rector of a church. Mr. Austen graduated from Oxford University and encouraged the love of learning in his children. And Austen's mother was a woman of ready wit, born in a prominent family. Austen was mostly educated at home. She was versed in French and British history. When she was still young, she began to read works of Fielding, Richardson and Byron. Living in an environment of creativity, she started writing at an early age. Also, she frequently attended balls and parties to pay attention to various people, while not engaging in reading and writing. In 1801, her father retired to Bath with the families. During their life in Bath, Austen observed all kinds of people which served as the valuable material for her novels. However, it was not a good place for her to focus her energies on writing. So, she moved into Chawton in 1809 and completed almost all of her famous novels. In her novels, she vividly depicted middle class life during the early 19th century. In later stages of Austen's writing, her brother Henry acted as her literary agent. Austen's health declined quickly and she finally died in 1817. Austen showed her belief in reason over passion, the sense of responsibility and good manners over Romantic tendencies of emotion and individuality, setting the stage for the 19th century Realism.

　　Charlotte Brontë (1816—1855) is an English novelist and poet. It is *Jane Eyre*, a semi-autobiographical novel that placed Charlotte in the ranks of the foremost English realistic writers. Charlotte was the third of the six children, who was born on 21 April 1816. Her father was a well-educated clergyman. In 1820, the family moved to Haworth of Yorkshire, isolated moorland, where the children often enjoyed themselves in its wildness. In 1821 her mother died of cancer. Charlotte was sent to a charity school in 1824. However, she went through a painful and tough time in this boarding school where kids were tortured by starvation and harsh rules. Her two elder sisters died of tuberculosis in 1825 mostly because of the terrible condition in the school and shortly after that she left school. In Charlotte's life, few years of a governess made her feel like a slave. So, she and Emily decided to study French in Brussels aiming to found a school but finally they failed to enroll students. In 1846, Charlotte and her two sisters, Emily and Anne, published a joint collection of poems with masculine pen names but only two copies were sold. Then they began to write novels and made successes in succession. She was especially fond of Byron and created some characters like Byron's brooding heroes. She died in 1855. Charlotte presented a vivid realistic picture of the English society by exposing the cruelty, hypocrisy and evils of the upper class. Furthermore, she presented a detailed inner life of characters. As a woman writer, she was concerned about women problems in Victorian England and spoke for women.

Pride and Prejudice

作品简介 (Introduction to the Work)

Pride and Prejudice, a novel by Jane Austen, published anonymously in three volumes in 1813. It centres on the burgeoning relationship between Elizabeth Bennet, the daughter of a country gentleman and the novel's heroine, and Fitzwilliam Darcy, an aristocratic landowner. It is set in rural England at the turn of the 19th century, and it follows the Bennet family, which includes five very different sisters, all of whom their mother is keen to see suitably married. The intersections of these sisters with several eligible bachelors drive the action of the novel. Despite initial friction between them, Elizabeth eventually accepts Darcy's proposal of marriage. Throughout the novel, Austen describes the personalities of the Bennet sisters and how they contend with their contemporary world in different ways. It's a novel that also deals with the issues of manners, upbringing, morality, education, and marriage in the society of the landed gentry in the north of England in the early 19th century. *Pride and Prejudice* was the second of four novels Austen published during her lifetime. It has remained popular since its first publication, and it has inspired various stage, film, and television productions.

The story opens with the arrival of Mr. Bingley, a wealthy, charming, and sociable young bachelor, into Netherfield Park in the neighborhood of the Bennet family. Without telling his family, Mr. Bennet visits Bingley. Back at home, Mr. Bennet teases his family by pretending to be uninterested in Bingley's arrival, only to then reveal his visit by asking Elizabeth when the next ball is scheduled and promising to introduce her to Bingley beforehand. Mrs. Bennet is delighted and praises her husband and his little joke. She promises all the girls that they'll get a chance to dance with Bingley.

(扫码阅读)
Pride and Prejudice
(excerpt)

Jane Eyre

▌ 作品简介 (Introduction to the Work)

Jane Eyre is a novel by the English writer Charlotte Brontë. It was published under her pen name "Currer Bell" on 19 October 1847, which is a male name, for nobody respected and valued woman writers in England in that period. It is a Bildungsroman which follows the experiences of its eponymous heroine, including her growth to adulthood and her love for Mr. Rochester, the brooding master of Thornfield Hall. *Jane Eyre*'s appeal was partly due to the fact that it was written in the first person and often addressed the reader, creating great immediacy. In addition, Jane is an unconventional heroine, an independent and self-reliant woman who overcomes both adversity and societal norms. Widely considered as a classic, *Jane Eyre* gave new truthfulness to the Victorian novel with its realistic portrayal of the inner life of a woman, noting her struggles with her natural desires and social condition.

Chapter 14 tells the following story: Jane barely sees Rochester, until one night after dinner he calls for Jane and Adèle to join him. He gives Adèle the gift from Paris that she's been impatiently waiting for, and she goes off to play. Rochester, who seems a bit drunk, chats amiably with Jane, and she answers with all of her usual directness. Rochester asks if Jane thinks he's handsome. Jane bluntly says no, even though she secretly admires his eyes. They converse about each other's personalities, about treating people directly and on equal terms. It seems to her that Rochester sometimes speaks as if he were reading her mind. Describing himself, Rochester claims to be a man of experience and unfortunate circumstances, hardened from flesh into "Indian-rubber". He makes obscure references to his past and his plans for reforming himself, but Jane gets confused by his vagueness and she stops the conversation. Adèle soon returns, dressed up in a new pink gown, and dances around. Rochester says that Adèle reminds him of her French mother, Céline Varens. Rochester promises to someday explain to Jane more about how and why Adèle became his ward.

作品选文 (Selected Reading)

Jane Eyre
(Excerpt)
Chapter 14

For several subsequent days I saw little of Mr. Rochester. In the mornings he seemed much engaged with business, and, in the afternoon, gentlemen from Millcote or the neighbourhood called, and sometimes stayed to dine with him. When his sprain was well enough to admit of horse exercise, he rode out a good deal; probably to return these visits, as he generally did not come back till late at night.

During this interval, even Adèle was seldom sent for to his presence, and all my acquaintance with him was confined to an occasional rencontre in the hall, on the stairs, or in the gallery, when he would sometimes pass me haughtily and coldly, just acknowledging my presence by a distant nod or a cool glance, and sometimes bow and smile with gentlemanlike affability. His changes of mood did not offend me, because I saw that I had nothing to do with their alternation; the ebb and flow depended on causes quite disconnected with me.

One day he had had company to dinner, and had sent for my portfolio; in order, doubtless, to exhibit its contents: the gentlemen went away early, to attend a public meeting at Millcote, as Mrs. Fairfax informed me; but the night being wet and inclement, Mr. Rochester did not accompany them. Soon after they were gone he rang the bell: a message came that I and Adèle were to go downstairs. I brushed Adèle's hair and made her neat, and having ascertained that I was myself in my usual Quaker[1] trim, where there was nothing to retouch—all being too close and plain, braided locks included, to admit of disarrangement—we descended, Adèle wondering whether the petit coffre[2] was at length come; for, owing to some mistake, its arrival had hitherto been delayed. She was gratified: there it stood, a little carton, on the table when we entered the dining-room. She appeared to know it by instinct.

"Ma[3] boite[4]! ma boite!" exclaimed she, running towards it.

"Yes, there is your 'boite' at last: take it into a corner, you genuine daughter of Paris, and amuse yourself with disembowelling it," said the deep and rather sarcastic voice of Mr. Rochester, proceeding from the depths of an immense easy-chair at the fireside. "And mind," he continued, "don't bother me with any details of the anatomical process, or any notice of the condition of the entrails: let your operation be conducted in silence; tiens-toi-tranquille[5], enfant[6]; comprends-tu[7]?"

Adèle seemed scarcely to need the warning; she had already retired to a sofa with her treasure, and was busy untying the cord which secured the lid. Having removed this impediment, and lifted certain silvery envelopes of tissue paper, she merely exclaimed—

"Oh ciel[8]! Que c'est beau![9]" and then remained absorbed in ecstatic contemplation.

"Is Miss Eyre there?" now demanded the master, half rising from his seat to look round to the door, near which I still stood.

"Ah! well, come forward; be seated here." He drew a chair near his own. "I am not fond of the prattle of children," he continued; "for, old bachelor as I am, I have no pleasant associations connected with their lisp. It would be intolerable to me to pass a whole evening tête-à-tête[10] with a brat. Don't draw that chair farther off, Miss Eyre; sit down exactly where I placed it—if you please, that is. Confound these civilities! I continually forget them. Nor do I particularly affect simple-minded old ladies. By-the-bye, I must have mine in mind; it won't do to neglect her; she is a Fairfax, or wed to one; and blood is said to be thicker than water."

He rang, and despatched an invitation to Mrs. Fairfax, who soon arrived, knitting-basket in hand.

"Good evening, madam; I sent to you for a charitable purpose. I have forbidden Adèle to talk to me about her presents, and she is bursting with repletion; have the goodness to serve her as auditress and interlocutrice; it will be one of the most benevolent acts you ever performed."

Adèle, indeed, no sooner saw Mrs. Fairfax, than she summoned her to her sofa, and there quickly filled her lap with the porcelain, the ivory, the waxen contents of her "boite;" pouring out, meantime, explanations and raptures in such broken English as she was mistress of.

"Now I have performed the part of a good host," pursued Mr. Rochester, "put my guests into the way of amusing each other, I ought to be at liberty to attend to my own pleasure. Miss Eyre, draw your chair still a little farther forward: you are yet too far back; I cannot see you without disturbing my position in this comfortable chair, which I have no mind to do."

I did as I was bid, though I would much rather have remained somewhat in the shade; but Mr. Rochester had such a direct way of giving orders, it seemed a matter of course to obey him promptly.

We were, as I have said, in the dining-room: the lustre, which had been lit for dinner, filled the room with a festal breadth of light; the large fire was all red and clear; the purple curtains hung rich and ample before the lofty window and loftier arch;

everything was still, save the subdued chat of Adèle (she dared not speak loud), and, filling up each pause, the beating of winter rain against the panes.

Mr. Rochester, as he sat in his damask-covered chair, looked different to what I had seen him look before; not quite so stern—much less gloomy. There was a smile on his lips, and his eyes sparkled, whether with wine or not, I am not sure; but I think it very probable. He was, in short, in his after-dinner mood; more expanded and genial, and also more self-indulgent than the frigid and rigid temper of the morning; still he looked preciously grim, cushioning his massive head against the swelling back of his chair, and receiving the light of the fire on his granite-hewn features, and in his great, dark eyes; for he had great, dark eyes, and very fine eyes, too—not without a certain change in their depths sometimes, which, if it was not softness, reminded you, at least, of that feeling.

He had been looking two minutes at the fire, and I had been looking the same length of time at him, when, turning suddenly, he caught my gaze fastened on his physiognomy.

"You examine me, Miss Eyre," said he: "do you think me handsome?"

I should, if I had deliberated, have replied to this question by something conventionally vague and polite; but the answer somehow slipped from my tongue before I was aware—"No, sir."

"Ah! By my word! there is something singular about you," said he: "you have the air of a little nonnette[11]; quaint, quiet, grave, and simple, as you sit with your hands before you, and your eyes generally bent on the carpet (except, by-the-bye, when they are directed piercingly to my face; as just now, for instance); and when one asks you a question, or makes a remark to which you are obliged to reply, you rap out a round rejoinder, which, if not blunt, is at least brusque. What do you mean by it?"

"Sir, I was too plain; I beg your pardon. I ought to have replied that it was not easy to give an impromptu answer to a question about appearances; that tastes mostly differ; and that beauty is of little consequence, or something of that sort."

"You ought to have replied no such thing. Beauty of little consequence, indeed! And so, under pretence of softening the previous outrage, of stroking and soothing me into placidity, you stick a sly penknife under my ear! Go on: what fault do you find with me, pray? I suppose I have all my limbs and all my features like any other man?"

"Mr. Rochester, allow me to disown my first answer: I intended no pointed repartee: it was only a blunder."

"Just so: I think so: and you shall be answerable for it. Criticise me: does my forehead not please you?"

He lifted up the sable waves of hair which lay horizontally over his brow, and showed a solid enough mass of intellectual organs, but an abrupt deficiency where the suave sign of benevolence should have risen.

"Now, ma'am, am I a fool?"

"Far from it, sir. You would, perhaps, think me rude if I inquired in return whether you are a philanthropist?"

"There again! Another stick of the penknife, when she pretended to pat my head: and that is because I said I did not like the society of children and old women (low be it spoken!). No, young lady, I am not a general philanthropist; but I bear a conscience;" and he pointed to the prominences which are said to indicate that faculty, and which, fortunately for him, were sufficiently conspicuous; giving, indeed, a marked breadth to the upper part of his head: "and, besides, I once had a kind of rude tenderness of heart. When I was as old as you, I was a feeling fellow enough; partial to the unfledged, unfostered, and unlucky; but Fortune has knocked me about since: she has even kneaded me with her knuckles, and now I flatter myself I am hard and tough as an India-rubber ball; pervious, though, through a chink or two still, and with one sentient point in the middle of the lump. Yes: does that leave hope for me?"

"Hope of what, sir?"

"Of my final re-transformation from India-rubber back to flesh?"

"Decidedly he has had too much wine," I thought; and I did not know what answer to make to his queer question: how could I tell whether he was capable of being retransformed?

"You looked very much puzzled, Miss Eyre; and though you are not pretty any more than I am handsome, yet a puzzled air becomes you; besides, it is convenient, for it keeps those searching eyes of yours away from my physiognomy, and busies them with the worsted flowers of the rug; so puzzle on. Young lady, I am disposed to be gregarious and communicative to-night."

With this announcement he rose from his chair, and stood, leaning his arm on the marble mantelpiece: in that attitude his shape was seen plainly as well as his face; his unusual breadth of chest, disproportionate almost to his length of limb. I am sure most people would have thought him an ugly man; yet there was so much unconscious pride in his port; so much ease in his demeanour; such a look of complete indifference to his own external appearance; so haughty a reliance on the power of other qualities, intrinsic or adventitious, to atone for the lack of mere personal attractiveness, that, in looking at him, one inevitably shared the indifference, and, even in a blind, imperfect sense, put faith in the confidence.

"I am disposed to be gregarious and communicative to-night," he repeated, "and that is why I sent for you: the fire and the chandelier were not sufficient company for me;

nor would Pilot have been, for none of these can talk. Adèle is a degree better, but still far below the mark; Mrs. Fairfax ditto; you, I am persuaded, can suit me if you will: you puzzled me the first evening I invited you down here. I have almost forgotten you since: other ideas have driven yours from my head; but to-night I am resolved to be at ease; to dismiss what importunes, and recall what pleases. It would please me now to draw you out—to learn more of you—therefore speak."

Instead of speaking, I smiled; and not a very complacent or submissive smile either.

"Speak," he urged.

"What about, sir?"

"Whatever you like. I leave both the choice of subject and the manner of treating it entirely to yourself."

Accordingly I sat and said nothing: "If he expects me to talk for the mere sake of talking and showing off, he will find he has addressed himself to the wrong person," I thought.

"You are dumb, Miss Eyre."

I was dumb still. He bent his head a little towards me, and with a single hasty glance seemed to dive into my eyes.

"Stubborn?" he said, "and annoyed. Ah! it is consistent. I put my request in an absurd, almost insolent form. Miss Eyre, I beg your pardon. The fact is, once for all, I don't wish to treat you like an inferior: that is" (correcting himself), "I claim only such superiority as must result from twenty years' difference in age and a century's advance in experience. This is legitimate, et j'y tiens[12], as Adèle would say; and it is by virtue of this superiority, and this alone, that I desire you to have the goodness to talk to me a little now, and divert my thoughts, which are galled with dwelling on one point—cankering as a rusty nail."

He had deigned an explanation, almost an apology, and I did not feel insensible to his condescension, and would not seem so.

"I am willing to amuse you, if I can, sir—quite willing; but I cannot introduce a topic, because how do I know what will interest you? Ask me questions, and I will do my best to answer them."

"Then, in the first place, do you agree with me that I have a right to be a little masterful, abrupt, perhaps exacting, sometimes, on the grounds I stated, namely, that I am old enough to be your father, and that I have battled through a varied experience with many men of many nations, and roamed over half the globe, while you have lived quietly with one set of people in one house?"

"Do as you please, sir."

"That is no answer; or rather it is a very irritating, because a very evasive one. Reply clearly."

"I don't think, sir, you have a right to command me, merely because you are older than I, or because you have seen more of the world than I have; your claim to superiority depends on the use you have made of your time and experience."

"Humph! Promptly spoken. But I won't allow that, seeing that it would never suit my case, as I have made an indifferent, not to say a bad, use of both advantages. Leaving superiority out of the question, then, you must still agree to receive my orders now and then, without being piqued or hurt by the tone of command. Will you?"

I smiled: I thought to myself Mr. Rochester is peculiar—he seems to forget that he pays me £30 per annum for receiving his orders.

"The smile is very well," said he, catching instantly the passing expression; "but speak too."

"I was thinking, sir, that very few masters would trouble themselves to inquire whether or not their paid subordinates were piqued and hurt by their orders."

"Paid subordinates! What! you are my paid subordinate, are you? Oh yes, I had forgotten the salary! Well then, on that mercenary ground, will you agree to let me hector a little?"

"No, sir, not on that ground; but, on the ground that you did forget it, and that you care whether or not a dependent is comfortable in his dependency, I agree heartily."

"And will you consent to dispense with a great many conventional forms and phrases, without thinking that the omission arises from insolence?"

"I am sure, sir, I should never mistake informality for insolence: one I rather like, the other nothing free-born would submit to, even for a salary."

"Humbug! Most things free-born will submit to anything for a salary; therefore, keep to yourself, and don't venture on generalities of which you are intensely ignorant. However, I mentally shake hands with you for your answer, despite its inaccuracy; and as much for the manner in which it was said, as for the substance of the speech; the manner was frank and sincere; one does not often see such a manner: no, on the contrary, affectation, or coldness, or stupid, coarse-minded misapprehension of one's meaning are the usual rewards of candour. Not three in three thousand raw school-girl-governesses would have answered me as you have just done. But I don't mean to flatter you: if you are cast in a different mould to the majority, it is no merit of yours: Nature did it. And then, after all, I go too fast in my conclusions: for what I yet know, you may be no better than the rest; you may have intolerable defects to counterbalance your few good points."

"And so may you," I thought. My eye met his as the idea crossed my mind: he seemed to read the glance, answering as if its import had been spoken as well as imagined—

"Yes, yes, you are right," said he; "I have plenty of faults of my own: I know it, and I don't wish to palliate them, I assure you. God wot I need not be too severe about others; I have a past existence, a series of deeds, a colour of life to contemplate within my own breast, which might well call my sneers and censures from my neighbours to myself. I started, or rather (for like other defaulters, I like to lay half the blame on ill fortune and adverse circumstances) was thrust on to a wrong tack at the age of one-and-twenty, and have never recovered the right course since: but I might have been very different; I might have been as good as you—wiser—almost as stainless. I envy you your peace of mind, your clean conscience, your unpolluted memory. Little girl, a memory without blot or contamination must be an exquisite treasure—an inexhaustible source of pure refreshment: is it not?"

"How was your memory when you were eighteen, sir?"

"All right then; limpid, salubrious: no gush of bilge water had turned it to fetid puddle. I was your equal at eighteen—quite your equal. Nature meant me to be, on the whole, a good man, Miss Eyre; one of the better kind, and you see I am not so. You would say you don't see it; at least I flatter myself I read as much in your eye (beware, by-the-bye, what you express with that organ; I am quick at interpreting its language). Then take my word for it,—I am not a villain: you are not to suppose that—not to attribute to me any such bad eminence; but, owing, I verily believe, rather to circumstances than to my natural bent, I am a trite commonplace sinner, hackneyed in all the poor petty dissipations with which the rich and worthless try to put on life. Do you wonder that I avow this to you? Know, that in the course of your future life you will often find yourself elected the involuntary confidant of your acquaintances' secrets: people will instinctively find out, as I have done, that it is not your forte to tell of yourself, but to listen while others talk of themselves; they will feel, too, that you listen with no malevolent scorn of their indiscretion, but with a kind of innate sympathy; not the less comforting and encouraging because it is very unobtrusive in its manifestations."

注释（Notes）

1. Quaker：贵格会，17 世纪成立的基督教派别，因宣称"听到上帝的话而发抖"得名，该派别反对战争和暴力，不敬重任何人。
2. petit coffre：法语，小箱子。
3. Ma：法语，我的。
4. boite：法语，箱子。

5. tiens-toi-tranquille：法语，保持安静。
6. enfant：法语，我的孩子。
7. comprends-tu：法语，明白了吗。
8. ciel：法语，天呐。
9. Que c'est beau!：法语，如此美丽!
10. tête-à-tête：法语，促膝长谈。
11. Nonnette：法语，年轻修女。
12. et j'y tiens：法语，我一定会把握住的。

主题探究（Themes）

（扫码阅读）

价值引领（Value Guidance）/ 中英比较（A Comparison between Chinese and English Literature）

夏洛蒂·勃朗特在《简·爱》中旗帜鲜明地提出了女性独立人格的问题，并指出独立人格是建立在经济独立的基础上的，她的作品凸显了女性自尊自爱的美好人格。通过简·爱这个人物，夏洛蒂否定了当时男性与女性的地位差异，正如简·爱对罗切斯特所说："在人格上我们是平等的。"遵循法律与道德底线，简拒绝诱惑，拒绝成为罗切斯特的情妇，她要以一种平等而受尊敬的姿态与罗切斯特走入婚姻，如果不能，那么她的选择就是离开，尽管这种选择让她痛彻心扉（如小说中所写："Hiring a mistress is the next worse thing to buying a slave: both are often by nature, and always by position, inferior; and to live familiarly with inferiors is degrading."[①]）。这种平等意识是女性意识的一大进步。这不禁让我们想起我国朦胧派诗人舒婷的《致橡树》，诗歌中所歌颂的也正是同样的比肩站立、风雨同舟的爱情。的确，爱情和婚姻需要以人格平等、个性独立、互相尊重为基础。

致橡树
（舒　婷）

我如果爱你——

---

① Charlotte Brontë. *Jane Eyre*[M]. Ware, Hertfordshire: Wordsworth Editions Limited, 1999: 275.

绝不学攀援的凌霄花,
借你的高枝炫耀自己;
我如果爱你——
绝不学痴情的鸟儿,
为绿荫重复单调的歌曲;
也不止像泉源,
常年送来清凉的慰藉;
也不止像险峰,
增加你的高度,衬托你的威仪。
甚至日光,
甚至春雨。
不,这些都还不够!
我必须是你近旁的一株木棉,
作为树的形象和你站在一起。
根,紧握在地下;
叶,相触在云里。
每一阵风过,
我们都互相致意,
但没有人,
听懂我们的言语。
你有你的铜枝铁干,
像刀,像剑,也像戟;
我有我红硕的花朵,
像沉重的叹息,
又像英勇的火炬。
我们分担寒潮、风雷、霹雳;
我们共享雾霭、流岚、虹霓。
仿佛永远分离,
却又终身相依。
这才是伟大的爱情,
坚贞就在这里:
爱——
不仅爱你伟岸的身躯,
也爱你坚持的位置,
足下的土地。

问题讨论(Questions for Discussion)

1. Jane is plain-looking in appearance. Can you list some inner beauty that might help her win Rochester's love?

2. If Jane and Rochester are "akin", then what is their "kind"? What do Jane and Rochester actually share, and what made them similar in the first place?

3. Marriage is one of the most important themes of the novel. What is marriage in your opinion? At what point in the novel does their marriage become *desirable*? Why?

4. Why does Jane want to go to school or learn anything in the first place? Why does education become such an important issue for her as a child?

5. As a novel, how does *Jane Eyre* depict with high society and wealthy aristocrats? And how does it imply about poverty?

6. Do you feel sorry for Bertha Mason? Does Rochester threat her fairly? Does she seem as bad as he suggests? Please write a sequel to the novel in about 150 words.

(请扫码观看视频 *Jane Eyre*)

Unit 11
Modernism in Poetry

W. B. Yeats: "When You Are Old"
T. S. Eliot: "The Love Song of J. Alfred Prufrock"
▽

作者简介 (Introduction to the Authors)

　　W. B. Yeats (1865—1939) is a dramatist and the foremost poet of the modern age. He is also the acknowledged leader of the Irish literary renaissance. He was born into an Anglo-Irish Protestant family in Dublin. Yeats always spent his holiday in his mother's native county of Sligo, where he gained access to Irish history and legends. In his life time, mysticism, spiritualism and astrology all had a lasting influence on him. It is viewed that his poetry can be divided into three periods. In the first period, his lyrical poems were much in debts to Edmund Spenser, Shelley and the poets of Pre-Raphaelite Brotherhood. But his Irish theme and special use of language distinguished him from others. In the middle of it, he wrote some modern poetry under the influence of Ezra Pound and T. S. Eliot. In 1889, he met and fell in love with Maude Gonne, an Irish nationalist, but the woman refused to marry him. Apparently, she had a significant effect on his works. Then, Yeats, Lady Gregory, Edward Martyn and other writers launched a campaign to revive Irish Literary, which led to the Abbey Theatre. And he wrote many plays for this theatre. He was awarded Nobel Prize in literature in 1923. In 1939 he died in France. His contribution to literature is the various kinds of poetry, extraordinary ranges of subjects, rich imagination and use of symbols. His plays based on Irish culture facilitate the Irish cultural transmission and promote the national awareness, thus becoming a drive for Irish independence.

　　T. S. Eliot (1888—1965) is a poet, playwright, prose writer and literary critic. And he is considered as one of the 20th century's major poet. His *The Waste Land* proved to be a milestone in modern poetry. Eliot was born in a wealthy merchant family in St. Louis, Missouri. It is his hometown that affected him deeply. Eliot once acknowledged that some imagery in his poems was created on the basis of St. Louis. When he was a kid, he became obsessed with books. Undoubtedly, Eliot received a good education. He attained the degrees of BA and MA at Harvard. Then he began to study philosophy. During his education, he was exposed to French Symbolist. Furthermore, New Criticism, argued by Irving Babbit, had a great influence on Eliot. So, he was usually viewed as an opponent of romanticism and an advocate of classical literature. In 1914, Eliot moved to England, and was introduced to Ezra Pound who helped him most. In 1927, he converted to Anglicanism and then took the British citizenship. On account of his frequent migration, Eliot had no sense of identity which formed a homeless atmosphere in his poems. He was awarded the Nobel Prize for literature and British Order of Merit in 1948. He died in 1965 in London. Eliot made decisive achievement in initiating New Criticism. He proposed the ideas of objective correlative and the impersonal theory. In his view, a poem should be an organic thing and it should reflect the fragmentary nature of modern life. His poetry was also noted for its fresh visual imagery, flexible tone, highly expressive rhythm and rich illusions.

When You Are Old

作品简介 (Introduction to the Work)

"When You Are Old" is a poem by the Irish poet William Butler Yeats, which is published in Yeats's second collection, *The Rose* (1893). In the poem, the speaker asks someone to think ahead to old age, strongly suggesting that the addressee will eventually regret being unwilling to return the speaker's love. The poem consists of three stanzas, each containing four lines. The rhyme scheme is very distinct and steady; the first stanza is abba; the second is cddc; the third is effe. Yeats uses this closed rhyming pattern to emphasize the idea of each stanza. Additionally, there are a total of ten syllables in each line. The stress falls on the second syllable of each foot. Hence, Yeats wrote the poem in iambic pentameter. This, coupled with the steady rhyme scheme, lends a sing-song quality to the poem.

"When You Are Old" is a bittersweet poem that reveals the complexities of love. The poem is generally taken to be addressed to Maud Gonne, an Irish actress with whom Yeats was infatuated throughout his life. Besides, the poem can also be interpreted more broadly, without specifying the names or genders of either the speaker or the addressee. In any case, the poem argues in favor of a kind of love based not on physical appearances—which fade over time—but on the deeper beauty of the soul.

作品选文 (Selected Reading)

When You Are Old[1]

When you are old and grey and full of sleep,
And nodding by the fire, take down this book[2],
And slowly read, and dream of the soft look

Your eyes had once³, and of their shadows deep⁴;

How many loved your moments of glad grace,
And loved your beauty with love false or true,
But one man loved the pilgrim Soul in you,
And loved the sorrows of your changing⁵ face;

And bending down beside the glowing bars,
Murmur, a little sadly, how Love fled
And paced upon the mountains overhead
And hid his face amid a crowd of stars.

作品译文(扫码阅读)

注释（Notes）

1. 此诗受到法国十六世纪诗人皮埃尔·德·龙沙一首十四行诗的启发。叶芝写此诗是献给他所热恋的女演员、爱尔兰民族主义者 Maud Gonne，但是他始终未能赢得她的爱。

2. this book：叶芝献给 Maud Gonne 的诗集。

3. had once：once had

4. their shadows deep：比喻双目深邃。

5. changing：aging

主题探究（Themes）

(扫码阅读)

问题讨论（Questions for Discussion）

1. Who do "you" allude to?
2. What life as "you" are old will be like?
3. The speaker uses the "pilgrim Soul" to describe his attitude towards "you", what

does it represents? Is there any difference between his love and others' love to "you"?

4. What do you think of the form and metre of this poem?

5. The image "fire" is repeatedly applied in this poem. What is the function of it?

6. What do "mountains" and "stars" symbolize? Please translate the last two lines in your own words.

7. Do you know any other poem in China that is similar with Yeats's "When You Are Old"? And please make a comparative study between them.

The Love Song of J. Alfred Prufrock

作品简介 (Introduction to the Work)

"The Love Song of J. Alfred Prufrock" is a poem written by T. S. Eliot and published in 1915. It is considered one of the quintessential works of modernism, a literary movement at the turn of the 20th century that emphasized themes of alienation, isolation, and the diminishing power of the traditional sources of authority. It isn't easy to decide what Prufrock is about; the fragmented poetic landscape of T. S. Eliot's poetry makes it difficult to pin down one exact feeling within "The Love Song of J. Alfred Prufrock". It is considered one of the most visceral, emotional poems and remains relevant today, particularly with millennials who are more than a little bit used to these feelings. It is primarily written in free verse. This means that most of the lines do not follow a specific rhyme scheme or metrical pattern. But, the poem is not without either. Eliot briefly uses various meters, such as the common iambic pentameter and less common spondaic and trochaic feet. For example, in lines seventy-three and seventy-four, the poet uses perfect iambic pentameter. The same can be said about the rhyme scheme. Although there is no perfect pattern, there are numerous couplets throughout the piece.

A free verse, stream-of-consciousness monologue from the perspective of an aging everyman, the poem portrays modern disillusionment with the social isolation and emptiness of the early 20th century world. Eliot's startling, precise imagery and his juxtaposition of classical allusions with banal, everyday concerns, established him as a voice of literary modernism, setting the stage for future his canonical works, like "The Waste Land" and "Preludes".

作品选文 (Selected Reading)

The Love Song of J. Alfred Prufrock

S'io credesse che mia risposta fosse

Modernism in Poetry | Unit 11

A persona che mai tornasse al mondo,
Questa fiamma staria senza piu scosse.
Ma percioche giammai di questo fondo
Non torno vivo alcun, s'i'odo il vero,
Senza tema d'infamia ti rispondo. [1]

Let us go then, you and I,
When the evening is spread out against the sky
Like a patient etherized upon a table;
Let us go, through certain half-deserted streets,
The muttering retreats
Of restless nights in one-night cheap hotels
And sawdust[2] restaurants with oyster-shells:
Streets that follow like a tedious argument
Of insidious intent
To lead you to an overwhelming question…
Oh, do not ask, "What is it?"
Let us go and make our visit.

In the room the women come and go
Talking of Michelangelo[3].

The yellow fog[4] that rubs its back upon the window-panes,
The yellow smoke that rubs its muzzle on the window-panes,
Licked its tongue into the corners of the evening,
Lingered upon the pools that stand in drains,
Let fall upon its back the soot that falls from chimneys,
Slipped by the terrace, made a sudden leap,
And seeing that it was a soft October night,
Curled once about the house, and fell asleep.

And indeed there will be time
For the yellow smoke that slides along the street,
Rubbing its back upon the window-panes;
There will be time, there will be time
To prepare a face to meet the faces that you meet;

There will be time to murder and create,
And time for all the works and days of hands
That lift and drop a question on your plate;
Time for you and time for me,
And time yet for a hundred indecisions,
And for a hundred visions and revisions,
Before the taking of a toast and tea.

In the room the women come and go
Talking of Michelangelo.

And indeed there will be time
To wonder, "Do I dare?" and, "Do I dare?"
Time to turn back and descend the stair,
With a bald spot in the middle of my hair —
(They will say: "How his hair is growing thin!")
My morning coat, my collar mounting firmly to the chin,
My necktie rich and modest, but asserted by a simple pin —
(They will say: "But how his arms and legs are thin!")
Do I dare
Disturb the universe?
In a minute there is time
For decisions and revisions which a minute will reverse.

For I have known them all already, known them all:
Have known the evenings, mornings, afternoons,
I have measured out my life with coffee spoons;
I know the voices dying with a dying fall[5]
Beneath the music from a farther room.
So how should I presume?

And I have known the eyes already, known them all—
The eyes that fix you in a formulated phrase,
And when I am formulated, sprawling on a pin,
When I am pinned and wriggling on the wall,
Then how should I begin

To spit out all the butt-ends of my days and ways?
And how should I presume?

And I have known the arms already, known them all—
Arms that are braceleted and white and bare
(But in the lamplight, downed with light brown hair!)
Is it perfume from a dress
That makes me so digress?
Arms that lie along a table, or wrap about a shawl.
And should I then presume?
And how should I begin?

Shall I say, I have gone at dusk through narrow streets
And watched the smoke that rises from the pipes
Of lonely men in shirt-sleeves, leaning out of windows? ...

I should have been a pair of ragged claws
Scuttling across the floors of silent seas.

And the afternoon, the evening, sleeps so peacefully!
Smoothed by long fingers,
Asleep... tired... or it malingers,
Stretched on the floor, here beside you and me.
Should I, after tea and cakes and ices,
Have the strength to force the moment to its crisis?
But though I have wept and fasted, wept and prayed,
Though I have seen my head (grown slightly bald) brought in upon a platter,
I am no prophet[6]— and here's no great matter;
I have seen the moment of my greatness flicker,
And I have seen the eternal Footman[7] hold my coat, and snicker,
And in short, I was afraid.

And would it have been worth it, after all,
After the cups, the marmalade, the tea,
Among the porcelain, among some talk of you and me,
Would it have been worth while,

To have bitten off the matter with a smile,
To have squeezed the universe into a ball[8]
To roll it towards some overwhelming question,
To say: "I am Lazarus[9], come from the dead,
Come back to tell you all, I shall tell you all"—
If one, settling a pillow by her head
Should say: "That is not what I meant at all;
That is not it, at all."

And would it have been worth it, after all,
Would it have been worth while,
After the sunsets and the dooryards and the sprinkled streets,
After the novels, after the teacups, after the skirts that trail along the floor—
And this, and so much more?—
It is impossible to say just what I mean!
But as if a magic lantern threw the nerves in patterns on a screen:
Would it have been worth while
If one, settling a pillow or throwing off a shawl,
And turning toward the window, should say:
"That is not it at all,
That is not what I meant, at all."

No! I am not Prince Hamlet[10], nor was meant to be;
Am an attendant lord, one that will do
To swell a progress, start a scene or two,
Advise the prince; no doubt, an easy tool,
Deferential, glad to be of use,
Politic, cautious, and meticulous;
Full of high sentence, but a bit obtuse;
At times, indeed, almost ridiculous—
Almost, at times, the Fool.

I grow old…I grow old…
I shall wear the bottoms of my trousers rolled.

Shall I part my hair behind? Do I dare to eat a peach?

I shall wear white flannel trousers, and walk upon the beach.
I have heard the mermaids singing, each to each.

I do not think that they will sing to me.

I have seen them riding seaward on the waves
Combing the white hair of the waves blown back
When the wind blows the water white and black.
We have lingered in the chambers of the sea
By sea-girls wreathed with seaweed red and brown
Till human voices wake us, and we drown.

作品译文(扫码阅读)

注释（Notes）

1. 这段话引自但丁的《神曲·地狱篇》，是在地狱的吉多对但丁说的话，大意为"如果这段话是对一个可以回到阳间的人说的，那我的火就要熄灭了，但是没有人可以从这里出去，所以我也就不害怕了。"暗示了本诗为叙述者不愿意让人知道的内心独白，同时也暗示这首"情歌"并非在人间吟唱，而普鲁弗洛克像被贬入地狱的吉多。

2. sawdust：旧时用木屑来清洁地板。

3. Michelangelo：米开朗基罗，意大利文艺复兴时期雕塑家，他的代表作《大卫》充满了人体的肌肉美，与中年并柔弱的普鲁弗洛克形成对比，暗示他并不是女人们喜好的对象。

4. The yellow fog…：在15—22行里，作者运用转喻的手法把黄色的雾浓缩为一个意象：一只慵懒的猫。

5. dying with a dying fall：指说话声音逐渐低微而至停歇。出自莎士比亚的著名戏剧《第十二夜》中的句子："That strain again! It had a dying fall." 这是一种模仿上流社会人士说话的语调(降调)。

6. prophet：《圣经·马太福音》中记载了施洗礼者约翰的故事。希律王因为约翰诅咒他娶自己的弟媳妇希罗底，而将约翰囚禁，但因百姓以约翰为先知，不敢杀他。希罗底的女儿莎乐美爱上约翰，但他拒绝了莎乐美。后来莎乐美得到希律王的欢心，要求希律把约翰杀掉，把他的头放在盘子上给她，希律王照办了。

7. Footman：男仆，在传统英国庄园中，男仆处于低等的位置，需要照顾主人的穿衣。这里指的是静静等待侍衣的死神。

8. squeezed the universe into a ball：17世纪的玄学派诗人马维尔的诗歌《致羞涩的情人》中，情人要"把我们所有的力量和柔情蜜意/滚卷成一枚球形弹"，冲破空间的限制，在时间中自由翱翔，以免青春被时间吞噬。

9. Lazarus：拉撒路，在《圣经·约翰福音》中，拉撒路病危时没等到耶稣的救治死了，但耶稣认定他会复活，四天后拉撒路果然从山洞中走了出来，证明了耶稣的神迹。

10. Prince Hamlet：莎士比亚著名戏剧《哈姆雷特》中的主角，与诗中的普鲁弗洛克一样犹豫不决。

主题探究 (Themes)

（扫码阅读）

中西比较 (A Comparison between Chinese and Western Literature)

英美意象派诗歌没有情感与景象的契合，只注重实物模仿和实景呈现，诗歌中的image总难免给人以理性与感性的疏离感。且看庞德的名作《地铁车站》："人群中这些脸庞的隐现；湿漉漉黑黝黝的树枝上的花瓣。"鲜活的脸庞，泛光的花瓣，交相闪现，形象具体，给人以鲜明的视觉美感，或许还有些让人惊异，然而总感觉少了些我们熟悉的中国古典诗歌的神韵和情趣。我国唐朝诗人崔护有诗《题都城南庄》："去年今日此门中，人面桃花相映红。人面不知何处去，桃花依旧笑春风。"同样是人面、花瓣意象，在这首诗里却融入了物是人非的感慨，给人吟咏不尽的回味。在理性与感性疏离的西方诗学体系中，image呈现的是表象，是形似，是视觉效果。意象，无论是在我国文论发展史，还是在我国古典诗歌的创作表现上，都是表象之景与心灵之情相融凝的特有审美概念。①

如果说意象派诗歌具有雕塑美和图画美，那么象征主义诗歌则具有音乐美和流动美。相比于叶芝的《当你老了》，在中国，戴望舒的《雨巷》也是象征主义的代表作，他曾因此而赢得了"雨巷诗人"的雅号。这首诗写于1927年夏天。当时全国处于白色恐怖之下，戴望舒因曾参加进步活动而不得不避居于松江的友人家中，在孤寂中咀嚼着大革命失败后的幻灭与痛苦，心中充满了迷惘的情绪和朦胧的希望。《雨巷》

---

① 魏瑾. 意象之辨：从imagism说起[J]. 外语与外语教学, 2008(11): 47-49.

一诗就是他的这种心情的表现,其中交织着失望和希望、幻灭和追求的双重情调。这种情怀在当时是有一定的普遍性的。《雨巷》运用了象征性的抒情手法,诗中那狭窄阴沉的雨巷,在雨巷中徘徊的独行者,以及那个像丁香一样结着愁怨的姑娘,都是寓意深邃的象征。这些又共同构成了一种象征性的意境,含蓄地暗示出作者既迷惘感伤又有期待的情怀,并给人一种朦胧而又幽深的美感。

雨 巷
(戴望舒)

撑着油纸伞,独自
彷徨在悠长,悠长
又寂寥的雨巷,
我希望逢着
一个丁香一样地
结着愁怨的姑娘。

她是有
丁香一样的颜色,
丁香一样的芬芳,
丁香一样的忧愁,
在雨中哀怨,
哀怨又彷徨。

她彷徨在这寂寥的雨巷,
撑着油纸伞
像我一样,
像我一样地
默默彳亍着
冷漠,凄清,又惆怅。

她静默地走近
走近,又投出
太息一般的眼光,
她飘过
像梦一般的,
像梦一般的凄婉迷茫。

像梦中飘过
一枝丁香的,
我身旁飘过这个女郎;
她默默地远了,远了,
到了颓圮的篱墙,
走尽这雨巷。

在雨的哀曲里,
消了她的颜色,
散了她的芬芳
消散了,甚至她的
太息般的眼光,
丁香般的惆怅。

撑着油纸伞,独自
彷徨在悠长,悠长
又寂寥的雨巷,
我希望飘过
一个丁香一样地
结着愁怨的姑娘。

问题讨论(Questions for Discussion)

1. What does Prufrock represent? What kind of person do you think he is?
2. What's up with the title? Is the title accurate in calling the poem a "love song"?
3. Do you think Prufrock is really in love?
4. Guido da Montefeltro only told Dante the story of his life because he thought Dante would not return to earth to repeat it. Is Prufrock doing the same thing in this poem?
5. Please comment on the view that although Prufrock mistrusts doctors and scientists, he acts like one when he "dissects" people in his perception.
6. What do you think of the form and meter of the poem?

(请扫码观看视频 Modernism in Poetry: Imagism and Symbolism)

Unit 12

Modernism in Fiction (Ⅰ):
Katherine Mansfield & Virginia Woolf

Katherine Mansfield: "The Garden Party"
Virginia Woolf: "The Mark on the Wall"; *Mrs. Dalloway*
▽

作者简介 (Introduction to the Authors)

Katherine Mansfield (1888—1923) is a writer, essayist and journalist. And she is viewed as one of the most influential and important authors of the modernist movement. Mansfield was born in New Zealand in 1888. Her father was the chairman of the Bank of New Zealand. And her mother was of genteel origins. She spent a happy childhood in suburbs of New Zealand which served as a rich source of material for her works. Mansfield developed an interest in the works of French Symbolists and Oscar Wilde in the Queen's college. Between 1903 and 1906, she travelled around Europe. In 1908, she left New Zealand and settled in England, where she made acquaintance of D. H. Lawrence, Virginia Woolf and others in Bloomsbury Group. Then, she began to write under the pseudonym of K. Mansfield. The death of her brother during the First World War affected her a lot. Thus, she immersed herself in nostalgic memories in New Zealand and then wrote *Prelude* and other stories. In 1918, Mansfield married John Murry, an editor. It is also worth noting that she was obsessed with Russian culture. So, most characters in her works were Russian style. She was diagnosed with tuberculosis in 1917 and died in France in 1923. Mansfield made the short story a legitimate and important genre of 20th century fiction. Her works were filled with some modern techniques, like interior monologue and psychological conflicts, which stimulated the innovation of short novels. She was praised for the compression and understatement of her prose. Portraying the plight of women in her short stories, Mansfield also made a contribution to feminism.

Virginia Woolf (1882—1941) is an English essayist, novelist, critic and feminist. She is known for her experimentation in novel writing and was one of the foremost modernist figures in 20th century. Woolf was born into an intellectual family in 1882. Her father was an editor, writer, critic and biographer. Therefore, she had the opportunity to be exposed to the thoughts of some intellectuals. She was self-educated to a great extent. After her father's death, her home in Bloomsbury became the center of Bloomsbury Group, where some artists and scholars always gathered together. Inspired by Joyce's *Ulysses* and Bergson's theory, she began to explore some new methods of writing. And Russian literature also had a major influence on her. For example, Woolf learned the way to depict characters' psychological state from Leo Tolstoy. She struggled with the mental illness for much of her life. Her parents' death and the sexual assault from her half-brothers led to her nervous breakdowns. She tried to suicide at least twice. In 1912, she married Leonard Woolf and her husband supported her a lot. They founded the Hogarth Press, which encouraged many young writers to make innovations. However, overwhelmed by the mental torture, Woolf drowned herself in 1941. Woolf was important in helping the development of modern literature. She believed that inner workings were more important than facts. Using the stream of consciousness technique, she totally broke with the traditional novel-writing. Her feminist ideas of androgyny and "a room of one's own" also played an significant role in feminine literary criticism.

The Garden Party

作品简介 (Introduction to the Work)

"The Garden Party" is a short story by Katherine Mansfield, collected in *The Garden Party and Other Stories*, which was first published in 1922. This book was well received upon publication and further cemented Mansfield's reputation as one of the most influential modernists of her time, joining the ranks of such notable authors as James Joyce, Virginia Woolf, and D. H. Lawrence. *The Garden Party and Other Stories* is considered a modern classic and contains several of Mansfield's greatest works. "The Garden Party" centres on the annual garden party held by the Sheridan family at their home, in New Zealand (the country where Mansfield had been born in 1888, though she later moved to England). It tells a fairly straightforward story of a young girl who gains greater understanding about life and death, her personal growth and developing class consciousness.

The story follows Laura, a teenaged daughter of the wealthy family, and the family were debating whether to proceed with a party following the news that their neighbor was just killed in an accident, leaving a wife and five small children. The story details the Sheridan's planning and execution of their idyllic garden party despite the news of the neighbor's tragic accident and subsequent death. Laura's concern for the dead man's family causes her to venture down the hill to the dingy, almost sinister, cottages of the working classes. While the style and narrative are compelling, the real reward of this story lies in the multiple layers of interpretation available to the careful reader. Whether one sees the tale as a simple coming of age quest, a commentary on class and society, or a reimagining of tales from Greek and Roman mythology, "The Garden Party" will never fail to reward readers with its rich symbolism and effortless complexity.

作品选文 (Selected Reading)

The Garden Party

And after all the weather was ideal. They could not have had a more perfect day for a garden-party if they had ordered it. Windless, warm, the sky without a cloud. Only the blue was veiled with a haze of light gold, as it is sometimes in early summer. The gardener had been up since dawn, mowing the lawns and sweeping them, until the grass and the dark flat rosettes where the daisy plants had been seemed to shine. As for the roses, you could not help feeling they understood that roses are the only flowers that impress people at garden-parties; the only flowers that everybody is certain of knowing. Hundreds, yes, literally hundreds, had come out in a single night; the green bushes bowed down as though they had been visited by archangels.

Breakfast was not yet over before the men came to put up the marquee[1].

"Where do you want the marquee put, mother?"

"My dear child, it's no use asking me. I'm determined to leave everything to you children this year. Forget I am your mother. Treat me as an honoured guest."

But Meg could not possibly go and supervise the men. She had washed her hair before breakfast, and she sat drinking her coffee in a green turban, with a dark wet curl stamped on each cheek. Jose, the butterfly, always came down in a silk petticoat and a kimono[2] jacket.

"You'll have to go, Laura; you're the artistic one."

Away Laura flew, still holding her piece of bread-and-butter. It's so delicious to have an excuse for eating out of doors, and besides, she loved having to arrange things; she always felt she could do it so much better than anybody else.

Four men in their shirt-sleeves stood grouped together on the garden path. They carried staves covered with rolls of canvas, and they had big tool-bags slung on their backs. They looked impressive. Laura wished now that she had not got the bread-and-butter, but there was nowhere to put it, and she couldn't possibly throw it away. She blushed and tried to look severe and even a little bit short-sighted as she came up to them.

"Good morning," she said, copying her mother's voice. But that sounded so fearfully affected that she was ashamed, and stammered like a little girl, "Oh—er—have you come—is it about the marquee?"

"That's right, miss," said the tallest of the men, a lanky, freckled fellow, and he shifted his tool-bag, knocked back his straw hat and smiled down at her. "That's about it."

His smile was so easy, so friendly that Laura recovered. What nice eyes he had, small, but such a dark blue! And now she looked at the others, they were smiling too. "Cheer up, we won't bite," their smile seemed to say. How very nice workmen were! And what a beautiful morning! She mustn't mention the morning; she must be businesslike. The marquee.

"Well, what about the lily-lawn? Would that do?"

And she pointed to the lily-lawn with the hand that didn't hold the bread-and-butter. They turned, they stared in the direction. A little fat chap thrust out his under-lip, and the tall fellow frowned.

"I don't fancy it," said he. "Not conspicuous enough. You see, with a thing like a marquee," and he turned to Laura in his easy way, "you want to put it somewhere where it'll give you a bang slap in the eye, if you follow me."

Laura's upbringing made her wonder for a moment whether it was quite respectful of a workman to talk to her of bangs slap in the eye. But she did quite follow him.

"A corner of the tennis-court," she suggested. "But the band's going to be in one corner."

"H'm, going to have a band, are you?" said another of the workmen. He was pale. He had a haggard look as his dark eyes scanned the tennis-court. What was he thinking?

"Only a very small band," said Laura gently. Perhaps he wouldn't mind so much if the band was quite small. But the tall fellow interrupted.

"Look here, miss, that's the place. Against those trees. Over there. That'll do fine."

Against the karakas. Then the karaka-trees[3] would be hidden. And they were so lovely, with their broad, gleaming leaves, and their clusters of yellow fruit. They were like trees you imagined growing on a desert island, proud, solitary, lifting their leaves and fruits to the sun in a kind of silent splendour. Must they be hidden by a marquee?

They must. Already the men had shouldered their staves and were making for the place. Only the tall fellow was left. He bent down, pinched a sprig of lavender, put his thumb and forefinger to his nose and snuffed up the smell. When Laura saw that gesture she forgot all about the karakas in her wonder at him caring for things like that—caring for the smell of lavender. How many men that she knew would have done such a thing? Oh, how extraordinarily nice workmen were, she thought. Why couldn't she have workmen for her friends rather than the silly boys she danced with and who came to Sunday night supper? She would get on much better with men like these.

It's all the fault, she decided, as the tall fellow drew something on the back of an envelope, something that was to be looped up or left to hang, of these absurd class distinctions. Well, for her part, she didn't feel them. Not a bit, not an atom... And now there came the chock-chock[4] of wooden hammers. Some one whistled, some one sang out, "Are you right there, matey?" "Matey!" The friendliness of it, the—the—Just to prove how happy she was, just to show the tall fellow how at home she felt, and how she despised stupid conventions, Laura took a big bite of her bread-and-butter as she stared at the little drawing. She felt just like a work-girl.

"Laura, Laura, where are you? Telephone, Laura!" a voice cried from the house.

"Coming!" Away she skimmed, over the lawn, up the path, up the steps, across the veranda, and into the porch. In the hall her father and Laurie were brushing their hats ready to go to the office.

"I say, Laura," said Laurie very fast, "you might just give a squiz at my coat before this afternoon. See if it wants pressing."

"I will," said she. Suddenly she couldn't stop herself. She ran at Laurie and gave him a small, quick squeeze. "Oh, I do love parties, don't you?" gasped Laura.

"Ra-ther," said Laurie's warm, boyish voice, and he squeezed his sister too, and gave her a gentle push. "Dash off to the telephone, old girl."

The telephone. "Yes, yes; oh yes. Kitty? Good morning, dear. Come to lunch? Do, dear. Delighted of course. It will only be a very scratch meal—just the sandwich crusts and broken meringue-shells and what's left over. Yes, isn't it a perfect morning? Your white? Oh, I certainly should. One moment-hold the line. Mother's calling." And Laura sat back. "What, mother? Can't hear."

Mrs. Sheridan's voice floated down the stairs. "Tell her to wear that sweet hat she had on last Sunday."

"Mother says you're to wear that sweet hat you had on last Sunday. Good. One o'clock. Bye-bye."

Laura put back the receiver, flung her arms over her head, took a deep breath, stretched and let them fall. "Huh," she sighed, and the moment after the sigh she sat up quickly. She was still, listening. All the doors in the house seemed to be open. The house was alive with soft, quick steps and running voices. The green baize door that led to the kitchen regions swung open and shut with a muffled thud. And now there came a long, chuckling absurd sound. It was the heavy piano being moved on its stiff castors. But the air! If you stopped to notice, was the air always like this? Little faint winds were playing chase in at the tops of the windows, out at the doors. And there were two tiny spots of sun, one on the inkpot, one on a silver photograph frame, playing too. Darling little spots. Especially the one on the inkpot lid. It was quite warm. A warm little silver star. She could have kissed it.

The front door bell pealed, and there sounded the rustle of Sadie's print skirt on the stairs. A man's voice murmured; Sadie answered, careless, "I'm sure I don't know. Wait. I'll ask Mrs Sheridan."

"What is it, Sadie?" Laura came into the hall.

"It's the florist, Miss Laura."

It was, indeed. There, just inside the door, stood a wide, shallow tray full of pots of pink lilies. No other kind. Nothing but lilies—canna lilies, big pink flowers, wide open, radiant, almost frighteningly alive on bright crimson stems.

"O-oh, Sadie!" said Laura, and the sound was like a little moan. She crouched down as if to warm herself at that blaze of lilies; she felt they were in her fingers, on her lips, growing in her breast.

"It's some mistake," she said faintly. "Nobody ever ordered so many. Sadie, go and find mother."

But at that moment Mrs. Sheridan joined them.

"It's quite right," she said calmly. "Yes, I ordered them. Aren't they lovely?" She pressed Laura's arm. "I was passing the shop yesterday, and I saw them in the window. And I suddenly thought for once in my life I shall have enough canna lilies. The garden-party will be a good excuse."

"But I thought you said you didn't mean to interfere," said Laura. Sadie had gone. The florist's man was still outside at his van. She put her arm round her mother's neck and gently, very gently, she bit her mother's ear.

"My darling child, you wouldn't like a logical mother, would you? Don't do that. Here's the man."

He carried more lilies still, another whole tray.

"Bank them up, just inside the door, on both sides of the porch, please," said Mrs. Sheridan. "Don't you agree, Laura?"

"Oh, I do, mother."

In the drawing-room Meg, Jose and good little Hans had at last succeeded in moving the piano.

"Now, if we put this chesterfield against the wall and move everything out of the room except the chairs, don't you think?"

"Quite."

"Hans, move these tables into the smoking-room, and bring a sweeper to take these marks off the carpet and—one moment, Hans—" Jose loved giving orders to the servants, and they loved obeying her. She always made them feel they were taking part in some drama. "Tell mother and Miss Laura to come here at once."

"Very good, Miss Jose."

She turned to Meg. "I want to hear what the piano sounds like, just in case I'm asked to sing this afternoon. Let's try over 'This life is Weary.'"

Pom! Ta-ta-ta Tee-ta![5] The piano burst out so passionately that Jose's face changed. She clasped her hands. She looked mournfully and enigmatically at her mother and Laura as they came in.

This Life is Wee-ary[6],

A Tear—a Sigh.

A Love that Chan-ges,

This Life is Wee-ary,

A Tear—a Sigh.

A Love that Chan-ges,

And then... Good-bye!

But at the word "Good-bye," and although the piano sounded more desperate than ever, her face broke into a brilliant, dreadfully unsympathetic smile.

"Aren't I in good voice, mummy?" she beamed.

This Life is Wee-ary,

Hope comes to Die.

A Dream—a Wa-kening.

But now Sadie interrupted them. "What is it, Sadie?"

"If you please, m'm[7], cook says have you got the flags for the sandwiches?"

"The flags for the sandwiches, Sadie?" echoed Mrs. Sheridan dreamily. And the children knew by her face that she hadn't got them. "Let me see." And she said to Sadie firmly, "Tell cook I'll let her have them in ten minutes."

Sadie went.

"Now, Laura," said her mother quickly, "come with me into the smoking-room. I've got the names somewhere on the back of an envelope. You'll have to write them out for me. Meg, go upstairs this minute and take that wet thing off your head. Jose, run and finish dressing this instant. Do you hear me, children, or shall I have to tell your father when he comes home tonight? And—and, Jose, pacify cook if you do go into the kitchen, will you? I'm terrified of her this morning."

The envelope was found at last behind the dining-room clock, though how it had got there Mrs. Sheridan could not imagine.

"One of you children must have stolen it out of my bag, because I remember vividly—cream cheese and lemon-curd. Have you done that?"

"Yes."

"Egg and—" Mrs. Sheridan held the envelope away from her. "It looks like mice. It can't be mice, can it?"

"Olive, pet," said Laura, looking over her shoulder.

"Yes, of course, olive. What a horrible combination it sounds. Egg and olive."

They were finished at last, and Laura took them off to the kitchen. She found Jose there pacifying the cook, who did not look at all terrifying.

"I have never seen such exquisite sandwiches," said Jose's rapturous voice. "How many kinds did you say there were, cook? Fifteen?"

"Fifteen, Miss Jose."

"Well, cook, I congratulate you."

Cook swept up crusts with the long sandwich knife and smiled broadly.

"Godber's has come," announced Sadie, issuing out of the pantry. She had seen the man pass the window.

That meant the cream puffs had come. Godber's were famous for their cream puffs. Nobody ever thought of making them at home.

"Bring them in and put them on the table, my girl," ordered cook.

Sadie brought them in and went back to the door. Of course Laura and Jose were far too grown-up to really care about such things. All the same, they couldn't help agreeing that the puffs looked very attractive. Very. Cook began arranging them, shaking off the extra icing sugar.

"Don't they carry one back to all one's parties?" said Laura.

"I suppose they do," said practical Jose, who never liked to be carried back. "They look beautifully light and feathery, I must say."

"Have one each, my dears," said cook in her comfortable voice. "Yer ma[8] won't know."

Oh, impossible. Fancy cream puffs so soon after breakfast. The very idea made one shudder. All the same, two minutes later Jose and Laura were licking their fingers with that absorbed inward look that only comes from whipped cream.

"Let's go into the garden, out by the back way," suggested Laura. "I want to see how the men are getting on with the marquee. They're such awfully nice men."

But the back door was blocked by cook, Sadie, Godber's man and Hans.

Something had happened.

"Tuk-tuk-tuk[9]," clucked cook like an agitated hen. Sadie had her hand clapped to her cheek as though she had toothache. Hans's face was screwed up in the effort to understand. Only Godber's man seemed to be enjoying himself; it was his story.

"What's the matter? What's happened?"

"There's been a horrible accident," said Cook. "A man killed."

"A man killed! Where? How? When?"

But Godber's man wasn't going to have his story snatched from under his nose.

"Know those little cottages just below here, miss?" Know them? Of course, she knew them. "Well, there's a young chap living there, name of Scott, a carter. His horse shied at a traction-engine, corner of Hawke Street this morning, and he was thrown out on the back of his head. Killed."

"Dead!" Laura stared at Godber's man.

"Dead when they picked him up," said Godber's man with relish. "They were taking the body home as I come up here." And he said to the cook, "He's left a wife and five little ones." "Jose, come here." Laura caught hold of her sister's sleeve and dragged her through the kitchen to the other side of the green baize door. There she paused and leaned against it. "Jose!" she said, horrified, "however are we going to stop everything?"

"Stop everything, Laura!" cried Jose in astonishment. "What do you mean?"

"Stop the garden-party, of course." Why did Jose pretend?

But Jose was still more amazed. "Stop the garden-party? My dear Laura, don't be so absurd. Of course we can't do anything of the kind. Nobody expects us to. Don't be so extravagant."

"But we can't possibly have a garden-party with a man dead just outside the front gate."

That really was extravagant, for the little cottages were in a lane to themselves at the very bottom of a steep rise that led up to the house. A broad road ran between. True, they were far too near. They were the greatest possible eyesore, and they had no right to be in that neighbourhood at all. They were little mean dwellings painted a chocolate brown. In the garden patches there was nothing but cabbage stalks, sick hens and tomato cans. The very smoke coming out of their chimneys was poverty-stricken. Little rags and shreds of smoke, so unlike the great silvery plumes that uncurled from the Sheridans' chimneys. Washerwomen lived in the lane and sweeps and a cobbler, and a man whose house-front was studded all over with minute bird-cages. Children swarmed. When the Sheridans were little they were forbidden to set foot there because of the revolting language and of what they might catch. But since they were grown up, Laura and Laurie on their prowls sometimes walked through. It was disgusting and sordid. They came out with a shudder. But still one must go everywhere; one must see everything. So through they went.

"And just think of what the band would sound like to that poor woman," said Laura.

"Oh, Laura!" Jose began to be seriously annoyed. "If you're going to stop a band playing every time some one has an accident, you'll lead a very strenuous life. I'm every bit as sorry about it as you. I feel just as sympathetic." Her eyes hardened. She looked at her sister just as she used to when they were little and fighting together. "You won't bring a drunken workman back to life by being sentimental," she said softly.

"Drunk! Who said he was drunk?" Laura turned furiously on Jose. She said just as they had used to say on those occasions, "I'm going straight up to tell mother."

"Do, dear," cooed Jose. "Mother, can I come into your room?" Laura turned the big glass door-knob. "Of course, child. Why, what's the matter? What's given you such a colour?" And Mrs. Sheridan turned round from her dressing-table. She was trying on a new hat.

"Mother, a man's been killed," began Laura.

"Not in the garden?" interrupted her mother.

"No, no!"

"Oh, what a fright you gave me!" Mrs. Sheridan sighed with relief, and took off the big hat and held it on her knees.

"But listen, mother," said Laura. Breathless, half-choking, she told the dreadful story. "Of course, we can't have our party, can we?" she pleaded. "The band and everybody arriving. They'd hear us, mother; they're nearly neighbours!"

To Laura's astonishment her mother behaved just like Jose; it was harder to bear because she seemed amused. She refused to take Laura seriously.

"But, my dear child, use your common sense. It's only by accident we've heard of it. If some one had died there normally—and I can't understand how they keep alive in those poky little holes-we should still be having our party, shouldn't we?"

Laura had to say "yes" to that, but she felt it was all wrong. She sat down on her mother's sofa and pinched the cushion frill.

"Mother, isn't it terribly heartless of us?" she asked.

"Darling!" Mrs. Sheridan got up and came over to her, carrying the hat. Before Laura could stop her she had popped it on. "My child!" said her mother, "the hat is yours. It's made for you. It's much too young for me. I have never seen you look such a picture. Look at yourself!" And she held up her hand-mirror.

"But, mother," Laura began again. She couldn't look at herself; she turned aside.

This time Mrs. Sheridan lost patience just as Jose had done.

"You are being very absurd, Laura," she said coldly. "People like that don't expect sacrifices from us. And it's not very sympathetic to spoil everybody's enjoyment as you're doing now."

"I don't understand," said Laura, and she walked quickly out of the room into her own bedroom. There, quite by chance, the first thing she saw was this charming girl in the mirror, in her black hat trimmed with gold daisies, and a long black velvet ribbon.

Never had she imagined she could look like that. Is mother right? she thought. And now she hoped her mother was right. Am I being extravagant? Perhaps it was extravagant. Just for a moment she had another glimpse of that poor woman and those little children, and the body being carried into the house. But it all seemed blurred, unreal, like a picture in the newspaper. I'll remember it again after the party's over, she decided. And somehow that seemed quite the best plan...

Lunch was over by half-past one. By half-past two they were all ready for the fray. The green-coated band had arrived and was established in a corner of the tennis-court.

"My dear!" trilled Kitty Maitland, "aren't they too like frogs for words? You ought to have arranged them round the pond with the conductor in the middle on a leaf."

Laurie arrived and hailed them on his way to dress. At the sight of him Laura remembered the accident again. She wanted to tell him. If Laurie agreed with the others, then it was bound to be all right. And she followed him into the hall.

"Laurie!"

"Hallo!" He was half-way upstairs, but when he turned round and saw Laura he suddenly puffed out his cheeks and goggled his eyes at her. "My word, Laura! You do look stunning," said Laurie. "What an absolutely topping hat!"

Laura said faintly "Is it?" and smiled up at Laurie, and didn't tell him after all.

Soon after that people began coming in streams. The band struck up; the hired waiters ran from the house to the marquee. Wherever you looked there were couples strolling, bending to the flowers, greeting, moving on over the lawn. They were like bright birds that had alighted in the Sheridans' garden for this one afternoon, on their way to-where? Ah, what happiness it is to be with people who all are happy, to press hands, press cheeks, smile into eyes.

"Darling Laura, how well you look!"

"What a becoming hat, child!"

"Laura, you look quite Spanish. I've never seen you look so striking."

And Laura, glowing, answered softly, "Have you had tea? Won't you have an ice? The passion-fruit ices really are rather special." She ran to her father and begged him. "Daddy darling, can't the band have something to drink?"

And the perfect afternoon slowly ripened, slowly faded, slowly its petals closed.

"Never a more delightful garden-party..." "The greatest success..." "Quite the most..."

Laura helped her mother with the good-byes. They stood side by side in the porch till it was all over.

"All over, all over, thank heaven," said Mrs. Sheridan. "Round up the others, Laura. Let's go and have some fresh coffee. I'm exhausted. Yes, it's been very successful. But oh, these parties, these parties! Why will you children insist on giving parties!" And they all of them sat down in the deserted marquee.

"Have a sandwich, daddy dear. I wrote the flag."

"Thanks." Mr. Sheridan took a bite and the sandwich was gone. He took another. "I suppose you didn't hear of a beastly accident that happened today?" he said.

"My dear," said Mrs. Sheridan, holding up her hand, "we did. It nearly ruined the party. Laura insisted we should put it off."

"Oh, mother!" Laura didn't want to be teased about it.

"It was a horrible affair all the same," said Mr. Sheridan. "The chap was married too. Lived just below in the lane, and leaves a wife and half a dozen kiddies, so they say."

An awkward little silence fell. Mrs. Sheridan fidgeted with her cup. Really, it was very tactless of father…

Suddenly she looked up. There on the table were all those sandwiches, cakes, puffs, all uneaten, all going to be wasted. She had one of her brilliant ideas.

"I know," she said. "Let's make up a basket. Let's send that poor creature some of this perfectly good food. At any rate, it will be the greatest treat for the children. Don't you agree? And she's sure to have neighbours calling in and so on. What a point to have it all ready prepared. Laura!" She jumped up. "Get me the big basket out of the stairs cupboard."

"But, mother, do you really think it's a good idea?" said Laura.

Again, how curious, she seemed to be different from them all. To take scraps from their party. Would the poor woman really like that?

"Of course! What's the matter with you today? An hour or two ago you were insisting on us being sympathetic, and now—"

Oh well! Laura ran for the basket. It was filled, it was heaped by her mother.

"Take it yourself, darling," said she. "Run down just as you are. No, wait, take the arum lilies too. People of that class are so impressed by arum lilies."

"The stems will ruin her lace frock," said practical Jose.

So they would. Just in time. "Only the basket, then. And, Laura!"—her mother followed her out of the marquee— "don't on any account—"

"What mother?"

No, better not put such ideas into the child's head! "Nothing! Run along."

It was just growing dusky as Laura shut their garden gates. A big dog ran by like a shadow. The road gleamed white, and down below in the hollow the little cottages were in deep shade. How quiet it seemed after the afternoon. Here she was going down the hill to somewhere where a man lay dead, and she couldn't realize it. Why couldn't she? She stopped a minute. And it seemed to her that kisses, voices, tinkling spoons, laughter, the smell of crushed grass were somehow inside her. She had no room for anything else. How strange! She looked up at the pale sky, and all she thought was, "Yes, it was the most successful party."

Now the broad road was crossed. The lane began, smoky and dark. Women in shawls and men's tweed caps hurried by. Men hung over the palings; the children played in the doorways. A low hum came from the mean little cottages. In some of them there was a flicker of light, and a shadow, crab-like, moved across the window. Laura bent her head and hurried on. She wished now she had put on a coat. How her frock shone! And the big hat with the velvet streamer-if only it was another hat! Were the people looking at her? They must be. It was a mistake to have come; she knew all along it was a mistake. Should she go back even now?

No, too late. This was the house. It must be. A dark knot of people stood outside. Beside the gate an old, old woman with a crutch sat in a chair, watching. She had her feet on a newspaper. The voices stopped as Laura drew near. The group parted. It was as though she was expected, as though they had known she was coming here.

Laura was terribly nervous. Tossing the velvet ribbon over her shoulder, she said to a woman standing by, "Is this Mrs. Scott's house?" and the woman, smiling queerly, said, "It is, my lass."

Oh, to be away from this! She actually said, "Help me, God," as she walked up the tiny path and knocked. To be away from those staring eyes, or to be covered up in anything, one of those women's shawls even. I'll just leave the basket and go, she decided. I shan't even wait for it to be emptied.

Then the door opened. A little woman in black showed in the gloom.

Laura said, "Are you Mrs. Scott?" But to her horror the woman answered, "Walk in, please, miss," and she was shut in the passage.

"No," said Laura, "I don't want to come in. I only want to leave this basket. Mother sent—"

The little woman in the gloomy passage seemed not to have heard her. "Step this way, please, miss," she said in an oily voice, and Laura followed her.

She found herself in a wretched little low kitchen, lighted by a smoky lamp. There was a woman sitting before the fire.

"Em," said the little creature who had let her in. "Em! It's a young lady." She turned to Laura. She said meaningly, "I'm'er[10] sister, miss. You'll excuse'er, won't you?"

"Oh, but of course!" said Laura. "Please, please don't disturb her. I—I only want to leave—"

But at that moment the woman at the fire turned round. Her face, puffed up, red, with swollen eyes and swollen lips, looked terrible. She seemed as though she couldn't understand why Laura was there. What did it mean? Why was this stranger standing in the kitchen with a basket? What was it all about? And the poor face puckered up again.

"All right, my dear," said the other. "I'll thenk the young lady."

And again she began, "You'll excuse her, miss, I'm sure," and her face, swollen too, tried an oily smile.

Laura only wanted to get out, to get away. She was back in the passage. The door opened. She walked straight through into the bedroom where the dead man was lying.

"You'd like a look at'im[11], wouldn't you?" said Em's sister, and she brushed past Laura over to the bed. "Don't be afraid, my lass,"—and now her voice sounded fond and sly, and fondly she drew down the sheet—"'e looks a picture. There's nothing to show. Come along, my dear."

Laura came.

There lay a young man, fast asleep—sleeping so soundly, so deeply, that he was far, far away from them both. Oh, so remote, so peaceful. He was dreaming. Never wake him up again. His head was sunk in the pillow, his eyes were closed; they were blind under the closed eyelids. He was given up to his dream. What did garden-parties and baskets and lace frocks matter to him? He was far from all those things. He was wonderful, beautiful. While they were laughing and while the band was playing, this marvel had come to the lane. Happy... happy... All is well, said that sleeping face. This is just as it should be. I am content.

But all the same you had to cry, and she couldn't go out of the room without saying something to him. Laura gave a loud childish sob.

"Forgive my hat," she said.

And this time she didn't wait for Em's sister. She found her way out of the door, down the path, past all those dark people. At the corner of the lane she met Laurie.

He stepped out of the shadow. "Is that you, Laura?"

"Yes."

"Mother was getting anxious. Was it all right?"

"Yes, quite. Oh, Laurie!" She took his arm, she pressed up against him.

"I say, you're not crying, are you?" asked her brother.

Laura shook her head. She was.

Laurie put his arm round her shoulder. "Don't cry," he said in his warm, loving voice. "Was it awful?"

"No," sobbed Laura. "It was simply marvellous. But Laurie—" She stopped, she looked at her brother. "Isn't life," she stammered, "isn't life—" But what life was she couldn't explain. No matter. He quite understood.

"Isn't it, darling?" said Laurie.

注释（Notes）

1. marquee: canvas shelter set up for outdoor parties' 大帐篷。
2. kimono: 日语,和服。
3. karaka-trees: 新西兰有毒植物,卡拉卡树。
4. chock-chock: 拟声词。
5. Ta-ta-ta Tee-ta: 音乐中的节拍。
6. Wee-ary: weary,累人的。
7. m'm: madam,女士。
8. Yer ma: your mum
9. Tuk-tuk-tuk: 拟声词。
10. 'er: her,下同。
11. 'im: him

主题探究（Themes）

（扫码阅读）

问题讨论（Questions for Discussion）

1. What do you think of the beginning of the story? Is it different from that of the realists' novels?

2. There is an open ending in the story. It is ambiguous. Concerning "Isn't life—", can you supplement something to complete the sentence?

3. Mansfield's glimpse and Joyce's epiphany are similar, but can you sense something different between the two?

4. Impression is a main feature of Mansfield's stories. Can you find some instance of the technique in the two stories?

5. Symbolism is another main feature of Mansfield's stories. What do the hat and the

mirror symbolize in the story?

6. There are many contrasts in the story. Can you list some?

价值引领 (Value Guidance)

我们经常听到这样的说法:女孩要富养,男孩要穷养。你同意这样的观点吗?事实上,无论是男孩还是女孩都要"丰富"地养,而这里的"丰富"更多指的是精神、内心的富足。内心丰盈的人,能活出无数种精彩、无数种姿态。内心的丰富,是我们抗拒这个同质化世界的最大力量。内心如果是一片荒芜,生命也会跟着俗气不堪与麻木。不断去丰富自己的精神世界,滋养自由的灵魂,才能在无数个看似平淡的日子里,仍然保持对生活的那份好奇心与探索的欲望,活出自己想要的人生。

The Mark on the Wall

作品简介 (Introduction to the Work)

"The Mark on the Wall" is the first published story by Virginia Woolf. It was published in 1917 as part of the first collection of short stories written by Virginia Woolf and her husband, Leonard Woolf, called *Two Stories*. It was later published in New York in 1921 as part of another collection entitled *Monday or Tuesday*. "The Mark on the Wall" is narrated by someone who recalls noticing a mark on the wall of their house. But the story is not really about the mark on the wall, but rather what it prompts the narrator to think about, muse upon and recollect. As well as speculating on what the mark on the wall might be—a small hole, or perhaps a leftover rose leaf—the narrator's mind wanders to much bigger questions and meditations, such as the aftermath of the war, the nature of life, and even what the afterlife might be like.

Woolf wrote "The Mark on the Wall" at the height of the First World War. The war touched the lives of English citizens, as Germany began strategically bombing England in 1915, and England began conscripting citizens to be soldiers in January of 1916 with the Military Service Bill. Woolf depicts the influence of the war on private citizens in this story, as her references to the war consistently interrupt her narrator's trains of thought. Additionally, the early 20th century showed drastic changes in social norms, technological development, and the confluence of citizens in urban areas (which had begun with the industrial revolution). Movements for women's rights, which played a central role in Woolf's work, saw great gains at the time, as women's suffrage was introduced in 1918 (just one year after the story's initial publication).

作品选文 (Selected Reading)

The Mark on the Wall

Perhaps it was the middle of January in the present year that I first looked up and saw the mark on the wall. In order to fix a date it is necessary to remember what one saw. So now I think of the fire; the steady film of yellow light upon the page of my book; the three chrysanthemums in the round glass bowl on the mantelpiece. Yes, it must have been the winter time, and we had just finished our tea, for I remember that I was smoking a cigarette when I looked up and saw the mark on the wall for the first time. I looked up through the smoke of my cigarette and my eye lodged for a moment upon the burning coals, and that old fancy of the crimson flag flapping from the castle tower came into my mind, and I thought of the cavalcade of red knights riding up the side of the black rock. Rather to my relief the sight of the mark interrupted the fancy, for it is an old fancy, an automatic fancy, made as a child perhaps. The mark was a small round mark, black upon the white wall, about six or seven inches above the mantelpiece.

How readily our thoughts swarm upon a new object, lifting it a little way, as ants carry a blade of straw so feverishly, and then leave it... If that mark was made by a nail, it can't have been for a picture, it must have been for a miniature—the miniature of a lady with white powdered curls, powder-dusted cheeks, and lips like red carnations. A fraud of course, for the people who had this house before us would have chosen pictures in that way—an old picture for an old room. That is the sort of people they were—very interesting people, and I think of them so often, in such queer places, because one will never see them again, never know what happened next. They wanted to leave this house because they wanted to change their style of furniture, so he said, and he was in process of saying that in his opinion art should have ideas behind it when we were torn asunder, as one is torn from the old lady about to pour out tea and the young man about to hit the tennis ball in the back garden of the suburban villa as one rushes past in the train.

But as for that mark, I'm not sure about it; I don't believe it was made by a nail after all; it's too big, too round, for that. I might get up, but if I got up and looked at it, ten to one I shouldn't be able to say for certain; because once a thing's done, no one ever knows how it happened. Oh! dear me, the mystery of life; The inaccuracy of thought! The ignorance of humanity! To show how very little control of our possessions we have—what an accidental affair this living is after all our civilization—let me just count over a few of the things lost in one lifetime, beginning, for that seems always the most mysterious of losses—what cat would gnaw, what rat would nibble—three pale blue canisters of book-binding tools? Then there were the bird cages, the iron hoops, the steel skates, the Queen

Anne[1] coal-scuttle, the bagatelle board, the hand organ-all gone, and jewels, too. Opals and emeralds, they lie about the roots of turnips. What a scraping paring affair it is to be sure! The wonder is that I've any clothes on my back, that I sit surrounded by solid furniture at this moment. Why, if one wants to compare life to anything, one must liken it to being blown through the Tube at fifty miles an hour—landing at the other end without a single hairpin in one's hair! Shot out at the feet of God entirely naked! Tumbling head over heels in the asphodel meadows like brown paper parcels pitched down a shoot in the post office! With one's hair flying back like the tail of a race-horse. Yes, that seems to express the rapidity of life, the perpetual waste and repair; all so casual, all so haphazard...

But after life. The slow pulling down of thick green stalks so that the cup of the flower, as it turns over, deluges one with purple and red light. Why, after all, should one not be born there as one is born here, helpless, speechless, unable to focus one's eyesight, groping at the roots of the grass, at the toes of the Giants? As for saying which are trees, and which are men and women, or whether there are such things, that one won't be in a condition to do for fifty years or so. There will be nothing but spaces of light and dark, intersected by thick stalks, and rather higher up perhaps, rose-shaped blots of an indistinct colour—dim pinks and blues—which will, as time goes on, become more definite, become—I don't know what...

And yet that mark on the wall is not a hole at all. It may even be caused by some round black substance, such as a small rose leaf, left over from the summer, and I, not being a very vigilant housekeeper—look at the dust on the mantelpiece, for example, the dust which, so they say, buried Troy three times over, only fragments of pots utterly refusing annihilation, as one can believe.

The tree outside the window taps very gently on the pane... I want to think quietly, calmly, spaciously, never to be interrupted, never to have to rise from my chair, to slip easily from one thing to another, without any sense of hostility, or obstacle. I want to sink deeper and deeper, away from the surface, with its hard separate facts. To steady myself, let me catch hold of the first idea that passes... Shakespeare... Well, he will do as well as another. A man who sat himself solidly in an arm-chair, and looked into the fire, so—A shower of ideas fell perpetually from some very high Heaven down through his mind. He leant his forehead on his hand, and people, looking in through the open door, —for this scene is supposed to take place on a summer's evening—But how dull this is, this historical fiction! It doesn't interest me at all. I wish I could hit upon a pleasant track of thought, a track indirectly reflecting credit upon myself, for those are the pleasantest thoughts, and very frequent even in the minds of modest mouse-coloured people, who believe genuinely that they dislike to hear their own praises. They are not thoughts directly praising oneself; that is the beauty of them; they are thoughts like this:

"And then I came into the room. They were discussing botany. I said how I'd seen a flower growing on a dust heap on the site of an old house in Kingsway. The seed, I said, must have been sown in the reign of Charles the First[2]. What flowers grew in the reign of Charles the First?" I asked—(but I don't remember the answer). Tall flowers with purple tassels to them perhaps. And so it goes on. All the time I'm dressing up the figure of myself in my own mind, lovingly, stealthily, not openly adoring it, for if I did that, I should catch myself out, and stretch my hand at once for a book in self-protection. Indeed, it is curious how instinctively one protects the image of oneself from idolatry or any other handling that could make it ridiculous, or too unlike the original to be believed in any longer. Or is it not so very curious after all? It is a matter of great importance. Suppose the looking glass smashes, the image disappears, and the romantic figure with the green of forest depths all about it is there no longer, but only that shell of a person which is seen by other people—what an airless, shallow, bald, prominent world it becomes! A world not to be lived in. As we face each other in omnibuses and underground railways we are looking into the mirror; that accounts for the vagueness, the gleam of glassiness, in our eyes. And the novelists in future will realize more and more the importance of these reflections, for of course there is not one reflection but an almost infinite number; those are the depths they will explore, those the phantoms they will pursue, leaving the description of reality more and more out of their stories, taking a knowledge of it for granted, as the Greeks did and Shakespeare perhaps—but these generalizations are very worthless. The military sound of the word is enough. It recalls leading articles, cabinet ministers—a whole class of things indeed which as a child one thought the thing itself, the standard thing, the real thing, from which one could not depart save at the risk of nameless damnation. Generalizations bring back somehow Sunday in London, Sunday afternoon walks, Sunday luncheons, and also ways of speaking of the dead, clothes, and habits—like the habit of sitting all together in one room until a certain hour, although nobody liked it. There was a rule for everything. The rule for tablecloths at that particular period was that they should be made of tapestry with little yellow compartments marked upon them, such as you may see in photographs of the carpets in the corridors of the royal palaces. Tablecloths of a different kind were not real tablecloths. How shocking, and yet how wonderful it was to discover that these real things, Sunday luncheons, Sunday walks, country houses, and tablecloths were not entirely real, were indeed half phantoms, and the damnation which visited the disbeliever in them was only a sense of illegitimate freedom. What now takes the place of those things I wonder, those real standard things? Men perhaps, should you be a woman; the masculine point of view which governs our lives, which sets the standard, which establishes Whitaker's Table of Precedency[3], which has become, I suppose, since the war half a phantom to many men and women, which soon, one may hope, will be laughed into the dustbin where the phantoms go, the mahogany sideboards and the Landseer prints, Gods and Devils, Hell and so forth, leaving us all with an intoxicating sense of illegitimate freedom—if freedom exists...

In certain lights that mark on the wall seems actually to project from the wall. Nor is it entirely circular. I cannot be sure, but it seems to cast a perceptible shadow, suggesting that if I ran my finger down that strip of the wall it would, at a certain point, mount and descend a small tumulus, a smooth tumulus like those barrows on the South Downs which are, they say, either tombs or camps. Of the two I should prefer them to be tombs, desiring melancholy like most English people, and finding it natural at the end of a walk to think of the bones stretched beneath the turf... There must be some book about it. Some antiquary must have dug up those bones and given them a name... What sort of a man is an antiquary, I wonder? Retired Colonels for the most part, I daresay, leading parties of aged labourers to the top here, examining clods of earth and stone, and getting into correspondence with the neighbouring clergy, which, being opened at breakfast time, gives them a feeling of importance, and the comparison of arrow-heads necessitates cross-country journeys to the county towns, an agreeable necessity both to them and to their elderly wives, who wish to make plum jam or to clean out the study, and have every reason for keeping that great question of the camp or the tomb in perpetual suspension, while the Colonel himself feels agreeably philosophic in accumulating evidence on both sides of the question. It is true that he does finally incline to believe in the camp; and, being opposed, indites a pamphlet which he is about to read at the quarterly meeting of the local society when a stroke lays him low, and his last conscious thoughts are not of wife or child, but of the camp and that arrowhead there, which is now in the case at the local museum, together with the foot of a Chinese murderess, a handful of Elizabethan nails, a great many Tudor[4] clay pipes, a piece of Roman pottery, and the wine-glass that Nelson drank out of—proving I really don't know what.

No, no, nothing is proved, nothing is known. And if I were to get up at this very moment and ascertain that the mark on the wall is really—what shall we say? —the head of a gigantic old nail, driven in two hundred years ago, which has now, owing to the patient attrition of many generations of housemaids, revealed its head above the coat of paint, and is taking its first view of modern life in the sight of a white-walled fire-lit room, what should I gain? —Knowledge? Matter for further speculation? I can think sitting still as well as standing up. And what is knowledge? What are our learned men save the descendants of witches and hermits who crouched in caves and in woods brewing herbs, interrogating shrew-mice and writing down the language of the stars? And the less we honour them as our superstitions dwindle and our respect for beauty and health of mind increases... Yes, one could imagine a very pleasant world. A quiet, spacious world, with the flowers so red and blue in the open fields. A world without professors or specialists or house-keepers with the profiles of policemen, a world which one could slice with one's thought as a fish slices the water with his fin, grazing the stems of the water-lilies, hanging suspended over nests of white sea eggs... How peaceful it is down here, rooted in the centre of the world and gazing up through the grey waters, with their sudden gleams of light, and their reflections—if it were not for Whitaker's Almanack—if it were not for the Table of Precedency!

I must jump up and see for myself what that mark on the wall really is—a nail, a rose-leaf, a crack in the wood?

Here is nature once more at her old game of self-preservation. This train of thought, she perceives, is threatening mere waste of energy, even some collision with reality, for who will ever be able to lift a finger against Whitaker's Table of Precedency? The Archbishop of Canterbury[5] is followed by the Lord High Chancellor[6]; the Lord High Chancellor is followed by the Archbishop of York. Everybody follows somebody, such is the philosophy of Whitaker; and the great thing is to know who follows whom. Whitaker knows, and let that, so Nature counsels, comfort you, instead of enraging you; and if you can't be comforted, if you must shatter this hour of peace, think of the mark on the wall.

I understand Nature's game—her prompting to take action as a way of ending any thought that threatens to excite or to pain. Hence, I suppose, comes our slight contempt for men of action—men, we assume, who don't think. Still, there's no harm in putting a full stop to one's disagreeable thoughts by looking at a mark on the wall.

Indeed, now that I have fixed my eyes upon it, I feel that I have grasped a plank in the sea; I feel a satisfying sense of reality which at once turns the two Archbishops and the Lord High Chancellor to the shadows of shades. Here is something definite, something real. Thus, waking from a midnight dream of horror, one hastily turns on the light and lies quiescent, worshipping the chest of drawers, worshipping solidity, worshipping reality, worshipping the impersonal world which is a proof of some existence other than ours. That is what one wants to be sure of... Wood is a pleasant thing to think about. It comes from a tree; and trees grow, and we don't know how they grow. For years and years they grow, without paying any attention to us, in meadows, in forests, and by the side of rivers—all things one likes to think about. The cows swish their tails beneath them on hot afternoons; they paint rivers so green that when a moorhen dives one expects to see its feathers all green when it comes up again. I like to think of the fish balanced against the stream like flags blown out; and of water-beetles slowly raising domes of mud upon the bed of the river. I like to think of the tree itself: first the close dry sensation of being wood; then the grinding of the storm; then the slow, delicious ooze of sap. I like to think of it, too, on winter's nights standing in the empty field with all leaves close-furled, nothing tender exposed to the iron bullets of the moon, a naked mast upon an earth that goes tumbling, tumbling, all night long. The song of birds must sound very loud and strange in June; and how cold the feet of insects must feel upon it, as they make laborious progresses up the creases of the bark, or sun themselves upon the thin green awning of the leaves, and look straight in front of them with diamond-cut red eyes… One by one the fibres snap beneath the immense cold pressure of the earth, then the last storm comes and, falling, the highest branches drive deep into the ground again. Even so, life isn't done with; there are a million patient, watchful lives still for a tree, all over the world, in bedrooms, in ships, on the pavement, lining rooms, where men and women sit after tea, smoking cigarettes. It is full of peaceful thoughts, happy thoughts, this tree. I should like to take each one separately-but something is getting in the way… Where was I? What has it all been about? A tree? A river? The Downs? Whitaker's Almanack? The fields of asphodel? I can't remember a thing. Everything's moving, falling, slipping, vanishing… There is a vast upheaval of matter. Someone is standing over me and saying—

"I'm going out to buy a newspaper."

"Yes?"

"Though it's no good buying newspapers… Nothing ever happens. Curse this war; God damn this war! … All the same, I don't see why we should have a snail on our wall."

Ah, the mark on the wall! It was a snail.

注释（Notes）

1. Queen Anne：安妮女王，1702—1714 年在位。
2. Charles the First：查理一世，1625—1649 年在位，因独裁与议会产生冲突，导致了英国资产阶级革命，最后落败于克伦威尔，被公开处死。
3. Whitaker's Table of Precedency：惠特克年鉴（尊卑序列表），1868 年创刊，被誉为英国最好的年鉴和一部微型百科全书。惠特克（1820—1895），英国出版商，创办过《书商》杂志。
4. Tudor：都铎王朝，1485—1603 年，当时英国处于从封建主义向资本主义的过渡时期，被认为是英国君主专制历史上的黄金时期。
5. Archbishop of Canterbury：坎特伯雷大主教，为全英格兰的首席主教。
6. Lord High Chancellor：英国大法官，大法官在一众国务官员中排行第二，有关任命由首相提出意见，再由君主委任。

主题探究 (Themes)

（扫码阅读）

问题讨论 (Questions for Discussion)

1. What does the mark on the wall turn out to be?

2. Why there is little information about the external objective world but more description of trifles and inner world of the protagonist?

3. Could you summarize the psychological activity of the protagonist?

4. What's the difference between Joyce's "epiphany" and Woolf's "moment of importance"?

5. Some people comment that Woolf cares too much about the society. What do you think of it?

6. Is it important to find out what the mark on the wall is? What's the function of the mark on the wall in the story?

Mrs. Dalloway

作品简介 (Introduction to the Work)

Mrs. Dalloway is a novel by Virginia Woolf, first published in 1925. One of the most celebrated and important modernist novels in English, it is perhaps Virginia Woolf's best novel. Originally titled *The Hours*, a title that Michael Cunningham would retrieve and use for his 1998 novel based on *Mrs. Dalloway* and Woolf's own life (a book that would in turn be adapted for the 2002 film starring Nicole Kidman in a prosthetic nose), *Mrs. Dalloway* is at once a powerful response to the First World War and a lyrical exploration of the role of memory itself. The technique of stream of consciousness narrative in this novel has led some people to compare it to Joyce's *Ulysses*. The themes of time and human connections, whether fleeting or more persistent, gives sway to the idea that there can be meaning in even the small details of life. This is accentuated in the novel in the way the characters are constantly reminded of things from their past by simple ideas and things.

Mrs. Dalloway takes the reader through a single day in the life and thoughts of 51-

year-old Clarissa Dalloway as she prepares for a party that she is hosting that evening. Going around London reminds her of her youth and as she goes about her day, the reader gets a glimpse into her past. Via her reminiscing, we are also introduced to other characters, such as Septimus Smith, who is a veteran of World War Ⅰ, who suffers from shell shock and PTSD. In the following excerpt, he is sitting with his wife in Regent's Park and thinks about his dead friend Evans, who was killed fighting in the war. Septimus fears that the world might burst into flames. His wife is frightened and embarrassed by him, especially since his doctor said there was nothing wrong with him. They get ready to see his new psychiatrist.

(扫码阅读)

Mrs. Dalloway

(Excerpt)

(请扫码观看视频 Modernism in Fiction)

Unit 13
Modernism in Fiction (Ⅱ): James Joyce & D. H. Lawrence

James Joyce: "A Little Cloud"
D. H. Lawrence: *Sons & Lovers*
▽

作者简介 (Introduction to the Authors)

James Joyce (1882—1941) is a novelist, poet and literary critic. He is regarded as the most prominent novelist using the stream of consciousness technique. His masterpiece *Ulysses* is viewed as a modern prose. It is a parallel to Homer's great epic *Odyssey*. Joyce was born into a Catholic family in Dublin on 2 February 1882. He studied at a Jesuit boarding school in 1888 and was intended to be a priest. But he renounced Catholicism at adolescence. With no good feelings to British traditional culture, Joyce spent most of his life in France, Italy and Switzerland. Nevertheless, all his works were written about Dublin. For one thing, Dublin was the place that he knew best. For another thing, getting to the heart of Dublin was equivalent to penetrating the heart of all cities of the world. Throughout his life, Joyce kept interest in Irish national politics. And his novels reflected socialist, anarchist and Irish nationalist issues. There are also some signs of Naturalism and Aestheticism in his works. He suffered from an eye disease in later years and lived a poor life. He died in 1941. Joyce made great contributions to English language and he is regarded as "second only to Shakespeare in his mastery of the English language". Joyce was free in his experiments with the English language and grammar. Many writers have been influenced by his meticulous attention to details, fragmentary sentences, use of interior monologue and radical transformation of plot. In his writing, the stream of consciousness reached the highest point.

D. H. Lawrence (1885—1930) is an English novelist, poet, writer, painter, playwright, essayist and literary critic. He is one of the most original and influential writers in the 20th century. Lawrence was born in 1885 in Eastwood, Nottinghamshire. He had a great affection for his homeland and later made it as a setting for much of his fiction. His father was a barely literate coal-miner who was coarse, energetic but often drunk. His mother used to be a teacher. She was refined, strong-willed and up-climbing who always looked down upon her husband. Lawrence's working class background and the tensions between his parents provided the raw material for his works. In 1910, his mother died of cancer, which became a major turning point in his life. Lawrence once worked as a clerk at a surgical appliances factory and as a teacher and then became a full time author in 1911. He eloped with Frieda in 1912 and they spent many years travelling to many countries such as Austria, Italy, France and Mexico. These experiences can be seen in his works. Influenced by Freud's psychology, he actively explored characters' unconscious activities and strongly opposed the repression. His novels were also known for Oedipal anxieties. He died of tuberculosis at the age of 45. His originality widely gained reputation. Lawrence criticized the dehumanizing effect of the capital industrialization on human nature. The social meanings in his novels reflected their association with the ideal of Realism in 19th century England. Besides, Lawrence acquired his fame as a modern writer for his technique of symbolism and use of psychological contents.

A Little Cloud

作品简介 (Introduction to the Work)

"A Little Cloud" is a short story by James Joyce, first published in his 1914 collection, *Dubliners*. It is the eighth of the 15 short stories that comprise *Dubliners*. This collection realistically portrays the lives of everyday people in Dublin in the early 1900s. Through their stories, Joyce criticizes social conventions and raises complex moral questions, often by portraying characters struggling to come to terms with their limited, even thwarted lives. "A Little Cloud" contrasts the life of the protagonist, Little Chandler, a Dubliner who remained in the city and married, with the life of his old friend Ignatius Gallaher, who had left Ireland to find success and excitement as a journalist and bachelor in London.

The story hinges on a reunion between the two friends after an eight-year separation. Gallaher, the bluff, worldly one, has "got on" in the world by leaving Dublin and becoming a journalist in London. Chandler has remained in Dublin, become a law-clerk, married, and had a son. Beside what he imagines to be Gallaher's glittering, licentious adventures in the heady world of Fleet Street, Chandler views his own life as inadequate, his ambitions thwarted, his talents neglected. He provides the focal point of the narration. Referred to throughout as "Little Chandler", he is not small in physical stature but gives the impression of smallness, and this diminutiveness ironically extends and echoes the pettiness and feebleness of his ambitions. Little Chandler is a pathetic figure but is at the same time a quasi-tragic one. He yearns to escape the confines of his dead-end life in Dublin but he lacks the ability to follow through on his dreams and he is ultimately left feeling trapped and alone.

作品选文 (Selected Reading)

A Little Cloud

Eight years before he had seen his friend off at the North Wall[1] and wished him God-speed. Gallaher had got on. You could tell that at once by his travelled air, his well-cut tweed suit, and fearless accent. Few fellows had talents like his, and fewer still could remain unspoiled by such success. Gallaher's heart was in the right place and he had deserved to win. It was something to have a friend like that.

Little Chandler's thoughts ever since lunch-time had been of his meeting with Gallaher, of Gallaher's invitation, and of the great city London where Gallaher lived. He was called Little Chandler because, though he was but slightly under the average stature, he gave one the idea of being a little man. His hands were white and small, his frame was fragile, his voice was quiet and his manners were refined. He took the greatest care of his fair silken hair and moustache, and used perfume discreetly on his handkerchief. The half-moons of his nails were perfect, and when he smiled you caught a glimpse of a row of childish white teeth.

As he sat at his desk in the King's Inns[2] he thought what changes those eight years had brought. The friend whom he had known under a shabby and necessitous guise had become a brilliant figure on the London Press. He turned often from his tiresome writing to gaze out of the office window. The glow of a late autumn sunset covered the grass plots and walks. It cast a shower of kindly golden dust on the untidy nurses and decrepit old men who drowsed on the benches; it flickered upon all the moving figures—on the children who ran screaming along the gravel paths and on everyone who passed through the gardens. He watched the scene and thought of life; and (as always happened when he thought of life) he became sad. A gentle melancholy took possession of him. He felt how useless it was to struggle against fortune, this being the burden of wisdom which the ages had bequeathed to him.

He remembered the books of poetry upon his shelves at home. He had bought them in his bachelor days and many an evening, as he sat in the little room off the hall, he had been tempted to take one down from the bookshelf and read out something to his wife. But shyness had always held him back; and so the books had remained on their shelves. At times he repeated lines to himself and this consoled him.

When his hour had struck he stood up and took leave of his desk and of his fellow-clerks punctiliously. He emerged from under the feudal arch of the King's Inns, a neat modest figure, and walked swiftly down Henrietta Street. The golden sunset was waning and the air had grown sharp. A horde of grimy children populated the street. They stood or ran in the roadway, or crawled up the steps before the gaping doors, or squatted like mice upon the thresholds. Little Chandler gave them no thought. He picked his way deftly through all that minute vermin-like life and under the shadow of the gaunt spectral mansions in which the old nobility of Dublin had roistered. No memory of the past touched him, for his mind was full of a present joy.

He had never been in Corless's, but he knew the value of the name. He knew that people went there after the theatre to eat oysters and drink liqueurs; and he had heard that the waiters there spoke French and German. Walking swiftly by at night he had seen cabs drawn up before the door and richly-dressed ladies, escorted by cavaliers, alight and enter quickly. They wore noisy dresses and many wraps. Their faces were powdered and they caught up their dresses, when they touched earth, like alarmed Atalantas[3]. He had always passed without turning his head to look. It was his habit to walk swiftly in the street even by day, and whenever he found himself in the city late at night he hurried on his way apprehensively and excitedly. Sometimes, however, he courted the causes of his fear. He chose the darkest and narrowest streets and, as he walked boldly forward, the silence that was spread about his footsteps troubled him; the wandering, silent figures troubled him; and at times a sound of low fugitive laughter made him tremble like a leaf.

He turned to the right towards Capel Street[4]. Ignatius Gallaher on the London Press! Who would have thought it possible eight years before? Still, now that he reviewed the past, Little Chandler could remember many signs of future greatness in his friend. People used to say that Ignatius Gallaher was wild. Of course, he did mix with a rakish set of fellows at that time; drank freely and borrowed money on all sides. In the end he had got mixed up in some shady affair, some money transaction: at least, that was one version of his flight. But nobody denied him talent. There was always a certain… something in Ignatius Gallaher that impressed you in spite of yourself. Even when he was out at elbows and at his wits' end for money he kept up a bold face. Little Chandler remembered (and the remembrance brought a slight flush of pride to his cheek) one of Ignatius Gallaher's sayings when he was in a tight corner:

"Half-time now, boys," he used to say light-heartedly. "Where's my considering cap?"

That was Ignatius Gallaher all out; and, damn it, you couldn't but admire him for it.

Little Chandler quickened his pace. For the first time in his life he felt himself superior to the people he passed. For the first time his soul revolted against the dull inelegance of Capel Street. There was no doubt about it: if you wanted to succeed you had to go away. You could do nothing in Dublin. As he crossed Grattan Bridge he looked down the river towards the lower quays and pitied the poor stunted houses. They seemed to him a band of tramps, huddled together along the river-banks, their old coats covered with dust and soot, stupefied by the panorama of sunset and waiting for the first chill of night to bid them arise, shake themselves and begone. He wondered whether he could write a poem to express his idea. Perhaps Gallaher might be able to get it into some London paper for him. Could he write something original? He was not sure what idea he wished to express, but the thought that a poetic moment had touched him took life within him like an infant hope. He stepped onward bravely.

Every step brought him nearer to London, farther from his own sober inartistic life. A light began to tremble on the horizon of his mind. He was not so old—thirty-two. His temperament might be said to be just at the point of maturity. There were so many different moods and impressions that he wished to express in verse. He felt them within him. He tried to weigh his soul to see if it was a poet's soul. Melancholy was the dominant note of his temperament, he thought, but it was a melancholy tempered by recurrences of faith and resignation and simple joy. If he could give expression to it in a book of poems perhaps men would listen. He would never be popular: he saw that. He could not sway the crowd, but he might appeal to a little circle of kindred minds. The English critics, perhaps, would recognize him as one of the Celtic[5] school by reason of the melancholy tone of his poems; besides that, he would put in allusions. He began to invent sentences and phrases from the notice which his book would get. "Mr Chandler has the gift of easy and graceful verse"... "A wistful sadness pervades these poems"... "The Celtic note". It was a pity his name was not more Irish-looking. Perhaps it would be better to insert his mother's name before the surname: Thomas Malone Chandler; or better still: T. Malone Chandler. He would speak to Gallaher about it.

He pursued his reverie so ardently that he passed his street and had to turn back. As he came near Corless's his former agitation began to overmaster him and he halted before the door in indecision. Finally he opened the door and entered.

The light and noise of the bar held him at the doorway for a few moments. He looked about him, but his sight was confused by the shining of many red and green wine-glasses. The bar seemed to him to be full of people and he felt that the people were observing him curiously. He glanced quickly to right and left (frowning slightly to make his errand appear serious), but when his sight cleared a little he saw that nobody had turned to look at him: and there, sure enough, was Ignatius Gallaher leaning with his back against the counter and his feet planted far apart.

"Hallo, Tommy, old hero, here you are! What is it to be? What will you have? I'm taking whisky: better stuff than we get across the water. Soda? Lithia[6]? No mineral? I'm the same. Spoils the flavour... Here, garcon[7], bring us two halves of malt whisky, like a good fellow... Well, and how have you been pulling along since I saw you last? Dear God, how old we're getting! Do you see any signs of ageing in me-eh, what? A little grey and thin on the top—what?"

Ignatius Gallaher took off his hat and displayed a large closely-cropped head. His face was heavy, pale, and clean-shaven. His eyes, which were of bluish slate-colour, relieved his unhealthy pallor and shone out plainly above the vivid orange tie[8] he wore. Between these rival features the lips appeared very long and shapeless and colourless. He bent his head and felt with two sympathetic fingers the thin hair at the crown. Little Chandler shook his head as a denial. Ignatius Gallaher put on his hat again.

"It pulls you down," he said. "Press life. Always hurry and scurry, looking for copy and sometimes not finding it: and then, always to have something new in your stuff. Damn proofs and printers, I say, for a few days. I'm deuced glad, I can tell you, to get back to the old country. Does a fellow good, a bit of a holiday. I feel a ton better since I landed again in dear, dirty Dublin... Here you are, Tommy. Water? Say when."

Little Chandler allowed his whisky to be very much diluted.

"You don't know what's good for you, my boy," said Ignatius Gallaher. "I drink mine neat."

"I drink very little as a rule," said Little Chandler modestly. "An odd half-one or so when I meet any of the old crowd: that's all."

"Ah well," said Ignatius Gallaher cheerfully, "here's to us and to old times and old acquaintance."

They clinked glasses and drank the toast.

"I met some of the old gang today," said Ignatius Gallaher. "O'Hara seems to be in a bad way. What's he doing?"

"Nothing," said Little Chandler. "He's gone to the dogs."

"But Hogan has a good sit, hasn't he?"

"Yes, he's in the Land Commission."

"I met him one night in London and he seemed to be very flush... Poor O'Hara! Booze, I suppose?"

"Other things, too," said Little Chandler shortly.

Ignatius Gallaher laughed.

"Tommy," he said, "I see you haven't changed an atom. You're the very same serious person that used to lecture me on Sunday mornings when I had a sore head and a fur on my tongue. You'd want to knock about a bit in the world. Have you never been anywhere even for a trip?"

"I've been to the Isle of Man[9]," said Little Chandler.

Ignatius Gallaher laughed.

"The Isle of Man!" he said. "Go to London or Paris: Paris, for choice. That'd do you good."

"Have you seen Paris?"

"I should think I have! I've knocked about there a little."

"And is it really so beautiful as they say?" asked Little Chandler.

He sipped a little of his drink while Ignatius Gallaher finished his boldly.

"Beautiful?" said Ignatius Gallaher, pausing on the word and on the flavour of his drink. "It's not so beautiful, you know. Of course it is beautiful… But it's the life of Paris; that's the thing. Ah, there's no city like Paris for gaiety, movement, excitement…"

Little Chandler finished his whisky and, after some trouble, succeeded in catching the barman's eye. He ordered the same again.

"I've been to the Moulin Rouge[10]," Ignatius Gallaher continued when the barman had removed their glasses, "and I've been to all the Bohemian cafes. Hot stuff! Not for a pious chap like you, Tommy."

Little Chandler said nothing until the barman returned with two glasses: then he touched his friend's glass lightly and reciprocated the former toast. He was beginning to feel somewhat disillusioned. Gallaher's accent and way of expressing himself did not please him. There was something vulgar in his friend which lie had not observed before. But perhaps it was only the result of living in London amid the bustle and competition of the Press. The old personal charm was still there under this new gaudy manner. And, after all, Gallaher had lived, he had seen the world. Little Chandler looked at his friend enviously.

"Everything in Paris is gay," said Ignatius Gallaher. "They believe in enjoying life—and don't you think they're right? If you want to enjoy yourself properly you must go to Paris. And, mind you, they've a great feeling for the Irish there. When they heard I was from Ireland they were ready to eat me, man."

Little Chandler took four or five sips from his glass.

"Tell me," he said, "is it true that Paris is so… immoral as they say?"

Ignatius Gallaher made a catholic gesture with his right arm.

"Every place is immoral," he said. "Of course you do find spicy bits in Paris. Go to one of the students' balls, for instance. That's lively, if you like, when the cocottes begin to let themselves loose. You know what they are, I suppose?"

"I've heard of them," said Little Chandler.

Ignatius Gallaher drank off his whisky and shook his head.

"Ah," he said, "you may say what you like. There's no woman like the Parisienne—

for style, for go."

"Then it is an immoral city," said Little Chandler, with timid insistence— "I mean, compared with London or Dublin?"

"London!" said Ignatius Gallaher. "It's six of one and half a dozen of the other. You ask Hogan, my boy. I showed him a bit about London when he was over there. He'd open your eye... I say, Tommy, don't make punch of that whisky: liquor up."

"No, really."

"O, come on, another one won't do you any harm. What is it? The same again, I suppose?"

"Well... all right."

"Francois, the same again... Will you smoke, Tommy?"

Ignatius Gallaher produced his cigar-case. The two friends lit their cigars and puffed at them in silence until their drinks were served.

"I'll tell you my opinion," said Ignatius Gallaher, emerging after some time from the clouds of smoke in which he had taken refuge, "it's a rum world. Talk of immorality! I've heard of cases—what am I saying? —I've known them: cases of... immorality..."

Ignatius Gallaher puffed thoughtfully at his cigar and then, in a calm historian's tone, he proceeded to sketch for his friend some pictures of the corruption which was rife abroad. He summarized the vices of many capitals and seemed inclined to award the palm to Berlin. Some things he could not vouch for (his friends had told him), but of others he had had personal experience. He spared neither rank nor caste. He revealed many of the secrets of religious houses on the Continent and described some of the practices which were fashionable in high society, and ended by telling, with details, a story about an English duchess—a story which he knew to be true. Little chandler was astonished.

"Ah, well," said Ignatius Gallaher, "here we are in old jog-along Dublin where nothing is known of such things."

"How dull you must find it," said Little Chandler, "after all the other places you've seen!"

"Well," said Ignatius Gallaher, "it's a relaxation to come over here, you know. And, after all, it's the old country, as they say, isn't it? You can't help having a certain feeling for it. That's human nature... But tell me something about yourself. Hogan told me you had... tasted the joys of connubial bliss. Two years ago, wasn't it?"

Little Chandler blushed and smiled.

"Yes," he said. "I was married last May twelve months."

"I hope it's not too late in the day to offer my best wishes," said Ignatius Gallaher. "I didn't know your address or I'd have done so at the time."

He extended his hand, which Little Chandler took.

"Well, Tommy," he said, "I wish you and yours every joy in life, old chap, and tons of money, and may you never die till I shoot you. And that's the wish of a sincere friend, an old friend. You know that?"

"I know that," said Little Chandler.

"Any youngsters?" said Ignatius Gallaher.

Little Chandler blushed again.

"We have one child," he said.

"Son or daughter?"

"A little boy."

Ignatius Gallaher slapped his friend sonorously on the back.

"Bravo," he said, "I wouldn't doubt you, Tommy."

Little Chandler smiled, looked confusedly at his glass and bit his lower lip with three childishly white front teeth.

"I hope you'll spend an evening with us," he said, "before you go back. My wife will be delighted to meet you. We can have a little music and—"

"Thanks awfully, old chap," said Ignatius Gallaher, "I'm sorry we didn't meet earlier. But I must leave tomorrow night."

"Tonight, perhaps... ?"

"I'm awfully sorry, old man. You see I'm over here with another fellow, clever young chap he is too, and we arranged to go to a little card-party. Only for that..."

"O, in that case..."

"But who knows?" said Ignatius Gallaher considerately. "Next year I may take a little skip over here now that I've broken the ice. It's only a pleasure deferred."

"Very well," said Little Chandler, "the next time you come we must have an evening together. That's agreed now, isn't it?"

"Yes, that's agreed," said Ignatius Gallaher. "Next year if I come, parole d'honneur[11]."

"And to clinch the bargain," said Little Chandler, "we'll just have one more now."

Ignatius Gallaher took out a large gold watch and looked at it.

"Is it to be the last?" he Said. "Because, you know, I have an a. p.[12]"

"O, yes, positively," said Little Chandler.

"Very well, then," said Ignatius Gallaher, "let us have another one as a deoc an doirus—that's good vernacular for a small whisky, I believe."

Little Chandler ordered the drinks. The blush which had risen to his face a few moments before was establishing itself. A trifle made him blush at any time; and now he felt warm and excited. Three small whiskies had gone to his head and Gallaher's strong cigar had confused his mind, for he was a delicate and abstinent person. The adventure of meeting Gallaher after eight years, of finding himself with Gallaher in Corless's surrounded by lights and noise, of listening to Gallaher's stories and of sharing for a brief space Gallaher's vagrant and triumphant life, upset the equipoise of his sensitive nature. He felt acutely the contrast between his own life and his friend's, and it seemed to him unjust. Gallaher was his inferior in birth and education. He was sure that he could do something better than his friend had ever done, or could ever do, something higher than mere tawdry journalism if he only got the chance. What was it that stood in his way? His unfortunate timidity! He wished to vindicate himself in some way, to assert his manhood. He saw behind Gallaher's refusal of his invitation. Gallaher was only patronizing him by his friendliness just as he was patronizing Ireland by his visit.

The barman brought their drinks. Little Chandler pushed one glass towards his friend and took up the other boldly.

"Who knows?" he said, as they lifted their glasses. "When you come next year I may have the pleasure of wishing long life and happiness to Mr and Mrs Ignatius Gallaher."

Ignatius Gallaher in the act of drinking closed one eye expressively over the rim of his glass. When he had drunk he smacked his lips decisively, set down his glass and said:

"No blooming fear of that, my boy. I'm going to have my fling first and see a bit of life and the world before I put my head in the sack—if I ever do."

"Some day you will," said Little Chandler calmly.

Ignatius Gallaher turned his orange tie and slate-blue eyes full upon his friend.

"You think so?" he said.

"You'll put your head in the sack," repeated Little Chandler stoutly, "like everyone else if you can find the girl."

He had slightly emphasized his tone, and he was aware that he had betrayed himself; but, though the colour had heightened in his cheek, he did not flinch from his friends' gaze. Ignatius Gallaher watched him for a few moments and then said:

"If ever it occurs, you may bet your bottom dollar there'll be no mooning and spooning about it. I mean to marry money. She'll have a good fat account at the bank or she won't do for me."

Little Chandler shook his head.

"Why, man alive," said Ignatius Gallaher, vehemently, "do you know what it is? I've only to say the word and tomorrow I can have the woman and the cash. You don't believe it? Well, I know it. There are hundreds—what am I saying?—thousands of rich Germans and Jews, rotten with money, that'd only be too glad… You wait a while, my boy. See if I don't play my cards properly. When I go about a thing I mean business, I tell you. You just wait."

He tossed his glass to his mouth, finished his drink and laughed loudly. Then he looked thoughtfully before him and said in a calmer tone:

"But I'm in no hurry. They can wait. I don't fancy tying myself up to one woman, you know."

He imitated with his mouth the act of tasting and made a wry face.

"Must get a bit stale, I should think," he said.

...

Little Chandler sat in the room off the hall, holding a child in his arms. To save money they kept no servant, but Annie's young sister Monica came for an hour or so in the morning and an hour or So in the evening to help. But Monica had gone home long ago. It was a quarter to nine. Little Chandler had come home late for tea and, moreover, he had forgotten to bring Annie home the parcel of coffee from Bewley's. Of course she was in a bad humour and gave him short answers. She said she would do without any tea, but when it came near he time at which the shop at the corner closed she decided to go out herself for a quarter of a pound of tea and two pounds of sugar. She put the sleeping child deftly in his arms and said:

"Here. Don't waken him."

A little lamp with a white china shade stood upon the table and its light fell over a photograph which was enclosed in a frame of crumpled horn. It was Annie's photograph. Little Chandler looked at it, pausing at the thin tight lips. She wore the pale blue summer blouse which he had brought her home as a present one Saturday. It had cost him ten and elevenpence; but what an agony of nervousness it had cost him! How he had suffered that day, waiting at the shop door until the shop was empty, standing at the counter and trying to appear at his ease while the girl piled ladies' blouses before him, paying at the desk and forgetting to take up the odd penny of his change, being called back by the cashier, and finally, striving to hide his blushes as he left the shop by examining the parcel to see if it was Securely tied. When he brought the blouse home Annie kissed him and said it was very pretty and stylish; but when she heard the price she threw the blouse on the table and said it was a regular swindle to charge ten and elevenpence for it. At first she wanted to take it back, but when she tried it on she was delighted with it, especially with the make of the sleeves, and kissed him and said he was very good to think of her.

Hm! ...

He looked coldly into the eyes of the photograph and they answered coldly. Certainly they were pretty and the face itself was pretty. But he found something mean in it. Why was it so unconscious and ladylike? The composure of the eyes irritated him. They repelled him and defied him: there was no passion in them, no rapture. He thought of what Gallaher had said about rich Jewesses. Those dark Oriental eyes, he thought, how full they are of passion, of voluptuous longing!... Why had he married the eyes in the photograph?

He caught himself up at the question and glanced nervously round the room. He found something mean in the pretty furniture which he had bought for his house on the hire system[13]. Annie had chosen it herself and it reminded him of her. It too was prim and pretty. A dull resentment against his life awoke within him. Could he not escape from his little house? Was it too late for him to try to live bravely like Gallaher? Could he go to London? There was the furniture still to be paid for. If he could only write a book and get it published, that might open the way for him.

A volume of Byron's poems lay before him on the table. He opened it cautiously with his left hand lest he should waken the child and began to read the first poem in the book:

Hushed are the winds and still the evening gloom,

Not e'en a Zephyr[14] wanders through the grove,

Whilst I return to view my Margaret's tomb

And scatter flowers on the dust I love.

He paused. He felt the rhythm of the verse about him in the room. How melancholy it was! Could he, too, write like that, express the melancholy of his soul in verse? There were so many things he wanted to describe: his sensation of a few hours before on Grattan Bridge, for example. If he could get back again into that mood...

The child awoke and began to cry. He turned from the page and tried to hush it: but it would not be hushed. He began to rock it to and fro in his arms, but its wailing cry grew keener. He rocked it faster while his eyes began to read the second stanza:

Within this narrow cell reclines her clay,

That clay where once...

It was useless. He couldn't read. He couldn't do anything. The wailing of the child pierced the drum of his ear. It was useless, useless! He was a prisoner for life. His arms trembled with anger and suddenly bending to the child's face he shouted:

"Stop!"

The child stopped for an instant, had a spasm of fright and began to scream. He jumped up from his chair and walked hastily up and down the room with the child in his arms. it began to sob piteously, losing its breath for four or five seconds, and then bursting out anew. The thin walls of the room echoed the sound. He tried to soothe it, but it sobbed more convulsively. He looked at the contracted and quivering face of the child and began to be alarmed. He counted seven sobs without a break between them and caught the child to his breast in fright. If it died! …

The door was burst open and a young woman ran in, panting.

"What is it? What is it?" she cried.

The child, hearing its mother's voice, broke out into a paroxysm of sobbing.

"It's nothing, Annie… it's nothing… He began to cry…"

She flung her parcels on the floor and snatched the child from him.

"What have you done to him?" she cried, glaring into his face.

Little Chandler sustained for one moment the gaze of her eyes and his heart closed together as he met the hatred in them. He began to stammer:

"It's nothing… He… he… began to cry… I couldn't… I didn't do anything… What?"

Giving no heed to him she began to walk up and down the room, clasping the child tightly in her arms and murmuring:

"My little man! My little mannie! Was 'ou frightened, love?'… There now, love! There now! … Lambabaun! Mamma's little lamb of the world! … There now!"

Little Chandler felt his cheeks suffused with shame and he stood back out of the lamplight. He listened while the paroxysm of the child's sobbing grew less and less; and tears of remorse started to his eyes.

注释（Notes）

1. the North Wall: cluster of docks and railway stations in Dublin

2. the King's Inns: offices and residences for lawyers comparable to London's Inns of Court,国王律师公会。亨利八世在位时,为了让爱尔兰成为英国附属地,在都柏林设立的一个律师公会,成为爱尔兰法律职业的中心。

3. Atalantas: Atalanta was a virgin huntress of classic mythology, who promised to marry the first man who could beat her in a foot race.

4. Capel Street: 卡佩尔街,位于都柏林市中心。

5. Celtic: 凯尔特人风格的。

6. :Lithia:原意为氧化锂,这里结合语境推测可能是含锂的某种饮品,比如锂盐矿泉水之类的。

7. garcon: waiter

8. the vivid orange tie: Wearing an orange tie, Gallaher seems to be flaunting his allegiance to England. Orangemen (called after William of Orange, last British conqueror of Ireland) were supporters of Anglo-Irish Protestantism.

9. the Isle of Man: in the Irish Sea, not far from Dublin

10. the Moulin Rouge：红磨坊，位于法国巴黎十八区皮加勒红灯区的酒吧，因屋顶上仿造的红风车而闻名于世。

11. parole d'honneur：my word of honor，法语，表承诺。

12. a. p. ：author's proof, i. e. trial printing which Gallaher as journalist would have to correct before sending it to press

13. the hire system：the installment plan

14. Zephyr：仄费罗斯，希腊神话中的西风之神。

主题探究（Themes）

（扫码阅读）

问题讨论（Questions for Discussion）

1. So many characters in these stories (e. g. little Chandler) want to leave Dublin, but no one ever gets out. Is this just a coincidence? What's holding everyone back?

2. There is a movement in the story, not just physical, but also psychological. Can you describe the psychological journey?

3. Concerning symbolism in the story, the most obvious one is the title. What does the "little cloud" symbolize? Then, how do you like the image of "window" which appears in many stories of "Dubliners".

4. Who is the narrator, can she or he read minds, and, more importantly, can we trust her or him?

Sons & Lovers

作品简介（Introduction to the Work）

Sons and Lovers, semiautobiographical novel by D. H. Lawrence, published in 1913. His first mature novel, it is a psychological study of the familial and love relationships of a working-class English family. It traces emotional conflicts through the protagonist, Paul Morel, and his suffocating relationships with a demanding mother and two very different lovers, which exert complex influences on the development of his manhood. While the novel initially received a lukewarm critical reception, along with allegations of obscenity, it is today regarded as a masterpiece by many critics and is often regarded as Lawrence's finest achievement. It tells us more about Lawrence's life and his phases, as his first was when he lost his mother in 1910 to whom he was particularly attached. And it was from then that he met Frieda Richthofen, and around this time that he began conceiving his two other great novels, *The Rainbow* and *Women In Love*, which had more sexual emphasis and maturity.

The novel opens with the description of settings. Gertrude Morel was pregnant with her third and unwanted child. While she was sleeping, Walter cut off his eldest son's hair like shorn sheep. They both have an argument over this. Later her husband comes home drunk, and their fight leads to locking Gertrude out of the house. A flashback scene also occurs, and Gertrude remembers how she and Walter met at a Christmas party, and she loved him not knowing that he was lying about himself. They both get married, and eventually, Gertrude gets to know about the betrayal of her husband and his poverty. They often have argued over his alcoholic nature. The novel progresses with the birth of Paul, an unwanted child. The parents keep on quarreling, and the father steals money from his wife's purse. In following excerpt, the he confrontation by the wife leads Walter to leave the house, but he comes back home at night. Walter pays no attention to his family, and the environment of the house gets more tensed.

(扫码阅读)

Sons & Lovers

(excerpt)

Unit 14
Poets after the Second World War (Contemporary Poets)

W. H. Auden: "As I Walked Out One Evening"
Philip Larkin: "Toads"
▽

作者简介 (Introduction to the Authors)

W. H. Auden (1907—1973) is a poet, editor and critic. He is considered as one of the most skilled and creative poets in 20th century. Auden was born in a middle class family in 1907. He spent his early years in an industrial section of northern England which left a deep impression on him. His father was a doctor and his mother was a nurse. His grandfathers were both Church of England clergyman. The religious atmosphere exerted great influence on him. Meanwhile, his interest in science earned him scholarship to Oxford University in 1925. But after a year's study, Auden switched to Old English. Nevertheless, some scientific references can still be found in his poetry. While at Oxford, he founded Auden Group or the Oxford Group with Stephen Spender, C. Day Lewis and others. Their works reflected social, political, and other concerns. After graduation, he studied German literature and arts and Freud's theories in Germany. So, the thoughts of Marx and Freud weighed heavily in Auden's early works. During his lifetime, he visited Germany, China, Iceland and served in the Spanish Civil War. In 1946, he became an American citizen, retaining his British citizenship. In 1948, Auden won the Pulitzer Prize. He died in Vienna in 1973. His collection *Poems* established him as the leading voice of a new generation. It made great contribution to English poetry in the content, direction and writing technique. His poetry was noted for its stylistic and technical achievement, its imaginable verse form, its engagement with politics, morals and religion, and its variety in tone and content.

Philip Larkin (1922—1985) is an English poet, novelist and librarian. He is one of post-war England's most famous poets. Larkin was born in Coventry in 1922. His father was a self-made man who had risen to be Coventry City Treasurer. He introduced many works of modernist writers to his son. Larkin didn't go to school until eight. It was at the local grammar school that he got attached to literature. Between 1933 and 1940, he made regular contributions to the school magazine. In 1940, he enrolled at Oxford. He made friends with those who shared his ideas, including Kingsley Amis and John Wain. During World War II, Larkin was exempted from service due to his poor eyesight. After graduation, he became a librarian and worked in different places. Larkin received many awards throughout his life. Actually, the poet disliked fame and was sick of being in the limelight. In 1984, he was offered, but declined the position of Poet Laureate. He was influenced by W. B. Yeats at an early stage and he chiefly credited his literary inspirations to the reading of Thomas Hardy's verse. Yet, most of his works showed concerns for the society. Larkin was unmarried and died of cancer in 1985. Larkin was noted for his poetic techniques. Borrowing some skills from Modernism, he got rid of its obscurity and ambiguity. And he was strict in meters and rhymes. His poems were filled with precise language, careful observation and tight structure. It was his poetry that marked an end to the reign of Modernism.

As I Walked Out One Evening

作品简介 (Introduction to the Work)

"As I Walked Out One Evening" is W. H. Auden's song of disillusionment, mortality, and love. This poem first appeared in Auden's 1940 collection *Another Time*. It reflects the anxiety he had about his own relationships in life and was one of a number of poems that were created around the time of the Second World War and all the uncertainty surrounding the future of the West. It is a fifteen-stanza poem. These fifteen stanzas are four lines each, known as quatrains. The poem takes the form of a ballad. This means that it uses a specific metrical pattern and rhyme scheme. It is also song-like in its descriptions and images. Throughout this piece, Auden chose to use iambic trimeter, which, in some instances, is used more loosely than others. In some examples of lines, there are three stressed beats, but not necessarily in the pattern of trochees or iambs.

The poem's speaker wanders out for an evening stroll and overhears a kind of debate between a young lover, who believes that "love has no ending", and all the city's clocks, which counter that "you cannot conquer time". These personified clocks sing of all life's disappointments and endings—but also suggest that, in spite of the fact that love does have an ending, one must nevertheless go on trying to "love your crooked neighbor / With your crooked heart". Love isn't a liberating, all-conquering force, as this poem says: it's a humble, brave task, taken on in the face of death itself.

作品选文（Selected Reading）

As I Walked Out One Evening

As I walked out one evening,
Walking down Bristol[1] Street,
The crowds upon the pavement
Were fields of harvest wheat.

And down by the brimming river[2]
I heard a lover sing
Under an arch of the railway:
'Love has no ending.

'I'll love you, dear, I'll love you
Till China and Africa meet,
And the river jumps over the mountain
And the salmon sing in the street,

'I'll love you till the ocean
Is folded and hung up to dry
And the seven stars go squawking
Like geese about the sky.

'The years shall run like rabbits,
For in my arms I hold
The Flower of the Ages,
And the first love of the world.'

But all the clocks in the city
Began to whirr and chime:
'O let not Time[3] deceive you,
You cannot conquer Time.

'In the burrows of the Nightmare
Where Justice naked is[4],
Time watches from the shadow
And coughs when you would kiss.

'In headaches and in worry
Vaguely life leaks away,
And Time will have his fancy
To-morrow or to-day.

'Into many a green valley
Drifts the appalling snow;
Time breaks the threaded dances[5]
And the diver's brilliant bow.

'O plunge your hands in water,
Plunge them in up to the wrist;
Stare, stare in the basin
And wonder what you've missed.

'The glacier knocks in the cupboard,
The desert sighs in the bed[6],
And the crack in the tea-cup opens
A lane to the land of the dead.

'Where the beggars raffle the banknotes
And the Giant is enchanting to Jack[7],
And the Lily-white Boy[8] is a Roarer,
And Jill[9] goes down on her back.

'O look, look in the mirror,
O look in your distress;
Life remains a blessing
Although you cannot bless.

'O stand, stand at the window
As the tears scald and start;
You shall love your crooked neighbour
With your crooked heart.'

It was late, late in the evening,

The lovers they were gone¹⁰;

The clocks had ceased their chiming,

And the deep river ran on.

作品译文(扫码阅读)

注释 (Notes)

1. Bristol：布里斯托尔，英格兰西南部的城市，是英格兰八大核心城市之一。

2. brimming river：满溢的河，象征生命力。

3. Time：这里大写的时间用了拟人的手法。

4. Where Justice naked is：Where Justice is naked，这里倒装与第四行的kiss形成了眼韵。

5. threaded dances：refer to traditional dances like the Maypole Dance，五朔节花柱舞。

6. The glacier knocks in the cupboard, / The desert sighs in the bed：Glaciers and deserts are barren places. Here are two examples of mixing the natural and man-made realms.

7. the Giant is enchanting to Jack："Jack the Giant Killer" is a Cornish/British fairy tale and legends about a plucky lad who slays a number of giants during King Arthur's reign.

8. Lily-white Boy：pure, innocent little boy

9. Jill：Jill (of "Jack and Jill Went Up the Hill" fame) is presented in a more grownup, subtly sexualized way.

10. gone：双关，可以指离开或者死亡。

主题探究 (Themes)

(扫码阅读)

问题讨论(Questions for Discussion)

1. You got three speakers in this poem. Who are they?
2. Please comment on the form and meter of this poem?
3. The poem starts and ends with a river, so what do you think of the image?
4. Auden set up comparisons between the man—made and the natural. Can you give some examples?
5. Where in the poem does Auden introduce the Death theme? Name a line and an image. How many images or symbols in the poem can you connect with Death?
6. Can you identify with the lover in this poem? Why or why not?

(请扫码观看视频 W. H. Auden &"As I Walked Out One Evening")

Toads

作品简介(Introduction to the Work)

"Toads" by Philip Larkin explores the confines of everyday life. Throughout, he uses a frog as a way to depict dual pressures in his life. Larkin wrote "Toads" in 1954, and it was published a year later in his second collection, *The Less Deceived*. This is a nine-stanza poem that is separated into sets of four lines, known as quatrains. These quatrains do not follow a specific pattern of rhyme. Instead, there are isolated moments of perfect and imperfect (or slant) rhymes. For instance, in the first stanza, the first and third lines are perfect, with the "-k" sound. The second and fourth lines are half, consonant rhymes, using the "f" sound. "Toads" is a cry of frustration that sees Larkin grumbling about having to devote his entire day to work, just so he could have an evening. He has to give up "six days" of his week to the toad work, which seems "out of proportion" for what he gets in return. Yet he ends up concluding that work is probably something he is well-suited to, and he wouldn't want to be one of those people who live without it. For he, too, is "toad-like".

This concept of the two toads, the one representing the institution of work itself and the one that lurks deep within Larkin, helps to explain the meaning of that final stanza: it's hard not to be a bit of a toad when you slave away at work all day, just as it would be difficult to chuck in the job when you harbor a toad-like approach to living as part of your nature.

作品选文 (Selected Reading)

Toads

Why should I let the toad work
Squat¹ on my life?
Can't I use my wit as a pitchfork
And drive the brute off?

Six days of the week it soils
With its sickening poison—
Just for paying a few bills!
That's out of proportion².

Lots of folk live on their wits:
Lecturers, lispers,
Losels, loblolly-men, louts—
They don't end as paupers;

Lots of folk live up lanes
With fires in a bucket,
Eat windfalls³ and tinned sardines—
They seem to like it.

Their nippers have got bare feet,
Their unspeakable wives
Are skinny as whippets—and yet
No one actually starves.

Ah, were I courageous enough
To shout Stuff your pension!⁴
But I know, all too well, that's the stuff
That dreams are made on:

For something sufficiently toad-like
Squats in me, too⁵;

Its hunkers are heavy as hard luck,
And cold as snow,

And will never allow me to blarney
My way of getting
The fame and the girl and the money
All at one sitting[6].

I don't say, one bodies the other
One's spiritual truth;
But I do say it's hard to lose either,
When you have both.

作品译文(扫码阅读)

注释（Notes）

1. Squat: This word creates the feeling of big, fat.
2. out of proportion: 付出的辛劳和获得的报酬不成比例。
3. windfalls: fruit knocked out of trees by the wind
4. To shout Stuff your pension: This kind of action is just a fantasy, a dream, something he knows just isn't going to happen.
5. For something sufficiently toad-like / Squats in me, too: Here is the internal-toad, the personal sense of obligation, duty or honesty. Now we find out why the speaker hasn't joined the merry ranks of the jobless.
6. at one sitting: 一次性.

主题探究（Themes）

(扫码阅读)

问题讨论（Questions for Discussion）

1. Why do you think Larkin chose to write this poem in slant rhymed quatrains? Does the poem's form reflect any of the poem's themes or ideas? How?

2. How do you picture this speaker? Is he young or old? Would you hang out with him or would you turn and walk the other way if he tried to corner you at a party? What in the poem creates the impression that you have of this speaker?

3. Larkin chose to use a toad to represent work. Did he make a good choice? Why or why not? If you think he made a bad choice, step up: what animal would have been better and why?

Unit 15
Novelists after the Second World War
(Contemporary Novelists)

Doris Lessing: *The Golden Notebook*
Kazuo Ishiguro: *An Artist of the Floating World*
▽

作者简介 (Introduction to the Authors)

Doris Lessing (1919—2013) is a British novelist and short story writer. She is one of the most creative contemporary women writers. She was born in 1919 in Iran. Her parents were both British. In 1925, the family moved to the Southern Rhodesia, where they lived in a farm. At that time, Lessing read a lot of European classics so as to ease her loneliness. She left school at 14 and then was self-educated. When she was 15, she began to sell her stories. Her life and experience in Rhodesia have provided excellent material for her African stories, which have been widely acclaimed. Lessing once worked as a nursemaid, typist, telephone operator and so on. She had two failed marriage before she moved to London in 1949. Throughout her life, she developed great interest in politics and engaged herself in many left-wing political campaigns. Lessing was strongly opposed to apartheid which got her banned from south Africa and Rhodesia for many years. Moreover, Lessing was not only influenced by Marxism but also by Freud's and Carl Jung's psychoanalysis and the Sufi. As a prolific writer, she had issued more than 50 novels. In 2007, she was awarded the Noble Prize in Literature. She died in 2013. Overall, her works dealt with many topics, for example, racism, communism, mysticism and feminism, reflecting the sign of that time. She showed women's struggles with their living condition and mental freedom in her novels which received highly praise from feminist. Trying to solve the modern spiritual crisis in her later years, she was more of a prophet.

Kazuo Ishiguro (1954—) is an English novelist, musician and short story writer. He is one of the most critically praised contemporary writers. Ishiguro was born in Nagasaki, Japan in 1954. His father, a physical oceanographer, was invited to do research at the National Institute of Oceanographer. Therefore, the family moved to Britain in 1960. Ishiguro's different perspective towards life was actually based on his experience as Japanese in the UK. He was educated at a grammar school in Surrey. After graduation in 1973, he travelled through the United States and Canada. He enjoyed music and worked as a grouse-beater for the Queen Mother. In 1974, Ishiguro began to study at the University of Kent, Canterbury, and he graduated with a Bachelor of Arts in English and Philosophy. He worked as a community worker and social worker for a period of time. Then he took the Creative Writing course at the University of East Anglia where he met Angela Carter, a famous English feminist. Ishiguro has been a full-time writer since 1982. In 1989, he won the Booker Prize for *The Remains of the Day*. He gained British citizenship in 1983. He was awarded the Nobel Prize in Literature in 2017. Now, he lives in London with his wife and daughter. Ishiguro focuses more on international themes rather than the survival state of immigrants, aiming to show some new elements in worldwide basis. His novels are filled with pieces of memories, their potential to distort, to digress, to forget, to silence, and to hunt.

The Golden Notebook

作品简介 (Introduction to the Work)

The Golden Notebook, novel by Doris Lessing, published in 1962. It is a multilayered novel that centrally concerns the life, memories, and writings of Anna Wulf in the 1950s, during her late twenties and early thirties in London and colonial Africa. The novel alternates between a linear narrative entitled *Free Women*, which follows the lives of Anna and her friend Molly, and Anna's four private notebooks: in the black notebook she recalls the time she spent in Africa, the novel she fashioned out of her experience, and her difficulties coping with the novel's reception; in the red notebook she recounts her ambivalent membership in and disavowal of the British Communist Party; in the yellow notebook, she starts a novel that closely mirrors her own pattern of unfulfilling relationships in London; and the blue notebook serves as her inconsistent personal diary, full of self-doubt and contradiction. As one of the most important books of the growing feminist movement of the 1950s, *The Golden Notebook* was brought to a wider public when Doris Lessing won the Nobel Prize in 2007. Anna's struggle to unify the various strands of her life—emotional, political, and professional—amasses into a fascinating encyclopedia of female experience in the 1950s. In this authentic, taboo-breaking novel, Lessing brings the plight of women's lives from obscurity behind closed doors into broad daylight. *The Golden Notebook* resonates with the concerns and experiences of a great many women and is a true modern classic, thoroughly deserving of its reputation as a feminist bible.

Free Women says, Anna, a talented but sheepish writer, tells Molly, the boisterous and "worldly-wise" actress that "everything's cracking up" in the world. Molly's ex-husband Richard, a wealthy businessman who now violently disdains the leftist politics that brought them together, visits to talk about finding a job for their son Tommy, who has spent the last few months brooding in his room. He also wants advice about his current wife, Marion, who has become an alcoholic due to his numerous affairs. Overhearing all of this, Tommy comes downstairs to refuse his father's offer. Anna tells Molly about her waning interest in writing another novel, Richard's attempts to have an affair with her, the state of their communist friends, and her inability to get over her married ex-lover, Michael.

作品选文 (Selected Reading)

The Golden Notebook
(Exerpt)
Free Women 1

Anna meets her friend Molly in the summer of 1957 after a separation...

The two women were alone in the London flat.

"The point is," said Anna, as her friend came back from the telephone on the landing, "the point is, that as far as I can see, everything's cracking up."

Molly was a woman much on the telephone. When it rang she had just enquired: "Well, what's the gossip?" Now she said, "That's Richard, and he's coming over. It seems today's his only free moment for the next month. Or so he insists."

"Well I'm not leaving," said Anna.

"No, you stay just where you are."

Molly considered her own appearance—she was wearing trousers and a sweater, both the worse for wear. "He'll have to take me as I come," she concluded, and sat down by the window. "He wouldn't say what it's about—another crisis with Marion, I suppose."

"Didn't he write to you?" asked Anna, cautious.

"Both he and Marion wrote—ever such bonhomous[1] letters. Odd, isn't it?"

This odd, isn't it? Was the characteristic note of the intimate conversations they designated gossip. But having struck the note, Molly swerved off with: "It's no use talking now, because he's coming right over, he says."

"He'll probably go when he sees me here," said Anna, cheerfully, but slightly aggressive. Molly glanced at her, keenly, and said: "Oh, but why?"

It had always been understood that Anna and Richard disliked each other; and before, Anna had always left when Richard was expected. Now Molly said: "Actually I think he rather likes you, in his heart of hearts. The point is, he's committed to liking me, on principle—he's such a fool he's always got to either like or dislike someone, so all the dislike he won't admit he has for me gets pushed off on to you."

It's a pleasure," said Anna. "But do you know something? I discovered while you were away that for a lot of people you and I are practically interchangeable."

"You've only just understood that?" said Molly, triumphant as always when Anna came up with—as far as she was concerned—facts that were self-evident.

In this relationship a balance had been struck early on: Molly was altogether more worldly-wise than Anna who, for her part, had a superiority of talent.

Anna held her own private views. Now she smiled, admitting that she had been very slow.

"When we're so different in every way," said Molly, "it's odd. I suppose because we both live the same kind of life—not getting married and so on. That's all they see."

"*Free women*," said Anna, wryly. She added, with an anger new to Molly, so that she earned another quick scrutinizing glance from her friend: "They still define us in terms of relationships with men, even the best of them."

"Well, we do, don't we?" said Molly, rather tart. "Well, it's awfully hard not to," she amended, hastily, because of the look of surprise Anna now gave her. There was a short pause, during which the women did not look at each other but reflected that a year apart was a long time, even for an old friendship.

Molly said at last, sighing: "Free. Do you know, when I was away, I was thinking about us, and I've decided that we're a completely new type of woman. We must be, surely?"

"There's nothing new under the sun," said Anna, in an attempt at a German accent. Molly, irritated—she spoke half a dozen languages well—said: "There's nothing new under the sun," in a perfect reproduction of a shrewd old woman's voice, German accented.

Anna grimaced, acknowledging failure. She could not learn languages, and was too self-conscious ever to become somebody else: for a moment Molly had even looked like Mother Sugar, otherwise Mrs Marks, to whom both had gone for psycho-analysis[2]. The reservations both had felt about the solemn and painful ritual were expressed by the pet name, "Mother Sugar"; which, as time passed, became a name for much more than a person, and indicated a whole way of looking at life—traditional, rooted, conservative, in spite of its scandalous familiarity with everything amoral. In spite was how Anna and Molly, discussing the ritual, had felt it; recently Anna had been feeling more and more it was because of; and this was one of the things she was looking forward to discussing with her friend.

But now Molly, reacting as she had often done in the past, to the slightest suggestion of a criticism from Anna of Mother Sugar, said quickly: "All the same, she was wonderful and I was in much too bad a shape to criticize."

"Mother Sugar used to say, 'You're Electra,' or 'You're Antigone,' and that was the end, as far as she was concerned," said Anna.

"Well, not quite the end," said Molly, wryly insisting on the painful probing hours both had spent.

"Yes," said Anna, unexpectedly insisting, so that Molly, for the third time, looked at her curiously. "Yes. Oh I'm not saying she didn't do me all the good in the world. I'm sure I'd never have coped with what I've had to cope with without her. But all the same... I remember quite clearly one afternoon, sitting there—the big room, and the discreet wall lights, and the Buddha and the pictures and the statues."

"Well?" said Molly, now very critical.

Anna, in the face of this unspoken but clear determination not to discuss it, said: "I've been thinking about it all during the last few months...no, I'd like to talk about it with you. After all, we both went through it, and with the same person..."

"Well?"

Anna persisted: "I remember that afternoon, knowing I'd never go back. It was all that damned art all over the place."

Molly drew in her breath, sharp. She said, quickly: "I don't know what you mean." As Anna did not reply, she said, accusing: "And have you written anything since I've been away?"

"No."

"I keep telling you," said Molly, her voice shrill, "I'll never forgive you if you throw that talent away. I mean it. I've done it, and I can't stand watching you—I've messed with painting and dancing and acting and scribbling, and now...you're so talented, Anna. Why? I simply don't understand."

"How can I ever say why, when you're always so bitter and accusing?"

Molly even had tears in her eyes, which were fastened in the most painful reproach on her friend. She brought out with difficulty: "At the back of my mind I always thought, well, I'll get married, so it doesn't matter my wasting all the talents I was born with. Until recently I was even dreaming about having more children—yes I know it's idiotic but it's true. And now I'm forty and Tommy's grown up. But the point is, if you're not writing simply because you're thinking about getting married..."

"But we both want to get married," said Anna, making it humorous; the tone restored reserve to the conversation; she had understood, with pain, that she was not, after all, going to be able to discuss certain subjects with Molly.

Molly smiled, drily, gave her friend an acute, bitter look, and said: "All right, but you'll be sorry later."

"Sorry," said Anna, laughing, out of surprise. "Molly, why is it you'll never believe other people have the disabilities you have?"

"You were lucky enough to be given one talent, and not four."

"Perhaps my one talent has had as much pressure on it as your four?"

"I can't talk to you in this mood. Shall I make you some tea while we're waiting for Richard?"

"I'd rather have beer or something." She added, provocative: "I've been thinking I might very well take to drink later on."

Molly said, in the older sister's tone Anna had invited: "You shouldn't make jokes, Anna. Not when you see what it does to people—look at Marion. I wonder if she's been drinking while I was away?"

"I can tell you. She has—yes, she came to see me several times."

"She came to see you?"

"That's what I was leading up to, when I said you and I seem to be interchangeable."

Molly tended to be possessive—she showed resentment, as Anna had known she would, as she said: "I suppose you're going to say Richard came to see you too?" Anna nodded; and Molly said, briskly, "I'll get us some beer." She returned from the kitchen with two long cold-beaded glasses, and said: "Well you'd better tell me all about it before Richard comes, hadn't you?"

Richard was Molly's husband; or rather, he had been her husband. Molly was the product of what she referred to as one of those 'twenties marriages'. Her mother and father had both glittered, but briefly, in the intellectual and bohemian[3] circles that had spun around the great central lights of Huxley[4], Lawrence, Joyce, etc. Her childhood had been disastrous, since this marriage only lasted a few months. She had married, at the age of eighteen, the son of a friend of her father's. She knew now she had married out of a need for security and even respectability. The boy Tommy was a product of this marriage. Richard at twenty had already been on the way to becoming the very solid businessman he had since proved himself; and Molly and he had stood their incompatibility for not much more than a year. He had then married Marion, and there were three boys. Tommy had remained with Molly. Richard and she, once the business of the divorce was over, became friends again. Later, Marion became her friend. This, then, was the situation to which Molly often referred as: "It's all very odd, isn't it?"

"Richard came to see me about Tommy," said Anna.

"What? Why?"

"Oh—idiotic! He asked me if I thought it was good for Tommy to spend so much time brooding. I said I thought it was good for everyone to brood, if by that he meant, thinking; and that since Tommy was twenty and grown up it was not for us to interfere anyway."

"Well it isn't good for him," said Molly.

"He asked me if I thought it would be good for Tommy to go off on some trip or other to Germany—a business trip, with him. I told him to ask Tommy, not me. Of course Tommy said no."

"Of course. Well I'm sorry Tommy didn't go."

"But the real reason he came, I think, was because of Marion. But Marion had just been to see me, and had a prior claim, so to speak. So I wouldn't discuss Marion at all. I think it's likely he's coming to discuss Marion with you."

Molly was watching Anna closely. "How many times did Richard come?"

"About five or six times."

After a silence, Molly let her anger spurt out with: "It's very odd he seems to expect me almost to control Marion. Why me? Or you? Well, perhaps you'd better go after all. It's going to be difficult if all sorts of complications have been going on while my back was turned."

Anna said firmly: "No, Molly. I didn't ask Richard to come and see me. I didn't ask Marion to come and see me. After all, it's not your fault or mine that we seem to play the same role for people. I said what you would have said—at least, I think so."

There was a note of humorous, even childish pleading in this. But it was deliberate. Molly, the older sister, smiled and said: "Well, all right." She continued to observe Anna narrowly; and Anna was careful to appear unaware of it. She did not want to tell Molly what had happened between her and Richard now; not until she could tell her the whole story of the last miserable year.

"Is Marion drinking badly?"

"Yes, I think she is."

"And she told you all about it?"

"Yes. In detail. And what's odd is, I swear she talked as if I were you—even making slips of the tongue, calling me Molly and so on."

"Well, I don't know," said Molly. "Who would ever have thought? And you and I are different as chalk and cheese."

"Perhaps not so different," said Anna, drily; but Molly laughed in disbelief.

She was a tallish woman, and big-boned, but she appeared slight, and even boyish. This was because of how she did her hair, which was a rough, streaky gold, cut like a boy's; and because of her clothes, for which she had a great natural talent. She took pleasure in the various guises she could use: for instance, being a hoyden in lean trousers and sweaters, and then a siren, her large green eyes made-up, her cheekbones prominent, wearing a dress which made the most of her full breasts.

This was one of the private games she played with life, which Anna envied her; yet in moments of self-rebuke she would tell Anna she was ashamed of herself, she so much enjoyed the different roles: "It's as if I were really different—don't you see? I even feel a different person. And there's something spiteful in it—that man, you know, I told you about him last week—he saw me the first time in my old slacks and my sloppy old jersey, and then I rolled into the restaurant, nothing less than a femme and he didn't know how to have me, he couldn't say a word all evening, and I enjoyed it. Well, Anna?"

"But you do enjoy it," Anna would say, laughing.

But Anna was small, thin, dark, brittle, with large black always-on-guard eyes, and a fluffy haircut. She was, on the whole, satisfied with herself, but she was always the same. She envied Molly's capacity to project her own changes of mood. Anna wore neat, delicate clothes, which tended to be either prim, or perhaps a little odd; and relied upon her delicate white hands, and her small, pointed white face to make an impression. But she was shy, unable to assert herself, and, she was convinced, easily overlooked.

When the two women went out together, Anna deliberately effaced herself and played to the dramatic Molly. When they were alone, she tended to take the lead. But this had by no means been true at the beginning of their friendship. Molly, abrupt, straightforward, tactless, had frankly domineered Anna. Slowly, and the offices of Mother Sugar had had a good deal to do with it, Anna learned to stand up for herself. Even now there were moments when she should challenge Molly when she did not. She admitted to herself she was a coward; she would always give in rather than have fights or scenes. A quarrel would lay Anna low for days, whereas Molly thrived on them. She would burst into exuberant tears, say unforgivable things, and have forgotten all about it half a day later. Meanwhile Anna would be limply recovering in her flat.

注释（Notes）

1. bonhomous：和蔼的，愉快的。
2. psycho-analysis：19世纪末由奥地利医生西格蒙德·弗洛伊德创立的学科。
3. bohemian：波西米亚风格，用来描述欧洲主要城市边缘化和贫困的艺术家、作家、记者、音乐家和演员的非传统生活方式。
4. Huxley：阿尔多斯·赫胥黎（Aldous Huxley，1894年07月26日—1963年11月22日）于1894年出生于英国南部名门世家。英国小说家、诗人、剧作家。

主题探究 (Themes)

（扫码阅读）

问题讨论 (Questions for Discussion)

1. Many scholars probe into this novel from four notebooks colored by black, red, yellow and blue. How do you like the symbolic meaning of each color?
2. In your opinion, what does the title "The Golden Notebook" represents?
3. What's the narrative time of this novel? Why does Lessing narrate in this way?
4. What are Anna's grounds for wanting a divorce? Could you give me your reasons? Do you agree with her behavior? If you were Anna, what would you do?
5. Does Anna stop her pursuit of love after her divorce?
6. Could you make a comparative study between Anna and Marion?

An Artist of the Floating World

作品简介 (Introduction to the Work)

An Artist of the Floating World is a novel by British author Kazuo Ishiguro. It is set in post-World War Ⅱ Japan and is narrated by Masuji Ono, an aging painter, who looks back on his life and how he has lived it. In this novel, Ono notices how his once great reputation has faltered since the war and how attitudes towards him and his paintings have changed. The chief conflict deals with Ono's need to accept responsibility for his past actions, rendered politically suspect in the context of post-War Japan, and it also deals with the role of people in a rapidly changing political environment and with the assumption and denial of guilt. Ono provides a highly subjective account of the events that shaped his career, family life, and reputation, grappling with his past as he tells his story. Though the narrative leaps in and out of different periods in Ono's life, from his first job to his childhood to his role working for the government in World-War Ⅱ era Japan, the strongest linear thread revolves around the marriage of Ono's daughter. In the years after the war, Ono works to negotiate a traditional arranged marriage for his younger daughter, Noriko. In light of a failed marriage negotiation for Noriko a year before, Ono's older daughter Setsuko suggests that he visit various old acquaintances. This way he can ensure that, if these acquaintances are interviewed about Ono and his family as part of the negotiation, they will provide positive testimony.

Ono believes that Setsuko is politely telling him to find a way to make his past less of a problem, since he became a propagandist for Japanese imperialism during the war and which has destroyed his reputation. Finally, Noriko has been successfully wed to a reputable man named Taro Saito. The novel ends with Ono expressing good will for the young white-collar workers on the streets at lunchbreak. He thinks that, despite the nation's mistakes, the new generation is starting afresh. He wishes them well.

（扫码阅读）

An Artist of the Floating World

(Exerpt)

（请扫码观看视频 Kazuo Ishiguro）

Unit 16
Despair and Absurdity in Contemporary
English Drama

Samuel Beckett: *Waiting for Godot*
▽

作者简介 (Introduction to the Author)

Samuel Beckett (1906—1989) is an Irish novelist, dramatist, poet, and theatre director. He is regarded as one of the key figures in the Theatre of the Absurd. Beckett was born in 1906 in Dublin. His father was a surveyor with whom he often walked around the countryside. His mother worked as a nurse. He studied English, French, Italian at Trinity College Dublin and graduated with a BA in 1927. Beckett was good at cricket and once played for Dublin University. When he taught in Paris, he was introduced to James Joyce who exerted great influence on him. He offered assistance in finishing Joyce's *Finnegans Wake* and translated a fragment of the book into French with the help of Joyce. After the death of his father, Beckett began to undergo psychoanalysis which lasted for two years. In 1938, he was stabbed because of his refusal of the solicitations from a villain. During his life, he travelled throughout the Europe. Beckett fought for the French Resistance and was awarded by the French government. From 1932, He began to settle in France. He wrote both in English and French. And in 1969 he won the Noble Prize in Literature. He died in 1989. Beckett had a wider influence on literature. Many writers, including Harold Pinter and John Banville, all credited their success to Samuel Beckett. Beckett's absurd theatre served as an example for the plays. His desolate stage setting, simplified characters, communicable rhythms and broken sentences, led to innovations of English drama. And the nihilistic, absurdist themes in his works also fitted with the zeitgeist.

作品简介 (Introduction to the Work)

Waiting for Godot is the most well-known play from the Theatre of the Absurd movement. It was written by Samuel Beckett and performed for the first time in Paris on January 5th, 1953. *Waiting for Godot* is a tragic play with two acts depicting the unbearable miserable condition of modern man. There are two tramps: Estragon and Vladimir. They are subject to an apparently endless wait expecting some sort of help from

Godot but he does not come except for a vague promise that Godot will come tomorrow. Nothing is certain or clearer in the play. The scope of time seems quite disturbed because a tomorrow could mean a day, a year, a season or even a whole of one's life in this play.

The second act of the play opens the next day—although, oddly, the tree has grown a number of leaves overnight, suggesting that more time than this has passed. Vladimir and Estragon discover Lucky's hat which he had left behind, and the two men role-play at pretending to be Lucky and Pozzo. They then throw insults at each other to pass the time. Lucky and Pozzo return, but they have changed overnight: Lucky can no longer speak, and Pozzo is blind. When Lucky and Pozzo fall to the ground, Vladimir and Estragon try to help them up, but end up falling down too. Pozzo has no memory of meeting the two men the day before. He and Lucky leave again, with Vladimir and Estragon left to wait for Godot.

(扫码阅读)

Waiting for Godot

(Excerpt)

Part II
American Literature

Unit 17
Colonial America

Anne Bradstreet: "To My Dear and Loving Husband"
▽

作者简介 (Introduction to the Author)

Anne Bradstreet (1612—1672) was a distinguished English poet and the first female Colonialist whose works to be published. Bradstreet was born in Northampton, England. She was born into a prominent and wealthy Puritan family, allowing her to grow up in a cultured environment where she was tutored in history, literature and language. Bradstreet was an extremely well-educated young woman, especially for her time when education was a field reserved specifically for men. She married Simon Bradstreet, a graduate of Cambridge University, at the age of 16. Two years later, Bradstreet, along with her husband and parents, immigrated to America with the Winthrop Puritan group, and the family settled in Ipswich, Massachusetts. There Bradstreet and her husband raised eight children, and she became one of the first poets to write English verse in the American colonies. It was during this time that Bradstreet penned many of the poems that would be taken to England by her brother-in-law, purportedly without her knowledge, and published in 1650 under the title *The Tenth Muse Lately Sprung Up in America*. It was the only collection of Bradstreet's poetry to appear during her lifetime. In 1644, the family moved to Andover, Massachusetts, where Bradstreet lived until her death in 1672. In 1678, the first American edition of The *Tenth Muse Lately Sprung Up in America* was published posthumously and expanded as *Several Poems Compiled with Great Variety of Wit and Learning*. Bradstreet's most highly regarded work, a sequence of religious poems entitled *Contemplations* was not published until the middle of the 19th century. As the first widely recognized woman poet in American literature, Anne Bradstreet is a model for future generations.

作品简介 (Introduction to the Work)

"To My Dear and Loving Husband" first appeared in the second edition of *The Tenth Muse Lately Sprung Up in America*, which came off the presses in 1678. Bradstreet's brother-in-law snagged a copy of her manuscript, took it to England with him in 1647, and had it first published in 1650, apparently without her knowledge. In the literature of ancient Greece and Rome there were, traditionally, nine muses, mythological figures who were thought to inspire art and poetry. The title of Bradstreet's book adds a tenth to the list, and boldly claims that Bradstreet herself is the tenth muse—the American one. This is a very brave move: It would have been like adding one to the list of "founding fathers". It's both a claim to superior artistic ability (I'm on par with the patron deities of art) and a claim to American, as opposed to European, artistic fertility (America as the new place for great poetry). But then again, Bradstreet herself wasn't planning on publishing the book. *The Tenth Muse Lately Sprung Up in America* was the first book of poetry published by someone living in the New World, giving her the unique distinction of being America's first poet. *The Tenth Muse* was Bradstreet's only publication during her lifetime.

"To My Dear and Loving Husband" is about what happens when one meets that perfect person. Anne Bradstreet felt that her husband was that perfect guy and wrote scads of poems about him. The whole poem is, essentially, one gigantic statement about how much the speaker loves her husband. Love is so powerful, and so complicated, that it defies words.

作品选文 (Selected Reading)

To My Dear and Loving Husband

If ever two were one, then surely we.
If ever man were loved by wife, then thee[1];
If ever wife was happy in a man,
Compare with me, ye[2] women, if you can.
I prize thy[3] love more than whole mines of gold
Or all the riches that the East doth[4] hold.
My love is such that rivers cannot quench[5],
Nor ought[6] but love from thee give recompense[7].
Thy love is such I can no way repay.
The heavens reward thee manifold[8], I pray.
Then while we live, in love let's so persever[e][9]
That when we live no more, we may live ever.

作品译文(扫码阅读)

注释 (Notes)

1. thee：古体，you 的单数的宾格。
2. ye：古体，you 的复数的主格，你们。
3. thy：古体，第二人称所有格，相当于 your。
4. doth：古体，does。
5. quench：扑灭，熄灭（火）。
6. ought：这里指 anything，任何事物。
7. recompense：赔偿，补偿。
8. manifold：繁多的，多种多样的。
9. persever[e]：坚持不懈。

主题探究 (Themes)

（扫码阅读）

文化延展 (Cultural Extension)

文学的历史和生活的历史一样，充满着埋没、堕落与忧伤。作为这个星球上最年轻的文明之一，美国在和其国家历史同样短暂的文学历史中，天才般地制造出了丝毫不亚于其他历史悠久的国家制造出来的血泪。美国文学是美国历史和文化的重要组成部分，因为它不仅生动地记载和描述了美国的历史，而且反映了美国人的思维和想象力。美国文学是在欧洲殖民者，特别是英国殖民者和本土传统共同影响下所形成的产物，渗透和彰显着美国自由主义和个人主义等典型特征。

问题讨论 (Questions for Discussion)

1. When the speaker says rivers cannot quench her love, to what does she compare her love? What does that comparison really mean, anyway?
2. Would you use some of the lines from the poem to declare your love for somebody? Or are they just too corny for your taste?
3. What's up with the language of payment (recompense, repay, etc.)? If it's so filled with love, why does the speaker make her marriage sound like some sort of business deal?
4. Does this poem's idea of marriage differ from our current ideas about marriage?

5. How does this poem suggest that one can cheat death?

6. Does death sound like a bad thing in this poem? Or could it be considered good because it brings the speaker and her husband to eternal life together?

7. Are the speaker's claims about love being the key to a life in heaven strange? How do you make sense of them?

Unit 18

American Romanticism

Washington Irving: "Rip Van Winkle"
▽

作者简介 (Introduction to the Author)

Washington Irving (1783—1859) is the most famous American writer, historian, diplomat and traveler in the 19th century. He is known as "the Father of American literature". His works are beautiful in writing, vivid in language and full of interest, reflecting the transformation of American literature from rationalism in the 18th century to Romanticism in the 19th century. Washington Irving was born into a wealthy merchant family in New York. He dropped out of school at the age of 16 and studied law in several law firms. However, Irving's interest was in literature rather than law. Since he was a child, he liked to read adventure stories such as *Robinson Crusoe* and *Gulliver's Travels*. He often went to the theater to watch plays. Irving made his literary debut in 1802 with a series of observational letters to the *Morning Chronicle*. He moved to England in 1815 and gained international acclaim with the success of *The Sketchbook of Geoffrey Crayon, Gent*. In 1820, Irving toured all the places of interest in Britain. With admiration for the ancient British civilization and longing for the former capitalist society, he published many essays and stories. Irving died of a heart attack in 1859, eight months after completing his significant biographical series on George Washington. Irving uses humor and exaggeration appropriately in his description, and the romantic atmosphere reflected in it adds infinite charm to his works. "The Legend of Sleepy Hollow" and "Rip Van Winkle" are two representative works of him. As a representative of American romantic literature, Irving activated the creative potential of American literature and laid a solid foundation for its development.

作品简介 (Introduction to the Work)

"Rip Van Winkle" is a short story in *The Sketch Book*, in full *The Sketch Book of Geoffrey Crayon, Gent*. The short story collection by Washington Irving first published in 1819—1820 in seven separate parts. Most of the book's 30 odd pieces concern Irving's impressions of England, but six chapters deal with American subjects. Of these the tales, "The Legend of Sleepy Hollow" and "Rip Van Winkle" have been called the first

American short stories, although both are actually Americanized versions of German folktales. In addition to the stories based on folklore, the collection contains travel sketches, literary essays, and miscellany. *The Sketch Book* was a celebrated event in American literary history. The collection was the first American work to gain international literary success and popularity. Its unprecedented success allowed Irving to devote himself to writing.

"Rip Van Winkle", though set in the Dutch culture of pre-Revolutionary War New York state, is based on a German folktale. Rip Van Winkle is an amiable farmer who wanders into the Catskill Mountains, where he comes upon a group of dwarfs playing ninepins. Rip accepts their offer of a drink of liquor and promptly falls asleep. When he awakens, 20 years later, he is an old man with a long white beard; the dwarfs are nowhere in sight. When Rip returns to town, he finds that everything is changed: his wife is dead, his children are grown, and George Washington's portrait hangs in place of King George III's. The old man entertains the townspeople with tales of the old days and of his encounter with the little men in the mountains.

作品选文 (Selected Reading)

RIP VAN WINKLE
A POSTHUMOUS WRITING OF DIEDRICH KNICKERBOCKER

By Woden, God of Saxons[1],
From whence[2] comes Wensday, that is Wodensday[3],
Truth is a thing that ever I will keep
Unto thylke[4] day in which I creep into
My sepulchre[5]—

—CARTWRIGHT

The following tale was found among the papers of the late Diedrich Knickerbocker, an old gentleman of New York, who was very curious in the Dutch history of the province, and the manners of the descendants from its primitive settlers. His historical researches, however, did not lie so much among books as among men; for the former are lamentably scanty on his favorite topics; whereas he found the old burghers[6], and still more their wives, rich in that legendary lore, so invaluable to true history. Whenever, therefore, he happened upon a genuine Dutch family, snugly shut up in its low-roofed farmhouse, under a spreading sycamore, he looked upon it as a little clasped volume of black-letter, and studied it with the zeal of a book-worm.

The result of all these researches was a history of the province during the reign of the Dutch governors, which he published some years since. There have been various opinions as to the literary character of his work, and, to tell the truth, it is not a whit better than it should be. Its chief merit is its scrupulous accuracy, which indeed was a little questioned on its first appearance, but has since been completely established; and it is now admitted into all historical collections, as a book of unquestionable authority.

The old gentleman died shortly after the publication of his work, and now that he is dead and gone, it cannot do much harm to his memory to say that his time might have been better employed in weightier labors. He, however, was apt to ride his hobby his own way; and though it did now and then kick up the dust a little in the eyes of his neighbors, and grieve the spirit of some friends, for whom he felt the truest deference and affection; yet his errors and follies are remembered "more in sorrow than in anger," and it begins to be suspected, that he never intended to injure or offend. But however his memory may be appreciated by critics, it is still held dear by many folks, whose good opinion is well worth having; particularly by certain biscuit-bakers, who have gone so far as to imprint his likeness on their New-Year cakes; and have thus given him a chance for immortality, almost equal to the being stamped on a Waterloo Medal[7], or a Queen Anne's Farthing[8].

* * *

Whoever has made a voyage up the Hudson must remember the Kaatskill Mountains[9]. They are a dismembered branch of the great Appalachian[10] family, and are seen away to the west of the river, swelling up to a noble height, and lording it over the surrounding country. Every change of season, every change of weather, indeed, every hour of the day, produces some change in the magical hues and shapes of these mountains, and they are regarded by all the good wives, far and near, as perfect barometers. When the weather is fair and settled, they are clothed in blue and purple, and print their bold outlines on the clear evening sky, but, sometimes, when the rest of the landscape is cloudless, they will gather a hood of gray vapors about their summits, which, in the last rays of the setting sun, will glow and light up like a crown of glory.

At the foot of these fairy mountains, the voyager may have descried[11] the light smoke curling up from a village, whose shingle-roofs gleam among the trees, just where the blue tints of the upland melt away into the fresh green of the nearer landscape. It is a little village of great antiquity, having been founded by some of the Dutch colonists, in the early times of the province, just about the beginning of the government of the good Peter Stuyvesant[12] (may he rest in peace!) and there were some of the houses of the original settlers standing within a few years, built of small yellow bricks brought from Holland, having latticed windows and gable fronts, surmounted with weather cocks.

In that same village, and in one of these very houses (which, to tell the precise truth, was sadly time-worn and weather-beaten), there lived many years since, while the country was yet a province of Great Britain, a simple, good-natured fellow, of the name of Rip Van Winkle. He was a descendant of the Van Winkles who figured so gallantly in the chivalrous days of Peter Stuyvesant, and accompanied him to the siege of Fort Christina[13]. He inherited, however, but little of the martial character of his ancestors. I have observed that he was a simple good-natured man; he was, moreover, a kind neighbor, and an obedient hen-pecked husband. Indeed, to the latter circumstance might be owing that meekness of spirit which gained him such universal popularity; for those men are most apt to be obsequious and conciliating abroad, who are under the discipline of shrews at home. Their tempers, doubtless, are rendered pliant and malleable in the fiery furnace of domestic tribulation; and a curtain lecture is worth all the sermons in the world for teaching the virtues of patience and long-suffering. A termagant[14] wife may, therefore, in some respects, be considered a tolerable blessing; and if so, Rip Van Winkle was thrice blessed.

Certain it is, that he was a great favorite among all the good wives of the village, who, as usual, with the amiable sex, took his part in all family squabbles; and never failed, whenever they talked those matters over in their evening gossipings, to lay all the blame on Dame Van Winkle. The children of the village, too, would shout with joy whenever he approached. He assisted at their sports, made their playthings, taught them to fly kites and shoot marbles, and told them long stories of ghosts, witches, and Indians. Whenever he went dodging about the village, he was surrounded by a troop of them, hanging on his skirts, clambering on his back, and playing a thousand tricks on him with impunity[15]; and not a dog would bark at him throughout the neighborhood.

The great error in Rip's composition was an insuperable aversion to all kinds of profitable labor. It could not be from the want of assiduity or perseverance; for he would sit on a wet rock, with a rod as long and heavy as a Tartar's lance, and fish all day without a murmur, even though he should not be encouraged by a single nibble. He would carry a fowling-piece on his shoulder for hours together, trudging through woods and swamps, and up hill and down dale, to shoot a few squirrels or wild pigeons. He would never refuse to assist a neighbor even in the roughest toil, and was a foremost man at all country frolics for husking Indian corn, or building stone-fences; the women of the village, too, used to employ him to run their errands, and to do such little odd jobs as their less obliging husbands would not do for them. In a word, Rip was ready to attend to anybody's business but his own; but as to doing family duty, and keeping his farm in order, he found it impossible.

In fact, he declared it was of no use to work on his farm; it was the most pestilent little piece of ground in the whole country; every thing about it went wrong, and would go wrong, in spite of him. His fences were continually falling to pieces; his cow would either go astray, or get among the cabbages; weeds were sure to grow quicker in his fields than anywhere else; the rain always made a point of setting in just as he had some out-door work to do; so that though his patrimonial[17] estate had dwindled away under his management, acre by acre, until there was little more left than a mere patch of Indian corn and potatoes, yet it was the worst conditioned farm in the neighborhood.

His children, too, were as ragged and wild as if they belonged to nobody. His son Rip, an urchin begotten in his own likeness, promised to inherit the habits, with the old clothes of his father. He was generally seen trooping like a colt at his mother's heels, equipped in a pair of his father's cast-off galligaskins[18], which he had much ado to hold up with one hand, as a fine lady does her train in bad weather.

Rip Van Winkle, however, was one of those happy mortals, of foolish, well-oiled dispositions, who take the world easy, eat white bread or brown, whichever can be got with least thought or trouble, and would rather starve on a penny than work for a pound. If left to himself, he would have whistled life away in perfect contentment; but his wife kept continually dinning in his ears about his idleness, his carelessness, and the ruin he was bringing on his family. Morning, noon, and night, her tongue was incessantly going, and everything he said or did was sure to produce a torrent of household eloquence. Rip had but one way of replying to all lectures of the kind, and that, by frequent use, had grown into a habit. He shrugged his shoulders, shook his head, cast up his eyes, but said nothing. This, however, always provoked a fresh volley from his wife; so that he was fain to draw off his forces, and take to the outside of the house—the only side which, in truth, belongs to a hen-pecked husband.

Rip's sole domestic adherent was his dog Wolf, who was as much hen-pecked as his master; for Dame Van Winkle regarded them as companions in idleness, and even looked upon Wolf with an evil eye, as the cause of his master's going so often astray. True it is, in all points of spirit befitting an honorable dog, he was as courageous an animal as ever scoured the woods—but what courage can withstand the ever-during and all-besetting terrors of a woman's tongue? The moment Wolf entered the house his crest fell, his tail drooped to the ground, or curled between his legs, he sneaked about with a gallows air, casting many a sidelong glance at Dame Van Winkle, and at the least flourish of a broomstick or ladle, he would fly to the door with yelping precipitation.

Times grew worse and worse with Rip Van Winkle as years of matrimony rolled on; a tart temper never mellows with age, and a sharp tongue is the only edged tool that grows keener with constant use. For a long while he used to console himself, when driven from home, by frequenting a kind of perpetual club of the sages, philosophers, and other idle personages of the village; which held its sessions on a bench before a small inn, designated by a rubicund[19] portrait of his Majesty George the Third. Here they used to sit in the shade through a long lazy summer's day, talking listlessly over village gossip, or telling endless sleepy stories about nothing. But it would have been worth any statesman's money to have heard the profound discussions that sometimes took place, when by chance an old newspaper fell into their hands from some passing traveller. How solemnly they would listen to the contents, as drawled out by Derrick Van Bummel, the schoolmaster, a dapper learned little man, who was not to be daunted by the most gigantic word in the dictionary; and how sagely they would deliberate upon public events some months after they had taken place.

The opinions of this junto[20] were completely controlled by Nicholas Vedder, a patriarch of the village, and landlord of the inn, at the door of which he took his seat from morning till night, just moving sufficiently to avoid the sun and keep in the shade of a large tree; so that the neighbors could tell the hour by his movements as accurately as by a sundial. It is true he was rarely heard to speak, but smoked his pipe incessantly. His adherents, however (for every great man has his adherents), perfectly understood him, and knew how to gather his opinions. When anything that was read or related displeased him, he was observed to smoke his pipe vehemently, and to send forth short, frequent and angry puffs; but when pleased, he would inhale the smoke slowly and tranquilly, and emit it in light and placid clouds; and sometimes, taking the pipe from his mouth, and letting the fragrant vapor curl about his nose, would gravely nod his head in token of perfect approbation.

From even this stronghold the unlucky Rip was at length routed by his termagant wife, who would suddenly break in upon the tranquillity of the assemblage and call the members all to naught; nor was that august personage, Nicholas Vedder himself, sacred from the daring tongue of this terrible virago[21], who charged him outright with encouraging her husband in habits of idleness.

Poor Rip was at last reduced almost to despair; and his only alternative, to escape from the labor of the farm and clamor of his wife, was to take gun in hand and stroll away into the woods. Here he would sometimes seat himself at the foot of a tree, and share the contents of his wallet with Wolf, with whom he sympathized as a fellow-sufferer in persecution. "Poor Wolf," he would say, "thy mistress leads thee a dog's life of it; but never mind, my lad, whilst I live thou shalt never want a friend to stand by thee!"[22] Wolf would wag his tail, look wistfuly in his master's face, and if dogs can feel pity I verily believe he reciprocated the sentiment with all his heart.

In a long ramble of the kind on a fine autumnal day, Rip had unconsciously scrambled to one of the highest parts of the Kaatskill Mountains. He was after his favorite sport of squirrel shooting, and the still solitudes had echoed and re-echoed with the reports of his gun. Panting and fatigued, he threw himself, late in the afternoon, on a green knoll, covered with mountain herbage, that crowned the brow of a precipice. From an opening between the trees he could overlook all the lower country for many a mile of rich woodland. He saw at a distance the lordly Hudson, far, far below him, moving on its silent but majestic course, with the reflection of a purple cloud, or the sail of a lagging bark, here and there sleeping on its glassy bosom, and at last losing itself in the blue highlands.

On the other side he looked down into a deep mountain glen, wild, lonely, and shagged, the bottom filled with fragments from the impending cliffs, and scarcely lighted by the reflected rays of the setting sun. For some time Rip lay musing on this scene; evening was gradually advancing; the mountains began to throw their long blue shadows over the valleys; he saw that it would be dark long before he could reach the village, and he heaved a heavy sigh when he thought of encountering the terrors of Dame Van Winkle.

As he was about to descend, he heard a voice from a distance, hallooing, "Rip Van Winkle! Rip Van Winkle!" He looked around, but could see nothing but a crow winging its solitary flight across the mountain. He thought his fancy must have deceived him, and turned again to descend, when he heard the same cry ring through the still evening air: "Rip Van Winkle! Rip Van Winkle!"—at the same time Wolf bristled up his back, and giving a low growl, skulked to his master's side, looking fearfully down into the glen. Rip now felt a vague apprehension stealing over him; he looked anxiously in the same direction, and perceived a strange figure slowly toiling up the rocks, and bending under the weight of something he carried on his back. He was surprised to see any human being in this lonely and unfrequented place, but supposing it to be some one of the neighborhood in need of his assistance, he hastened down to yield it.

On nearer approach he was still more surprised at the singularity of the stranger's appearance. He was a short square-built[23] old fellow, with thick bushy hair, and a grizzled beard. His dress was of the antique Dutch fashion—a cloth jerkin strapped round the waist—several pair of breeches, the outer one of ample volume, decorated with rows of buttons down the sides, and bunches at the knees. He bore on his shoulder a stout keg[24], that seemed full of liquor, and made signs for Rip to approach and assist him with the load. Though rather shy and distrustful of this new acquaintance, Rip complied with his usual alacrity; and mutually relieving one another, they clambered up a narrow gully, apparently the dry bed of a mountain torrent. As they ascended, Rip every now and then heard long rolling peals, like distant thunder, that seemed to issue out of a deep ravine[25], or rather cleft, between lofty rocks, toward which their rugged path conducted. He paused for an instant, but supposing it to be the muttering of one of those transient thunder-showers which often take place in mountain heights, he proceeded. Passing through the ravine, they came to a hollow, like a small amphitheatre[26], surrounded by perpendicular precipices, over the brinks of which impending trees shot their branches, so that you only caught glimpses of the azure[27] sky and the bright evening cloud. During the whole time Rip and his companion had labored on in silence; for though the former marvelled greatly what could be the object of carrying a keg of liquor up this wild mountain, yet there was something strange and incomprehensible about the unknown, that inspired awe and checked familiarity.

On entering the amphitheatre, new objects of wonder presented themselves. On a level spot in the centre was a company of odd-looking personages playing at nine-pins. They were dressed in a quaint outlandish fashion; some wore short doublets, others jerkins, with long knives in their belts, and most of them had enormous breeches, of similar style with that of the guide's. Their visages, too, were peculiar: one had a large beard, broad face, and small piggish eyes: the face of another seemed to consist entirely of nose, and was surmounted by a white sugar-loaf hat set off with a little red cock's tail. They all had beards, of various shapes and colors. There was one who seemed to be the commander. He was a stout old gentleman, with a weather-beaten countenance; he wore a laced doublet, broad belt and hanger, high-crowned hat and feather, red stockings, and high-heeled shoes, with roses in them. The whole group reminded Rip of the figures in an old Flemish[28] painting, in the parlor of Domine Van Schaick, the village parson, and which had been brought over from Holland at the time of the settlement.

What seemed particularly odd to Rip was, that though these folks were evidently amusing themselves, yet they maintained the gravest faces, the most mysterious silence, and were, withal, the most melancholy party of pleasure he had ever witnessed. Nothing interrupted the stillness of the scene but the noise of the balls, which, whenever they were rolled, echoed along the mountains like rumbling peals of thunder.

As Rip and his companion approached them, they suddenly desisted from their play, and stared at him with such a fixed statue-like gaze, and such strange, uncouth, lack-lustre countenances, that his heart turned within him, and his knees smote together. His companion now emptied the contents of the keg into large flagons[29], and made signs to him to wait upon the company. He obeyed with fear and trembling; they quaffed the liquor in profound silence, and then returned to their game.

By degrees Rip's awe and apprehension subsided. He even ventured, when no eye was fixed upon him, to taste the beverage, which he found had much of the flavor of excellent Hollands. He was naturally a thirsty soul, and was soon tempted to repeat the draught. One taste provoked another; and he reiterated his visits to the flagon so often that at length his senses were overpowered, his eyes swam in his head, his head gradually declined, and he fell into a deep sleep.

On waking, he found himself on the green knoll whence he had first seen the old man of the glen. He rubbed his eyes—it was a bright sunny morning. The birds were hopping and twittering among the bushes, and the eagle was wheeling aloft, and breasting the pure mountain breeze. "Surely," thought Rip, "I have not slept here all night." He recalled the occurrences before he fell asleep. The strange man with a keg of liquor—the mountain ravine—the wild retreat among the rocks—the woe-begone party at nine-pins—the flagon—"Oh! that flagon! that wicked flagon!" thought Rip—"what excuse shall I make to Dame Van Winkle!"

He looked round for his gun, but in place of the clean well-oiled fowling-piece, he found an old firelock lying by him, the barrel encrusted with rust, the lock falling off, and the stock worm-eaten. He now suspected that the grave roysterers of the mountain had put a trick upon him, and having dosed him with liquor, had robbed him of his gun. Wolf, too, had disappeared, but he might have strayed away after a squirrel or partridge[30]. He whistled after him and shouted his name, but all in vain; the echoes repeated his whistle and shout, but no dog was to be seen.

He determined to revisit the scene of the last evening's gambol, and if he met with any of the party, to demand his dog and gun. As he rose to walk, he found himself stiff in the joints, and wanting in his usual activity. "These mountain beds do not agree with me," thought Rip, "and if this frolic should lay me up with a fit of the rheumatism[31], I shall have a blessed time with Dame Van Winkle." With some difficulty he got down into the glen: he found the gully up which he and his companion had ascended the preceding evening; but to his astonishment a mountain stream was now foaming down it, leaping from rock to rock, and filling the glen with babbling murmurs. He, however, made shift to scramble up its sides, working his toilsome way through thickets of birch, sassafras, and witch-hazel[32], and sometimes tripped up or entangled by the wild grapevines that twisted their coils or tendrils from tree to tree, and spread a kind of network in his path.

At length he reached to where the ravine had opened through the cliffs to the amphitheatre; but no traces of such opening remained. The rocks presented a high impenetrable wall over which the torrent came tumbling in a sheet of feathery foam, and fell into a broad deep basin, black from the shadows of the surrounding forest. Here, then, poor Rip was brought to a stand. He again called and whistled after his dog; he was only answered by the cawing of a flock of idle crows, sporting high in the air about a dry tree that overhung a sunny precipice; and who, secure in their elevation, seemed to look down and scoff at the poor man's perplexities. What was to be done? The morning was passing away, and Rip felt famished[33] for want of his breakfast. He grieved to give up his dog and gun; he dreaded to meet his wife; but it would not do to starve among the mountains. He shook his head, shouldered the rusty firelock, and, with a heart full of trouble and anxiety, turned his steps homeward.

As he approached the village he met a number of people, but none whom he knew, which somewhat surprised him, for he had thought himself acquainted with every one in the country round. Their dress, too, was of a different fashion from that to which he was accustomed. They all stared at him with equal marks of surprise, and whenever they cast their eyes upon him, invariably stroked their chins. The constant recurrence of this gesture induced Rip, involuntarily, to do the same, when to his astonishment, he found his beard had grown a foot long!

He had now entered the skirts of the village. A troop of strange children ran at his heels, hooting after him, and pointing at his gray beard. The dogs, too, not one of which he recognized for an old acquaintance, barked at him as he passed. The very village was altered; it was larger and more populous. There were rows of houses which he had never seen before, and those which had been his familiar haunts had disappeared. Strange names were over the doors—strange faces at the windows—every thing was strange. His mind now misgave him; he began to doubt whether both he and the world around him were not bewitched. Surely this was his native village, which he had left but the day before. There stood the Kaatskill Mountains—there ran the silver Hudson at a distance—there was every hill and dale precisely as it had always been—Rip was sorely perplexed—"That flagon last night," thought he, "has addled my poor head sadly!"

It was with some difficulty that he found the way to his own house, which he approached with silent awe, expecting every moment to hear the shrill voice of Dame Van Winkle. He found the house gone to decay—the roof fallen in, the windows shattered, and the doors off the hinges. A half-starved dog that looked like Wolf was skulking about it. Rip called him by name, but the cur snarled, showed his teeth, and passed on. This was an unkind cut indeed—"My very dog," sighed poor Rip, "has forgotten me!"

He entered the house, which, to tell the truth, Dame Van Winkle had always kept in neat order. It was empty, forlorn, and apparently abandoned. This desolateness overcame all his connubial[34] fears—he called loudly for his wife and children—the lonely chambers rang for a moment with his voice, and then all again was silence.

He now hurried forth, and hastened to his old resort, the village inn—but it too was gone. A large rickety wooden building stood in its place, with great gaping windows, some of them broken and mended with old hats and petticoats, and over the door was painted, "The Union Hotel, by Jonathan Doolittle." Instead of the great tree that used to shelter the quiet little Dutch inn of yore, there now was reared a tall naked pole, with something on the top that looked like a red night-cap, and from it was fluttering a flag, on which was a singular assemblage of stars and stripes—all this was strange and incomprehensible. He recognized on the sign, however, the ruby face of King George, under which he had smoked so many a peaceful pipe; but even this was singularly metamorphosed. The red coat was changed for one of blue and buff, a sword was held in the hand instead of a sceptre, the head was decorated with a cocked hat, and underneath was painted in large characters, GENERAL WASHINGTON.

There was, as usual, a crowd of folk about the door, but none that Rip recollected. The very character of the people seemed changed. There was a busy, bustling, disputatious tone about it, instead of the accustomed phlegm[35] and drowsy tranquillity. He looked in vain for the sage Nicholas Vedder, with his broad face, double chin, and fair long pipe, uttering clouds of tobacco-smoke instead of idle speeches; or Van Bummel, the schoolmaster, doling forth the contents of an ancient newspaper. In place of these, a lean, bilious-looking fellow, with his pockets full of handbills, was haranguing vehemently about rights of citizens—election—members of congress—liberty—Bunker's Hill—heroes of seventy-six—and other words, which were a perfect Babylonish jargon to the bewildered Van Winkle.

The appearance of Rip, with his long grizzled beard, his rusty fowling-piece, his uncouth dress, and an army of women and children at his heels, soon attracted the attention of the tavern politicians. They crowded round him, eyeing him from head to foot with great curiosity. The orator bustled up to him, and, drawing him partly aside, inquired "on which side he voted?" Rip stared in vacant stupidity. Another short but busy little fellow pulled him by the arm, and, rising on tiptoe, inquired in his ear, "Whether he was Federal or Democrat?" Rip was equally at a loss to comprehend the question; when a knowing, self-important old gentleman, in a sharp cocked hat, made his way through the crowd, putting them to the right and left with his elbows as he passed, and planting himself before Van Winkle, with one arm akimbo[36], the other resting on his cane, his keen eyes and sharp hat penetrating, as it were, into his very soul, demanded in an austere tone, "what brought him to the election with a gun on his shoulder, and a mob at his heels, and whether he meant to breed a riot in the village?" "Alas! gentlemen," cried Rip, somewhat dismayed, "I am a poor quiet man, a native of the place, and a loyal subject of the king, God bless him!"

Here a general shout burst from the by standers—"A tory! a tory! a spy! a refugee! hustle him! away with him!" It was with great difficulty that the self-important man in the cocked hat restored order; and, having assumed a tenfold austerity of brow, demanded again of the unknown culprit, what he came there for, and whom he was seeking? The poor man humbly assured him that he meant no harm, but merely came there in search of some of his neighbors, who used to keep about the tavern.

"Well—who are they?—name them."

Rip bethought himself a moment, and inquired, "Where's Nicholas Vedder?"

There was a silence for a little while, when an old man replied, in a thin piping voice, "Nicholas Vedder! why, he is dead and gone these eighteen years! There was a wooden tombstone in the church-yard that used to tell all about him, but that's rotten and gone too."

"Where's Brom Dutcher?"

"Oh, he went off to the army in the beginning of the war; some say he was killed at the storming of Stony Point—others say he was drowned in a squall at the foot of Antony's Nose[37]. I don't know—he never came back again."

"Where's Van Bummel, the schoolmaster?"

"He went off to the wars too, was a great militia general, and is now in congress."

Rip's heart died away at hearing of these sad changes in his home and friends, and finding himself thus alone in the world. Every answer puzzled him too, by treating of such enormous lapses of time, and of matters which he could not understand: war—congress—Stony Point;—he had no courage to ask after any more friends, but cried out in despair, "Does nobody here know Rip Van Winkle?"

"Oh, Rip Van Winkle!" exclaimed two or three, "Oh, to be sure! that's Rip Van Winkle yonder, leaning against the tree."

Rip looked, and beheld a precise counterpart of himself, as he went up the mountain: apparently as lazy, and certainly as ragged. The poor fellow was now completely confounded. He doubted his own identity, and whether he was himself or another man. In the midst of his bewilderment, the man in the cocked hat demanded who he was, and what was his name?

"God knows," exclaimed he, at his wit's end; "I'm not myself—I'm somebody else—that's me yonder—no—that's somebody else got into my shoes—I was myself last night, but I fell asleep on the mountain, and they've changed my gun, and every thing's changed, and I'm changed, and I can't tell what's my name, or who I am!"

The by standers began now to look at each other, nod, wink significantly, and tap their fingers against their foreheads. There was a whisper also, about securing the gun, and keeping the old fellow from doing mischief, at the very suggestion of which the self-important man in the cocked hat retired with some precipitation. At this critical moment a fresh comely woman pressed through the throng to get a peep at the gray-bearded man. She had a chubby child in her arms, which, frightened at his looks, began to cry. "Hush, Rip," cried she, "hush, you little fool; the old man won't hurt you." The name of the child, the air of the mother, the tone of her voice, all awakened a train of recollections in his mind. "What is your name, my good woman?" asked he.

"Judith Gardenier."

"And your father's name?"

"Ah, poor man, Rip Van Winkle was his name, but it's twenty years since he went away from home with his gun, and never has been heard of since—his dog came home without him; but whether he shot himself, or was carried away by the Indians, nobody can tell. I was then but a little girl."

Rip had but one question more to ask; but he put it with a faltering voice: "Where's your mother?"

"Oh, she too had died but a short time since; she broke a blood-vessel in a fit of passion at a New-England peddler."

There was a drop of comfort, at least, in this intelligence. The honest man could contain himself no longer. He caught his daughter and her child in his arms. "I am your father!" cried he—"Young Rip Van Winkle once—old Rip Van Winkle now! —Does nobody know poor Rip Van Winkle?"

All stood amazed, until an old woman, tottering out from among the crowd, put her hand to her brow, and peering under it in his face for a moment, exclaimed, "Sure enough! it is Rip Van Winkle—it is himself! Welcome home again, old neighbor—Why, where have you been these twenty long years?"

Rip's story was soon told, for the whole twenty years had been to him but as one night. The neighbors stared when they heard it; some were seen to wink at each other, and put their tongues in their cheeks: and the self-important man in the cocked hat, who, when the alarm was over, had returned to the field, screwed down the corners of his mouth, and shook his head—upon which there was a general shaking of the head throughout the assemblage.

It was determined, however, to take the opinion of old Peter Vanderdonk, who was seen slowly advancing up the road. He was a descendant of the historian of that name, who wrote one of the earliest accounts of the province. Peter was the most ancient inhabitant of the village, and well versed in all the wonderful events and traditions of the neighborhood. He recollected Rip at once, and corroborated his story in the most satisfactory manner. He assured the company that it was a fact, handed down from his ancestor the historian, that the Kaatskill Mountains had always been haunted by strange beings. That it was affirmed that the great Hendrick Hudson, the first discoverer of the river and country, kept a kind of vigil there every twenty years, with his crew of the Half-moon; being permitted in this way to revisit the scenes of his enterprise, and keep a guardian eye upon the river, and the great city called by his name. That his father had once seen them in their old Dutch dresses playing at nine-pins in a hollow of the mountain; and that he himself had heard, one summer afternoon, the sound of their balls, like distant peals of thunder.

To make a long story short, the company broke up, and returned to the more important concerns of the election. Rip's daughter took him home to live with her; she had a snug, well-furnished house, and a stout cheery farmer for a husband, whom Rip recollected for one of the urchins that used to climb upon his back. As to Rip's son and heir, who was the ditto of himself, seen leaning against the tree, he was employed to work on the farm; but evinced a hereditary disposition to attend to anything else but his business.

Rip now resumed his old walks and habits; he soon found many of his former cronies, though all rather the worse for the wear and tear of time; and preferred making friends among the rising generation, with whom he soon grew into great favor.

Having nothing to do at home, and being arrived at that happy age when a man can be idle with impunity, he took his place once more on the bench at the inn door, and was reverenced as one of the patriarchs of the village, and a chronicle of the old times "before the war." It was some time before he could get into the regular track of gossip, or could be made to comprehend the strange events that had taken place during his torpor. How that there had been a revolutionary war-that the country had thrown off the yoke of old England-and that, instead of being a subject of his Majesty George the Third, he was now a free citizen of the United States. Rip, in fact, was no politician; the changes of states and empires made but little impression on him; but there was one species of despotism under which he had long groaned, and that was-petticoat government[38]. Happily that was at an end; he had got his neck out of the yoke of matrimony, and could go in and out whenever he pleased, without dreading the tyranny of Dame Van Winkle. Whenever her name was mentioned, however, he shook his head, shrugged his shoulders, and cast up his eyes; which might pass either for an expression of resignation to his fate, or joy at his deliverance.

He used to tell his story to every stranger that arrived at Mr. Doolittle's hotel. He was observed, at first, to vary on some points every time he told it, which was, doubtless, owing to his having so recently awaked. It at last settled down precisely to the tale I have related, and not a man, woman, or child in the neighborhood, but knew it by heart. Some always pretended to doubt the reality of it, and insisted that Rip had been out of his head, and that this was one point on which he always remained flighty. The old Dutch inhabitants, however, almost universally gave it full credit. Even to this day they never hear a thunderstorm of a summer afternoon about the Kaatskill, but they say Hendrick Hudson and his crew are at their game of nine-pins; and it is a common wish of all hen-pecked husbands in the neighborhood, when life hangs heavy on their hands, that they might have a quieting draught out of Rip Van Winkle's flagon.

NOTE—The foregoing tale, one would suspect, had been suggested to Mr. Knickerbocker by a little German superstition about the Emperor Frederick der Rothbart, and the Kypphauser mountain: the subjoined note, however, which he had appended to the tale, shows that it is an absolute fact, narrated with his usual fidelity:

"The story of Rip Van Winkle may seem incredible to many, but nevertheless I give it my full belief, for I know the vicinity of our old Dutch settlements to have been very subject to marvellous events and appearances. Indeed, I have heard many stranger stories than this, in the villages along the Hudson; all of which were too well authenticated to admit of a doubt. I have even talked with Rip Van Winkle myself who, when last I saw him, was a very venerable old man, and so perfectly rational and consistent on every other point, that I think no conscientious person could refuse to take this into the bargain; nay, I have seen a certificate on the subject taken before a country justice and signed with a cross, in the justice's own handwriting. The story, therefore, is beyond the possibility of doubt. D. K."

POSTSCRIPT

The following are travelling notes from a memorandum-book of Mr. Knickerbocker:

The Kaatsberg or Kaatskill mountains have always been a region full of fable. The Indians considered them the abode of spirits, who influenced the weather, spreading sunshine or clouds over the landscape, and sending good or bad hunting seasons. They were ruled by an old squaw spirit, said to be their mother. She dwelt on the highest peak of the Kaatskill, and had charge of the doors of day and night to open and shut them at the proper hour. She hung up the new moons in the skies, and cut up the old ones into stars. In times of drought, if properly propitiated, she would spin light summer clouds out of cobwebs and morning dew, and send them off from the crest of the mountain, flake after flake, like flakes of carded cotton, to float in the air; until, dissolved by the heat of the sun, they would fall in gentle showers, causing the grass to spring, the fruits to ripen, and the corn to grow an inch an hour. If displeased, however, she would brew up clouds black as ink, sitting in the midst of them like a bottle-bellied spider in the midst of its web; and when these clouds broke, woe betide the valleys!

In old times, say the Indian traditions, there was a kind of Manitou[39] or Spirit, who kept about the wildest recesses of the Catskill mountains, and took a mischievous pleasure in wreaking all kind of evils and vexations upon the red men. Sometimes he would assume the form of a bear, a panther, or a deer, lead the bewildered hunter a weary chase through tangled forests and among ragged rocks, and then spring off with a loud ho! ho! leaving him aghast on the brink of a beetling precipice or raging torrent.

The favorite abode of this Manitou is still shown. It is a rock or cliff on the loneliest port of the mountains, and, from the flowering vines which clamber about it, and the wild flowers which abound in its neighborhood, is known by the name of the Garden Rock. Near the foot of it is a small lake, the haunt of the solitary bittern, with water-snakes basking in the sun on the leaves of the pond-lilies which lie on the surface. This place was held in great awe by the Indians, insomuch that the boldest hunter would not pursue his game within its precincts. Once upon a time, however, a hunter who had lost his way penetrated to the Garden Rock, where he beheld a number of gourds placed in the crotches of trees. One of these he seized and made off with it, but in the hurry of his retreat he let it fall among the rocks, when a great stream gushed forth, which washed him away and swept him down precipices, where he was dashed to pieces, and the stream made its way to the Hudson, and continues to flow to the present day, being the identical stream known by the name of the Kaaterskill.

注释 (Notes)

1. Woden, God of Saxons：北欧神话中的盎格鲁-撒克逊至高神，象征着宇宙间无所不在的精神。
2. whence：何处。
3. Wodensday：Wednesday, 周三。
4. thylke：the
5. sepulchre：坟墓。
6. burgher：市民；尤指当地的富人或有脸面的人。
7. Waterloo Medal：滑铁卢战役奖章。
8. Farthing：法寻；英国旧时铜币，币值为 1/4 便士, 1961 年被取消。
9. Caatskill mountains：同 Catskill Mountains，卡茨基尔山（位于美国纽约州）。
10. Appalachian：阿巴拉契亚山脉。
11. descried：descry, 看见，看出，辨认出。

12. Peter Stuyvesant：彼得·史蒂文森,荷兰殖民总督。

13. Fort Christina：克里斯蒂娜堡,美国在瑞典的第一个殖民地——新瑞典。

14. termagant：凶悍的,泼辣的。

15. impunity：不受惩罚。

16. assiduity：勤勉,殷勤。

17. patrimonial：祖传的,世袭的。

18. galligaskins：宽松马裤,尤指17世纪男人穿的。

19. rubicund：(脸色)红润的,容光焕发的。

20. junto：政治集团,秘密结社,团体。

21. virago：泼妇,悍妇。

22. thy：古语,your 你的;thee：古语,你;thou：古语,你;shalt：shall,应该。

23. square-built：粗壮的。

24. keg：(装啤酒或其他酒类饮品的)小桶。

25. ravine：沟壑,深谷。

26. amphitheatre：圆形露天竞技场。

27. azure：蔚蓝色。

28. Flemish：佛兰德的,佛兰德人的。

29. flagon：酒壶,大肚酒瓶。

30. partridge：[鸟]鹧鸪,松鸡。

31. rheumatism：风湿病。

32. birch：桦树;sassafras：黄樟树;witch-hazel：金缕梅。

33. famish：使挨饿。

34. connubial：婚姻的。

35. phlegm：痰。

36. akimbo：双手叉腰的。

37. Stony Point：斯托尼角;Antony's Nose：安东尼的鼻子山,属于阿巴拉契亚山脉最东的分支。

38. petticoat government：女性当权。

39. Manito：(阿尔衮琴印第安人的)神灵,超自然力。

主题探究（Themes）

（扫码阅读）

问题讨论 (Questions for Discussion)

1. In the story, Rip is described as a simple, good-natured, and warm-hearted man, but he is by no means free from demerits. Can you name some?

2. Please find examples in the short story to show that Irving is a sexist.

3. Can you prove that Dame Van Winkle is a hardworking, capable and responsible woman from a feminist perspective?

4. Can you analyze the story using the theory of archetypal criticism?

5. Irving used "irony" in the story, can you find some examples?

(请扫码观看视频"Rip Van Winkle")

Unit 19
New England Transcendentalism

Ralph Waldo Emerson: *Nature*
▽

作者简介 (Introduction to the Author)

Ralph Waldo Emerson (1803—1882), American thinker, writer, poet, was born in Boston. He was the representative of American Transcendentalism in the 19th century. Emerson was born into a pastoral family and his father was a devout minister. However, Emerson's father died when he was 8 years old, and his mother and aunt raised him. Emerson attended Harvard Divinity School, but was forced to terminate his studies due to vision problems. In 1829 Emerson was ordained minister of the Second Church in Boston, and soon he married Alan Tucker. In 1832, shortly after his wife died of tuberculosis, Emerson resigned and then traveled to various countries in Europe, where he met Wordsworth and Coleridge, the pioneers of romanticism, and accepted their transcendental ideas, which had a great impact on the formation of his ideological system. In 1835, he married Lydia Jackson. They settled in Concord and had four children. In 1840, Emerson founded *The Dial* Magazine to further promote transcendental ideas. In 1842, Emerson was hit hard by the death of his 5-year-old son. Emerson, in his middle and late years, focused on giving lectures across the United States to promote his ideas. In 1882, the great writer died of pneumonia. As a representative of American cultural spirit, Emerson's greatest contribution to American literature is that he firmly advocated the establishment of an independent national culture and literature. He preached the spiritual independence of the New World. It is no wonder that US President Lincoln called him "the Confucius of America" and "the father of American civilization".

作品简介 (Introduction to the Work)

Nature is a little book of essays written by Ralph Waldo Emerson, published in 1836. In the essays Emerson put forth the foundation of transcendentalism. Within the book, Emerson divides nature into four usages: Commodity, Beauty, Language and Discipline. These distinctions define the ways by which humans use nature for their basic needs, their desire for delight, their communication with one another and their understanding of the world. Emerson asserts that all our questions about the order of the universe—about the relationships between God, man, and nature—may be answered by our experience of life and by the world around us. Each individual is a manifestation of creation and as such holds the key to unlocking the mysteries of the universe. Nature, too, is both an expression of the divine and a means of understanding it. Emerson defines nature (the "NOT ME") as everything separate from the inner individual—nature, art, other men, our own bodies. In common usage, nature refers to the material world unchanged by man. Art is nature in combination with the will of man. Emerson explains that he will use the word "nature" in both its common and its philosophical meanings in the essay.

At the beginning of Chapter Ⅰ, Emerson describes true solitude as going out into nature and leaving behind all preoccupying activities as well as society. When a man gazes at the stars, he becomes aware of his own separateness. The stars were made to allow him to perceive the "perpetual presence of the sublime". We retain our original sense of wonder even when viewing familiar aspects of nature anew. Emerson discusses the poetical approach to nature—the perception of the encompassing whole made up of many individual components. Our delight in the landscape, which is made up of many particular forms, provides an example of this integrated vision.

作品选文 (Selected Reading)

Nature
(Excerpt)
Chapter Ⅰ NATURE

To go into solitude, a man needs to retire as much from his chamber as from society. I am not solitary whilst I read and write, though nobody is with me. But if a man would be alone, let him look at the stars. The rays that come from those heavenly worlds, will separate between him and what he touches. One might think the atmosphere was made transparent with this design, to give man, in the heavenly bodies, the perpetual presence of the sublime. Seen in the streets of cities, how great they are! If the stars should appear one night in a thousand years, how would men believe and adore; and preserve for many generations the remembrance of the city of God[1] which had been shown! But every night come out these envoys[2] of beauty, and light the universe with their admonishing smile.

The stars awaken a certain reverence, because though always present, they are inaccessible; but all natural objects make a kindred impression, when the mind is open to their influence. Nature never wears a mean appearance. Neither does the wisest man extort her secret, and lose his curiosity by finding out all her perfection. Nature never became a toy to a wise spirit. The flowers, the animals, the mountains, reflected the wisdom of his best hour, as much as they had delighted the simplicity of his childhood.

When we speak of nature in this manner, we have a distinct but most poetical sense in the mind. We mean the integrity of impression made by manifold natural objects. It is this which distinguishes the stick of timber of the wood-cutter, from the tree of the poet. The charming landscape which I saw this morning, is indubitably[3] made up of some twenty or thirty farms. Miller owns this field, Locke that, and Manning the woodland beyond. But none of them owns the landscape. There is a property in the horizon which no man has but he whose eye can integrate all the parts, that is, the poet. This is the best part of these men's farms, yet to this their warranty-deeds give no title.

To speak truly, few adult persons can see nature. Most persons do not see the sun. At least they have a very superficial seeing. The sun illuminates only the eye of the man, but shines into the eye and the heart of the child. The lover of nature is he whose inward and outward senses are still truly adjusted to each other; who has retained the spirit of infancy even into the era of manhood. His intercourse with heaven and earth, becomes part of his daily food. In the presence of nature, a wild delight runs through the man, in spite of real sorrows. Nature says,—he is my creature, and maugre[4] all his impertinent griefs, he shall be glad with me. Not the sun or the summer alone, but every hour and season yields its tribute of delight; for every hour and change corresponds to and authorizes a different state of the mind, from breathless noon to grimmest midnight. Nature is a setting that fits equally well a comic or a mourning piece. In good health, the air is a cordial[5] of incredible virtue. Crossing a bare common, in snow puddles, at twilight, under a clouded sky, without having in my thoughts any occurrence of special good fortune, I have enjoyed a perfect exhilaration. I am glad to the brink of fear. In the woods too, a man casts off his years, as the snake his slough[6], and at what period soever of life, is always a child. In the woods, is perpetual youth. Within these plantations of God, a decorum and sanctity reign, a perennial festival is dressed, and the guest sees not how he should tire of them in a thousand years. In the woods, we return to reason and faith. There I feel that nothing can befall me in life,—no disgrace, no calamity, (leaving me my eyes,) which nature cannot repair. Standing on the bare ground,—my head bathed by the blithe air, and uplifted into infinite space,—all mean egotism vanishes. I become a transparent eye-ball; I am nothing; I see all; the currents of the Universal Being circulate through me; I am part or particle of God. The name of the nearest friend sounds then foreign and accidental: to be brothers, to be acquaintances,—master or servant, is then a trifle and a disturbance. I am the lover of uncontained and immortal beauty. In the wilderness, I find something more dear and connate[7] than in streets or villages. In the tranquil landscape, and especially in the distant line of the horizon, man beholds somewhat as beautiful as his own nature.

The greatest delight which the fields and woods minister, is the suggestion of an occult[8] relation between man and the vegetable. I am not alone and unacknowledged. They nod to me, and I to them. The waving of the boughs in the storm, is new to me and old. It takes me by surprise, and yet is not unknown. Its effect is like that of a higher thought or a better emotion coming over me, when I deemed I was thinking justly or doing right.

Yet it is certain that the power to produce this delight, does not reside in nature, but in man, or in a harmony of both. It is necessary to use these pleasures with great temperance. For, nature is not always tricked in holiday attire[9], but the same scene which yesterday breathed perfume and glittered as for the frolic of the nymphs[10], is overspread with melancholy today. Nature always wears the colors of the spirit. To a man laboring under calamity, the heat of his own fire hath sadness in it. Then, there is a kind of contempt of the landscape felt by him who has just lost by death a dear friend. The sky is less grand as it shuts down over less worth in the population.

注释（Notes）

1. the city of God：上帝之城。
2. envoys：使者，代表。这里指星星。
3. indubitably：无疑地，不容置疑地。
4. maugre：尽管。
5. cordial：友善的。
6. slough：蜕下的皮（或壳）。
7. connate：天生的。
8. occult：神秘的。
9. attire：服装。
10. nymphs：古希腊和罗马神话中居于山林水泽的自然女神，常常化身为年轻女子。

主题探究（Themes）

（扫码阅读）

文化延展(Cultural Extension)

超验主义作为具有广泛影响的一股浪漫主义改革思潮,产生于美国 19 世纪 30 至 40 年代的波士顿地区,其基本精神是挑战传统的理性主义和怀疑论哲学,特别是挑战作为清教主义理论基础的加尔文主义。在哲学上,超验主义思想受到唯心主义的影响,同时也受到英国浪漫主义文学家和印度、中国等东方民族古典哲学思想的影响。

爱默生以超前的眼光看到了自然的精神价值。在他的心目中,自然不仅是精神的象征,同时,也是教导人们高尚品行的良师,美国文化艺术的源泉,人类汲取知识的读本。爱默生相信,人与宇宙是和谐的,是一个完整的统一体,因此,每个人都能够与宇宙保持最原始的关系。爱默生对美国这个自然之国的优势充满了自信。爱默生在自然中的追求,基本上仍是一种精神之追求,对他而言,理智和心灵都需要荒野和乡村的景色来滋润。自然界的每一种景观,都与人的某种心境相呼应。爱默生的自然,是一种带有浓郁的说教和道德色彩的自然。自然服务于人,是为了让他履行职责,恪守道义,而不是让他沉湎于欢乐之中①。

梭罗的一生中,似乎都在寻求一种与自然的最淳朴、最直接的接触。他几乎放弃了世人所追求的一切——财富、名利和安逸。实际上他也很少懂得世间人们习以为常的欢乐与享受,因为他像爱默生所说的那样,一生都在追求那种常人望而却步的美。让自然融于自身,同时也让自身融于自然,是梭罗不同寻常的人生追求。梭罗和惠特曼都是个性突出、强调自我的人,无论从他们的经历还是作品,我们不难看出两者的"习相近"——即他们对旷野的迷恋、对自由的向往、对陈规世俗的挑战。他们以不同的方式,让高雅的文学和土地荒野、山川河流、飞禽走兽联结在一起,才能携手成为爱默生理论的大胆实践者。②

问题讨论(Questions for Discussion)

1. How does Ralph Waldo Emerson define nature, as opposed to art?

2. Compare Emerson's descriptions of the bonds between people in society and those people and nature. Which bonds would Emerson say are more important? Explain.

3. What effect does nature have on Emerson? What does he mean when he says "I become a transparent eye-ball"?

4. What can human beings learn from nature? How does this learning affect the individual's spirituality?

5. How can you identify the elements of transcendentalism in Emerson's *Nature*?

---

① 程虹. 寻归荒野[M]. 增订版. 北京:生活·读书·新知三联书店,2011: 81-92.
② 程虹. 寻归荒野[M]. 增订版. 北京:生活·读书·新知三联书店,2011: 92-119.

Unit 20
Nathaniel Hawthorne & Herman Melville

Nathaniel Hawthorne: "The Minister's Black Veil"; *The Scarlet Letter*
Herman Melville: *Moby Dick*
▽

作者简介 (Introduction to the Authors)

Nathaniel Hawthorne (1804—1864) was a nineteenth-century American novelist and short story writer. He is recognized, with his close contemporaries Herman Melville and Walt Whitman, as a key figure in the development of American literature. Nathaniel Hawthorne was born in Salem, Massachusetts. His father was a sea captain and descendant of John Hawthorne, one of the judges who oversaw the Salem Witch Trials. Hawthorne's father died in 1808 of yellow fever when Hawthorne was only four years old, so he was raised by his mother. Hawthorne attended Bowdoin College in Maine from 1821 to 1824, becoming friends with Henry Wadsworth Longfellow and future president Franklin Pierce. Hawthorne anonymously published his first work *Fanshawe* in 1828. In 1837, he published *Twice-Told Tales* and became engaged to painter and illustrator Sophia Peabody the next year. He worked at a Custom House and joined a Transcendentalist Utopian community before marrying Peabody in 1842. The couple moved to The Old Manse in Concord, Massachusetts, later moving to Salem, the Berkshires, then to The Wayside in Concord. *The Scarlet Letter* was published in 1850, followed by a succession of other novels. A political appointment took Hawthorne and his family to Europe before returning to The Wayside in 1860. Hawthorne died on May 19, 1864, leaving behind his wife and their three children. As the pioneer of American psychoanalytic novels, Hawthorne is good at using symbols, metaphors and other artistic techniques. He also influenced a number of outstanding writers in the history of American literature, such as Faulkner, Fitzgerald, Hemingway, etc. Therefore, Hawthorne is recognized as the greatest American romantic writer in the 19th century.

Herman Melville (1819—1891) is a famous American novelist, essayist and poet in the 19th century. He was born in a prestigious family in New York in 1819 and received a good education when he was young. At the age of 12, his father died and the family fell into poverty. Melville dropped out of school at the age of 15 to support his family. He once worked as a farmer, clerk, primary school teacher, sailor, etc. In 1837, Melville set sail for Liverpool, England. In 1841 Melville became a whaling sailor and set out from Massachusetts. The five years from the age of 20 to 25 were the years he spent wandering on the sea. These years have had a great impact on his creation. Melville began to write novels in 1845. In 1846, he published the novel *Typee* in London and the novel *Omoo* the next year. Herman Melville married Elizabeth Shaw in 1847 and spent his honeymoon in Canada. They have four children. From 1847 to 1850, he was influenced by Emerson's transcendentalism. In 1850, he became friends with Hawthorne and carefully read Hawthorne's novel *The Scarlet Letter*. In February 1850, he began to create *Moby Dick* based on his sea experience. It took him 17 months to complete this masterpiece and finally published it in 1851. Melville presented *Moby Dick* to Hawthorne. Melville died on September 28, 1891. He was not recognized by the world before his death, but was rediscovered after his death, and was even regarded as the "Shakespeare" of the United States.

The Minister's Black Veil

作品简介 (Introduction to the Work)

"The Minister's Black Veil" is one of the best-known and most widely studied short stories written by the American writer Nathaniel Hawthorne. Subtitled 'A Parable', the story originally appeared in a gift book titled *The Token and Atlantic Souvenir* in 1836, before being collected in Hawthorne's short story collection *Twice-Told Tales*, the following year. The story is about Reverend Hooper, a pastor in the town of Milford, Connecticut, stuns his parishioners one Sunday when he goes up to convey his lesson wearing a dark veil. This hazy cover to a great extent darkens a lot of his face, leaving just his mouth completely noticeable. His parishioners are amazed by this, and start to chatter about why he has started wearing such a veil. Hooper offers no explanation for the black veil, nor does he appear to behave any differently. At first, the veil frightens and confuses his congregation, making Hooper appear ghostlike from head to foot. Yet the veil has the strange effect of making his sermons and his spiritual leadership more powerful. Hawthorne's use of symbolism and extended metaphor create a parable that transcends the written page. Written in a gothic style and haunting tone, "The Minister's Black Veil" challenges the ideas of good versus evil and scrutinizes the values of personal truth and self-sacrifice.

作品选文 (Selected Reading)

The Minister's Black Veil

A Parable[1]

The sexton[2] stood in the porch of Milford meeting-house, pulling busily at the bell-rope. The old people of the village came stooping along the street. Children, with bright faces, tripped merrily beside their parents, or mimicked a graver gait, in the conscious dignity of their Sunday clothes[3]. Spruce[4] bachelors looked sidelong at the pretty maidens, and fancied that the Sabbath[5] sunshine made them prettier than on week days. When the throng had mostly streamed into the porch, the sexton began to toll the bell, keeping his eye on the Reverend Mr. Hooper's door. The first glimpse of the clergyman's figure was the signal for the bell to cease its summons.

"But what has good Parson[6] Hooper got upon his face?" cried the sexton in astonishment.

All within hearing immediately turned about, and beheld the semblance[7] of Mr. Hooper, pacing slowly his meditative way towards the meetinghouse. With one accord they started, expressing more wonder than if some strange minister were coming to dust the cushions of Mr. Hooper's pulpit.

"Are you sure it is our parson?" inquired Goodman Gray of the sexton.

"Of a certainty it is good Mr. Hooper," replied the sexton. "He was to have exchanged pulpits with Parson Shute, of Westbury; but Parson Shute sent to excuse himself yesterday, being to preach a funeral sermon."

The cause of so much amazement may appear sufficiently slight. Mr. Hooper, a gentlemanly person, of about thirty, though still a bachelor, was dressed with due clerical neatness, as if a careful wife had starched[8] his band, and brushed the weekly dust from his Sunday's garb. There was but one thing remarkable in his appearance. Swathed about his forehead, and hanging down over his face, so low as to be shaken by his breath, Mr. Hooper had on a black veil. On a nearer view it seemed to consist of two folds of crape, which entirely concealed his features, except the mouth and chin, but probably did not intercept his sight, further than to give a darkened aspect to all living and inanimate things. With this gloomy shade before him, good Mr. Hooper walked onward, at a slow and quiet pace, stooping somewhat, and looking on the ground, as is customary with abstracted men, yet nodding kindly to those of his parishioners[9] who still waited on the meeting-house steps. But so wonder-struck were they that his greeting hardly met with a return.

"I can't really feel as if good Mr. Hooper's face was behind that piece of crape," said the sexton.

"I don't like it," muttered an old woman, as she hobbled into the meeting-house. "He has changed himself into something awful, only by hiding his face."

"Our parson has gone mad!" cried Goodman Gray, following him across the threshold.

A rumor of some unaccountable phenomenon had preceded Mr. Hooper into the meeting-house, and set all the congregation astir. Few could refrain from twisting their heads towards the door; many stood upright, and turned directly about; while several little boys clambered upon the seats, and came down again with a terrible racket. There was a general bustle, a rustling of the women's gowns and shuffling of the men's feet, greatly at variance with that hushed repose which should attend the entrance of the minister. But Mr. Hooper appeared not to notice the perturbation[10] of his people. He entered with an almost noiseless step, bent his head mildly to the pews on each side, and bowed as he passed his oldest parishioner, a white-haired great grandsire, who occupied an arm-chair in the centre of the aisle. It was strange to observe how slowly this venerable man became conscious of something singular in the appearance of his pastor. He seemed not fully to partake of the prevailing wonder, till Mr. Hooper had ascended the stairs, and showed himself in the pulpit, face to face with his congregation, except for the black veil. That mysterious emblem was never once withdrawn. It shook with his measured breath, as he gave out the psalm[11]; it threw its obscurity between him and the holy page, as he read the Scriptures[12]; and while he prayed, the veil lay heavily on his uplifted countenance. Did he seek to hide it from the dread Being whom he was addressing?

Such was the effect of this simple piece of crape, that more than one woman of delicate nerves was forced to leave the meeting-house. Yet perhaps the pale-faced congregation was almost as fearful a sight to the minister, as his black veil to them.

Mr. Hooper had the reputation of a good preacher, but not an energetic one: he strove to win his people heavenward by mild, persuasive influences, rather than to drive them thither[13] by the thunders of the Word. The sermon which he now delivered was marked by the same characteristics of style and manner as the general series of his pulpit oratory. But there was something, either in the sentiment of the discourse itself, or in the imagination of the auditors, which made it greatly the most powerful effort that they had ever heard from their pastor's lips. It was tinged, rather more darkly than usual, with the gentle gloom of Mr. Hooper's temperament. The subject had reference to secret sin, and those sad mysteries which we hide from our nearest and dearest, and would fain conceal from our own consciousness, even forgetting that the Omniscient[14] can detect them. A subtle power was breathed into his words. Each member of the congregation, the most innocent girl, and the man of hardened breast, felt as if the preacher had crept upon them, behind his awful veil, and discovered their hoarded iniquity[15] of deed or thought. Many spread their clasped hands on their bosoms. There was nothing terrible in what Mr. Hooper said, at least, no violence; and yet, with every tremor of his melancholy voice, the hearers quaked. An unsought pathos came hand in hand with awe. So sensible were the audience of some unwonted attribute in their minister, that they longed for a breath of wind to blow aside the veil, almost believing that a stranger's visage would be discovered, though the form, gesture, and voice were those of Mr. Hooper.

 At the close of the services, the people hurried out with indecorous[16] confusion, eager to communicate their pent-up[17] amazement, and conscious of lighter spirits the moment they lost sight of the black veil. Some gathered in little circles, huddled closely together, with their mouths all whispering in the centre; some went homeward alone, wrapt in silent meditation; some talked loudly, and profaned the Sabbath day with ostentatious laughter. A few shook their sagacious[18] heads, intimating that they could penetrate the mystery; while one or two affirmed that there was no mystery at all, but only that Mr. Hooper's eyes were so weakened by the midnight lamp, as to require a shade. After a brief interval, forth came good Mr. Hooper also, in the rear of his flock. Turning his veiled face from one group to another, he paid due reverence to the hoary heads, saluted the middle aged with kind dignity as their friend and spiritual guide, greeted the young with mingled authority and love, and laid his hands on the little children's heads to bless them. Such was always his custom on the Sabbath day. Strange and bewildered looks repaid him for his courtesy. None, as on former occasions, aspired to the honor of walking by their pastor's side. Old Squire Saunders, doubtless by an accidental lapse of memory, neglected to invite Mr. Hooper to his table, where the good clergyman had been wont to bless the food, almost every Sunday since his settlement. He returned, therefore, to the parsonage, and, at the moment of closing the door, was observed to look back upon the people, all of whom had their eyes fixed upon the minister. A sad smile gleamed faintly from beneath the black veil, and flickered about his mouth, glimmering as he disappeared.

 "How strange," said a lady, "that a simple black veil, such as any woman might wear on her bonnet, should become such a terrible thing on Mr. Hooper's face!"

 "Something must surely be amiss with Mr. Hooper's intellects," observed her husband, the physician of the village. "But the strangest part of the affair is the effect of this vagary[19], even on a sober-minded man like myself. The black veil, though it covers only our pastor's face, throws its influence over his whole person, and makes him ghostlike from head to foot. Do you not feel it so?"

 "Truly do I," replied the lady; "and I would not be alone with him for the world. I wonder he is not afraid to be alone with himself!"

 "Men sometimes are so," said her husband.

 The afternoon service was attended with similar circumstances. At its conclusion, the bell tolled for the funeral of a young lady. The relatives and friends were assembled in the house, and the more distant acquaintances stood about the door, speaking of the good qualities of the deceased, when their talk was interrupted by the appearance of Mr. Hooper, still covered with his black veil. It was now an appropriate emblem. The clergyman stepped into the room where the corpse was laid, and bent over the coffin, to take a last farewell of his deceased parishioner. As he stooped, the veil hung straight down from his forehead, so that, if her eyelids had not been closed forever, the dead maiden might have seen his face. Could Mr. Hooper be fearful of her glance, that he so hastily caught back the black veil? A person who watched the interview between the dead and living, scrupled[20] not to affirm, that, at the instant when the clergyman's features were disclosed, the corpse had slightly shuddered, rustling the shroud and muslin cap, though the countenance retained the composure of death. A superstitious old woman was the only witness of this prodigy[21]. From the coffin Mr. Hooper passed into the chamber of the mourners, and thence[22] to the head of the staircase, to make the funeral prayer. It was a tender and heart-dissolving prayer, full of sorrow, yet so imbued with celestial hopes, that the music of a heavenly harp, swept by the fingers of the dead, seemed faintly to be heard among the saddest accents of the minister. The people trembled, though they but darkly understood him when he prayed that they, and himself, and all of mortal race, might be ready, as he trusted this young maiden had been, for the dreadful hour that should snatch the veil from their faces. The bearers went heavily forth, and the mourners followed, saddening all the street, with the dead before them, and Mr. Hooper in his black veil behind.

"Why do you look back?" said one in the procession to his partner.

"I had a fancy," replied she, "that the minister and the maiden's spirit were walking hand in hand."

"And so had I, at the same moment," said the other.

That night, the handsomest couple in Milford village were to be joined in wedlock. Though reckoned a melancholy man, Mr. Hooper had a placid cheerfulness for such occasions, which often excited a sympathetic smile where livelier merriment would have been thrown away. There was no quality of his disposition which made him more beloved than this. The company at the wedding awaited his arrival with impatience, trusting that the strange awe, which had gathered over him throughout the day, would now be dispelled. But such was not the result. When Mr. Hooper came, the first thing that their eyes rested on was the same horrible black veil, which had added deeper gloom to the funeral, and could portend nothing but evil to the wedding. Such was its immediate effect on the guests that a cloud seemed to have rolled duskily from beneath the black crape, and dimmed the light of the candles. The bridal pair stood up before the minister. But the bride's cold fingers quivered in the tremulous hand of the bridegroom, and her deathlike paleness caused a whisper that the maiden who had been buried a few hours before was come from her grave to be married. If ever another wedding were so dismal, it was that famous one where they tolled the wedding knell. After performing the ceremony, Mr. Hooper raised a glass of wine to his lips, wishing happiness to the new married couple in a strain of mild pleasantry that ought to have brightened the features of the guests, like a cheerful gleam from the hearth. At that instant, catching a glimpse of his figure in the looking-glass, the black veil involved his own spirit in the horror with which it overwhelmed all others. His frame shuddered, his lips grew white, he spilt the untasted wine upon the carpet, and rushed forth into the darkness. For the Earth, too, had on her Black Veil.

The next day, the whole village of Milford talked of little else than Parson Hooper's black veil. That, and the mystery concealed behind it, supplied a topic for discussion between acquaintances meeting in the street, and good women gossiping at their open windows. It was the first item of news that the tavern-keeper told to his guests. The children babbled of it on their way to school. One imitative little imp covered his face with an old black handkerchief, thereby so affrighting his playmates that the panic seized himself, and he well-nigh lost his wits by his own waggery[23].

It was remarkable that all of the busybodies and impertinent people in the parish, not one ventured to put the plain question to Mr. Hooper, wherefore he did this thing. Hitherto, whenever there appeared the slightest call for such interference, he had never lacked advisers, nor shown himself averse to be guided by their judgment. If he erred at all, it was by so painful a degree of self-distrust, that even the mildest censure would lead him to consider an indifferent action as a crime. Yet, though so well acquainted with this amiable weakness, no individual among his parishioners chose to make the black veil a subject of friendly remonstrance[24]. There was a feeling of dread, neither plainly confessed nor carefully concealed, which caused each to shift the responsibility upon another, till at length it was found expedient to send a deputation of the church, in order to deal with Mr. Hooper about the mystery, before it should grow into a scandal. Never did an embassy so ill discharge its duties. The minister received then with friendly courtesy, but became silent, after they were seated, leaving to his visitors the whole burden of introducing their important business. The topic, it might be supposed, was obvious enough. There was the black veil swathed round Mr. Hooper's forehead, and concealing every feature above his placid mouth, on which, at times, they could perceive the glimmering of a melancholy smile. But that piece of crape, to their imagination, seemed to hang down before his heart, the symbol of a fearful secret between him and them. Were the veil but cast aside, they might speak freely of it, but not till then. Thus they sat a considerable time, speechless, confused, and shrinking uneasily from Mr. Hooper's eye, which they felt to be fixed upon them with an invisible glance. Finally, the deputies returned abashed to their constituents, pronouncing the matter too weighty to be handled, except by a council of the churches, if, indeed, it might not require a general synod[25].

But there was one person in the village unappalled by the awe with which the black veil had impressed all beside herself. When the deputies returned without an explanation, or even venturing to demand one, she, with the calm energy of her character, determined to chase away the strange cloud that appeared to be settling round Mr. Hooper, every moment more darkly than before. As his plighted wife, it should be her privilege to know what the black veil concealed. At the minister's first visit, therefore, she entered upon the subject with a direct simplicity, which made the task easier both for him and her. After he had seated himself, she fixed her eyes steadfastly upon the veil, but could discern nothing of the dreadful gloom that had so overawed the multitude: it was but a double fold of crape, hanging down from his forehead to his mouth, and slightly stirring with his breath.

"No," said she aloud, and smiling, "there is nothing terrible in this piece of crape, except that it hides a face which I am always glad to look upon. Come, good sir, let the sun shine from behind the cloud. First lay aside your black veil: then tell me why you put it on."

Mr. Hooper's smile glimmered faintly.

"There is an hour to come," said he, "when all of us shall cast aside our veils. Take it not amiss, beloved friend, if I wear this piece of crape till then."

"Your words are a mystery, too," returned the young lady. "Take away the veil from them, at least."

"Elizabeth, I will," said he, "so far as my vow may suffer me. Know, then, this veil is a type and a symbol, and I am bound to wear it ever, both in light and darkness, in solitude and before the gaze of multitudes, and as with strangers, so with my familiar friends. No mortal eye will see it withdrawn. This dismal shade must separate me from the world: even you, Elizabeth, can never come behind it!"

"What grievous affliction hath befallen you," she earnestly inquired, "that you should thus darken your eyes forever?"

"If it be a sign of mourning," replied Mr. Hooper, "I, perhaps, like most other mortals, have sorrows dark enough to be typified by a black veil."

"But what if the world will not believe that it is the type of an innocent sorrow?" urged Elizabeth. "Beloved and respected as you are, there may be whispers that you hide your face under the consciousness of secret sin. For the sake of your holy office, do away this scandal!"

The color rose into her cheeks as she intimated the nature of the rumors that were already abroad in the village. But Mr. Hooper's mildness did not forsake him. He even smiled again—that same sad smile, which always appeared like a faint glimmering of light, proceeding from the obscurity beneath the veil.

"If I hide my face for sorrow, there is cause enough," he merely replied; "and if I cover it for secret sin, what mortal might not do the same?"

And with this gentle, but unconquerable obstinacy[26] did he resist all her entreaties. At length Elizabeth sat silent. For a few moments she appeared lost in thought, considering, probably, what new methods might be tried to withdraw her lover from so dark a fantasy, which, if it had no other meaning, was perhaps a symptom of mental disease. Though of a firmer character than his own, the tears rolled down her cheeks. But, in an instant, as it were, a new feeling took the place of sorrow: her eyes were fixed insensibly on the black veil, when, like a sudden twilight in the air, its terrors fell around her. She arose, and stood trembling before him.

"And do you feel it then, at last?" said he mournfully.

She made no reply, but covered her eyes with her hand, and turned to leave the room. He rushed forward and caught her arm.

"Have patience with me, Elizabeth!" cried he, passionately. "Do not desert me, though this veil must be between us here on earth. Be mine, and hereafter there shall be no veil over my face, no darkness between our souls! It is but a mortal veil—it is not for eternity! O! you know not how lonely I am, and how frightened, to be alone behind my black veil. Do not leave me in this miserable obscurity forever!"

"Lift the veil but once, and look me in the face," said she.

"Never! It cannot be!" replied Mr. Hooper.

"Then farewell!" said Elizabeth.

She withdrew her arm from his grasp, and slowly departed, pausing at the door, to give one long shuddering gaze, that seemed almost to penetrate the mystery of the black veil. But, even amid his grief, Mr. Hooper smiled to think that only a material emblem had separated him from happiness, though the horrors, which it shadowed forth, must be drawn darkly between the fondest of lovers.

From that time no attempts were made to remove Mr. Hooper's black veil, or, by a direct appeal, to discover the secret which it was supposed to hide. By persons who claimed a superiority to popular prejudice, it was reckoned merely an eccentric whim, such as often mingles with the sober actions of men otherwise rational, and tinges them all with its own semblance of insanity. But with the multitude, good Mr. Hooper was irreparably a bugbear[27]. He could not walk the street with any peace of mind, so conscious was he that the gentle and timid would turn aside to avoid him, and that others would make it a point of hardihood to throw themselves in his way. The impertinence of the latter class compelled him to give up his customary walk at sunset to the burial ground; for when he leaned pensively over the gate, there would always be faces behind the gravestones, peeping at his black veil. A fable went the rounds that the stare of the dead people drove him thence. It grieved him, to the very depth of his kind heart, to observe how the children fled from his approach, breaking up their merriest sports, while his melancholy figure was yet afar off. Their instinctive dread caused him to feel more strongly than aught else, that a preternatural horror was interwoven with the threads of the black crape. In truth, his own antipathy to the veil was known to be so great, that he never willingly passed before a mirror, nor stooped to drink at a still fountain, lest, in its peaceful bosom, he should be affrighted by himself. This was what gave plausibility to the whispers, that Mr. Hooper's conscience tortured him for some great crime too horrible to be entirely concealed, or otherwise than so obscurely intimated. Thus, from beneath the black veil, there rolled a cloud into the sunshine, an ambiguity of sin or sorrow, which enveloped the poor minister, so that love or sympathy could never reach him. It was said that ghost and fiend[28] consorted with him there. With self-shudderings and outward terrors, he walked continually in its shadow, groping darkly within his own soul, or gazing through a medium that saddened the whole world. Even the lawless wind, it was believed, respected his dreadful secret, and never blew aside the veil. But still good Mr. Hooper sadly smiled at the pale visages of the worldly throng as he passed by.

Among all its bad influences, the black veil had the one desirable effect, of making its wearer a very efficient clergyman. By the aid of his mysterious emblem—for there was no other apparent cause—he became a man of awful power over souls that were in agony for sin. His converts always regarded him with a dread peculiar to themselves, affirming, though but figuratively, that, before he brought them to celestial light, they had been with him behind the black veil. Its gloom, indeed, enabled him to sympathize with all dark affections. Dying sinners cried aloud for Mr. Hooper, and would not yield their breath till he appeared; though ever, as he stooped to whisper consolation, they shuddered at the veiled face so near their own. Such were the terrors of the black veil, even when Death had bared his visage! Strangers came long distances to attend service at his church, with the mere idle purpose of gazing at his figure, because it was forbidden them to behold his face. But many were made to quake ere they departed! Once, during Governor Belcher's administration, Mr. Hooper was appointed to preach the election sermon. Covered with his black veil, he stood before the chief magistrate, the council, and the representatives, and wrought so deep an impression, that the legislative measures of that year were characterized by all the gloom and piety of our earliest ancestral sway.

In this manner Mr. Hooper spent a long life, irreproachable in outward act, yet shrouded in dismal suspicions; kind and loving, though unloved, and dimly feared; a man apart from men, shunned in their health and joy, but ever summoned to their aid in mortal anguish. As years wore on, shedding their snows above his sable veil, he acquired a name throughout the New England churches, and they called him Father[29] Hooper. Nearly all his parishioners, who were of mature age when he was settled, had been borne away by many a funeral: he had one congregation in the church, and a more crowded one in the churchyard; and having wrought so late into the evening, and done his work so well, it was now good Father Hooper's turn to rest.

Several persons were visible by the shaded candlelight, in the death chamber of the old clergyman. Natural connections he had none. But there was the decorously grave, though unmoved physician, seeking only to mitigate the last pangs of the patient whom he could not save. There were the deacons[30], and other eminently pious members of his church. There, also, was the Reverend Mr. Clark, of Westbury, a young and zealous divine, who had ridden in haste to pray by the bedside of the expiring minister. There was the nurse, no hired handmaiden of death, but one whose calm affection had endured thus long in secrecy, in solitude, amid the chill of age, and would not perish, even at the dying hour. Who, but Elizabeth! And there lay the hoary head of good Father Hooper upon the death pillow, with the black veil still swathed about his brow, and reaching down over his face, so that each more difficult gasp of his faint breath caused it to stir. All through life that piece of crape had hung between him and the world: it had separated him from cheerful brotherhood and woman's love, and kept him in that saddest of all prisons, his own heart; and still it lay upon his face, as if to deepen the gloom of his darksome chamber, and shade him from the sunshine of eternity.

For some time previous, his mind had been confused, wavering doubtfully between the past and the present, and hovering forward, as it were, at intervals, into the indistinctness of the world to come. There had been feverish turns, which tossed him from side to side, and wore away what little strength he had. But in his most convulsive struggles, and in the wildest vagaries of his intellect, when no other thought retained its sober influence, he still showed an awful solicitude lest the black veil should slip aside. Even if his bewildered soul could have forgotten, there was a faithful woman at this pillow, who, with averted eyes, would have covered that aged face, which she had last beheld in the comeliness of manhood. At length the death-stricken old man lay quietly in the torpor[31] of mental and bodily exhaustion, with an imperceptible pulse, and breath that grew fainter and fainter, except when a long, deep, and irregular inspiration seemed to prelude the flight of his spirit.

The minister of Westbury approached the bedside.

"Venerable Father Hooper," said he, "the moment of your release is at hand. Are you ready for the lifting of the veil that shuts in time from eternity?"

Father Hooper at first replied merely by a feeble motion of his head; then, apprehensive, perhaps, that his meaning might be doubted, he exerted himself to speak.

"Yea," said he, in faint accents, "my soul hath a patient weariness until that veil be lifted."

"And is it fitting," resumed the Reverend Mr. Clark, "that a man so given to prayer, of such a blameless example, holy in deed and thought, so far as mortal judgment may pronounce; is it fitting that a father in the church should leave a shadow on his memory, that may seem to blacken a life so pure? I pray you, my venerable brother, let not this thing be! Suffer us to be gladdened by your triumphant aspect as you go to your reward. Before the veil of eternity be lifted, let me cast aside this black veil from your face!"

And thus speaking, the Reverend Mr. Clark bent forward to reveal the mystery of so many years. But, exerting a sudden energy, that made all the beholders stand aghast, Father Hooper snatched both his hands from beneath the bedclothes, and pressed them strongly on the black veil, resolute to struggle, if the minister of Westbury would contend with a dying man.

"Never!" cried the veiled clergyman. "On earth, never!"

"Dark old man!" exclaimed the affrighted minister, "with what horrible crime upon your soul are you now passing to the judgment?"

Father Hooper's breath heaved; it rattled in his throat; but, with a mighty effort, grasping forward with his hands, he caught hold of life, and held it back till he should speak. He even raised himself in bed; and there he sat, shivering with the arms of death around him, while the black veil hung down, awful, at that last moment, in the gathered terrors of a lifetime. And yet the faint, sad smile, so often there, now seemed to glimmer from its obscurity, and linger on Father Hooper's lips.

"Why do you tremble at me alone?" cried he, turning his veiled face round the circle of pale spectators. "Tremble also at each other! Have men avoided me, and women shown no pity, and children screamed and fled, only for my black veil? What, but the mystery which it obscurely typifies, has made this piece of crape so awful? When the friend shows his inmost heart to his friend; the lover to his best beloved; when man does not vainly shrink from the eye of his Creator, loathsomely treasuring up the secret of his sin; then deem me a monster, for the symbol beneath which I have lived, and die! I look around me, and, lo! on every visage a Black Veil!"

While his auditors shrank from one another, in mutual affright, Father Hooper fell back upon his pillow, a veiled corpse, with a faint smile lingering on the lips. Still veiled, they laid him in his coffin, and a veiled corpse they bore him to the grave. The grass of many years has sprung up and withered on that grave, the burial stone is moss-grown, and good Mr. Hooper's face is dust; but awful is still the thought that it mouldered[32] beneath the Black Veil!

注释（Notes）

1. Parable：（尤指道德或宗教）寓言故事。
2. sexton：教堂司事（负责看管教堂及其墓地，有时也负责敲钟）。
3. Sunday clothes：节日盛装。
4. spruce：整洁清爽的。
5. the Sabbath：安息日（大部分基督徒的安息日是星期日，犹太教徒的安息日是星期六，穆斯林的安息日是星期五）。
6. Parson：牧师。
7. semblance：近似，相似，假象。
8. starch：上浆（用淀粉浆硬衣服）。
9. parishioner：教区居民。
10. perturbation：不安，扰动。
11. psalm：圣诗，圣歌，赞美诗；（尤指《圣经·诗篇》中的一篇）诗篇。
12. Scriptures：圣经。
13. thither：到那儿。
14. the Omniscient：全知全能者。
15. iniquity：邪恶，不公。
16. indecorous：不得体的，不雅的，粗鲁的。
17. pent-up：（感情）被压抑的，被抑制的。
18. sagacious：聪慧的，洞察事理的，睿智的。
19. vagary：奇特行为。
20. scruple：对……有顾忌（顾虑）。
21. prodigy：奇观。
22. thence：然后，接着。
23. waggery：玩笑。
24. remonstrance：抱怨，抗议。
25. synod：教会会议。
26. obstinacy：固执，顽固。
27. bugbear：怪物。
28. fiend：魔鬼。
29. Father：（尤指天主教或东正教的）神父。

30. deacon:(某些宗教团体由非神职人员担任的)辅祭,助祭。
31. torpor:不活跃,萎靡,迟钝。
32. moulder:腐烂。

主题探究(Themes)

(扫码阅读)

价值引领(Value Guidance)

霍桑的浪漫主义被称为黑暗浪漫主义(dark romanticism),因为他认为恶是人性的一部分,他的作品"缺少阳光"。在学习他的短篇小说《牧师的黑面纱》时,作品主题所涉及的清教主义的原罪和人性恶等观念,难免会让人产生压抑和绝望的情绪。此时,我们要意识到世界本身就是包含诸如美好和丑恶、光明和黑暗等这些相反和相对事物,每个人都不可能一直生活在充满阳光和鲜花的虚幻世界里,就像英国作家曼斯菲尔德的短篇小说《园会》中的那句话:"But still one must go everywhere; one must see everything"①。刘意青指出:"每个人的内心都要经历从天真出发穿越黑洞的一个途程,黑洞象征邪恶。那些成功走出黑洞的人是胜利者,他们战胜了邪恶;而有些人永远走不出黑洞,就成为了失败者。……生活在世界上要能够接受恶的存在。"②在生活中面对各种各样的考验时,必须学会坚韧;经历生活的艰辛与痛苦,体味人性的自私与阴暗,但依然热爱生命和人类,这才是真正的勇敢和成熟。

问题讨论(Questions for Discussion)

1. Why the short story is called a "parable"?

2. How do you understand people's fancy "that the minister and the maiden's spirit were walking hand in hand" in Paragraph 20? Why is it appropriate that we never learn the precise reason or fact?

3. On his deathbed, what does Reverend Hooper say men, women, and children have done? What does he say he sees on every face? What might he mean by saying so?

4. Please list possible reasons Reverend Hooper might have for wearing the veil?

---

① Katherine Mansfield. *The Collected Stories of Katherine Mansfield*. Hertfordshire: Wordsworth Editions Limited, 2006: 204.
② 刘意青. 如何看待人生的善与恶——对梅尔维尔和霍桑的比较探讨[J]. 浙江外国语学院学报,3: 5.

5. How do you understand the "smile" of Reverend Hooper?

6. Symbolism is a noticeable feature of Hawthorne's short story. What does the veil symbolize? And what does Reverend Hooper symbolize?

(请扫码观看视频"The Minister's Black Veil")

The Scarlet Letter

作品简介 (Introduction to the Work)

The Scarlet Letter is a work by Nathaniel Hawthorne, published in 1850. The novel is set in a village in Puritan New England. The main character is Hester Prynne, a young woman who has borne a child out of wedlock. Hester believes herself a widow, but her husband, Roger Chillingworth, arrives in New England very much alive and conceals his identity. He finds his wife forced to wear the scarlet letter A on her dress as punishment for her adultery. After Hester refuses to name her lover, Chillingworth becomes obsessed with finding his identity. When he learns that the man in question is Arthur Dimmesdale, a saintly young minister who is the leader of those exhorting her to name the child's father, Chillingworth proceeds to torment him. Stricken by guilt, Dimmesdale becomes increasingly ill. Hester herself is revealed to be a self-reliant heroine who is never truly repentant for committing adultery with the minister; she feels that their act was consecrated by their deep love for each other. Although she is initially scorned, over time her compassion and dignity silence many of her critics. Chillingworth is morally degraded by his monomaniacal pursuit of revenge. Dimmesdale is broken by his own sense of guilt. Only Hester can face the future bravely. In the following excerpt, after Dimmesdale mounts the scaffold after delivering a memorable sermon, he publicly confesses his adultery before dying in Hester's arms.

(扫码阅读)

The Scarlet Letter
(Excerpt)

(请扫码观看视频 *The Scarlet Letter*)

Moby Dick

作品简介 (Introduction to the Work)

Published in 1851, *Moby Dick* was based in part on author Herman Melville's own experiences on a whaleship. The novel tells the story of Ahab, the captain of a whaling vessel called The Pequod, who has a three-year mission to collect and sell the valuable oil of whales at the behest of the ship's owners. Instead, the furious Ahab takes the ship on his own personal journey through hell, seeking revenge against the eponymous white whale who took his leg leading to alienation, rebellion, doubt, and doom for all aboard. The novel is narrated by Ishmael, a dreamy and disaffected man who tells the tale with his own unique opinions and digressions, ranging on subjects of literature, philosophy, science, and sailing. In the following excerpt, Ishmael is about to take his first turn at the masthead, looking constantly at the sea for signs of whales. Ishmael notes, half-comically, that "mast-head-standing" has a long history: the Babylonians did something similar when they built the tower of Babel, and stone carvings of Napoleon, Admiral Nelson, and George Washington sit atop tall columns in the Western world and America. He also considers how "young philosophers" might not do a diligent job of sighting the whales. He admits that it is difficult to maintain your focus on watching for whales when you are constantly getting caught up in philosophical thoughts. Melville adopts a historical view of whaling, citing developments in the industry and changes to it in this chapter.

(扫码阅读)

Moby Dick

(Excerpt)

Unit 21
Edgar Allan Poe

Edgar Allan Poe: "The Raven"; "The Fall of the House of Usher"

作者简介 (Introduction to the Author)

Edgar Allan Poe (1809—1849), an American poet, novelist and literary critic in the 19th century, is one of the representative figures of American Romanticism. Edgar Allan Poe was born in Boston, Massachusetts. His parents died when he was young, and then he was adopted by John Allan and Frances Allan from Richmond, Virginia. In 1826, Poe went to the University of Virginia to study and began to fall into the bad habit of drinking and even taking drugs. He left the university after just one year's study. He then stayed in the army for several years and entered the "The United States Military Academy" in 1830. Edgar Allan Poe began his writing career in a low-key manner. He anonymously published a collection of poems *Tamerlane and Other Poems*. He married his 13-year-old cousin Virginia Clem in Baltimore in 1835. *The narrative of Arthur Gordon Pym* was published in 1838 and received widespread attention. In the summer of 1839, Poe became an assistant to *Burton's Gentleman's Magazine*. During this period, he published many essays, novels, and reviews, which reinforced his reputation. In January 1845, Edgar Allan Poe published the poem "*The Raven*", which gained instant fame. On October 3, 1849, Poe was found unconscious in a street in Baltimore. On October 7, he died of cerebral congestion in the hospital at the age of 40. As the founder of mystery novels, Edgar Allan Poe is no doubt one of America's greatest writers. His novels and poems have an immortal place in the history of the Western literature.

作品简介 (Introduction to the Work)

"The Raven" is a poem published in 1845 by Poe. His poetry wasn't especially popular during his lifetime, but "The Raven" was among the few of Poe's poems to grab the attention of his contemporaries, as well as future poetry lovers. In the poem, An unnamed speaker sits in his chamber on a dreary December night, reading old, esoteric books. He dearly misses his love, Lenore, who presumably died recently, and he hopes that reading will distract him from his loss. He has nearly fallen asleep when he suddenly hears someone—or something—knocking on the door. He's instantly uneasy but reassures himself that it's probably just a visitor. He calls out, apologizing for his delayed response. However, when he opens the door, no one is there. He whispers, "Lenore," to the darkness outside but hears only his words echo back at him. Ominously, the knocking continues, this time from the window. The speaker assumes it is the wind but still feels uneasy. He opens the window shutters, and a raven hops in, perching on a bust of the Greek goddess Pallas Athena above the chamber door. The sight of the bird relieves the speaker momentarily. He jokingly asks the bird's name. To his utter shock, the raven cries out, "Nevermore."

作品选文 (Selected Reading)

The Raven

Once upon a midnight dreary, while I pondered, weak and weary,
Over many a quaint and curious volume of forgotten lore[1]—
While I nodded, nearly napping, suddenly there came a tapping,
As of some one gently rapping, rapping at my chamber door.
"'Tis[2] some visitor," I muttered, "tapping at my chamber door—
Only this, and nothing more."

Ah, distinctly I remember it was in the bleak December;
And each separate dying ember[3] wrought its ghost upon the floor.
Eagerly I wished the morrow;—vainly I had sought to borrow
From my books surcease of sorrow—sorrow for the lost Lenore—
For the rare and radiant maiden whom the angels name Lenore—
Nameless here for evermore.

And the silken, sad, uncertain rustling of each purple curtain
Thrilled me—filled me with fantastic terrors never felt before;
So that now, to still the beating of my heart, I stood repeating
"'Tis some visitor entreating entrance at my chamber door—
Some late visitor entreating entrance at my chamber door;—
This it is and nothing more."

Presently my soul grew stronger; hesitating then no longer,
"Sir," said I, "or Madam, truly your forgiveness I implore;
But the fact is I was napping, and so gently you came rapping,
And so faintly you came tapping, tapping at my chamber door,

That I scarce was sure I heard you"—here I opened wide the door;—
Darkness there and nothing more.

Deep into that darkness peering, long I stood there wondering, fearing,
Doubting, dreaming dreams no mortal ever dared to dream before;
But the silence was unbroken, and the stillness gave no token,
And the only word there spoken was the whispered word, "Lenore?"
This I whispered, and an echo murmured back the word, "Lenore!"—
Merely this and nothing more.

Back into the chamber turning, all my soul within me burning,
Soon again I heard a tapping somewhat louder than before.
"Surely," said I, "surely that is something at my window lattice[4];
Let me see, then, what thereat is, and this mystery explore—
Let my heart be still a moment and this mystery explore;—
'Tis the wind and nothing more!"

Open here I flung the shutter, when, with many a flirt and flutter,
In there stepped a stately Raven of the saintly days of yore[5];
Not the least obeisance[6] made he; not a minute stopped or stayed he;
But, with mien of lord or lady, perched[7] above my chamber door—
Perched upon a bust of Pallas[8] just above my chamber door—
Perched, and sat, and nothing more.

Then this ebony bird beguiling my sad fancy into smiling[9],
By the grave and stern decorum of the countenance it wore,
"Though thy crest be shorn and shaven, thou," I said, "art sure no craven[10],
Ghastly grim and ancient Raven wandering from the Nightly shore—
Tell me what thy lordly name is on the Night's Plutonian shore[11]!"
Quoth the Raven, "Nevermore."

Much I marvelled this ungainly fowl to hear discourse so plainly,
Though its answer little meaning—little relevancy bore;
For we cannot help agreeing that no living human being
Ever yet was blessed with seeing bird above his chamber door—
Bird or beast upon the sculptured bust above his chamber door,

With such name as "Nevermore."

But the Raven, sitting lonely on the placid bust, spoke only
That one word, as if his soul in that one word he did outpour.
Nothing further then he uttered—not a feather then he fluttered—
Till I scarcely more than muttered "Other friends have flown before—
On the morrow he will leave me, as my Hopes have flown before."
Then the bird said "Nevermore."

Startled at the stillness broken by reply so aptly spoken,
"Doubtless," said I, "what it utters is its only stock and store,
Caught from some unhappy master whom unmerciful Disaster
Followed fast and followed faster till his songs one burden bore—
Till the dirges[12] of his Hope that melancholy burden bore
Of 'Never—nevermore'."

But the Raven still beguiling all my fancy into smiling,
Straight I wheeled a cushioned seat in front of bird, and bust and door;
Then, upon the velvet sinking, I betook myself to linking
Fancy unto fancy, thinking what this ominous bird of yore—
What this grim, ungainly, ghastly, gaunt[13] and ominous bird of yore
Meant in croaking "Nevermore."

This I sat engaged in guessing, but no syllable expressing
To the fowl whose fiery eyes now burned into my bosom's core;
This and more I sat divining, with my head at ease reclining
On the cushion's velvet lining that the lamp-light gloated o'er,
But whose velvet-violet lining with the lamp-light gloating o'er,
She shall press, ah, nevermore!

Then methought the air grew denser, perfumed from an unseen censer
Swung by Seraphim[14] whose footfalls tinkled on the tufted floor.
"Wretch," I cried, "thy God hath lent thee—by these angels he hath sent thee
Respite—respite and nepenthe[15] from thy memories of Lenore;
Quaff, oh quaff this kind nepenthe and forget this lost Lenore!"
Quoth the Raven "Nevermore."

"Prophet[16]!" said I, "thing of evil! —prophet still, if bird or devil! —
Whether Tempter sent, or whether tempest tossed thee here ashore,
Desolate yet all undaunted, on this desert land enchanted—
On this home by Horror haunted—tell me truly, I implore—
Is there—is there balm in Gilead?[17]—tell me—tell me, I implore!"
Quoth the Raven "Nevermore."

"Prophet!" said I, "thing of evil! —prophet still, if bird or devil!
By that Heaven that bends above us—by that God we both adore—
Tell this soul with sorrow laden if, within the distant Aidenn[18],
It shall clasp a sainted maiden whom the angels name Lenore—
Clasp a rare and radiant maiden whom the angels name Lenore."
Quoth the Raven "Nevermore."

"Be that word our sign in parting, bird or fiend," I shrieked, upstarting—
"Get thee back into the tempest and the Night's Plutonian shore!
Leave no black plume[19] as a token of that lie thy soul hath spoken!
Leave my loneliness unbroken! —quit the bust above my door!
Take thy beak from out my heart, and take thy form from off my door!"
Quoth the Raven "Nevermore."

And the Raven, never flitting, still is sitting, still is sitting
On the pallid bust of Pallas just above my chamber door;
And his eyes have all the seeming of a demon's that is dreaming,
And the lamp-light o'er him streaming throws his shadow on the floor;
And my soul from out that shadow that lies floating on the floor
Shall be lifted—nevermore!

作品译文(扫码阅读)

注释 (Notes)

1. lore：知识，学问。
2. 'Tis：it's，这是。
3. ember：余烬。
4. window lattice：窗格子。
5. yore：往昔，过去。
6. obeisance：敬意，尊敬。
7. perch：（鸟）栖息。
8. Pallas：帕拉斯，智慧女神雅典娜。
9. ebony：乌黑的；beguile：使陶醉，使着迷，哄骗。
10. thy：your，你的；thou：you，你；art：are，是。
11. the Night's Plutonian shore：黑夜中的冥界海岸。
12. dirge：哀乐，挽歌。
13. gaunt：very thin especially from disease or hunger，憔悴的。
14. Seraphim：撒拉弗，六翼天使（等级最高的天使），天使之首炽天使，爱和想象力的精灵，做歌颂神。
15. nepenthe：（据传说古希腊人用的）忘忧药。
16. Prophet：预言家，先知。
17. Is there—is there balm in Gilead："基列有香膏吗?"语出《旧约·耶利米书》第8章第22节"难道基列没有镇痛香膏吗？难道那里没有治病的医生吗？"这里用于讽刺。
18. Aidenn：Eden，伊甸园。
19. plume：羽毛。

主题探究 (Themes)

（扫码阅读）

问题讨论 (Questions for Discussion)

1. Do you think this poem is supposed to be funny? Do you find the speaker's tale intense and dramatic, or ridiculous and over-the-top?
2. This is a really carefully organized poem. What do you think of the rhyme, form

and meter of the poem?

3. How would you describe the speaker's feelings for Lenore? Do you find his love for Lenore touching? Or maybe a little cheesy?

4. How does Poe represent the spooky side of nature? Why is that so important for this poem?

5. Do you think the speaker is insane? Do you see it in the poem? Where?

6. Does the talking Raven actually seem supernatural to you?

The Fall of the House of Usher

作品简介 (Introduction to the Work)

Edgar Allan Poe wrote the Gothic short story "The Fall of the House of Usher" in 1839. It first appeared in *Burton's Gentleman's Magazine* published in 1839 and in Poe's collection of short stories *Tales of the Grotesque and Arabesque* in 1840. "The Fall of the House of Usher" is a foundational Gothic text and helped to cement the Gothic aesthetic. In the story, an unnamed narrator is summoned to the remote mansion of his boyhood friend, Roderick Usher. Filled with a sense of dread by the sight of the house itself, the narrator reunites with his old companion, who is suffering from a strange mental illness and whose sister Madeline is near death due to a mysterious disease. The narrator provides company to Usher while he paints and plays guitar, spending all his days inside, avoiding the sunlight and obsessing over the sentience of the non-living. When Madeline dies, Usher decides to bury her temporarily in one of his house's large vaults. A few days later, however, she emerges from her provisional tomb, killing her brother while the narrator flees for his life. The House of Usher splits apart and collapses, wiping away the last remnants of the ancient family.

(扫码阅读)

"The Fall of the House of Usher"

Unit 22
Walt Whitman & Emily Dickinson

Walt Whitman: "Song of Myself"
Emily Dickinson: "Success"; "I'm Nobody! Who Are You?"
▽

作者简介 (Introduction to the Authors)

Walt Whitman (1819—1892) was the greatest romantic poet of the 19th century in the United States and the most outstanding singer of freedom and democracy. Whitman was born in a farmer's family on Long Island, New York. Due to the financial constraints of his family, he had only been in primary school for a few years and dropped out at the age of 11. Whitman has engaged in a variety of occupations, including apprenticeship, typesetter, rural primary school teacher, reporter, editor, etc. In 1836, 17-year-old Whitman became a teacher on Long Island. In 1841, he became a full-time journalist. Since 1850, Whitman, on the one hand, had been engaged in manual labor as a carpenter and architect. On the other hand, he had launched his vigorous poetry creation activities. He began to publish free poems in newspapers to express his love for nature and praise for free and democratic life. After the outbreak of the Civil War, he actively supported Lincoln's idea of liberating black slaves and got involved in the battle. During the Civil War, Whitman, as a freelance journalist, went to the New York Hospital to take care of the wounded. In December 1862, he went to Washington, D. C. to take care of his brother who was injured in the war. In 1873, Whitman suffered a stroke, which led to his partial paralysis. A few months later, he moved to Camden, New Jersey to recuperate. On 1892, Whitman died of serious illness. After his death, he was buried in a tomb designed by himself. Along with Emily Dickinson, he is considered one of the most important poets in America.

Emily Dickinson (1830—1886) is an American legendary poet. She is regarded as one of the pioneers of modernist poetry in the 20th century. Dickinson was born into a famous family in Amherst, Massachusetts. Her father, Edward Dickinson, was a lawyer, politician and heir to Amherst College. Dickinson ranks second in the family, with an older brother (William Austin) and a younger sister (Lavinia). At the insistence of her father, Dickinson received more strict and orthodox education than many other girls of the same age. As a teenager, she studied at Amherst College and Mount Holyoke Female

Seminary. Although her academic requirements were strict and challenging at that time, Dickinson still performed well in her studies, learning literature, science, history, philosophy and Latin. However, at the age of 23, Dickinson began to withdraw from society. By the age of 30, she had become a relative recluse, spending most of her time indoors. Dickinson only received guests occasionally, and traveled to New England once to visit relatives. The most frequent way for her to contact with the outside world is to write to her relatives and friends. She often communicated with her close friend Susan Gilbert to discuss her poems. Dickinson was a prolific poet, but it was not until her death that the world really realized her talent. She published only seven poems in her life. After her death, her sister Lavinia found nearly a thousand poems she had written in a pile of pamphlets. Marbel Todd and Thomas Higginson, the critics, edited these poems extensively and published them in three volumes in 1890, 1891 and 1896 respectively. Along with Whitman, Dickinson is recognized as a milestone in a new era of American poetry, laying an important foundation for the development of American literature.

Song of Myself

作品简介 (Introduction to the Work)

"Song of Myself" might be the most egotistical poem ever written: it's all about me, myself, and I. In the first line, Walt Whitman kindly informs us that he is going to celebrate himself throughout 52 glorious sections. First published in 1855, without a title, as part of his collection *Leaves of Grass*, the work we now call "Song of Myself" just might be the most important and influential American poem out there. For one thing, it represents a huge break from the formal traditions of the past. Whitman wrote his verses without a regular form, meter, or rhythm. His lines are highly rhythmic, and they have a mesmerizing chant-like quality. Few poems are as fun to read aloud as this one. The poem has also helped shape the idea of what it means to be an American. It is a "democratic" poem that draws all different kinds of people and places into itself and tries to forge them into a unity. Section 1 begins in the middle of the poet's life. In Section 6, a child asks the narrator "What is the grass?" The answer to this question is, in a sense, the answer to the whole poem because it is formally structured around the grass. The bunches of grass in the child's hands may symbolize the regeneration in nature. But they may also signify a common thing that unites disparate people in the United States: grass, the ultimate symbol of democracy, grows and spreads everywhere.

作品选文（Selected Reading）

Song of Myself
(Excerpt)

1

I celebrate myself, and sing myself,
And what I assume you shall assume,
For every atom belonging to me as good belongs to you.

I loafe[1] and invite my soul,
I lean and loafe at my ease observing a spear of summer grass.

My tongue, every atom of my blood, form'd[2] from this soil, this air,
Born here of parents born here from parents the same, and their parents the same,
I, now thirty-seven years old in perfect health begin,
Hoping to cease not till death.

Creeds and schools in abeyance[3],
Retiring back a while sufficed at what they are, but never forgotten,
I harbor for good or bad, I permit to speak at every hazard,
Nature without check with original energy.

6

A child said *What is the grass?* fetching it to me with full hands;
How could I answer the child? I do not know what it is any more than he.

I guess it must be the flag of my disposition, out of hopeful green stuff woven.

Or I guess it is the handkerchief of the Lord,
A scented gift and remembrancer designedly dropt,
Bearing the owner's name someway in the corners, that we may see and remark, and say *Whose?*

Or I guess the grass is itself a child, the produced babe of the vegetation.

Or I guess it is a uniform hieroglyphic[4],
And it means, Sprouting alike in broad zones and narrow zones,
Growing among black folks as among white,
Kanuck, Tuckahoe, Congressman, Cuff[5], I give them the same, I receive them the same.

And now it seems to me the beautiful uncut hair of graves.

Tenderly will I use you curling grass,
It may be you transpire from the breasts of young men,
It may be if I had known them I would have loved them,
It may be you are from old people, or from offspring taken soon out of their mothers' laps,
And here you are the mothers' laps.

This grass is very dark to be from the white heads of old mothers,
Darker than the colorless beards of old men,
Dark to come from under the faint red roofs of mouths.

O I perceive after all so many uttering tongues,
And I perceive they do not come from the roofs of mouths for nothing.

I wish I could translate the hints about the dead young men and women,
And the hints about old men and mothers, and the offspring taken soon out of their laps.

What do you think has become of the young and old men?
And what do you think has become of the women and children?

They are alive and well somewhere,
The smallest sprout shows there is really no death,
And if ever there was it led forward life, and does not wait at the end to arrest it,
And ceas'd the moment life appear'd.

All goes onward and outward, nothing collapses,

And to die is different from what any one supposed, and luckier.

作品译文(扫码阅读)

注释 (Notes)

1. loafe：loaf，闲游。
2. form'd：formed，由……组成。
3. abeyance：中止，暂时搁置。
4. hieroglyphic：象形文字。
5. Kanuck：开纳克人；Tuckahoe：塔卡河人；Congressman：国会议员；Cuff：贫苦人民。

主题探究 (Themes)

(扫码阅读)

问题讨论 (Questions for Discussion)

1. What do you think of the image of "grass"?
2. What are the features of form and meter in the poem?
3. Does Whitman have different identities at different points in the poem, or does he maintain the same basic identity throughout?
4. What are the central elements of Whitman's ideal of America?
5. How would you put the distinction between "priests" and "prophets" in your own words? If Whitman were to fall into one of these groups, which would it be?
6. The speaker is eager to become fast friends with any kind of stranger. Do you think it's possible to become friends with people you've never met, as the speaker claims to be?

Success

作品简介 (Introduction to the Work)

The poem "Success is counted sweetest" is written by Emily Dickinson. She wrote eighteen hundred poems in total but only seven of them were published during her life. "Success is counted sweetest" is one of those seven poems which were published during her lifetime. It was written in 1859, first published anonymously in 1864 and republished in 1878, with the title "Success" in the anthology *A Masque of Poets*. The poem is written about the significance of success. It emphasizes the fact that one must lose something in order to truly appreciate it. It explains its theme by providing an image of a battlefield.

作品选文 (Selected Reading)

Success

Success is counted sweetest
By those who ne'er[1] succeed.
To comprehend a nectar[2]
Requires sorest need.

Not one of all the purple host[3]
Who took the flag[4] today
Can tell the definition
So clear, of victory

As he defeated—dying—
On whose forbidden ear
The distant strains of triumph
Burst agonized and clear!

作品译文(扫码阅读)

注释 (Notes)

1. ne'er: never,永不,从未。
2. nectar: the drink of gods
3. the purple host: victorious arm,紫袍加身的胜利之师。
4. took the flag: won the victory,取得胜利。

主题探究(Themes)

(扫码阅读)

价值引领(Value Guidance)

失败是痛苦的,但是人在情绪谷底时不要怕,失败和痛苦是人生的重要组成部分。相信自己,坚持下去,终将"柳暗花明又一村"。

当我确定自己的身体健康和情绪都在谷底的时候,我想不管怎么做,都是在向上走,只要自己拥有想好起来的愿望,就会从内心升发出力量。同时明白反弹需要力量,需要充电,需要积累。每天把情绪"垃圾"变成垫脚石。有负面情绪没关系,每个人都有,它是老天爷送给我们的"礼物"。只是这个礼物需要我们有足够的耐心、足够的信心、足够的勇气,才能拿到。相信我们每个人都可以绽放如花,而痛苦,却是滋养我们最好的养料。①

"我宁可痛苦,我不要麻木。"陕西女子刘小样的这句话令人震撼。有时候,"痛"则"通",失败和痛苦会促使你去思考、去反思,进而获得领悟,也许会让你看清事实的真相,变得更加通透,使你洞悉人生,令你成长。所以,在某种程度上,或许失败和痛苦这些令人恐惧的东西也是一种幸事(a blessing)。

问题讨论(Questions for Discussion)

1. Do you agree with the speaker's argument that you can only appreciate something when it's gone? Why or why not?

2. What about the form and/or meter of this poem emphasizes the idea of dissatisfaction?

3. Do you think Dickinson's lack of publishing in her lifetime influenced the way she represents ambition and success in this poem? Why or why not?

---

① 参见 https://www.jianshu.com/p/407e67537b0b

4. How comforting would this poem be to someone who's suffering? Why do you think so?
5. Are there any drawbacks to the suffering depicted in this poem?

I'm Nobody! Who Are You?

作品简介 (Introduction to the Work)

"I'm Nobody! Who are you?" is a short lyric poem by Emily Dickinson first published in 1891 in *Poems, Series 2*. It is one of Dickinson's most popular poems. In the poem, a speaker introduces themselves—perhaps to the reader—as "Nobody" before excitedly realizing that the addressee is "Nobody" too. Paradoxically, this hints at a community of "Nobodies" out there. These people just don't make as much noise as all the "Somebodies" who crave attention and admiration. The poem, then, calls out to its readers to say that being humble, withdrawn, shy, or private is just fine. In fact, such a way of life has many virtues of its own. The poem is one of a number of Dickinson poems that questions the value of public admiration—something which eluded Dickinson in her own lifetime.

作品选文 (Selected Reading)

I'm Nobody! Who Are You?

I'm Nobody! Who are you?
Are you—Nobody—too?
Then there's a pair of us!
Don't tell! they'd banish us[1]—you know!

How dreary—to be—Somebody!
How public—like a Frog—
To tell one's name—the livelong June—
To an admiring Bog[2]!

作品译文(扫码阅读)

注释（Notes）

1. banish us：这里有版本为 advertise。banish：drive out，放逐，驱逐。
2. Bog：wet, spongy ground made up of partly decayed plants，沼泽，泥塘。

主题探究（Themes）

（扫码阅读）

问题讨论（Questions for Discussion）

1. Discuss the use of irony in "I'm Nobody! Who Are You?".
2. Does the word "bog" have positive or negative connotations?
3. Some readers who are modest and self-effacing or who lack confidence feel validated by this poem. Why?
4. What is the significance of Line 3 in the overall meaning of the poem?
5. How do we interpret Dickinson's use of punctuation in the poem "I'm Nobody! Who Are You?"
6. What does the speaker mean by "Nobody" and "Somebody"?
7. What does Emily Dickinson's "I'm Nobody! Who Are You?" have in common with Walt Whitman's "Song of Myself"?

Unit 23
The Age of Realism

Mark Twain: The Adventures of Tom Sawyer
Kate Chopin: "A Pair of Stockings"
▽

作者简介 (Introduction to the Authors)

Mark Twain (1835—1910), pseudonym of Samuel Langhorne Clemens, is the founder of American critical realist literature and a world-famous short story master. Mark Twain is known as "the Lincoln in American Literature". His father was a local lawyer with a meager income. When little Twain went to school, he had to work at the same time to make a living. Unfortunately, in 1847, Mark Twain's father died of pneumonia. As a result, Mark Twain had to start his independent working life. He first worked as an apprentice in a printing factory, then as a newspaper messenger and typesetter, and later as a sailor and coxswain on the Mississippi River. In the autumn of 1839, Mark Twain's family moved to a port city in Missouri. In 1862, Mark Twain worked in a newspaper office in Virginia City, Nevada. In 1863, he began to use the pseudonym "Mark Twain". In 1876, the novel *The Adventures of Tom Sawyer* was published. In 1884, Mark Twain's another important novel *The Adventures of Huckleberry Finn* was published. This novel has been highly praised by critics and welcomed by readers at home and abroad. In October 1900, nearly ten years after he left the United States, Mark Twain and his family returned to America and were warmly welcomed. In 1904, his wife died in Italy. Mark Twain entered the final stage of his career. Pessimism had now become the main theme of some of his works. On April 21, 1910, Mark Twain died of illness. As the first writer to "Americanize" literary creation and nationalize literary language, Mark Twain is worthy of being an outstanding representative of American critical realist literature in the late 19th century.

Kate Chopin (1851—1904), born Katherine O'Flaherty in St. Louis, Missouri, is considered one of the first feminist authors of the 20th century. Her father, Thomas, was a highly successful Irish-born businessman; he died when Kate was five years old. She grew up in a household dominated by women: her mother, great-grandmother, and the female slaves her mother owned. Kate attended Academy of the Sacred Heart from age five to eighteen. In 1869, Kate married Oscar Chopin, a French cotton merchant, and they had six children. When Oscar's cotton brokerage business failed due to drought and his mismanagement, they moved to Louisiana where Oscar had family and a small amount of land. Her husband died in 1882, leaving a huge debt. Mother also died in 1883. The death of her husband and mother made Kate Chopin nervous. The doctor advised her to write to ease her mood. In the late 1890s, Kate wrote short stories, essays and engaged in translation. The novel *Awakening* was published in 1899 and was criticized from the literary and moral perspectives. This book is Kate's most famous work and widely valued for its literary status as an early feminist work. Deeply hit by the criticism, Kate turned to short story writing. In 1900, she wrote *New Orleans Gentlemen*. However, she never gained much from her writing so she still relied on the investment in Louisiana and St. Louis to survive. On August 22, 1904, Kate Chopin died of cerebral hemorrhage at the age of 54. As a pioneer of feminist literature, Kate Chopin is undoubtedly recognized as one of the greatest American writers.

The Adventures of Tom Sawyer

作品简介 (Introduction to the Work)

The Adventures of Tom Sawyer is a novel written by Mark Twain and published in 1876. The novel sets in the 1840s in the town of St. Petersburg, which is largely based on Twain's own memories of his childhood hometown, Hannibal, a river town in Missouri. The novel isn't quite as successful as its sequel, *The Adventures of Huckleberry Finn*, which skyrocketed Twain to the role of noteworthy American author. *The Adventures of Tom Sawyer* includes themes of youth, race, religion, visions of America, the supernatural, language and communication, morality and maturity, and the hopes, plans, and dreams of the young boys who are its protagonists. The story begins with an imaginative, clever, and mischievous boy named Tom Sawyer. He lives with his Aunt Polly and half-brother Sid in the fictional town of St. Petersburg, Missouri. In the first chapter, after playing hookey from school and being caught messing up his clothes in a fight, Tom must face a punishment: he must whitewash the fence on Saturday.

作品选文 (Selected Reading)

The Adventures of Tom Sawyer

(Excerpt)

Chapter 1

"TOM!"

No answer.

"TOM!"

No answer.

"What's gone with that boy, I wonder? You TOM!"

No answer.

The old lady pulled her spectacles down and looked over them about the room; then she put them up and looked out under them. She seldom or never looked through them for so small a thing as a boy; they were her state pair, the pride of her heart, and were built for "style," not service—she could have seen through a pair of stove-lids[1] just as well. She looked perplexed for a moment, and then said, not fiercely, but still loud enough for the furniture to hear:

"Well, I lay if I get hold of you I'll—"

She did not finish, for by this time she was bending down and punching under the bed with the broom, and so she needed breath to punctuate the punches with. She resurrected[2] nothing but the cat.

"I never did see the beat of that boy!"

She went to the open door and stood in it and looked out among the tomato vines and "jimpson" weeds[3] that constituted the garden. No Tom. So she lifted up her voice at an angle calculated for distance and shouted:

"Y-o-u-u TOM!"

There was a slight noise behind her and she turned just in time to seize a small boy by the slack of his roundabout and arrest his flight.

"There! I might 'a' thought of that closet. What you been doing in there?"

"Nothing."

"Nothing! Look at your hands. And look at your mouth. What is that truck?"

"I don't know, aunt."

"Well, I know. It's jam—that's what it is. Forty times I've said if you didn't let that jam alone I'd skin you. Hand me that switch."

The switch hovered in the air—the peril was desperate—

"My! Look behind you, aunt!"

The old lady whirled round, and snatched her skirts out of danger. The lad fled on the instant, scrambled up the high board-fence, and disappeared over it.

His aunt Polly stood surprised a moment, and then broke into a gentle laugh.

"Hang the boy, can't I never learn anything? Ain't[4] he played me tricks enough like that for me to be looking out for him by this time? But old fools is the biggest fools there is. Can't learn an old dog new tricks[5], as the saying is. But my goodness, he never plays them alike, two days, and how is a body to know what's coming? He 'pears to know just how long he can torment me before I get my dander up[6], and he knows if he can make out to put me off for a minute or make me laugh, it's all down again and I can't hit him a lick[7]. I ain't doing my duty by that boy, and that's the Lord's truth, goodness knows. Spare the rod and spile the child[8], as the Good Book says. I'm a laying up sin and suffering for us both, I know. He's full of the Old Scratch, but laws-a-me[9]! he's my own dead sister's boy, poor thing, and I ain't got the heart to lash him, somehow. Every time I let him off[10], my conscience does hurt me so, and every time I hit him my old heart most breaks. Well-a-well, man that is born of woman is of few days and full of trouble, as the Scripture says, and I reckon it's so. He'll play hookey[12] this evening, and I'll just be obleeged[13] to make him work, tomorrow, to punish him. It's mighty hard to make him work Saturdays, when all the boys is having holiday, but he hates work more than he hates anything else, and I've got to do some of my duty by him, or I'll be the ruination of the child."

Tom did play hookey, and he had a very good time. He got back home barely in season to help Jim, the small colored boy, saw next-day's wood and split the kindlings[14] before supper—at least he was there in time to tell his adventures to Jim while Jim did three-fourths of the work. Tom's younger brother (or rather half-brother) Sid was already through with his part of the work (picking up chips), for he was a quiet boy, and had no adventurous, trouble-some ways.

While Tom was eating his supper, and stealing sugar as opportunity offered, Aunt Polly asked him questions that were full of guile, and very deep—for she wanted to trap him into damaging revealments. Like many other simple-hearted souls, it was her pet vanity to believe she was endowed with a talent for dark and mysterious diplomacy, and she loved to contemplate her most transparent devices as marvels of low cunning. Said she:

"Tom, it was middling warm in school, warn't it[15]?"

"Yes'm.[16]"

"Powerful warm, warn't it?"

"Yes'm."

"Didn't you want to go in a-swimming, Tom?"

A bit of a scare shot through Tom—a touch of uncomfortable suspicion. He searched Aunt Polly's face, but it told him nothing. So he said:

"No'm—well, not very much."

The old lady reached out her hand and felt Tom's shirt, and said:

"But you ain't too warm now, though." And it flattered her to reflect that she had discovered that the shirt was dry without anybody knowing that that was what she had in her mind. But in spite of her, Tom knew where the wind lay, now. So he forestalled what might be the next move:

"Some of us pumped on our heads—mine's damp yet. See?"

Aunt Polly was vexed to think she had overlooked that bit of circumstantial evidence, and missed a trick. Then she had a new inspiration:

"Tom, you didn't have to undo your shirt collar where I sewed it, to pump on your head, did you? Unbutton your jacket!"

The trouble vanished out of Tom's face. He opened his jacket. His shirt collar was securely sewed.

"Bother! Well, go 'long with you. I'd made sure you'd played hookey and been a-swimming. But I forgive ye, Tom. I reckon you're a kind of a singed cat, as the saying is—better'n you look[17]. This time."

She was half sorry her sagacity had miscarried, and half glad that Tom had stumbled into obedient conduct for once.

But Sidney said:

"Well, now, if I didn't think you sewed his collar with white thread, but it's black."

"Why, I did sew it with white! Tom!"

But Tom did not wait for the rest. As he went out at the door he said:

"Siddy, I'll lick you for that."

In a safe place Tom examined two large needles which were thrust into the lapels[18] of his jacket, and had thread bound about them—one needle carried white thread and the other black. He said:

"She'd never noticed if it hadn't been for Sid. Confound it! sometimes she sews it with white, and sometimes she sews it with black. I wish to gee-miny[19] she'd stick to one or t'other—I can't keep the run of 'em[20]. But I bet you I'll lam Sid for that. I'll learn him!"

He was not the Model Boy of the village. He knew the model boy very well though—and loathed him.

Within two minutes, or even less, he had forgotten all his troubles. Not because his troubles were one whit less heavy and bitter to him than a man's are to a man, but because a new and powerful interest bore them down and drove them out of his mind for the time—just as men's misfortunes are forgotten in the excitement of new enterprises. This new interest was a valued novelty in whistling, which he had just acquired from a negro, and he was suffering to practise it undisturbed. It consisted in a peculiar bird-like turn, a sort of liquid warble[21], produced by touching the tongue to the roof of the mouth at short intervals in the midst of the music—the reader probably remembers how to do it, if he has ever been a boy. Diligence and attention soon gave him the knack[22] of it, and he strode down the street with his mouth full of harmony and his soul full of gratitude. He felt much as an astronomer feels who has discovered a new planet—no doubt, as far as strong, deep, unalloyed pleasure is concerned, the advantage was with the boy, not the astronomer.

The summer evenings were long. It was not dark, yet. Presently Tom checked his whistle. A stranger was before him—a boy a shade larger than himself. A new-comer of any age or either sex was an impressive curiosity in the poor little shabby village of St. Petersburg. This boy was well dressed, too—well dressed on a week-day. This was simply astounding. His cap was a dainty[23] thing, his close-buttoned blue cloth roundabout was new and natty[24], and so were his pantaloons[25]. He had shoes on—and it was only Friday. He even wore a necktie, a bright bit of ribbon. He had a citified air about him that ate into Tom's vitals. The more Tom stared at the splendid marvel, the higher he turned up his nose at his finery and the shabbier and shabbier his own outfit seemed to him to grow. Neither boy spoke. If one moved, the other moved—but only sidewise, in a circle; they kept face to face and eye to eye all the time. Finally Tom said:

"I can lick you!"

"I'd like to see you try it."

"Well, I can do it."

"No you can't, either."

"Yes I can."

"No you can't."

"I can."

"You can't."

"Can!"

"Can't!"

An uncomfortable pause. Then Tom said:

"What's your name?"

"'Tisn't[26] any of your business, maybe."

"Well I 'low[27] I'll make it my business."

"Well why don't you?"

"If you say much, I will."

"Much—much—much. There now."

"Oh, you think you're mighty smart, don't you? I could lick you with one hand tied behind me, if I wanted to."

"Well why don't you do it? You say you can do it."

"Well I will, if you fool with me."

"Oh yes—I've seen whole families in the same fix."

"Smarty! You think you're some, now, don't you? Oh, what a hat!"

"You can lump that hat if you don't like it. I dare you to knock it off—and anybody that'll take a dare will suck eggs[28]."

"You're a liar!"

"You're another."

"You're a fighting liar and dasn't[29] take it up."

"Aw—take a walk!"

"Say—if you give me much more of your sass I'll take and bounce a rock off'n your head."

"Oh, of course you will."

"Well I will."

"Well why don't you do it then? What do you keep saying you will for? Why don't you do it? It's because you're afraid."

"I ain't afraid."

"You are."

"I ain't."

"You are."

注释（Notes）

1. stove-lids：炉盖,但是经常被用来比喻"眼镜"。

2. resurrect：找出。

3. jimpson weeds：曼陀罗草。

4. Ain't：可被用来替代 am not、aren't、isn't、haven't 和 hasn't。许多人认为该用法不规范,这也突出了马克·吐温的口语书写特点。

5. Can't learn an old dog new tricks：老狗学不了新把戏,即老年人很难适应新事物。

6. get my dander up：生气,发脾气。

7. hit him a lick：打一顿,揍一顿。

8. Spare the rod and spile the child：不打不成器。

9. full of Old Scratch：满是鬼主意；laws-a-me：天啊。

10. let off：宽恕。

11. man that is born...full of trouble：出自《圣经》,人为妇人所生,时日不多却充满苦难。

12. play hookey：逃学。
13. obleeged：(obliged 的方言)，有责任的，必须的。
14. kindlings：引火柴。
15. warn't it：wasn't it，是吗。
16. Yes'm：Yes ma'am，是的姨妈。
17. a singed cat...better'n you look：一只烧焦的猫，并不像表面看起来那么坏。
18. lapel：翻领。
19. gee-miny：语气词，天啊。
20. t'other：the other；of 'em：of them
21. warble：颤音。
22. knack：诀窍。
23. dainty：讲究的，精致的。
24. natty：整洁时髦的。
25. pantaloons：马裤。
26. 'Tisn't：It isn't，这不是。
27. I'low：I know，我知道。
28. I dare you...will suck eggs：我谅你也不敢——谁敢的话，我就揍扁谁。
29. dasn't：doesn't

主题探究（Themes）

（扫码阅读）

融通中西（Integrating Chinese Literature with Western Literature）

美国现实主义作家中，马克·吐温等为代表的地方色彩主义作家因注重本土特色而出名，他们对乡土生活的细致描写和怀旧情绪成为突出特征。在我国，鲁迅被认为是中国乡土文学的鼻祖，他以浙江绍兴农村生活为题材创作了大量优秀作品。与鲁迅同时代的沈从文和萧红等的作品也都带有浓厚的乡土和地域色彩，恰如明丽的风俗画。当代作家中，从莫言、贾平凹、陈忠实到王安忆和叶兆言等人的作品中，都能读出浓郁的乡土味和地方文化，表现出巨大的风土人情描写能力和区域文化自觉。

问题讨论 (Questions for Discussion)

1. Who is the narrator, can she or he read minds, and, more importantly, can we trust her or him?

2. How does Injun Joe' race the fact that he is part Native American, affect the story as a whole? How does Injun Joe think about his racial identity?

3. Tom Sawyer lives with Aunt Polly; he is the son of her deceased sister. Why does Twain choose to place him in this family situation?

4. Is *The Adventures of Tom Sawyer* simply a comical retelling of Twain's youth in Missouri, or is it something more? What does it say about American culture in the middle of the nineteenth century?

5. How does Twain's presence, as narrator, influence our perceptions of Tom's actions, of his age, and his growth as a character?

(请扫码观看视频 *The Adventures of Tom Sawyer*)

A Pair of Stockings

作品简介 (Introduction to the Work)

"A Pair of Stockings" by Kate Chopin is a short story originally published in the September 1897 issue of *Vogue*. The main character is Mrs. Sommers, who receives a windfall of money and chooses not to spend it on her children, but rather on herself. The windfall itself is fifteen dollars, a sum equivalent to over 400 dollars in 2016. Initially, she plans to buy her children new clothes with the money. Before she can buy clothing for her children, she comes upon a pair of silk stockings. They are smooth enough to entice her to forego buying children's clothes and purchase the stockings instead. Yet, she doesn't stop there. Mrs. Sommers also buys herself boots, gloves, magazines, an expensive lunch, chocolates, and theater tickets. After the show ends, she makes her way home on a cable car, wishing that it would never stop. For once it does, not only must she return to more modest means, but she must see her children, whom she denied new clothes in favor of spoiling herself for an afternoon. The story was well received, as were Chopin's other short stories (many of which were published in *Vogue*). The stockings represent consumerism and the temporary joy found in the self-satisfying act of pursuing enjoyment.

作品选文 (Selected Reading)

A Pair of Silk Stockings

Little Mrs. Sommers one day found herself the unexpected possessor of fifteen dollars. It seemed to her a very large amount of money, and the way in which it stuffed and bulged her worn old porte-monnaie[1] gave her a feeling of importance such as she had not enjoyed for years.

The question of investment was one that occupied her greatly. For a day or two she walked about apparently in a dreamy state, but really absorbed in speculation and calculation. She did not wish to act hastily, to do anything she might afterward regret. But it was during the still hours of the night when she lay awake revolving plans in her mind that she seemed to see her way clearly toward a proper and judicious use of the money.

A dollar or two should be added to the price usually paid for Janie's shoes, which would insure their lasting an appreciable time longer than they usually did. She would buy so and so many yards of percale[2] for new shirt waists for the boys and Janie and Mag. She had intended to make the old ones do by skilful patching. Mag should have another gown. She had seen some beautiful patterns, veritable bargains in the shop windows. And still there would be left enough for new stockings—two pairs apiece—and what darning that would save for a while! She would get caps for the boys and sailor-hats[3] for the girls. The vision of her little brood looking fresh and dainty and new for once in their lives excited her and made her restless and wakeful with anticipation.

The neighbors sometimes talked of certain "better days" that little Mrs. Sommers had known before she had ever thought of being Mrs. Sommers. She herself indulged in no such morbid[4] retrospection. She had no time—no second of time to devote to the past. The needs of the present absorbed her every faculty. A vision of the future like some dim, gaunt monster sometimes appalled her, but luckily to-morrow never comes.

Mrs. Sommers was one who knew the value of bargains; who could stand for hours making her way inch by inch toward the desired object that was selling below cost. She could elbow her way[5] if need be; she had learned to clutch a piece of goods and hold it and stick to it with persistence and determination till her turn came to be served, no matter when it came.

But that day she was a little faint and tired. She had swallowed a light luncheon— no! when she came to think of it, between getting the children fed and the place righted, and preparing herself for the shopping bout, she had actually forgotten to eat any luncheon at all!

She sat herself upon a revolving stool before a counter that was comparatively deserted, trying to gather strength and courage to charge through an eager multitude that was besieging[6] breastworks of shirting and figured lawn. An all-gone limp feeling had come over her and she rested her hand aimlessly upon the counter. She wore no gloves. By degrees she grew aware that her hand had encountered something very soothing, very pleasant to touch. She looked down to see that her hand lay upon a pile of silk stockings. A placard[7] near by announced that they had been reduced in price from two dollars and fifty cents to one dollar and ninety-eight cents; and a young girl who stood behind the counter asked her if she wished to examine their line of silk hosiery[8]. She smiled, just as if she had been asked to inspect a tiara[9] of diamonds with the ultimate view of purchasing it. But she went on feeling the soft, sheeny[10] luxurious things—with both hands now, holding them up to see them glisten, and to feel them glide serpent-like through her fingers.

Two hectic blotches came suddenly into her pale cheeks. She looked up at the girl. "Do you think there are any eights-and-a-half among these?"

There were any number of eights-and-a-half. In fact, there were more of that size than any other. Here was a light-blue pair; there were some lavender, some all black and various shades of tan and gray. Mrs. Sommers selected a black pair and looked at them very long and closely. She pretended to be examining their texture, which the clerk assured her was excellent.

"A dollar and ninety-eight cents," she mused aloud. "Well, I'll take this pair." She handed the girl a five-dollar bill and waited for her change and for her parcel. What a very small parcel it was! It seemed lost in the depths of her shabby old shopping-bag.

Mrs. Sommers after that did not move in the direction of the bargain counter. She took the elevator, which carried her to an upper floor into the region of the ladies' waiting-rooms. Here, in a retired corner, she exchanged her cotton stockings for the new silk ones which she had just bought. She was not going through any acute mental process or reasoning with herself, nor was she striving to explain to her satisfaction the motive of her action. She was not thinking at all. She seemed for the time to be taking a rest from that laborious and fatiguing function and to have abandoned herself to some mechanical impulse that directed her actions and freed her of responsibility.

How good was the touch of the raw silk to her flesh! She felt like lying back in the cushioned[11] chair and reveling for a while in the luxury of it. She did for a little while. Then she replaced her shoes, rolled the cotton stockings together and thrust them into her bag. After doing this she crossed straight over to the shoe department and took her seat to be fitted.

She was fastidious[12]. The clerk could not make her out; he could not reconcile her shoes with her stockings, and she was not too easily pleased. She held back her skirts and turned her feet one way and her head another way as she glanced down at the polished, pointed-tipped[13] boots. Her foot and ankle looked very pretty. She could not realize that they belonged to her and were a part of herself. She wanted an excellent and stylish fit, she told the young fellow who served her, and she did not mind the difference of a dollar or two more in the price so long as she got what she desired.

It was a long time since Mrs. Sommers had been fitted with gloves. On rare occasions when she had bought a pair they were always "bargains," so cheap that it would have been preposterous[14] and unreasonable to have expected them to be fitted to the hand.

Now she rested her elbow on the cushion of the glove counter, and a pretty, pleasant young creature, delicate and deft[15] of touch, drew a long-wristed "kid" over Mrs. Sommers' hand. She smoothed it down over the wrist and buttoned it neatly, and both lost themselves for a second or two in admiring contemplation of the little symmetrical gloved hand. But there were other places where money might be spent.

There were books and magazines piled up in the window of a stall a few paces down the street. Mrs. Sommers bought two high-priced magazines such as she had been accustomed to read in the days when she had been accustomed to other pleasant things. She carried them without wrapping. As well as she could she lifted her skirts at the crossings. Her stockings and boots and well fitting gloves had worked marvels in her bearing—had given her a feeling of assurance, a sense of belonging to the well-dressed multitude.

She was very hungry. Another time she would have stilled the cravings for food until reaching her own home, where she would have brewed herself a cup of tea and taken a snack of anything that was available. But the impulse that was guiding her would not suffer her to entertain any such thought.

There was a restaurant at the corner. She had never entered its doors; from the outside she had sometimes caught glimpses of spotless damask[16] and shining crystal, and soft-stepping waiters serving people of fashion.

When she entered her appearance created no surprise, no consternation[17], as she had half feared it might. She seated herself at a small table alone, and an attentive waiter at once approached to take her order. She did not want a profusion; she craved a nice and tasty bite—a half dozen blue-points, a plump chop with cress, a something sweet—a crème-frappée, for instance; a glass of Rhine wine[18], and after all a small cup of black coffee.

While waiting to be served she removed her gloves very leisurely and laid them beside her. Then she picked up a magazine and glanced through it, cutting the pages with a blunt edge of her knife. It was all very agreeable. The damask was even more spotless than it had seemed through the window, and the crystal more sparkling. There were quiet ladies and gentlemen, who did not notice her, lunching at the small tables like her own. A soft, pleasing strain of music could be heard, and a gentle breeze was blowing through the window. She tasted a bite, and she read a word or two, and she sipped the amber wine and wiggled her toes in the silk stockings. The price of it made no difference. She counted the money out to the waiter and left an extra coin on his tray, whereupon he bowed before her as before a princess of royal blood.

There was still money in her purse, and her next temptation presented itself in the shape of a matinée[19] poster.

It was a little later when she entered the theatre, the play had begun and the house seemed to her to be packed. But there were vacant seats here and there, and into one of them she was ushered, between brilliantly dressed women who had gone there to kill time and eat candy and display their gaudy[20] attire. There were many others who were there solely for the play and acting. It is safe to say there was no one present who bore quite the attitude which Mrs. Sommers did to her surroundings. She gathered in the whole—stage and players and people in one wide impression, and absorbed it and enjoyed it. She laughed at the comedy and wept—she and the gaudy woman next to her wept over the tragedy. And they talked a little together over it. And the gaudy woman wiped her eyes and sniffled on a tiny square of filmy[21], perfumed lace and passed little Mrs. Sommers her box of candy.

The play was over, the music ceased, the crowd filed out. It was like a dream ended.

People scattered in all directions. Mrs. Sommers went to the corner and waited for the cable car.

A man with keen eyes, who sat opposite to her, seemed to like the study of her small, pale face. It puzzled him to decipher[22] what he saw there. In truth, he saw nothing—unless he were wizard enough to detect a poignant[23] wish, a powerful longing that the cable car would never stop anywhere, but go on and on with her forever.

注释（Notes）

1. bulge: swell or protrude outward, 膨胀, 充满; porte-monnaie: 钱包。
2. percale: 高级密织棉布。
3. sailor-hats: 水手帽。
4. morbid: 病态的。

5. elbow her way：用胳膊肘挤来挤去为自己开道，挤着向前走。

6. besiege：包围。

7. placard：海报，标语牌，布告。

8. hosiery：（尤指商店里出售的）袜类。

9. tiara：女式冕状头饰。

10. sheeny：有光泽的，光亮的。

11. cushioned：有软垫的。

12. fastidious：挑剔的。

13. pointed-tipped：尖头的。

14. preposterous：荒谬的，可笑的。

15. deft：灵巧的。

16. damask：织锦，锦缎。

17. consternation：恐慌。

18. blue-points：牡蛎；a plump chop with cress：一份水芹牛排；crème-frappée：冰激凌；Rhine wine：莱茵白葡萄酒。

19. matinée：（电影或戏剧的）下午场。

20. gaudy：华丽的。

21. filmy：薄的。

22. decipher：辨认。

23. poignant：producing a sharp feeling of sadness or pity，painful and deeply felt，令人伤心的，辛酸的。

主题探究（Themes）

（扫码阅读）

价值引领（Value Guidance）

文学的世界是一个广阔的精神空间，如何寻求女性的独立？如何实现女性的个人价值？女性又如何在自我追求和家庭责任间达到一种平衡？诸如此类的问题，文学能够触及，也许无法提供鲜明的答案，但有一点是确定的，那就是可以促使读者去思考、去反思。回到自己的内心，反思在建立各种关系的同时，是否逐渐丧失自我的主体性。

肖邦通过一系列的女性形象,描写了19世纪夫权主义统治下中产阶级妇女的生活。她们受到男性社会的压抑,又在压抑中觉醒,在觉醒中反叛。肖邦的新女性对文化价值观念的反叛与抗争是积极勇敢的,是震撼人心的。《觉醒》中的艾德娜是一个向社会传统势力、向19世纪的女性生活模式挑战的"社会叛逆",是一个敢于大胆表达女性情欲的"新女性"。她极大地挑战了读者在文化、道德与伦理等方面的观念,否定了女性传统的生存价值观念和女性的理想范式:家里的天使,男性的奉献者,自我的牺牲者。她所追求的女性自我意识是对女性自我的肯定,也是对女性本质的重新界定,都是对女性的历史命运与历史界定的否定,具有很强的颠覆性。①

艾德娜与托尔斯泰笔下的安娜·卡列尼娜有颇多相似之处。感情出位后的她们很难再重新回到原来的生活轨道,追求自我独立人格的尝试只能是短暂的,她们很难摆脱原有家庭和孩子的牵绊,而且触犯道德规范所带来的社会性死亡使其失去存在的空间。她们最终不得不承认自己争取女性自我意识的反抗是微不足道和孤立无援的。正如《觉醒》中的赖斯小姐曾提醒的"翱翔于传统与偏见上的鸟必须具有强壮的翅膀"。她们虽具有"勇敢的精神",但她们并没有"强壮的翅膀"飞得更远、更自由。她们注定只能"像一只断了羽翼的海鸟在空中扑打旋转……无力地画着圈子下坠"。艾德娜和卡列尼娜早逝的命运暗示了追求女性主体性的旅程是艰难甚至是危险的。叛逆的她们不是胜利者,她们的几个层面的觉醒只能是一个"觉"而未"醒"的历程,具有明显的不彻底性。②

问题讨论(Questions for Discussion)

1. What did neighbors say about Mrs. Sommers, according to the fourth paragraph? Why didn't Mrs. Sommers indulge in such "morbid retrospection"?

2. Describe Mrs. Sommers' life as a wife and mother. Does her life seem to have been different before she married? If so, how was it different?

3. How would you explain the motivation for Mrs. Sommers' shopping spree in "A Pair of Silk Stockings"?

4. Why is this day special for Mrs. Sommers?

5. Why did she long for the cable car to "go on and on with her forever"? Why was this wish called "poignant"?

6. Do you consider Mrs. Sommers justified in thinking of her own needs and desires? Why or why not?

---

① 刘红卫."觉"而未"醒":解读小说《觉醒》中的"觉醒"[J]. 武汉大学学报(人文科学版),2007:358-362.
② 刘红卫."觉"而未"醒":解读小说《觉醒》中的"觉醒"[J]. 武汉大学学报(人文科学版),2007:358-362.

Unit 24
American Naturalism

Stephen Crane: *The Red Badge of Courage*
Theodore Dreiser: *Sister Carrie*
▽

作者简介 (Introduction to the Authors)

Stephen Crane (1871—1900) was an American novelist, poet, and journalist who is now considered to be one of the most important writers of American realism. Born in Newark, New Jersey, Crane is the youngest child in his family. His father died when he was nine years old. In 1885, Crane entered the Pennington Seminary and Female Collegiate Institute to study. He began his higher education in 1888 at Claverack College and Hudson River Institute, a military school where he nurtured his interest in Civil War studies and military training. In 1891, Crane moved to his brother Edmund's home in New Jersey. In order to create, he often travelled to New York City and worked as a reporter. Crane also paid special attention to the situation of Bowery and the slums in Manhattan's rich neighborhoods. In 1893, he wrote the novel *Maggie: A Girl of the Streets*, which was based on the life in the slums of New York. In 1895, Crane published another novel, *The Red Badge of Courage*, which won him a great reputation in Europe and the United States. In 1896, Crane encountered a storm on his way to Cuba for an interview. Based on this experience, he wrote the short story *The Open Boat* (1898), which describes how four people struggle and fight in the vast sea. In 1898, he went to Cuba again to report the Spanish American War. Because of the deterioration of his marriage, Crane left the United States to settle in Britain and became good friends with Joseph Conrad and James Joyce. He died of lung disease in Germany in 1900. On the whole, Crane, despite his tragically short life and small overall output, is one of the most important American writers in the late 19th century.

Theodore Herman Albert Dreiser (1871—1945), a representative writer of American realism, is known as the three giants of American modern novels together with Hemingway and Faulkner. His famous works include *Sister Carrie*, *Jenny Gerhardt*, *American Tragedy* and etc. Theodore Dreiser was born in Terre Haute, Indiana. He grew up in a poor Catholic family with nine siblings and a father constantly underemployed. The poverty of his family made Dreiser realize the difficulty of survival when he was very young. Despite his hard work, Dreiser failed to finish high school. In 1892, Dreiser entered the press to start his career as a journalist and worked in several newspapers. In 1898, he married Sarah Osborne White, a teacher from St. Louis, but their marriage was not happy. In 1895, Dreiser moved to New York to write and edit magazines. Encouraged by his friends, Dreiser began to write his first novel, which was officially published in 1900. *The Financier* and *Giant*, the first two of Dreiser's *Trilogy of Desire* published in 1912 and 1914, respectively, had a great impact on the American society at that time and established Dreiser's position in the American literary world. In 1915, Dreiser published *The Genius*, which was his most satisfactory novel. In 1925, he published the novel *American Tragedy* with the theme of real criminal cases, which immediately stirred the United States. This work marks the new achievement of Dreiser's realistic creation, which makes him famous all over the world. In 1945, at the age of 74, Dreiser joined the Communist Party of America headed by Foster, and died the same year. All in all, Dreiser deserve to be called a pioneer of modern American novels and a great naturalist writer.

The Red Badge of Courage

作品简介 (Introduction to the Work)

Stephen Crane, a twenty-year old who had never been to war, wrote *The Red Badge of Courage* in 1895. Regardless, the book is considered one of the most accurate portrayals of the physical and psychological effects of intense battle. This book covers just two days of a heated battle between the Union and Confederate soldiers during the American Civil War. The novel traces the emotional trajectory of one young recruit, Henry, as he strains to cope with all of the feelings and behaviors of which he is guilty. Stephen Crane is a master of creating vastly realistic scenes of combat and death, and of the strange and varied emotions that accompany these experiences. Before *The Red Badge of Courage*, war novels were generally written from a vantage point in the sky, dealing with issues like tactical movements of large groups of men rather than getting into the psyche of one particular soldier. By doing this, Crane rejected the grandeur and poetry of war and portrayed instead its harsh reality. In Chapter 5, Henry encounters his first war action and spends the beginning of Chapter 6 reflecting on his accomplishments. He didn't run away, and because of this feat, Henry is beginning to feel a sense of pride that overtakes him. Henry and his fellow soldiers are now unified from their victory and bask in the glory together. But just as Henry begins to feel he is a Greek hero, gunfire starts up again and the opposing forces charge the field. The men groan dejectedly and prepare to repel the attack. This time, Henry does not feel as though he is part of a machine. He thinks that the enemy soldiers must be awe-inspiring men to have such persistence, and he panics. One by one, soldiers from Henry's regiment begin to jump up and flee from the line, and after a moment, Henry too runs away.

作品选文 (Selected Reading)

The Red Badge of Courage
(Excerpt)
Chapter 6

The youth awakened slowly. He came gradually back to a position from which he could regard himself. For moments he had been scrutinizing his person in a dazed way as if he had never before seen himself. Then he picked up his cap from the ground. He wriggled in his jacket to make a more comfortable fit, and kneeling relaced[1] his shoe. He thoughtfully mopped his reeking features.

So it was all over at last! The supreme trial had been passed. The red, formidable[2] difficulties of war had been vanquished.

He went into an ecstasy[3] of self-satisfaction. He had the most delightful sensations of his life. Standing as if apart from himself, he viewed that last scene. He perceived that the man who had fought thus was magnificent.

He felt that he was a fine fellow. He saw himself even with those ideals which he had considered as far beyond him. He smiled in deep gratification.

Upon his fellows he beamed[4] tenderness and good will. "Gee! ain't it hot, hey?" he said affably to a man who was polishing his streaming face with his coat sleeves.

"You bet!" said the other, grinning sociably. "I never seen sech dumb hotness." He sprawled out luxuriously on the ground. "Gee, yes! An' I hope we don't have no more fightin' till a week from Monday."[5]

There were some handshakings and deep speeches with men whose features were familiar, but with whom the youth now felt the bonds of tied hearts. He helped a cursing comrade[6] to bind up a wound of the shin[7].

But, of a sudden, cries of amazement broke out along the ranks of the new regiment[8]. "Here they come ag'in! Here they come ag'in!" The man who had sprawled upon the ground started up and said, "Gosh!"

The youth turned quick eyes upon the field. He discerned forms begin to swell in masses out of a distant wood. He again saw the tilted flag speeding forward.

The shells, which had ceased to trouble the regiment for a time, came swirling again, and exploded in the grass or among the leaves of the trees. They looked to be strange war flowers bursting into fierce bloom.

The men groaned. The luster faded from their eyes. Their smudged countenances now expressed a profound dejection[9]. They moved their stiffened bodies slowly, and watched in sullen mood the frantic approach of the enemy. The slaves toiling in the temple of this god began to feel rebellion at his harsh tasks.

They fretted and complained each to each. "Oh, say, this is too much of a good thing! Why can't somebody send us supports?"

"We ain't never goin' to stand this second banging. I didn't come here to fight the hull damn' rebel army."

There was one who raised a doleful[10] cry. "I wish Bill Smithers had trod on my hand, insteader me treddin' on his'n." The sore joints of the regiment creaked as it painfully floundered into position to repulse.

The youth stared. Surely, he thought, this impossible thing was not about to happen. He waited as if he expected the enemy to suddenly stop, apologize, and retire bowing. It was all a mistake.

But the firing began somewhere on the regimental line and ripped along in both directions. The level sheets of flame developed great clouds of smoke that tumbled and tossed in the mild wind near the ground for a moment, and then rolled through the ranks as through a gate. The clouds were tinged an earthlike yellow in the sunrays and in the shadow were a sorry blue. The flag was sometimes eaten and lost in this mass of vapor, but more often it projected, sun-touched, resplendent[11].

Into the youth's eyes there came a look that one can see in the orbs of a jaded horse. His neck was quivering with nervous weakness and the muscles of his arms felt numb and bloodless. His hands, too, seemed large and awkward as if he was wearing invisible mittens[12]. And there was a great uncertainty about his knee joints.

The words that comrades had uttered previous to the firing began to recur to him. "Oh, say, this is too much of a good thing! What do they take us for—why don't they send supports? I didn't come here to fight the hull damned rebel army."

He began to exaggerate the endurance, the skill, and the valor[13] of those who were coming. Himself reeling from exhaustion, he was astonished beyond measure at such persistency. They must be machines of steel. It was very gloomy struggling against such affairs, wound up perhaps to fight until sundown.

He slowly lifted his rifle and catching a glimpse of the thick spread field he blazed at a cantering cluster. He stopped then and began to peer as best as he could through the smoke. He caught changing views of the ground covered with men who were all running like pursued imps[14], and yelling.

To the youth it was an onslaught[15] of redoubtable dragons. He became like the man who lost his legs at the approach of the red and green monster. He waited in a sort of a horrified, listening attitude. He seemed to shut his eyes and wait to be gobbled.

A man near him who up to this time had been working feverishly at his rifle suddenly stopped and ran with howls. A lad whose face had borne an expression of exalted courage, the majesty of he who dares give his life, was, at an instant, smitten abject[16]. He blanched[17] like one who has come to the edge of a cliff at midnight and is suddenly made aware. There was a revelation. He, too, threw down his gun and fled. There was no shame in his face. He ran like a rabbit.

Others began to scamper away[18] through the smoke. The youth turned his head, shaken from his trance[19] by this movement as if the regiment was leaving him behind. He saw the few fleeting forms.

He yelled then with fright and swung about. For a moment, in the great clamor, he was like a proverbial chicken. He lost the direction of safety. Destruction threatened him from all points.

Directly he began to speed toward the rear in great leaps. His rifle and cap were gone. His unbuttoned coat bulged in the wind. The flap of his cartridge box[20] bobbed wildly, and his canteen, by its slender cord, swung out behind. On his face was all the horror of those things which he imagined.

The lieutenant sprang forward bawling. The youth saw his features wrathfully red, and saw him make a dab with his sword. His one thought of the incident was that the lieutenant was a peculiar creature to feel interested in such matters upon this occasion.

He ran like a blind man. Two or three times he fell down. Once he knocked his shoulder so heavily against a tree that he went headlong[21].

Since he had turned his back upon the fight his fears had been wondrously magnified. Death about to thrust him between the shoulder blades was far more dreadful than death about to smite him between the eyes. When he thought of it later, he conceived the impression that it is better to view the appalling than to be merely within hearing. The noises of the battle were like stones; he believed himself liable to be crushed.

As he ran on he mingled with others. He dimly saw men on his right and on his left, and he heard footsteps behind him. He thought that all the regiment was fleeing, pursued by those ominous crashes.

In his flight the sound of these following footsteps gave him his one meager[22] relief. He felt vaguely that death must make a first choice of the men who were nearest; the initial morsels[23] for the dragons would be then those who were following him. So he displayed the zeal of an insane sprinter in his purpose to keep them in the rear. There was a race.

As he, leading, went across a little field, he found himself in a region of shells. They hurtled[24] over his head with long wild screams. As he listened he imagined them to have rows of cruel teeth that grinned at him. Once one lit before him and the livid[25] lightning of the explosion effectually barred the way in his chosen direction. He groveled on the ground and then springing up went careering off through some bushes.

He experienced a thrill of amazement when he came within view of a battery in action. The men there seemed to be in conventional moods, altogether unaware of the impending annihilation. The battery was disputing with a distant antagonist and the gunners were wrapped in admiration of their shooting. They were continually bending in coaxing postures over the guns. They seemed to be patting them on the back and encouraging them with words. The guns, stolid[26] and undaunted, spoke with dogged valor.

The precise gunners were coolly enthusiastic. They lifted their eyes every chance to the smoke-wreathed hillock[27] from whence the hostile battery addressed them. The youth pitied them as he ran. Methodical idiots! Machine-like fools! The refined joy of planting shells in the midst of the other battery's formation would appear a little thing when the infantry came swooping out of the woods.

The face of a youthful rider, who was jerking his frantic horse with an abandon of temper he might display in a placid barnyard[28], was impressed deeply upon his mind. He knew that he looked upon a man who would presently be dead.

Too, he felt a pity for the guns, standing, six good comrades, in a bold row.

He saw a brigade[29] going to the relief of its pestered fellows. He scrambled upon a wee hill and watched it sweeping finely, keeping formation in difficult places. The blue of the line was crusted with steel color, and the brilliant flags projected. Officers were shouting.

This sight also filled him with wonder. The brigade was hurrying briskly to be gulped into the infernal mouths of the war god. What manner of men were they, anyhow? Ah, it was some wondrous breed! Or else they didn't comprehend—the fools.

A furious order caused commotion in the artillery. An officer on a bounding horse made maniacal motions with his arms. The teams went swinging up from the rear, the guns were whirled about, and the battery scampered away. The cannon with their noses poked slantingly at the ground grunted and grumbled like stout men, brave but with objections to hurry.

The youth went on, moderating his pace since he had left the place of noises.

Later he came upon a general of division seated upon a horse that pricked its ears in an interested way at the battle. There was a great gleaming of yellow and patent leather about the saddle and bridle[30]. The quiet man astride looked mouse-colored upon such a splendid charger.

A jingling staff was galloping hither and thither. Sometimes the general was surrounded by horsemen and at other times he was quite alone. He looked to be much harassed. He had the appearance of a business man whose market is swinging up and down.

The youth went slinking around this spot. He went as near as he dared trying to overhear words. Perhaps the general, unable to comprehend chaos, might call upon him for information. And he could tell him. He knew all concerning it. Of a surety the force was in a fix, and any fool could see that if they did not retreat while they had opportunity—why—

He felt that he would like to thrash[31] the general, or at least approach and tell him in plain words exactly what he thought him to be. It was criminal to stay calmly in one spot and make no effort to stay destruction. He loitered[32] in a fever of eagerness for the division commander to apply to him.

As he warily moved about, he heard the general call out irritably: "Tompkins, go over an' see Taylor, an' tell him not t' be in such an all-fired hurry; tell him t' halt his brigade in th' edge of th' woods; tell him t' detach a reg'ment—say I think th' center'll break if we don't help it out some; tell him t' hurry up."

A slim youth on a fine chestnut horse caught these swift words from the mouth of his superior. He made his horse bound into a gallop[33] almost from a walk in his haste to go upon his mission. There was a cloud of dust.

A moment later the youth saw the general bounce excitedly in his saddle.

"Yes, by heavens, they have!" The officer leaned forward. His face was aflame with excitement. "Yes, by heavens, they've held'im! They've held'im!"

He began to blithely roar at his staff: "We'll wallop[34]'im now. We'll wallop'im now. We've got'em sure." He turned suddenly upon an aide: "Here—you—Jones—quick—ride after Tompkins—see Taylor—tell him t' go in—everlastingly—like blazes—anything."

As another officer sped his horse after the first messenger, the general beamed upon the earth like a sun. In his eyes was a desire to chant a paean[35]. He kept repeating, "They've held'em, by heavens!"

His excitement made his horse plunge, and he merrily kicked and swore at it. He held a little carnival of joy on horseback.

注释（Notes）

1. relace：再次系上。

2. formidable：可怕的。

3. ecstasy：狂喜。

4. beam：绽开笑容。

5. sech：such，这种；An' I：And I；fightin'：fighting。

6. comrade：伙伴，战友。

7. shin：胫骨。

8. regiment：(军队的)团。

9. dejection：沮丧。

10. doleful：悲伤的，哀伤的。

11. resplendent：华丽的，灿烂的。

12. mitten：连指手套。

13. valor：英勇，勇猛。

14. imp：恶魔。

15. onslaught：猛攻，攻击。

16. abject：糟糕透顶的。

17. blanch：脸色变苍白。

18. scamper away：奔逃。

19. trance：恍惚，出神。

20. cartridge box：子弹盒。

21. headlong：迅猛地。

22. meager：微薄的，短暂的。

23. morsel：食物。

24. hurtle：猛冲。

25. livid：暗紫色的。

26. stolid：冷漠的。

27. hillock：小山丘。

28. barnyard：谷仓前的空场地。

29. brigade：(军队的)旅。

30. saddle and bridle：马鞍和缰绳。

31. thrash：打。

32. loiter：徘徊。

33. gallop：(马)飞跑，疾驰；(人)骑马奔驰。

34. wallop：重击。

35. paean：颂歌。

主题探究（Themes）

（扫码阅读）

问题讨论（Questions for Discussion）

1. Which of Henry's actions reveals the most courage? The least?
2. Does Henry define courage differently than the other soldiers in the novel? Which one is "correct"?
3. How do we know what Crane thinks about war? Where are his opinions/feelings most evident?
4. Why is Jim Conklin's death so important to Henry and to the book as a whole?
5. What are Henry's mother's notions of "manhood?"
6. Which event changes Henry more than any other?
7. What are the key events in the course of Henry's transformation?
8. Is Henry's transformation a positive or negative one? Is he better off at the start or the end of the novel?

Sister Carrie

作品简介（Introduction to the Work）

Sister Carrie, first novel by Theodore Dreiser, published in 1900 but suppressed until 1912. *Sister Carrie* tells the story of a pretty small-town girl who comes to the big city filled with vague ambitions. She meets Charles Drouet, a traveling salesman, on the train. Drouet is attracted by her because of her simple beauty and unspoiled manner. After arriving in Chicago, she finds a job in a shoe factory, but the poor income and hard work oppress her imagination. She quits the job. Lonely and distressed, she becomes Drouet's mistress. Carrie meets George Hurstwood, a married manager. He becomes infatuated with Carrie's youth and beauty instantly and before long they start an affair. Carrie and Hurstwood's affair is uncovered, and they elope. They rent a flat in New York and live together for more than three years. In these three years, Carrie's dissatisfaction with Hurstwood increases and she finally walks out on him. Hurstwood joins the homeless, falls ill with pneumonia, becomes a beggar, and finally commits suicide. Carrie becomes a popular star of musical comedies. In her massive success, she finds that money and fame do not bring her happiness and that nothing will. In chapter I, Carrie decides to leave her life in Wisconsin behind and takes a train to Chicago to live with her sister and her sister's husband, Minnie and Steve Hanson. On the train, Carrie meets traveling salesman Charles Drouet. In the last chapter, we will see what things are going for Hurstwood, Carrie and Drouet as the book ends.

Sister Carrie
(Excerpt)
Chapter I The Magnet Attracting: A Waif Amid Forces

When Caroline Meeber boarded the afternoon train for Chicago, her total outfit consisted of a small trunk, a cheap imitation alligator-skin satchel[1], a small lunch in a paper box, and a yellow leather snap purse, containing her ticket, a scrap of paper with her sister's address in Van Buren Street, and four dollars in money. It was in August, 1889. She was eighteen years of age, bright, timid, and full of the illusions of ignorance and youth. Whatever touch of regret at parting characterised her thoughts, it was certainly not for advantages now being given up. A gush of tears at her mother's farewell kiss, a touch in her throat when the cars clacked by the flour mill where her father worked by the day, a pathetic sigh as the familiar green environs[2] of the village passed in review, and the threads which bound her so lightly to girlhood and home were irretrievably broken.

To be sure there was always the next station, where one might descend and return. There was the great city, bound more closely by these very trains which came up daily. Columbia City was not so very far away, even once she was in Chicago. What, pray, is a few hours—a few hundred miles? She looked at the little slip bearing her sister's address and wondered. She gazed at the green landscape, now passing in swift review, until her swifter thoughts replaced its impression with vague conjectures of what Chicago might be.

When a girl leaves her home at eighteen, she does one of two things. Either she falls into saving hands and becomes better, or she rapidly assumes the cosmopolitan standard of virtue and becomes worse. Of an intermediate balance, under the circumstances, there is no possibility. The city has its cunning wiles, no less than the infinitely smaller and more human tempter. There are large forces which allure with all the soulfulness of expression possible in the most cultured human. The gleam of a thousand lights is often as effective as the persuasive light in a wooing and fascinating eye. Half the undoing of the unsophisticated and natural mind is accomplished by forces wholly superhuman. A blare of sound, a roar of life, a vast array of human hives, appeal to the astonished senses in equivocal³ terms. Without a counsellor at hand to whisper cautious interpretations, what falsehoods may not these things breathe into the unguarded ear! Unrecognised for what they are, their beauty, like music, too often relaxes, then weakens, then perverts the simpler human perceptions.

Caroline, or Sister Carrie, as she had been half affectionately termed by the family, was possessed of a mind rudimentary in its power of observation and analysis. Self-interest with her was high, but not strong. It was, nevertheless, her guiding characteristic. Warm with the fancies of youth, pretty with the insipid⁴ prettiness of the formative period, possessed of a figure promising eventual shapeliness and an eye alight with certain native intelligence, she was a fair example of the middle American class—two generations removed from the emigrant. Books were beyond her interest—knowledge a sealed book. In the intuitive graces she was still crude. She could scarcely toss her head gracefully. Her hands were almost ineffectual. The feet, though small, were set flatly. And yet she was interested in her charms, quick to understand the keener pleasures of life, ambitious to gain in material things. A half-equipped little knight she was, venturing to reconnoitre⁵ the mysterious city and dreaming wild dreams of some vague, far-off supremacy, which should make it prey and subject—the proper penitent⁶, grovelling at a woman's slipper.

"That," said a voice in her ear, "is one of the prettiest little resorts in Wisconsin⁷."

"Is it?" she answered nervously.

The train was just pulling out of Waukesha⁸. For some time she had been conscious of a man behind. She felt him observing her mass of hair. He had been fidgeting⁹, and with natural intuition she felt a certain interest growing in that quarter. Her maidenly reserve, and a certain sense of what was conventional under the circumstances, called her to forestall and deny this familiarity, but the daring and magnetism of the individual, born of past experiences and triumphs, prevailed. She answered.

He leaned forward to put his elbows upon the back of her seat and proceeded to make himself volubly agreeable.

"Yes, that is a great resort for Chicago people. The hotels are swell. You are not familiar with this part of the country, are you?"

"Oh, yes, I am," answered Carrie. "That is, I live at Columbia City. I have never been through here, though."

"And so this is your first visit to Chicago," he observed.

All the time she was conscious of certain features out of the side of her eye. Flush, colourful cheeks, a light moustache, a grey fedora hat¹⁰. She now turned and looked upon him in full, the instincts of self-protection and coquetry¹¹ mingling confusedly in her brain.

"I didn't say that," she said.

"Oh," he answered, in a very pleasing way and with an assumed air of mistake, "I thought you did."

Here was a type of the travelling canvasser[12] for a manufacturing house—a class which at that time was first being dubbed by the slang of the day "drummers[13]." He came within the meaning of a still newer term, which had sprung into general use among Americans in 1880, and which concisely expressed the thought of one whose dress or manners are calculated to elicit the admiration of susceptible young women—a "masher[14]." His suit was of a striped and crossed pattern of brown wool, new at that time, but since become familiar as a business suit. The low crotch of the vest revealed a stiff shirt bosom of white and pink stripes. From his coat sleeves protruded a pair of linen cuffs of the same pattern, fastened with large, gold plate buttons, set with the common yellow agates known as "cat's-eyes."[15] His fingers bore several rings—one, the ever-enduring heavy seal—and from his vest dangled a neat gold watch chain, from which was suspended the secret insignia[16] of the Order of Elks[17]. The whole suit was rather tight-fitting, and was finished off with heavy-soled tan shoes, highly polished, and the grey fedora hat. He was, for the order of intellect represented, attractive, and whatever he had to recommend him, you may be sure was not lost upon Carrie, in this, her first glance.

Lest this order of individual should permanently pass, let me put down some of the most striking characteristics of his most successful manner and method. Good clothes, of course, were the first essential, the things without which he was nothing. A strong physical nature, actuated by a keen desire for the feminine, was the next. A mind free of any consideration of the problems or forces of the world and actuated not by greed, but an insatiable[18] love of variable pleasure. His method was always simple. Its principal element was daring, backed, of course, by an intense desire and admiration for the sex. Let him meet with a young woman once and he would approach her with an air of kindly familiarity, not unmixed with pleading, which would result in most cases in a tolerant acceptance. If she showed any tendency to coquetry he would be apt to straighten her tie, or if she "took up" with him at all, to call her by her first name. If he visited a department store it was to lounge familiarly over the counter and ask some leading questions. In more exclusive circles, on the train or in waiting stations, he went slower. If some seemingly vulnerable object appeared he was all attention—to pass the compliments of the day, to lead the way to the parlor car, carrying her grip, or, failing that, to take a seat next her with the hope of being able to court her to her destination. Pillows, books, a footstool[19], the shade lowered; all these figured in the things which he could do. If, when she reached her destination he did not alight and attend her baggage for her, it was because, in his own estimation, he had signally failed.

A woman should some day write the complete philosophy of clothes. No matter how young, it is one of the things she wholly comprehends. There is an indescribably faint line in the matter of man's apparel which somehow divides for her those who are worth glancing at and those who are not. Once an individual has passed this faint line on the way downward he will get no glance from her. There is another line at which the dress of a man will cause her to study her own. This line the individual at her elbow now marked for Carrie. She became conscious of an inequality. Her own plain blue dress, with its black cotton tape trimmings, now seemed to her shabby. She felt the worn state of her shoes.

"Let's see," he went on, "I know quite a number of people in your town. Morgenroth the clothier and Gibson the dry goods man."

"Oh, do you?" she interrupted, aroused by memories of longings their show windows had cost her.

At last he had a clew to her interest, and followed it deftly. In a few minutes he had come about into her seat. He talked of sales of clothing, his travels, Chicago, and the amusements of that city.

"If you are going there, you will enjoy it immensely. Have you relatives?"

"I am going to visit my sister," she explained.

"You want to see Lincoln Park," he said, "and Michigan Boulevard[20]. They are putting up great buildings there. It's a second New York—great. So much to see—theatres, crowds, fine houses—oh, you'll like that."

There was a little ache in her fancy of all he described. Her insignificance in the presence of so much magnificence faintly affected her. She realised that hers was not to be a round of pleasure, and yet there was something promising in all the material prospect he set forth. There was something satisfactory in the attention of this individual with his good clothes. She could not help smiling as he told her of some popular actress of whom she reminded him. She was not silly, and yet attention of this sort had its weight.

"You will be in Chicago some little time, won't you?" he observed at one turn of the now easy conversation.

"I don't know," said Carrie vaguely—a flash vision of the possibility of her not securing employment rising in her mind.

"Several weeks, anyhow," he said, looking steadily into her eyes.

There was much more passing now than the mere words indicated. He recognised the indescribable thing that made up for fascination and beauty in her. She realised that she was of interest to him from the one standpoint which a woman both delights in and fears. Her manner was simple, though for the very reason that she had not yet learned the many little affectations with which women conceal their true feelings. Some things she did appeared bold. A clever companion—had she ever had one—would have warned her never to look a man in the eyes so steadily.

"Why do you ask?" she said.

"Well, I'm going to be there several weeks. I'm going to study stock at our place and get new samples. I might show you'round."

"I don't know whether you can or not. I mean I don't know whether I can. I shall be living with my sister, and—"

"Well, if she minds, we'll fix that." He took out his pencil and a little pocket notebook as if it were all settled. "What is your address there?"

She fumbled[21] her purse which contained the address slip.

He reached down in his hip pocket and took out a fat purse. It was filled with slips of paper, some mileage books[22], a roll of greenbacks[23]. It impressed her deeply. Such a purse had never been carried by any one attentive to her. Indeed, an experienced traveller, a brisk man of the world, had never come within such close range before. The purse, the shiny tan shoes, the smart new suit, and the air with which he did things, built up for her a dim world of fortune, of which he was the centre. It disposed her pleasantly toward all he might do.

He took out a neat business card, on which was engraved Bartlett, Caryoe & Company, and down in the left-hand corner, Chas. H. Drouet.

"That's me," he said, putting the card in her hand and touching his name. "It's pronounced Drew-eh. Our family was French, on my father's side."

She looked at it while he put up his purse. Then he got out a letter from a bunch in his coat pocket. "This is the house I travel for," he went on, pointing to a picture on it, "corner of State and Lake." There was pride in his voice. He felt that it was something to be connected with such a place, and he made her feel that way.

"What is your address?" he began again, fixing his pencil to write.

She looked at his hand.

"Carrie Meeber," she said slowly. "Three hundred and fifty-four West Van Buren Street, care S. C. Hanson."

He wrote it carefully down and got out the purse again. "You'll be at home if I come around Monday night?" he said.

"I think so," she answered.

How true it is that words are but the vague shadows of the volumes we mean. Little audible links, they are, chaining together great inaudible feelings and purposes. Here were these two, bandying little phrases, drawing purses, looking at cards, and both unconscious of how inarticulate all their real feelings were. Neither was wise enough to be sure of the working of the mind of the other. He could not tell how his luring succeeded. She could not realise that she was drifting, until he secured her address. Now she felt that she had yielded something—he, that he had gained a victory. Already they felt that they were somehow associated. Already he took control in directing the conversation. His words were easy. Her manner was relaxed.

They were nearing Chicago. Signs were everywhere numerous. Trains flashed by them. Across wide stretches of flat, open prairie they could see lines of telegraph poles stalking across the fields toward the great city. Far away were indications of suburban towns, some big smokestacks[24] towering high in the air.

Frequently there were two-story frame houses standing out in the open fields, without fence or trees, lone outposts of the approaching army of homes.

To the child, the genius with imagination, or the wholly untravelled, the approach to a great city for the first time is a wonderful thing. Particularly if it be evening—that mystic period between the glare and gloom of the world when life is changing from one sphere or condition to another. Ah, the promise of the night. What does it not hold for the weary! What old illusion of hope is not here forever repeated! Says the soul of the toiler to itself, "I shall soon be free. I shall be in the ways and the hosts of the merry. The streets, the lamps, the lighted chamber set for dining, are for me. The theatre, the halls, the parties, the ways of rest and the paths of song—these are mine in the night." Though all humanity be still enclosed in the shops, the thrill runs abroad. It is in the air. The dullest feel something which they may not always express or describe. It is the lifting of the burden of toil.

Sister Carrie gazed out of the window. Her companion, affected by her wonder, so contagious are all things, felt anew some interest in the city and pointed out its marvels.

"This is Northwest Chicago," said Drouet. "This is the Chicago River," and he pointed to a little muddy creek, crowded with the huge masted wanderers from far-off waters nosing the black-posted banks. With a puff, a clang, and a clatter of rails it was gone. "Chicago is getting to be a great town," he went on. "It's a wonder. You'll find lots to see here."

She did not hear this very well. Her heart was troubled by a kind of terror. The fact that she was alone, away from home, rushing into a great sea of life and endeavour, began to tell. She could not help but feel a little choked for breath—a little sick as her heart beat so fast. She half closed her eyes and tried to think it was nothing, that Columbia City was only a little way off.

"Chicago! Chicago!" called the brakeman, slamming open the door. They were rushing into a more crowded yard, alive with the clatter and clang of life. She began to gather up her poor little grip[25] and closed her hand firmly upon her purse. Drouet arose, kicked his legs to straighten his trousers, and seized his clean yellow grip.

"I suppose your people will be here to meet you?" he said. "Let me carry your grip."

"Oh, no," she said. "I'd rather you wouldn't. I'd rather you wouldn't be with me when I meet my sister."

"All right," he said in all kindness. "I'll be near, though, in case she isn't here, and take you out there safely."

"You're so kind," said Carrie, feeling the goodness of such attention in her strange situation.

"Chicago!" called the brakeman, drawing the word out long. They were under a great shadowy train shed, where the lamps were already beginning to shine out, with passenger cars all about and the train moving at a snail's pace. The people in the car were all up and crowding about the door.

"Well, here we are," said Drouet, leading the way to the door. "Good-bye, till I see you Monday."

"Good-bye," she answered, taking his proffered hand.

"Remember, I'll be looking till you find your sister."

She smiled into his eyes.

They filed out, and he affected to take no notice of her. A lean-faced, rather commonplace woman recognised Carrie on the platform and hurried forward.

"Why, Sister Carrie!" she began, and there was embrace of welcome.

Carrie realised the change of affectional atmosphere at once. Amid all the maze, uproar, and novelty she felt cold reality taking her by the hand. No world of light and merriment[26]. No round of amusement. Her sister carried with her most of the grimness of shift and toil[27].

"Why, how are all the folks at home?" she began; "how is father, and mother?"

Carrie answered, but was looking away. Down the aisle, toward the gate leading into the waiting-room and the street, stood Drouet. He was looking back. When he saw that she saw him and was safe with her sister he turned to go, sending back the shadow of a smile. Only Carrie saw it. She felt something lost to her when he moved away. When he disappeared she felt his absence thoroughly. With her sister she was much alone, a lone figure in a tossing[28], thoughtless sea.

注释 (Notes)

1. alligator-skin satchel: 鳄鱼皮小背包。
2. environs: 周围。

3. equivocal：模棱两可的,含糊其辞的。

4. insipid：枯燥乏味的。

5. reconnoitre：侦查。

6. penitent：忏悔者。

7. Wisconsin：美国威斯康星州。

8. Waukesha：沃基肖。

9. fidgeting：坐立不安,动来动去。

10. fedora hat：软呢帽。

11. coquetry：撒娇。

12. canvasser：兜揽生意的人,游说者。

13. drummers：旅行推销员。

14. masher：小白脸。

15. yellow agates：黄色玛瑙;cat's-eyes：猫眼。

16. insignia：徽章。

17. the Order of Elks：麋鹿会。1868年于纽约市创立的一个以兴办慈善事业为主的组织,其内部徽章上有一只指着十一点的钟,这是会员们举杯怀念已去世的会员的时间。

18. insatiable：无法满足的,贪得无厌的。

19. footstool：脚凳。

20. Lincoln Park：林肯公园;Michigan Boulevard：密歇根大道。

21. fumble：笨拙地摸索。

22. mileage books：里程簿。

23. greenback：美钞。

24. smokestacks：高烟囱。

25. grip：旅行袋。

26. merriment：欢乐。

27. shift and toil：艰辛劳作。

28. tossing：翻滚的,颠簸的。

Chapter XL VII　The Way of the Beaten：a Harp in the Wind（扫码阅读）

主题探究（Themes）

（扫码阅读）

文化延展（Cultural Extension）/ 价值引领（Value Guidance）

美国自然主义文学出现在19世纪末,是工业化和各种社会文化因素相互作用的产物,习惯于农业文明的美国人面对新的工业文明产生了心理震荡。城市和消费主义作为美国工业化文化的代表元素成为自然主义文学关注的焦点。美国这个时期的工业化进程和转型阶段与我国当前的阶段很相似,对《嘉莉妹妹》的学习可以帮助我们正确面对当今的消费社会、金钱和欲望等,并认识到金钱不等于幸福。这个在20世纪初的美国人狂热追求美国梦的悲剧事实,揭示了本能驱使人们享乐却最终幻灭的主题,说明了在以金钱为中心的社会里不可能有真正的幸福。其实追求高标准、高品位的生活,是没有错的,但物质生活的追求不是目的,人应该过有意义的生活,有真正推心置腹的朋友,有一个和睦温馨的家,有自己的责任和义务,这样的生活,才是幸福的。

另外,关于这个时期被自然主义作家认同和推崇的社会达尔文主义,我们应该批判性地去看待。社会达尔文主义是19世纪出现的一种资产阶级社会学理论,因把达尔文的生物学理论运用于解释社会现象而得名。著名代表人物有英国社会学家斯宾塞和德国唯心主义哲学家朗格等。他们认为,自然选择、生存斗争、适者生存等生物原则同样适用于人类社会。能符合"适者生存"的民族就是最优等的民族,理所应当地成为世界的统治者；反之,就是劣等民族,注定要被淘汰的民族。社会达尔文主义的错误就在于,混淆了人类社会发展规律和生物界发展规律。这种理论为推行殖民主义、种族压迫制造了理论依据,备受帝国主义者推崇。我们常说,一个社会的文明程度可以从它对待弱势群体的态度来判断。人不是普通的动物,人有理性、有观念、有同理心、有悲悯,推崇"物竞天择"这样的价值观根本不符合文明的基本原则。文明的基本原则是秩序和协作,而不是丛林法则,人们用秩序杜绝了动物世界的弱肉强食。

问题讨论（Questions for Discussion）

1. Please comment on the fact that the leading female character is alive while the leading male character is not at the end of the novel is a really big deal.

2. What do morality and ethics mean in this novel? What do the narrator's asides tell

us about morals or ethics, and how do they relate to the story?

3. Do you agree to the view that *Sister Carrie* is a scathing critique of wealth and conspicuous consumption?

4. What's up with the ending?

5. What's the implication of animal and insect imagery in the novel?

6. What's up with the title?

(请扫码观看视频 *Sister Carrie*)

Unit 25
Imagism

E. E. Cummings: "r-p-o-p-h-e-s-s-a-g-r"; [in Just-]

作者简介 (Introduction to the Author)

Edward Estlin Cummings (1894—1962) is a famous American poet, painter, critic, writer and playwright. Cummings was born in Cambridge, Massachusetts in 1894. He began to write poetry as early as 1904, and studied Latin and Greek at Cambridge Latin High School. Cummings received his bachelor's degree and master's degree both from Harvard University. During the First World War, Cummings went to France to work as an ambulance driver. There he was detained for some time on suspicion of spying. After the war, Cummings often lived on Happy Farm in New Hampshire. In the 1920s and 1930s, Cummings traveled throughout Europe and met many artists and poets, including Picasso, whom Cummings admired very much. During his life, Cummings won many honors, including the American Poet's Academy Scholarship, the Guggenheim Fellowships, the Bollingen Prize in Poetry and so on. Cummings died on September 3, 1962 and was buried in the Forest Hills Cemetery in Boston, Massachusetts. At the time of his death in 1962, he was the second most widely read poet in the United States, after Robert Frost. Cummings is considered to be the spokesman of poetry in the 20th century. He was deeply influenced by modern art, and completely transformed poetry, creating a new kind of Cummings style poetry.

"r-p-o-p-h-e-s-s-a-g-r"

作品简介 (Introduction to the Work)

E. E. Cummings is known for his innovative versification. "r-p-o-p-h-e-s-s-a-g-r" is the extreme form of poetical experimentation conveyed through multiple permutations. This poem contains typographical, grammatical, and syntactical eccentricities. Written in free-verse form, the poem generates a deep connection between the display of the poem and its words. The poet takes the text to another level by giving the form the main relevance. The central aspect of "r-p-o-p-h-e-s-s-a-g-r" is how the words, and its meanings, play with the drawing that the poem makes, generating a new significance that arises from this relationship between form and content. Cummings displaces the "r" from its terminal position, creating a sense of movement with his usage of rearrangement and punctuation, mimicking the movement of a grasshopper. It's a very unconventional poem and possesses great philosophical meaning if you look closely.

作品选文 (Selected Reading)

<pre>
                    r-p-o-p-h-e-s-s-a-g-r[1]
          who
     a)s w(e loo)k[2]
     upnowgath
          PPEGORHRASS
                    eringint(o-
     aThe)[3]:l
      eA
         !p:
     S   a
           (r
     rIvInG   .gRrEaPsPhOs[4])
                         to
     rea(be)rran(com)gi(e)ngly[5]
     ,grasshopper[6];
</pre>

作品译文(扫码阅读)

注释 (Notes)

1. r-p-o-p-h-e-s-s-a-g-r:"蚱蜢";出现在诗歌之首,字母支离破碎,拼写前后颠倒,意指"蚱蜢"刚被发现时影影绰绰,作者的意识也朦朦胧胧,标点符号"-"用来表示"蚱蜢"断断续续的叫声。

2. a)s w(e loo)k:括号用来描述作者循声寻觅"蚱蜢"时蹑手蹑脚/躲躲藏藏/悄悄张望的神态。

3. (o-aThe):表示惊叹和唏嘘。

4. gRrEaPsPhOs：作者有意将其"肢解"为两部分，小写的 grass 一词清晰可认，表明蚱蜢飞入草丛，忽东忽西，大写的 REPPO（指 hOPPER）意在说明作者的关注点依然是蚱蜢本身。

5. rea(be)rran(com)gi(e)ngly：指的是作者屏住呼吸，重新调整位置姿态。

6. grasshopper：最后落在地上，终于看清"蚱蜢"的全貌。

问题讨论（Questions for Discussion）

1. How does the poem look like?
2. What is it about? Can you explain in your own words?

[in Just-]

作品简介（Introduction to the Work）

Within [in Just-], E. E. Cummings uses his characteristic style that has made his poems so memorable and engaging to read. He plays with spacing, capitalization, indention, and syntax while at the same time creating a semi-clear image of spring. [in Just-] encompasses everything we love about spring (even puddles for the children). Children are outdoors playing games. People are whistling and happy. In the poem, cummings celebrates the thrills, pleasures, and subtle dangers of spring—both the literal season and the symbolic time of life. Childhood, in this free verse poem, has a lot in common with the very earliest part of spring, when the world feels full of delicious, muddy potential. But the strange old "balloonman" who whistles his way through the landscape reminds readers that neither the springtime of the year nor the springtime of childhood lasts forever.

作品选文（Selected Reading）

[in Just-]

in Just-
spring   when the world is mud-
luscious the little
lame balloonman

whistles[1]   far[2]   and wee[3]

and eddieandbill come

running from marbles and
piracies and it's
spring

when the world is puddle-wonderful

the queer
old balloonman whistles
far   and   wee
and bettyandisbel come dancing

from hop-scotch and jump-rope and

it's
spring
and

       the

               goat-footed

balloonMan[4]   whistles
far
and
wee

作品译文(扫码阅读)

注释(Notes)

1. whistles：指的是卖气球的人吹的哨声。
2. far：暗指声音空间传播距离。
3. wee：暗指声音传播时间。

4. goat-footed balloonMan："长着山羊脚的人"是古希腊神话中的潘神 Pan。潘神长着山羊的后臀、大腿、脚和角，由于他被公认为牧地、树林和灌木山谷之神，因此潘神也常被人与农业和春季联系起来。

主题探究（Themes）

（扫码阅读）

问题讨论（Questions for Discussion）

1. Is the use of lower-case letters related to the subject matter of the poem (children)? If so, how?

2. Is the balloonman innocent? Why or why not?

3. Does the balloonman seem to be a part of spring or not?

4. Amidst all this chaos, however, is there a tiny bit of order?

5. Many critics compare the balloonman to Pan, the half-man, half-goat god of the satyrs. Do you agree with them?

6. Does this draw you back into your childhood? Is it spoken as the voice of a child, or does it seem more like the voice of a person remembering childhood?

Unit 26
Modern Fiction (I)

Sherwood Anderson: "Paper Pills";
F. Scott Fitzgerald: *The Great Gatsby*
▽

作者简介 (Introduction to the Authors)

Sherwood Anderson (1876—1941) was born in Camden, Ohio. He is considered to be one of the greatest writers in the United States. He published many novels, short stories, poems and memoirs in his life, but his most famous work was *Winesburg, Ohio* (1919). Set in a small town in Ohio, a series of interrelated short stories have influenced a generation of writers, including Ernest Hemingway and William Faulkner. The son of a day labor, Anderson left school early and took various jobs to support his family. He studied at Wittenberg College in Springfield, Ohio for just one year. His mother died when he was 20. After his mother's death, Anderson moved to Chicago to work in advertising. He returned to Ohio in 1906 to become a businessman, writing novels in his spare time and running his own manufacturing business. After his mental breakdown in 1912, Anderson left his wife and children and returned to Chicago, where he met writers such as Carl Sandberg, Ben Hecht and Floyd Dell. He began to publish short stories in small magazines such as the *Little Review* and the *Masses*. Anderson was influenced by modernist writers, such as his friend Gertrude Stein. In *Winesburg, Ohio*, his concise and exploratory prose skillfully evokes a sense of alienation from small town life. In his old age, Anderson moved to Marion, Virginia, where he ran two newspaper agencies. He died unexpectedly in Panama on his way to South America and was buried in Marion. Although being criticized in his later life, Anderson was still an important and influential figure in American literature in the early 20th century.

Francis Scott Key Fitzgerald (1896—1940) is known as "the Poet Laureate of the Jazz Age". Fitzgerald was born in St. Paul, Minnesota. His father is a furniture dealer. He tried writing screenplays when he was young. After high school, Fitzgerald was admitted to Princeton University. When he was in Princeton, he organized his own troupe and wrote for the school's literary publications. He dropped out of school due to poor health. He joined the army in 1917 but did not go abroad to fight. After leaving the army, Fitzgerald insisted on writing. In 1920, Fitzgerald published the novel, *This Side of*

Paradise and became famous since then. After the novel was published, he married Zelda Sayre. After marriage, he moved to Paris with his wife and met many American writers such as Anderson and Hemingway. The publication of *The Great Gatsby* in 1925 established his place in the history of modern American literature. Fitzgerald continued to write diligently after he became famous. However, his wife was extravagant and became insane. This caused him great pain. He had to go to Hollywood to write scripts to earn a living. Unfortunately, in 1936, he contracted a lung disease, and his wife became ill again. On December 21, 1940, Fitzgerald suffered a heart attack and died in Los Angeles at the age of 44. In addition to the above two works, the main works of the writer include *Tender is the Night* (1934) and *The Love of the Last Tycoon* (1941). His novels vividly reflected the shattering of the "American Dream" in the 1920s, and showed the spiritual side of the "Wild Age" of the American upper class during the Great Depression. Although Fitzgerald achieved temporary wealth and success in the 1920s, it was only after his death that he received widespread criticism and popular acclaim. Being the representative of The Lost Generation, Fitzgerald is considered to be one of the greatest American writers of the 20th century.

Paper Pills

作品简介 (Introduction to the Work)

"Paper Pills" is a short story collected in *Winesburg, Ohio: A Group of Tales of Ohio Small Town Life* by Sherwood Anderson. Doctor Reefy is described as wearing the same old shabby clothes all the time, and inhabiting an equally unkempt office. The tale of Doctor Reefy and his deceased wife is "delicious, like the twisted little apples" left behind on the trees in the frosts of early winter after all the other apples have been picked and sent to the cities. These rejected apples are described as gnarled "like the knuckles of Doctor Reefy's hands." One day, the daughter of wealthy land-owning parents had consulted Doctor Reefy because she was afraid she has become pregnant. Her mother and father have died, leaving her alone, wealthy and pursued by suitors. She is torn between the son of a jeweler who talks at great length about virginity, and a silent but persuasive lover who "always managed to get her into the darkness where he began to kiss her." Perceiving both suitors as equally lustful and eager to use her for her wealth, the girl marries the older Doctor Reefy instead. He spends the winter before she dies reading to her everything he had written on the bits of paper.

作品选文 (Selected Reading)

Paper Pills[1]

He was an old man with a white beard and huge nose and hands. Long before the time during which we will know him, he was a doctor and drove a jaded white horse[2] from house to house through the streets of Winesburg. Later he married a girl who had money. She had been left a large fertile farm when her father died. The girl was quiet, tall, and dark, and to many people she seemed very beautiful. Everyone in Winesburg wondered why she married the doctor. Within a year after the marriage she died.

The knuckles[3] of the doctor's hands were extraordinarily large. When the hands were closed they looked like clusters of unpainted wooden balls as large as walnuts fastened together by steel rods. He smoked a cob pipe[4] and after his wife's death sat all day in his empty office close by a window that was covered with cobwebs. He never opened the window. Once on a hot day in August he tried but found it stuck fast[5] and after that he forgot all about it.

Winesburg had forgotten the old man, but in Doctor Reefy there were the seeds of something very fine. Alone in his musty[6] office in the Heffner Block above the Paris Dry Goods Company's store, he worked ceaselessly[7], building up something that he himself destroyed. Little pyramids of truth he erected and after erecting knocked them down[8] again that he might have the truths to erect other pyramids.

Doctor Reefy was a tall man who had worn one suit of clothes for ten years. It was frayed[9] at the sleeves and little holes had appeared at the knees and elbows. In the office he wore also a linen duster[10] with huge pockets into which he continually stuffed scraps of paper[11]. After some weeks the scraps of paper became little hard round balls, and when the pockets were filled he dumped them out upon the floor. For ten years he had but one friend, another old man named John Spaniard who owned a tree nursery[12]. Sometimes, in a playful mood[13], old Doctor Reefy took from his pockets a handful of the paper balls and threw them at the nursery man. "That is to confound[14] you, you blathering old sentimentalist[15]," he cried, shaking with laughter.

The story of Doctor Reefy and his courtship of the tall dark girl who became his wife and left her money to him is a very curious story. It is delicious, like the twisted little apples[16] that grow in the orchards of Winesburg. In the fall one walks in the orchards and the ground is hard with frost underfoot. The apples have been taken from the trees by the pickers. They have been put in barrels and shipped to the cities where they will be eaten in apartments that are filled with books, magazines, furniture, and people. On the trees are only a few gnarled[17] apples that the pickers have rejected. They look like the knuckles of Doctor Reefy's hands. One nibbles at them and they are delicious. Into a little round place at the side of the apple has been gathered all of its sweetness. One runs from tree to tree over the frosted ground picking the gnarled, twisted apples and filling his pockets with them. Only the few know the sweetness of the twisted apples.

The girl and Doctor Reefy began their courtship on a summer afternoon. He was forty-five then and already he had begun the practice of filling his pockets with the scraps of paper that became hard balls and were thrown away. The habit had been formed as he sat in his buggy[18] behind the jaded white horse and went slowly along country roads. On the papers were written thoughts, ends of thoughts, beginnings of thoughts.

One by one the mind of Doctor Reefy had made the thoughts. Out of many of them he formed a truth that arose gigantic in his mind. The truth clouded the world. It became terrible and then faded away and the little thoughts began again.

The tall dark girl came to see Doctor Reefy because she was in the family way[19] and had become frightened. She was in that condition because of a series of circumstances also curious.

The death of her father and mother and the rich acres of land that had come down to her had set a train of suitors on her heels[20]. For two years she saw suitors almost every evening. Except two they were all alike. They talked to her of passion and there was a strained eager quality[21] in their voices and in their eyes when they looked at her. The two who were different were much unlike each other. One of them, a slender young man with white hands, the son of a jeweler in Winesburg, talked continually of virginity. When he was with her he was never off the subject[22]. The other, a black-haired boy with large ears, said nothing at all but always managed to get her into the darkness, where he began to kiss her.

For a time the tall dark girl thought she would marry the jeweler's son. For hours she sat in silence listening as he talked to her and then she began to be afraid of something. Beneath his talk of virginity she began to think there was a lust[23] greater than in all the others. At times it seemed to her that as he talked he was holding her body in his hands. She imagined him turning it slowly about in the white hands and staring at it. At night she dreamed that he had bitten into her body and that his jaws were dripping[24]. She had the dream three times, then she became in the family way to the one who said nothing at all but who in the moment of his passion actually did bite her shoulder so that for days the marks of his teeth showed.

After the tall dark girl came to know Doctor Reefy it seemed to her that she never wanted to leave him again. She went into his office one morning and without her saying anything he seemed to know what had happened to her.

In the office of the doctor there was a woman, the wife of the man who kept the bookstore in Winesburg. Like all old-fashioned country practitioners[25], Doctor Reefy pulled teeth, and the woman who waited held a handkerchief to her teeth and groaned. Her husband was with her and when the tooth was taken out they both screamed and blood ran down on the woman's white dress. The tall dark girl did not pay any attention. When the woman and the man had gone the doctor smiled. "I will take you driving into the country with me," he said.

For several weeks the tall dark girl and the doctor were together almost every day. The condition that had brought her to him passed in an illness, but she was like one who has discovered the sweetness of the twisted apples, she could not get her mind fixed again upon the round perfect fruit that is eaten in the city apartments. In the fall after the beginning of her acquaintanceship[26] with him she married Doctor Reefy and in the following spring she died. During the winter he read to her all of the odds and ends of thoughts[27] he had scribbled on the bits of paper. After he had read them he laughed and stuffed them away in his pockets to become round hard balls.

注释（Notes）

1. paper pills：纸团。
2. a jaded white horse：一匹疲惫的白马，jaded 意思是 exhausted。
3. knuckles：指关节。
4. a cob pipe：一种用玉米之类的植物做成的烟斗，质地很次，价格也很便宜。
5. stuck fast：死死地卡住。
6. musty：发霉的；有霉味的。
7. ceaselessly：不停地。
8. knocked them down：打倒。
9. frayed：磨损的。
10. a linen duster：麻布防尘外衣，麻布风衣。
11. stuffed scraps of paper：塞进纸片。
12. a tree nursery：苗圃。
13. in a playful mood：以一种开玩笑的神情。
14. confound：使……困惑不解。
15. blathering old sentimentalist：喋喋不休、多愁善感的老家伙。
16. the twisted little apple：长得不够圆溜的小苹果。
17. gnarled：（树等）多节瘤的。
18. buggy：（四轮单车轻便）马车。
19. in the family way：怀孕。
20. set a…her heels：引来一大批追求者追随其左右。

21. a strained eager quality：内心紧张而急不可耐。
22. he was...the subject：他总是也离不开这个话题。
23. lust：欲望，情欲。
24. dripping：滴下，滴落。这里指滴血，血往下滴。
25. practitioners：开业医师。
26. acquaintanceship：相识，交往。
27. odds and ends of thoughts：零星琐碎的思想。

主题探究（Themes）

（扫码阅读）

问题讨论（Questions for Discussion）

Symbolism is an important feature of the story. What do "paper pills" and "twisted apples" symbolize?

The Great Gatsby

作品简介（Introduction to the Work）

The Great Gatsby, third novel by F. Scott Fitzgerald, published in 1925. Set in Jazz Age New York, the novel tells the tragic story of Jay Gatsby, a self-made millionaire, and his pursuit of Daisy Buchanan, a wealthy young woman whom he loved in his youth. Chapter one introduces the narrator, Nick Carraway, and establishes the context and setting of the novel. Nick begins by explaining his own situation. He has moved from the Midwest to West Egg, a town on Long Island, NY. The novel is set in the years following WWI, and begins in 1922. Nick served in the army in WWI, and now that he is home and he has decided to move east and try to become a bond trader on Wall Street. Nick has rented a small house that is nestled between many large mansions. The mansion next door to his house belongs to the title character, Jay Gatsby. There is a large bay in front of Nick's house, and across that bay live Nick's cousin, Daisy and her husband Tom Buchanan. Nick is invited to Tom and Daisy's for dinner. He discovers that Daisy's husband, Tom, is still as aggressive and assertive as he was when they went to college together. When he gets back to his own house after dinner, Nick spies his neighbor, Gatsby, for the first time. Gatsby is standing on the lawn, looking at a small green light at the end of the dock at Daisy and Tom's house. Gatsby's arms are stretched out, as though he is reaching for the light.

The Great Gatsby
(Excerpt)
Chapter 1

In my younger and more vulnerable years my father gave me some advice that I've been turning over in my mind ever since.

"Whenever you feel like criticizing anyone," he told me, "just remember that all the people in this world haven't had the advantages that you've had."

He didn't say any more, but we've always been unusually communicative in a reserved way, and I understood that he meant a great deal more than that. In consequence, I'm inclined to reserve all judgements, a habit that has opened up many curious natures to me and also made me the victim of not a few veteran bores. The abnormal mind is quick to detect and attach itself to this quality when it appears in a normal person, and so it came about that in college I was unjustly accused of being a politician, because I was privy[1] to the secret griefs of wild, unknown men. Most of the confidences were unsought—frequently I have feigned sleep, preoccupation, or a hostile levity when I realized by some unmistakable sign that an intimate revelation was quivering on the horizon[2]; for the intimate revelations of young men, or at least the terms in which they express them, are usually plagiaristic[3] and marred by obvious suppressions[4]. Reserving judgements is a matter of infinite hope. I am still a little afraid of missing something if I forget that, as my father snobbishly suggested, and I snobbishly repeat, a sense of the fundamental decencies is parcelled out[5] unequally at birth.

And, after boasting this way of my tolerance, I come to the admission that it has a limit. Conduct may be founded on the hard rock or the wet marshes, but after a certain point I don't care what it's founded on. When I came back from the East last autumn I felt that I wanted the world to be in uniform and at a sort of moral attention forever; I wanted no more riotous excursions with privileged glimpses into the human heart. Only Gatsby, the man who gives his name to this book, was exempt from my reaction—Gatsby, who represented everything for which I have an unaffected scorn. If personality is an unbroken series of successful gestures, then there was something gorgeous about him, some heightened sensitivity to the promises of life, as if he were related to one of those intricate machines that register earthquakes ten thousand miles away. This responsiveness had nothing to do with that flabby[6] impressionability[7] which is dignified under the name of the "creative temperament"—it was an extraordinary gift for hope, a romantic readiness such as I have never found in any other person and which it is not likely I shall ever find again. No—Gatsby turned out all right at the end; it is what preyed on Gatsby, what foul dust floated in the wake of his dreams that temporarily closed out my interest in the abortive sorrows and short-winded[8] elations of men.

My family have been prominent, well-to-do people in this Middle Western city for three generations. The Carraways are something of a clan, and we have a tradition that we're descended from the Dukes of Buccleuch[9], but the actual founder of my line was my grandfather's brother, who came here in fifty-one, sent a substitute to the Civil War, and started the wholesale hardware business that my father carries on today.

I never saw this great-uncle, but I'm supposed to look like him—with special reference to the rather hard-boiled painting that hangs in father's office. I graduated from New Haven[10] in 1915, just a quarter of a century after my father, and a little later I participated in that delayed Teutonic migration[11] known as the Great War. I enjoyed the counter-raid so thoroughly that I came back restless. Instead of being the warm centre of the world, the Middle West now seemed like the ragged edge of the universe—so I decided to go East and learn the bond business[12]. Everybody I knew was in the bond business, so I supposed it could support one more single man. All my aunts and uncles talked it over as if they were choosing a prep school[13] for me, and finally said, "Why—ye-es," with very grave, hesitant faces. Father agreed to finance me for a year, and after various delays I came East, permanently, I thought, in the spring of twenty-two.

The practical thing was to find rooms in the city, but it was a warm season, and I had just left a country of wide lawns and friendly trees, so when a young man at the office suggested that we take a house together in a commuting town, it sounded like a great idea. He found the house, a weather-beaten cardboard bungalow[14] at eighty a month, but at the last minute the firm ordered him to Washington, and I went out to the country alone. I had a dog—at least I had him for a few days until he ran away—and an old Dodge[15] and a Finnish woman, who made my bed and cooked breakfast and muttered Finnish wisdom to herself over the electric stove.

It was lonely for a day or so until one morning some man, more recently arrived than I, stopped me on the road.

"How do you get to West Egg village?" he asked helplessly.

I told him. And as I walked on I was lonely no longer. I was a guide, a pathfinder, an original settler. He had casually conferred on[16] me the freedom of the neighbourhood.

And so with the sunshine and the great bursts of leaves growing on the trees, just as things grow in fast movies, I had that familiar conviction that life was beginning over again with the summer.

There was so much to read, for one thing, and so much fine health to be pulled down out of the young breath-giving air. I bought a dozen volumes on banking and credit and investment securities, and they stood on my shelf in red and gold like new money from the mint, promising to unfold the shining secrets that only Midas[17] and Morgan[18] and Maecenas[19] knew. And I had the high intention of reading many other books besides. I was rather literary in college—one year I wrote a series of very solemn and obvious editorials for *the Yale News*[20]—and now I was going to bring back all such things into my life and become again that most limited of all specialists, the "well-rounded man." This isn't just an epigram—life is much more successfully looked at from a single window, after all.

It was a matter of chance that I should have rented a house in one of the strangest communities in North America. It was on that slender riotous island which extends itself due east of New York—and where there are, among other natural curiosities, two unusual formations of land. Twenty miles from the city a pair of enormous eggs, identical in contour and separated only by a courtesy bay, jut out into the most domesticated body of salt water in the Western hemisphere, the great wet barnyard of Long Island Sound[21]. They are not perfect ovals—like the egg in the Columbus story, they are both crushed flat at the contact end—but their physical resemblance must be a source of perpetual wonder to the gulls that fly overhead. To the wingless a more interesting phenomenon is their dissimilarity in every particular except shape and size.

I lived at West Egg, the—well, the less fashionable of the two, though this is a most superficial tag to express the bizarre and not a little sinister[22] contrast between them. My house was at the very tip of the egg, only fifty yards from the Sound, and squeezed between two huge places that rented for twelve or fifteen thousand a season. The one on my right was a colossal affair by any standard—it was a factual imitation of some Hôtel de Ville in Normandy[23], with a tower on one side, spanking new under a thin beard of raw ivy, and a marble swimming pool, and more than forty acres of lawn and garden. It was Gatsby's mansion. Or, rather, as I didn't know Mr. Gatsby, it was a mansion inhabited by a gentleman of that name. My own house was an eyesore, but it was a small eyesore, and it had been overlooked, so I had a view of the water, a partial view of my neighbour's lawn, and the consoling proximity of millionaires—all for eighty dollars a month.

Across the courtesy bay the white palaces of fashionable East Egg glittered along the water, and the history of the summer really begins on the evening I drove over there to have dinner with the Tom Buchanans. Daisy was my second cousin once removed, and I'd known Tom in college. And just after the war I spent two days with them in Chicago.

Her husband, among various physical accomplishments[24], had been one of the most powerful ends that ever played football at New Haven—a national figure in a way, one of those men who reach such an acute limited excellence at twenty-one that everything afterward savours of anticlimax. His family were enormously wealthy—even in college his freedom with money was a matter for reproach—but now he'd left Chicago and come East in a fashion that rather took your breath away[25]: for instance, he'd brought down a string of polo[26] ponies from Lake Forest[27]. It was hard to realize that a man in my own generation was wealthy enough to do that.

Why they came East I don't know. They had spent a year in France for no particular reason, and then drifted here and there unrestfully wherever people played polo and were rich together. This was a permanent move, said Daisy over the telephone, but I didn't believe it—I had no sight into Daisy's heart[28], but I felt that Tom would drift on forever seeking, a little wistfully, for the dramatic turbulence of some irrecoverable football game.

And so it happened that on a warm windy evening I drove over to East Egg to see two old friends whom I scarcely knew at all. Their house was even more elaborate than I expected, a cheerful red-and-white Georgian Colonial mansion, overlooking the bay. The lawn started at the beach and ran towards the front door for a quarter of a mile, jumping over sundials and brick walks and burning gardens—finally when it reached the house drifting up the side in bright vines as though from the momentum of its run. The front was broken by a line of French windows, glowing now with reflected gold and wide open to the warm windy afternoon, and Tom Buchanan in riding clothes was standing with his legs apart on the front porch.

注释（Notes）

1. privy：私人的，不公开的。
2. on the horizon：即将来临的。
3. plagiaristic：抄袭的。
4. suppressions：（心理）压抑。
5. parcelled out：分配。
6. flabby：虚弱的。
7. impressionability：易感性，敏感性。
8. short-winded：瞬间的。
9. the Dukes of Buccleuch：苏格兰贵族。
10. New Haven：纽黑文，耶鲁大学所在地。

11. Teutonic migration：条顿民族大迁移。

12. the bond business：债券生意。

13. a prep school：为富家子弟办的私立寄宿学校。

14. a weather-beaten cardboard bungalow：经历风雨剥蚀的木板平房。

15. Dodge：道奇车。

16. conferred on：授予，赋予（权利、荣誉等）。

17. Midas：迈达斯，希腊神话中的国王，曾求神赐予点金术。

18. Morgan：美国财阀。

19. Maecenas：米赛纳斯，古罗马大财主。

20. the Yale News：《耶鲁新闻》，报纸名称。

21. Long Island Sound：长岛海峡。

22. sinister：邪恶的；不详的。

23. Normandy：诺曼底；法国北部一地区，多古色古香的城堡。

24. accomplishments：技能，才艺。

25. took your breath away：使大吃一惊，令人屏息。

26. polo：马球。

27. Lake Forest：森林湖，伊利诺伊州东北部的小城。

28. I had no sight into Daisy's heart：我并不了解黛西的心思。

主题探究（Themes）

（扫码阅读）

价值引领（Value Guidance）

　　过去一个多世纪以来，美国梦随着美国强势崛起、走向"一超"而广为人知。"美国梦"是美国文学作品中时常出现的主题。如今，我们的中国梦随着中国的和平发展而走入全世界人民的视野。国家主席习近平访美时指出，中国梦要实现国家富强、民族复兴、人民幸福，是和平、发展、合作、共赢的梦，与包括美国梦在内的世界各国人民的美好梦想相通。那么，中国梦和美国梦究竟有何区别？中国社会科学院副院长、当代中国研究所所长李捷在一次专题报告中指出，中国梦和美国梦存在四大本质区别：

　　一是历史渊源不同。中国梦从反抗外部侵略和摆脱封建统治中产生，从一开始就有民族独立和人民解放的内容;而美国在摆脱英国的殖民统治后,很快走上了独立的道路。没有封建包袱的美国,在黑奴解放运动后,走上了资本主义经济快速发展的道路,并从20世纪初开始对外掠夺扩张。

二是发展道路有别。美国在独立战争和南北战争后形成了资本主义政治、经济和文化制度,以实用主义和自由主义为核心,其内外发展环境都比较好。而新中国成立后,内部发展起点低,外部受到西方列强的封锁和包围。在这样的环境下,要在一穷二白的基础上建设现代化国家,从农业国向工业国转变,中国只能走社会主义道路,坚持中国共产党的坚强领导,提倡爱国主义精神。同时,为了避免教条式搞社会主义出现的失误,我们必须坚持中国特色社会主义道路,坚持改革开放。实践也充分证明,关门、教条式搞社会主义都是行不通的,实现中国梦必须坚持改革开放。

三是个人奋斗和国家奋斗的关系不同。美国梦的一个重要内容是西部开发,这是美国个人奋斗的重要途径。从落后走向发达,美国的西部精神起到了一定作用。因此,美国梦更多地强调个人奋斗,即个人梦。与之相比,中华民族复兴的中国梦是国家和人民的奋斗史,也是中国共产党的奋斗史,离开了党、国家和人民整体利益,中国梦是无法实现的。因此,中国梦更强调个人奋斗和国家奋斗的结合。

四是与世界关系存在区别。美国梦在实现过程中走上了对外扩张的道路。尤其是冷战结束后"一超"格局下,美国梦在处理与世界关系上以强迫别国接受它的价值观、制度和理念为前提。而中国梦是希望中国好,同时友邻也好。中国乐意看到发展中国家和中国一样发展,发展中国家人民同样过上幸福的生活。

复旦大学中国研究院院长张维为说:"实际上中国梦也好,美国梦也好,我觉得在生活层面还是有很多相似之处的。美国梦最经典的一个表述,就是美国著名历史学家詹姆斯·亚当斯曾经讲过的:在这片土地上,每个人都能通过自己的努力实现自己的梦想。很多移民去美国的人也是怀着这样的梦想,用今天中国梦的表述方法就是,只要你努力,每个人都有人生出彩的机会。所以就这个意义而言,在生活层面上,中国梦和美国梦的差别似乎不是特别大。"

张维为认为,中国梦和美国梦的差别主要体现在以下方面:当讨论美国梦时,美国的主流精英一般都认为美国梦得以实现的背后是美国的政治制度,特别是美国人自己界定的所谓民主、自由、人权……这一套制度安排,至于中国梦,即国家富强、民族振兴、人民幸福。如果要谈制度原因的话,会强调中国特色社会主义制度是实现中国梦的最好的保障。中国正在重新界定现代性,一个21世纪的现代性的理想政治制度,应该远远超出美国这种所谓"三权分立"的范畴,超出政治本身的范畴;它要在一个更大的范围内,实现政治力量、社会力量、资本力量三者之间的某种平衡。如果这三种力量之间失衡的话,比如像美国这样资本力量独大,就是美国梦被出卖的主要原因。也正是在这个意义上,中国人今天的眼光已经远远超出了美国模式。不少西方国家的民主制度日益演变成了"钱主",特别是美国的民主。改革开放40年,随着中国的迅速崛起,中国经济和社会力量也都有了长足发展。我们也形成了政治力量、社会力量、资本力量之间的一种平衡。中国这三种力量的总体平衡,应该是中国可以避免美式金融危机和经济危机的主要原因,也是为什么中国普通老百姓的"中国梦"前景比"美国梦"前景更为精彩的主要原因。

问题讨论(Questions for Discussion)

1. Does Gatsby achieve the American Dream? If yes, when exactly can he say that he reaches it? If no, what prevents him from truly achieving it?

2. Nick comments on an "unmistakable air of natural intimacy" around Daisy and Tom after Myrtle is killed. Do these two share intimacy? More so than Daisy and Gatsby?

3. Do you agree that Gatsby ends up dead because he can't live in the present—so he can't live at all?

4. What does Gatsby mean when he says that Daisy's voice is "full of money?" Does he mean this negatively? Why does Nick agree with him? Does this comment say more about Daisy or Jay Gatsby?

5. In *The Great Gatsby*, are social norms insurmountable barriers between people? Are Inter-class relationships impossible?

6. Do you agree that love in *The Great Gatsby* is only the result of self-deception and denial?

7. Is Nick Carraway necessary? If we got the story through a third person omniscient narrator, what would we lose? Gain?

8. Is Gatsby great? In what way? How might he not be great? Does his greatness evolve over the course of the novel? What is the difference, in this text, between perceived greatness and actual greatness?

(请扫码观看视频 *The Great Gatsby*)

Unit 27
Modern Fiction (II)

Ernest Hemingway: *A Farewell to Arms*; *The Old Man and the Sea*; "A Clean, Well-Lighted Place"; "Hills like White Elephants"

▽

作者简介 (Introduction to the Author)

Ernest Miller Hemingway (1899—1961), born in Oak Park, Illinois, is an American writer and journalist. He is considered to be one of the most famous novelists in the 20th century. Hemingway began his career as a writer at the age of 17 in a newspaper agency in Kansas City. After the United States joined the First World War, he joined the volunteer ambulance team of the Italian army. While serving in the front line, he was injured and spent a long time in hospitals. After returning to the United States, he became a reporter for Canadian and American newspapers and was soon sent back to Europe to report on the Greek Revolution and other events. During the twenties, Hemingway became a member of the group of expatriate Americans in Paris, which he described in his first important work, *The Sun Also Rises* (1926). Equally successful was *A Farewell to Arms* (1929), the study of an American ambulance officer's disillusionment in the war and his role as a deserter. Hemingway used his experiences as a reporter during the civil war in Spain as the background for his most ambitious novel, *For Whom the Bell Tolls* (1940). Among his later works, the most outstanding is the short novel, *The Old Man and the Sea* (1952), which tells the story of an old fisherman's long and lonely struggle with a fish and the sea. Hemingway has always been known as a tough man in the literary world. He is the spiritual monument of the American nation. Hemingway's works mark the formation of his unique writing style and occupy an important position in the history of American literature and even the world literature.

A Farewell to Arms

作品简介 (Introduction to the Work)

A Farewell to Arms, the third novel by Ernest Hemingway, published in 1929. The novel, set against the backdrop of World War I, describes a love affair between the expatriate Henry and an English nurse, Catherine Barkley. *A Farewell to Arms* is particularly notable for its autobiographical elements. Its depiction of the existential disillusionment of the "Lost Generation" echoes his early short stories and his first major novel, *The Sun Also Rises*. In the last chapter, Catherine goes into labor and Henry takes her to the hospital. Her delivery did not go well. When Catherine's death comes, Henry reports it in the baldest, most unadorned terms: "It seems she had one hemorrhage after another. They couldn't stop it. I went into the room and stayed with Catherine until she died." Although Hemingway shows only the tip of the iceberg, the reader feels the immeasurable grief that extends below the surface. Here, in its ability to evoke so much by using so little, is the power of Hemingway's writing.

作品选文 (Selected Reading)

A Farewell to Arms
(An Excerpt)
Chapter 41

One morning I awoke about three o'clock hearing Catherine stirring in the bed.

"Are you all right, Cat?"

"I've been having some pains, darling."

"Regularly?"

"No, not very."

"If you have them at all regularly we'll go to the hospital."

I was very sleepy and went back to sleep. A little while later I woke again.

"Maybe you'd better call up the doctor," Catherine said. "I think maybe this is it."

I went to the phone and called the doctor. "How often are the pains coming?" he asked.

"How often are they coming, Cat?"

"I should think every quarter of an hour."

"You should go to the hospital then," the doctor said. "I will dress and go there right away myself."

I hung up and called the garage near the station to send up a taxi. No one answered the phone for a long time. Then I finally got a man who promised to send up a taxi at once. Catherine was dressing. Her bag was all packed with the things she would need at the hospital and the baby things. Outside in the hall I rang for the elevator. There was no answer. I went downstairs. There was no one downstairs except the night-watchman. I brought the elevator up myself, put Catherine's bag in it, she stepped in and we went down. The night-watchman opened the door for us and we sat outside on the stone slabs beside the stairs down to the driveway and waited for the taxi. The night was clear and the stars were out. Catherine was very excited.

"I'm so glad it's started," she said. "Now in a little while it will be all over."

"You're a good brave girl."

"I'm not afraid. I wish the taxi would come, though."

We heard it coming up the street and saw its headlights. It turned into the driveway and I helped Catherine in and the driver put the bag up in front.

"Drive to the hospital," I said.

We went out of the driveway and started up the hill.

At the hospital we went in and I carried the bag. There was a woman at the desk who wrote down Catherine's name, age, address, relatives and religion, in a book. She said she had no religion and the woman drew a line in the space after that word. She gave her name as Catherine Henry.

"I will take you up to your room," she said. We went up in an elevator. The woman stopped it and we stepped out and followed her down a hall. Catherine held tight to my arm.

"This is the room," the woman said. "Will you please undress and get into bed? Here is a nightgown for you to wear."

"I have a nightgown," Catherine said.

"It is better for you to wear this nightgown," the woman said.

I went outside and sat on a chair in the hallway.

"You can come in now," the woman said from the doorway. Catherine was lying in the narrow bed wearing a plain, square-cut nightgown that looked as though it were made of rough sheeting. She smiled at me.

"I'm having fine pains now," she said. The woman was holding her wrist and timing the pains with a watch.

"That was a big one," Catherine said. I saw it on her face.

"Where's the doctor?" I asked the woman.

"He's lying down sleeping. He will be here when he is needed."

"I must do something for Madame, now," the nurse said. "Would you please step out again?"

I went out into the hall. It was a bare hall with two windows and closed doors all down the corridor. It smelled of hospital. I sat on the chair and looked at the floor and prayed for Catherine.

"You can come in," the nurse said. I went in.

"Hello, darling," Catherine said.

"How is it?"

"They are coming quite often now." Her face drew up. Then she smiled.

"That was a real one. Do you want to put your hand on my back again, nurse?"

"If it helps you," the nurse said.

"You go away, darling," Catherine said. "Go out and get something to eat. I may do this for a long time the nurse says."

"The first labor is usually protracted[1]," the nurse said.

"Please go out and get something to eat," Catherine said. "I'm fine, really."

"I'll stay awhile," I said.

The pains came quite regularly, then slackened[2] off. Catherine was very excited. When the pains were bad she called them good ones. When they started to fall off she was disappointed and ashamed.

"You go out, darling," she said. "I think you are just making me self-conscious." Her face tied up. "There. That was better. I so want to be a good wife and have this child without any foolishness. Please go and get some breakfast, darling, and then come back. I won't miss you. Nurse is splendid to me."

"You have plenty of time for breakfast," the nurse said.

"I'll go then. Good-by, sweet."

"Good-by," Catherine said, "and have a fine breakfast for me too."

"Where can I get breakfast?" I asked the nurse.

"There's a café down the street at the square," she said. "It should be open now."

Outside it was getting light. I walked down the empty street to the café. There was a light in the window. I went in and stood at the zinc[3] bar and an old man served me a glass of white wine and a brioche[4]. The brioche was yesterday's. I dipped it in the wine and then drank a glass of coffee.

"What do you do at this hour?" the old man asked.

"My wife is in labor at the hospital."

"So. I wish you good luck."

"Give me another glass of wine."

He poured it from the bottle slopping[5] it over a little so some ran down on the zinc. I drank this glass, paid and went out. Outside along the street were the refuse cans from the houses waiting for the collector. A dog was nosing at one of the cans.

"What do you want?" I asked and looked in the can to see if there was anything I could pull out for him; there was nothing on top but coffee-grounds, dust and some dead flowers.

"There isn't anything, dog," I said. The dog crossed the street. I went up the stairs in the hospital to the floor Catherine was on and down the hall to her room. I knocked on the door. There was no answer. I opened the door; the room was empty, except for Catherine's bag on a chair and her dressing-gown hanging on a hook on the wall. I went out and down the hall, looking for somebody. I found a nurse.

"Where is Madame Henry?"

"A lady has just gone to the delivery room."

"Where is it?"

"I will show you."

She took me down to the end of the hall. The door of the room was partly open. I could see Catherine lying on a table, covered by a sheet. The nurse was on one side and the doctor stood on the other side of the table beside some cylinders. The doctor held a rubber mask attached to a tube in one hand.

"I will give you a gown and you can go in," the nurse said. "Come in here, please."

She put a white gown on me and pinned it at the neck in back with a safety pin.

"Now you can go in," she said. I went into the room.

"Hello, darling," Catherine said in a strained voice. "I'm not doing much."

"You are Mr. Henry?" the doctor asked.

"Yes. How is everything going, doctor?"

"Things are going very well," the doctor said. "We came in here where it is easy to give gas for the pains."

"I want it now," Catherine said. The doctor placed the rubber mask over her face and turned a dial and I watched Catherine breathing deeply and rapidly. Then she pushed the mask away. The doctor shut off the petcock[6].

"That wasn't a very big one. I had a very big one a while ago. The doctor made me go clear out, didn't you, doctor?" Her voice was strange. It rose on the word doctor.

The doctor smiled.

"I want it again," Catherine said. She held the rubber tight to her face and breathed fast. I heard her moaning a little. Then she pulled the mask away and smiled.

"That was a big one," she said. "That was a very big one. Don't you worry, darling. You go away. Go have another breakfast."

"I'll stay," I said.

We had gone to the hospital about three o'clock in the morning. At noon Catherine was still in the delivery room. The pains had slackened again. She looked very tired and worn now but she was still cheerful.

"I'm not any good, darling," she said. "I'm so sorry. I thought I would do it very easily. Now—there's one—" she reached out her hand for the mask and held it over her face. The doctor moved the dial and watched her. In a little while it was over.

"It wasn't much," Catherine said. She smiled. "I'm a fool about the gas. It's wonderful."

"We'll get some for the home," I said.

"There one comes," Catherine said quickly. The doctor turned the dial and looked at his watch.

"What is the interval now?" I asked.

"About a minute."

"Don't you want lunch?"

"I will have something pretty soon," he said.

"You must have something to eat, doctor," Catherine said. "I'm so sorry I go on so long. Couldn't my husband give me the gas?"

"If you wish," the doctor said. "You turn it to the numeral two."

"I see," I said. There was a marker on a dial that turned with a handle.

"I want it now," Catherine said. She held the mask tight to her face. I turned the dial to number two and when Catherine put down the mask I turned it off. It was very good of the doctor to let me do something.

"Did you do it, darling?" Catherine asked. She stroked my wrist.

"Sure."

"You're so lovely." She was a little drunk from the gas.

"I will eat from a tray in the next room," the doctor said. "You can call me any moment." While the time passed I watched him eat, then, after a while, I saw that he was lying down and smoking a cigarette. Catherine was getting very tired.

"Do you think I'll ever have this baby?" she asked.

"Yes, of course you will."

"I try as hard as I can. I push down but it goes away. There it comes. Give it to me."

At two o'clock I went out and had lunch. There were a few men in the café sitting with coffee and glasses of kirsch or marc on the tables. I sat down at a table.

"Can I eat?" I asked the waiter.

"It is past time for lunch."

"Isn't there anything for all hours?"

"You can have choucroute[7]."

"Give me choucroute and beer."

"A demi[8] or a bock[9]?"

"A light demi."

The waiter brought a dish of sauerkraut with a slice of ham over the top and a sausage buried in the hot wine-soaked cabbage. I ate it and drank the beer. I was very hungry. I watched the people at the tables in the café. At one table they were playing cards. Two men at the table next to me were talking and smoking. The café was full of smoke. The zinc bar, where I had breakfasted, had three people behind it now; the old man, a plump[10] woman in a black dress who sat behind a counter and kept track of everything served to the tables, and a boy in an apron. I wondered how many children the woman had and what it had been like.

When I was through with the choucroute I went back to the hospital. The street was all clean now. There were no refuse cans out. The day was cloudy but the sun was trying to come through. I rode upstairs in the elevator, stepped out and went down the hall to Catherine's room, where I had left my white gown. I put it on and pinned it in back at the neck. I looked in the glass and saw myself looking like a fake doctor with a beard. I went down the hall to the delivery room. The door was closed and I knocked. No one answered so I turned the handle and went in. The doctor sat by Catherine. The nurse was doing something at the other end of the room.

"Here is your husband," the doctor said.

"Oh, darling, I have the most wonderful doctor," Catherine said in a very strange voice. "He's been telling me the most wonderful story and when the pain came too badly he put me all the way out. He's wonderful. You're wonderful, doctor."

"You're drunk," I said.

"I know it," Catherine said. "But you shouldn't say it." Then "Give it to me. Give it to me." She clutched hold of the mask and breathed short and deep, pantingly, making the respirator click. Then she gave a long sigh and the doctor reached with his left hand and lifted away the mask.

"That was a very big one," Catherine said. Her voice was very strange. "I'm not going to die now, darling. I'm past where I was going to die. Aren't you glad?"

"Don't you get in that place again."

"I won't. I'm not afraid of it though. I won't die, darling."

"You will not do any such foolishness," the doctor said. "You would not die and leave your husband."

"Oh, no. I won't die. I wouldn't die. It's silly to die. There it comes. Give it to me."

After a while the doctor said, "You will go out, Mr. Henry, for a few moments and I will make an examination."

"He wants to see how I am doing," Catherine said. "You can come back afterward, darling, can't he, doctor?"

"Yes," said the doctor. "I will send word when he can come back."

I went out the door and down the hall to the room where Catherine was to be after the baby came. I sat in a chair there and looked at the room. I had the paper in my coat that I had bought when I went out for lunch and I read it. It was beginning to be dark outside and I turned the light on to read. After a while I stopped reading and turned off the light and watched it get dark outside. I wondered why the doctor did not send for me. Maybe it was better I was away. He probably wanted me away for a while. I looked at my watch. If he did not send for me in ten minutes I would go down anyway.

Poor, poor dear Cat. And this was the price you paid for sleeping together. This was the end of the trap. This was what people got for loving each other. Thank God for gas, anyway. What must it have been like before there were anaesthetics[11]? Once it started, they were in the mill-race. Catherine had a good time in the time of pregnancy. It wasn't bad. She was hardly ever sick. She was not awfully uncomfortable until toward the last. So now they got her in the end. You never got away with anything. Get away hell! It would have been the same if we had been married fifty times. And what if she should die? She won't die. People don't die in childbirth nowadays. That was what all husbands thought. Yes, but what if she should die? She won't die. She's just having a bad time. The initial labor is usually protracted. She's only having a bad time. Afterward we'd say what a bad time and Catherine would say it wasn't really so bad. But what if she should die? She can't die. Yes, but what if she should die? She can't, I tell you. Don't be a fool. It's just a bad time. It's just nature giving her hell. It's only the first labor, which is almost always protracted. Yes, but what if she should die? She can't die. Why would she die? What reason is there for her to die? There's just a child that has to be born, the by-product of good nights in Milan. It makes trouble and is born and then you look after it and get fond of it maybe. But what if she should die? She won't die. But what if she should die? She won't. She's all right. But what if she should die? She can't die. But what if she should die? Hey, what about that? What if she should die?

The doctor came into the room.

"How does it go, doctor?"

"It doesn't go," he said.

"What do you mean?"

"Just that. I made an examination—" He detailed the result of the examination. "Since then I've waited to see. But it doesn't go."

"What do you advise?"

"There are two things. Either a high forceps[12] delivery which can tear and be quite dangerous besides being possibly bad for the child, and a Caesarean[13]."

"What is the danger of a Caesarean?" What if she should die!

"It should be no greater than the danger of an ordinary delivery."

"Would you do it yourself?"

"Yes. I would need possibly an hour to get things ready and to get the people I would need. Perhaps a little less."

"What do you think?"

"I would advise a Caesarean operation. If it were my wife I would do a Caesarean."

"What are the after effects?"

"There are none. There is only the scar."

"What about infection?"

"The danger is not so great as in a high forceps delivery."

"What if you just went on and did nothing?"

"You would have to do something eventually. Mrs. Henry is already losing much of her strength. The sooner we operate now the safer."

"Operate as soon as you can," I said.

"I will go and give the instructions."

I went into the delivery room. The nurse was with Catherine who lay on the table, big under the sheet, looking very pale and tired.

"Did you tell him he could do it?" she asked.

"Yes."

"Isn't that grand. Now it will be all over in an hour. I'm almost done, darling. I'm going all to pieces. Please give me that. It doesn't work. Oh, it doesn't work!"

"Breathe deeply."

"I am. Oh, it doesn't work any more. It doesn't work!"

"Get another cylinder[14]," I said to the nurse.

"That is a new cylinder."

"I'm just a fool, darling," Catherine said. "But it doesn't work any more." She began to cry. "Oh, I wanted so to have this baby and not make trouble, and now I'm all done and all gone to pieces and it doesn't work. Oh, darling, it doesn't work at all. I don't care if I die if it will only stop. Oh, please, darling, please make it stop. There it comes. Oh Oh Oh!" She breathed sobbingly in the mask. "It doesn't work. It doesn't work. It doesn't work. Don't mind me, darling. Please don't cry. Don't mind me. I'm just gone all to pieces. You poor sweet. I love you so and I'll be good again. I'll be good this time. Can't they give me something? If they could only give me something."

"I'll make it work. I'll turn it all the way."

"Give it to me now."

I turned the dial all the way and as she breathed hard and deep her hand relaxed on the mask. I shut off the gas and lifted the mask. She came back from a long way away.

"That was lovely, darling. Oh, you're so good to me."

"You be brave, because I can't do that all the time. It might kill you."

"I'm not brave any more, darling. I'm all broken. They've broken me. I know it now."

"Everybody is that way."

"But it's awful. They just keep it up till they break you."

"In an hour it will be over."

"Isn't that lovely? Darling, I won't die, will I?"

"No. I promise you won't."

"Because I don't want to die and leave you, but I get so tired of it and I feel I'm going to die."

"Nonsense. Everybody feels that."

"Sometimes I know I'm going to die."

"You won't. You can't."

"But what if I should?"

"I won't let you."

"Give it to me quick. Give it to me!"

Then afterward, "I won't die. I won't let myself die."

"Of course you won't."

"You'll stay with me?"

"Not to watch it."

"No, just to be there."

"Sure. I'll be there all the time."

"You're so good to me. There, give it to me. Give me some more. It's not working!"

I turned the dial to three and then four. I wished the doctor would come back. I was afraid of the numbers above two.

Finally a new doctor came in with two nurses and they lifted Catherine onto a wheeled stretcher and we started down the hall. The stretcher went rapidly down the hall and into the elevator where every one had to crowd against the wall to make room; then up, then an open door and out of the elevator and down the hall on rubber wheels to the operating room. I did not recognize the doctor with his cap and mask on. There was another doctor and more nurses.

"They've got to give me something," Catherine said. "They've got to give me something. Oh please, doctor, give me enough to do some good!"

One of the doctors put a mask over her face and I looked through the door and saw the bright small amphitheatre[15] of the operating room.

"You can go in the other door and sit up there," a nurse said to me. There were benches behind a rail that looked down on the white table and the lights. I looked at Catherine. The mask was over her face and she was quiet now. They wheeled the stretcher forward. I turned away and walked down the hall. Two nurses were hurrying toward the entrance to the gallery.

"It's a Caesarean," one said. "They're going to do a Caesarean."

The other one laughed, "We're just in time. Aren't we lucky?" They went in the door that led to the gallery.

Another nurse came along. She was hurrying too.

"You go right in there. Go right in," she said.

"I'm staying outside."

She hurried in. I walked up and down the hall. I was afraid to go in. I looked out the window. It was dark but in the light from the window I could see it was raining. I went into a room at the far end of the hall and looked at the labels on bottles in a glass case. Then I came out and stood in the empty hall and watched the door of the operating room.

A doctor came out followed by a nurse. He held something in his two hands that looked like a freshly skinned rabbit and hurried across the corridor with it and in through another door. I went down to the door he had gone into and found them in the room doing things to a new-born child. The doctor held him up for me to see. He held him by the heels and slapped him.

"Is he all right?"

"He's magnificent. He'll weigh five kilos."

I had no feeling for him. He did not seem to have anything to do with me. I felt no feeling of fatherhood.

"Aren't you proud of your son?" the nurse asked. They were washing him and wrapping him in something. I saw the little dark face and dark hand, but I did not see him move or hear him cry. The doctor was doing something to him again. He looked upset.

"No," I said. "He nearly killed his mother."

"It isn't the little darling's fault. Didn't you want a boy?"

"No," I said. The doctor was busy with him. He held him up by the feet and slapped him. I did not wait to see it. I went out in the hall. I could go in now and see. I went in the door and a little way down the gallery. The nurses who were sitting at the rail motioned for me to come down where they were. I shook my head. I could see enough where I was.

I thought Catherine was dead. She looked dead. Her face was gray, the part of it that I could see. Down below, under the light, the doctor was sewing up the great long, forcep-spread, thick-edged, wound. Another doctor in a mask gave the anaesthetic. Two nurses in masks handed things. It looked like a drawing of the Inquisition[16]. I knew as I watched I could have watched it all, but I was glad I hadn't. I do not think I could have watched them cut, but I watched the wound closed into a high welted ridge with quick skilful-looking stitches like a cobbler's, and was glad. When the wound was closed I went out into the hall and walked up and down again. After a while the doctor came out.

"How is she?"

"She is all right. Did you watch?"

He looked tired.

"I saw you sew up. The incision looked very long."

"You thought so?"

"Yes. Will that scar flatten out?"

"Oh, yes."

After a while they brought out the wheeled stretcher and took it very rapidly down the hallway to the elevator. I went along beside it. Catherine was moaning. Downstairs they put her in the bed in her room. I sat in a chair at the foot of the bed. There was a nurse in the room. I got up and stood by the bed. It was dark in the room. Catherine put out her hand, "Hello, darling," she said. Her voice was very weak and tired.

"Hello, you sweet."

"What sort of baby was it?"

"Sh—don't talk," the nurse said.

"A boy. He's long and wide and dark."

"Is he all right?"

"Yes," I said. "He's fine."

I saw the nurse look at me strangely.

"I'm awfully tired," Catherine said. "And I hurt like hell. Are you all right, darling?"

"I'm fine. Don't talk."

"You were lovely to me. Oh, darling, I hurt dreadfully. What does he look like?"

"He looks like a skinned rabbit with a puckered-up[17] old-man's face."

"You must go out," the nurse said. "Madame Henry must not talk."

"I'll be outside," I said.

"Go and get something to eat."

"No. I'll be outside." I kissed Catherine. She was very gray and weak and tired.

"May I speak to you?" I said to the nurse. She came out in the hall with me. I walked a little way down the hall.

"What's the matter with the baby?" I asked.

"Didn't you know?"

"No."

"He wasn't alive."

"He was dead?"

"They couldn't start him breathing. The cord was caught around his neck or something."

"So he's dead."

"Yes. It's such a shame. He was such a fine big boy. I thought you knew."

"No," I said. "You better go back in with Madame."

I sat down on the chair in front of a table where there were nurses' reports hung on clips at the side and looked out of the window. I could see nothing but the dark and the rain falling across the light from the window. So that was it. The baby was dead. That was why the doctor looked so tired. But why had they acted the way they did in the room with him? They supposed he would come around and start breathing probably. I had no religion but I knew he ought to have been baptized. But what if he never breathed at all. He hadn't. He had never been alive. Except in Catherine. I'd felt him kick there often enough. But I hadn't for a week. Maybe he was choked all the time. Poor little kid. I wished the hell I'd been choked like that. No I didn't. Still there would not be all this dying to go through. Now Catherine would die. That was what you did. You died. You did not know what it was about. You never had time to learn. They threw you in and told you the rules and the first time they caught you off base they killed you[18]. Or they killed you gratuitously like Aymo. Or gave you the syphilis like Rinaldi. But they killed you in the end. You could count on that. Stay around and they would kill you.

Once in camp I put a log on top of the fire and it was full of ants. As it commenced to burn, the ants swarmed out and went first toward the centre where the fire was; then turned back and ran toward the end. When there were enough on the end they fell off into the fire. Some got out, their bodies burnt and flattened, and went off not knowing where they were going. But most of them went toward the fire and then back toward the end and swarmed on the cool end and finally fell off into the fire. I remember thinking at the time that it was the end of the world and a splendid chance to be a messiah[19] and lift the log off the fire and throw it out where the ants could get off onto the ground. But I did not do anything but throw a tin cup of water on the log, so that I would have the cup empty to put whiskey in before I added water to it. I think the cup of water on the burning log only steamed the ants.

So now I sat out in the hall and waited to hear how Catherine was. The nurse did not come out, so after a while I went to the door and opened it very softly and looked in. I could not see at first because there was a bright light in the hall and it was dark in the room. Then I saw the nurse sitting by the bed and Catherine's head on a pillow, and she all flat under the sheet. The nurse put her finger to her lips, then stood up and came to the door.

"How is she?" I asked.

"She's all right," the nurse said. "You should go and have your supper and then come back if you wish."

I went down the hall and then down the stairs and out the door of the hospital and down the dark street in the rain to the café. It was brightly lighted inside and there were many people at the tables. I did not see a place to sit, and a waiter came up to me and took my wet coat and hat and showed me a place at a table across from an elderly man who was drinking beer and reading the evening paper. I sat down and asked the waiter what the plat du jour was.

"Veal[20] stew—but it is finished."

"What can I have to eat?"

"Ham and eggs, eggs with cheese, or choucroute."

"I had choucroute this noon," I said.

"That's true," he said. "That's true. You ate choucroute this noon." He was a middle-aged man with a bald top to his head and his hair slicked over it. He had a kind face.

"What do you want? Ham and eggs or eggs with cheese?"

"Ham and eggs," I said, "and beer."

"A demi-blonde?"

"Yes," I said.

"I remembered," he said. "You took a demi-blonde this noon."

I ate the ham and eggs and drank the beer. The ham and eggs were in a round dish— the ham underneath and the eggs on top. It was very hot and at the first mouthful I had to take a drink of beer to cool my mouth. I was hungry and I asked the waiter for another order. I drank several glasses of beer. I was not thinking at all but read the paper of the man opposite me. It was about the break through on the British front. When he realized I was reading the back of his paper he folded it over. I thought of asking the waiter for a paper, but I could not concentrate. It was hot in the café and the air was bad. Many of the people at the tables knew one another. There were several card games going on. The waiters were busy bringing drinks from the bar to the tables. Two men came in and could find no place to sit. They stood opposite the table where I was. I ordered another beer. I was not ready to leave yet. It was too soon to go back to the hospital. I tried not to think and to be perfectly calm. The men stood around but no one was leaving, so they went out. I drank another beer. There was quite a pile of saucers now on the table in front of me. The man opposite me had taken off his spectacles, put them away in a case, folded his paper and put it in his pocket and now sat holding his liqueur glass and looking out at the room. Suddenly I knew I had to get back. I called the waiter, paid the reckoning, got into my coat, put on my hat and started out the door. I walked through the rain up to the hospital.

Upstairs I met the nurse coming down the hall.

"I just called you at the hotel," she said. Something dropped inside me.

"What is wrong?"

"Mrs. Henry has had a hemorrhage[21]."

"Can I go in?"

"No, not yet. The doctor is with her."

"Is it dangerous?"

"It is very dangerous." The nurse went into the room and shut the door. I sat outside in the hall. Everything was gone inside of me. I did not think. I could not think. I knew she was going to die and I prayed that she would not. Don't let her die. Oh, God, please don't let her die. I'll do anything for you if you won't let her die. Please, please, please, dear God, don't let her die. Dear God, don't let her die. Please, please, please don't let her die. God please make her not die. I'll do anything you say if you don't let her die. You took the baby but don't let her die. That was all right but don't let her die. Please, please, dear God, don't let her die.

The nurse opened the door and motioned with her finger for me to come. I followed her into the room. Catherine did not look up when I came in. I went over to the side of the bed. The doctor was standing by the bed on the opposite side. Catherine looked at me and smiled. I bent down over the bed and started to cry.

"Poor darling," Catherine said very softly. She looked gray.

"You're all right, Cat," I said. "You're going to be all right."

"I'm going to die," she said; then waited and said, "I hate it."

I took her hand.

"Don't touch me," she said. I let go of her hand. She smiled. "Poor darling. You touch me all you want."

"You'll be all right, Cat. I know you'll be all right."

"I meant to write you a letter to have if anything happened, but I didn't do it."

"Do you want me to get a priest or any one to come and see you?"

"Just you," she said. Then a little later, "I'm not afraid. I just hate it."

"You must not talk so much," the doctor said.

"All right," Catherine said.

"Do you want me to do anything, Cat? Can I get you anything?"

Catherine smiled, "No." Then a little later, "You won't do our things with another girl, or say the same things, will you?"

"Never."

"I want you to have girls, though."

"I don't want them."

"You are talking too much," the doctor said. "Mr. Henry must go out. He can come back again later. You are not going to die. You must not be silly."

"All right," Catherine said. "I'll come and stay with you nights," she said. It was very hard for her to talk.

"Please go out of the room," the doctor said. "You cannot talk." Catherine winked at me, her face gray. "I'll be right outside," I said.

"Don't worry, darling," Catherine said. "I'm not a bit afraid. It's just a dirty trick."

"You dear, brave sweet."

I waited outside in the hall. I waited a long time. The nurse came to the door and came over to me. "I'm afraid Mrs. Henry is very ill," she said. "I'm afraid for her."

"Is she dead?"

"No, but she is unconscious."

It seems she had one hemorrhage after another. They couldn't stop it. I went into the room and stayed with Catherine until she died. She was unconscious all the time, and it did not take her very long to die.

Outside the room, in the hall, I spoke to the doctor, "is there anything I can do tonight?"

"No. There is nothing to do. Can I take you to your hotel?"

"No, thank you. I am going to stay here a while."

"I know there is nothing to say. I cannot tell you—"

"No," I said. "There's nothing to say."

"Good-night," he said. "I cannot take you to your hotel?"

"No, thank you."

"It was the only thing to do," he said. "The operation proved—"

"I do not want to talk about it," I said.

"I would like to take you to your hotel."

"No, thank you."

He went down the hall. I went to the door of the room.

"You can't come in now," one of the nurses said.

"Yes I can," I said.

"You can't come in yet."

"You get out," I said. "The other one too."

But after I had got them out and shut the door and turned off the light it wasn't any good. It was like saying good-by to a statue. After a while I went out and left the hospital and walked back to the hotel in the rain.

注释（Notes）

1. protracted：延长的,拖延的。
2. slackened：使松弛,放松。
3. zinc：锌。
4. brioche：奶油蛋卷。
5. slopping：(液体)溢出,溅出,泼出。
6. petcock：小龙头,小旋阀。
7. choucroute：酸泡菜。
8. A demi：这里指小杯。
9. a bock：这里指大杯。
10. plump：饱满的,丰满的,圆润的。
11. anaesthetics：麻醉药,麻醉剂。
12. forceps：钳子,镊子。
13. Caesarean：剖腹产的。
14. cylinder：(尤指用作容器的)圆筒状物,这里指气罐。
15. amphitheatre：阶梯式座位大厅(或剧场)。
16. the Inquisition：宗教裁判是欧洲中世纪的一种残酷的审判,用酷刑逼口供,惨无人道。封建势力利用它来镇压人民。
17. puckered-up：(尤指某人脸部或面貌)起皱,起褶。
18. They threw you in and told you the rules and the first time they caught you off base they killed you：作者借棒球来象征人生的残酷,也就是资本主义社会的残酷。棒球中一个基本活动是偷垒,如偷不成就被逼出局。
19. messiah：(基督徒心目中的)救世主耶稣。
20. veal：(食用)小牛肉。

21. hemorrhage:(大)出血。

主题探究 (Themes)

(扫码阅读)

问题讨论 (Questions for Discussion)

1. What's up with the title?

2. What do you think of the ending?

3. Does the novel challenge your ideas of masculinity? If so, how? If not, where does it present views similar to your own?

4. Some critics say that the female characters are all flat and underdeveloped, even Catherine. How do you feel about this?

5. What are some of the ways alcohol is used in the novel?

6. Frederic Henry feels like a criminal when he "deserts" the Italian army during the retreat, but some people believe that his so-called desertion is an act of bravery and heroism. What's your opinion?

(请扫码观看视频 *A Farewell to Arms*)

The Old Man and the Sea

作品简介 (Introduction to the Work)

The Old Man and the Sea is a novella written in 1951 and published in 1952. In *The Old Man and the Sea*, for eighty-four days Santiago does not catch a single fish, but he does not give up. On the eighty-fifth day, he sails out before dawn, fishing alone in a skiff in the Gulf Stream. He goes far out into the sea and at last hooks a giant marlin. The hooked fish moves away slowly and steadily as they travel on the calm sea. A desperate struggle ensues in which Santiago is almost exhausted and he tries to kill the fish and tie it to his small boat. But when he is ready for home, sharks come up from the deep water. Santiago's struggle with the giant sharks is even more breathtaking than with the marlin. He first uses his knife then his club, and then his oar handle to fight against the sharks. In the end the marlin is consumed by the sharks and only a skeleton remains. Santiago brings the skeleton home and goes to bed almost dead from exhaustion. In his sleep, a lion comes into his dream.

(扫码阅读)

The Old Man and the Sea

(Excerpt)

A Clean, Well-Lighted Place

作品简介 (Introduction to the Work)

"A Clean, Well-Lighted Place" was published in 1926, but the story appeared again in 1933 in *Winner Take Nothing*, a collection of Hemingway short stories. Late at night, a deaf old man is the sole patron in a café. Nearby, two waiters, one young, the other older, talk about him. When the old man orders another brandy, the young waiter purposely overfills his glass. The waiters speculate about the old man's recent suicide attempt. The young waiter wants the patron to go home, and complains that he never gets to bed before three o'clock, while the older waiter is more understanding of the old man's plight. Again the old man asks for another brandy, but this time the young man tells him the cafe is closed. After he leaves, the waiters resume their discussion. The young waiter wants to hurry home to his wife; the older waiter is more thoughtful. He muses on youth and observes that he is now one "of those who like to stay late in the cafe", likening himself to the old man. He mentions the importance to some people of having "a clean, well-lighted place" in which they can spend time. After the young waiter leaves, the older waiter reflects on the emptiness of his own life and returns to his home and his insomnia. In only a few pages, the story deals with several of the hard-hitting themes we see in many of Hemingway's works—namely, loneliness, isolation, and the futility of modern society.

Critics often see these themes emerge as reflections of the cultural and spiritual malaise of the disillusioned, post-World War I Western world. This story, with its suggestion of war (the presence of the soldier and the guard) and disconnected, lonely characters, manages to bring three vast concepts—loneliness, age, and death—to the reader in an incredibly effective, tragic yet subdued way.

作品选文 (Selected Reading)

A Clean, Well-Lighted Place

It was late and every one had left the café except an old man who sat in the shadow the leaves of the tree made against the electric light. In the daytime the street was dusty, but at night the dew settled the dust and the old man liked to sit late because he was deaf and now at night it was quiet and he felt the difference. The two waiters inside the café knew that the old man was a little drunk, and while he was a good client they knew that if he became too drunk he would leave without paying, so they kept watch on him.

"Last week he tried to commit suicide," one waiter said.

"Why?"

"He was in despair."

"What about?"

"Nothing."

"How do you know it was nothing?"

"He has plenty of money."

They sat together at a table that was close against the wall near the door of the café and looked at the terrace where the tables were all empty except where the old man sat in the shadow of the leaves of the tree that moved slightly in the wind. A girl and a soldier went by in the street. The street light shone on the brass number on his collar. The girl wore no head covering and hurried beside him.

"The guard will pick him up[1]," one waiter said.

"What does it matter if he gets what he's after?"

"He had better get off the street now. The guard will get him. They went by five minutes ago."

The old man sitting in the shadow rapped on his saucer with his glass. The younger waiter went over to him.

"What do you want?"

The old man looked at him. "Another brandy," he said.

"You'll be drunk," the waiter said. The old man looked at him. The waiter went away.

"He'll stay all night," he said to his colleague. "I'm sleepy now. I never get into bed before three o'clock. He should have killed himself last week."

The waiter took the brandy bottle and another saucer from the counter inside the café and marched out to the old man's table. He put down the saucer and poured the glass full of brandy.

"You should have killed yourself last week," he said to the deaf man. The old man motioned with his finger. "A little more," he said. The waiter poured on into the glass so that the brandy slopped over and ran down the stem into the top saucer of the pile. "Thank you," the old man said. The waiter took the bottle back inside the café. He sat down at the table with his colleague again.

"He's drunk now," he said.

"He's drunk every night."

"What did he want to kill himself for?"

"How should I know."

"How did he do it?"

"He hung himself with a rope."

"Who cut him down[2]?"

"His niece."

"Why did they do it?"

"Fear for his soul[3]."

"How much money has he got?"

"He's got plenty."

"He must be eighty years old."

"Anyway I should say he was eighty."

"I wish he would go home. I never get to bed before three o'clock. What kind of hour is that to go to bed?"

"He stays up because he likes it."

"He's lonely. I'm not lonely. I have a wife waiting in bed for me."

"He had a wife once too."

"A wife would be no good to him now."

"You can't tell. He might be better with a wife."

"His niece looks after him."

"I know. You said she cut him down."

"I wouldn't want to be that old. An old man is a nasty thing."

"Not always. This old man is clean. He drinks without spilling. Even now, drunk. Look at him."

"I don't want to look at him. I wish he would go home. He has no regard for those who must work."

The old man looked from his glass across the square, then over at the waiters.

"Another brandy," he said, pointing to his glass. The waiter who was in a hurry came over.

"Finished," he said, speaking with that omission of syntax stupid people employ when talking to drunken people or foreigners. "No more tonight. Close now."

"Another," said the old man.

"No. Finished." The waiter wiped the edge of the table with a towel and shook his head.

The old man stood up, slowly counted the saucers[4], took a leather coin purse from his pocket and paid for the drinks, leaving half a peseta[5] tip.

The waiter watched him go down the street, a very old man walking unsteadily but with dignity.

"Why didn't you let him stay and drink?" the unhurried waiter asked. They were putting up the shutters. "It is not half-past two."

"I want to go home to bed."

"What is an hour?"

"More to me than to him[6]."

"An hour is the same."

"You talk like an old man yourself. He can buy a bottle and drink at home."

"It's not the same."

"No, it is not," agreed the waiter with a wife. He did not wish to be unjust. He was only in a hurry.

"And you? You have no fear of going home before your usual hour?"

"Are you trying to insult me?"

"No, hombre[7], only to make a joke."

"No," the waiter who was in a hurry said, rising from pulling down the metal shutters. "I have confidence. I am all confidence."

"You have youth, confidence, and a job," the older waiter said. "You have everything."

"And what do you lack?"

"Everything but work."

"You have everything I have."

"No. I have never had confidence and I am not young."

"Come on. Stop talking nonsense and lock up."

"I am of those who like to stay late at the café," the older waiter said. "With all those who do not want to go to bed. With all those who need a light for the night."

"I want to go home and into bed."

"We are of two different kinds," the older waiter said. He was now dressed to go home. "It is not only a question of youth and confidence although those things are very beautiful. Each night I am reluctant to close up because there may be some one who needs the café."

"Hombre, there are bodegas open all night long."

"You do not understand. This is a clean and pleasant café. It is well lighted. The light is very good and also, now, there are shadows of the leaves."

"Good night," said the younger waiter.

"Good night," the other said. Turning off the electric light he continued the conversation with himself. It is the light of course but it is necessary that the place be clean and pleasant. You do not want music. Certainly you do not want music. Nor can you stand before a bar with dignity although that is all that is provided for these hours. What did he fear? It was not a fear or dread. It was a nothing that he knew too well. It was all a nothing and a man was a nothing too. It was only that and light was all it needed and a certain cleanness and order. Some lived in it and never felt it but he knew it all was nada[8] y[9] pues[10] nada y nada y pues nada. Our nada who art in nada, nada be thy name thy kingdom nada thy will be nada in nada as it is in nada. Give us this nada our daily nada and nada us our nada as we nada our nadas and nada us not into nada but deliver us from nada; pues nada. Hail nothing full of nothing, nothing is with thee.[11] He smiled and stood before a bar with a shining steam pressure coffee machine.

"What's yours?" asked the barman.

"Nada."

"Otro loco mas[12]," said the barman and turned away.

"A little cup," said the waiter.

The barman poured it for him.

"The light is very bright and pleasant but the bar is unpolished," the waiter said.

The barman looked at him but did not answer. It was too late at night for conversation.

"You want another copita[13]?" the barman asked.

"No, thank you," said the waiter and went out. He disliked bars and bodegas. A clean, well-lighted café was a very different thing. Now, without thinking further, he would go home to his room. He would lie in the bed and finally, with daylight, he would go to sleep. After all, he said to himself, it is probably only insomnia. Many must have it.

注释（Notes）

1. The guard will pick him up：(宵禁)卫兵会逮捕他的。
2. Who cut him down：是谁把绳子切断救他下来的？
3. Fear for his soul：为他的灵魂不能得救而担心。基督教认为自杀是一种犯罪，是对上帝行为的干预。
4. The old man…counted the saucers，…顾客根据碟子的数量计算自己要了多少杯酒。
5. peseta：比塞塔(西班牙货币单位)
6. More to me than to him：对我比对他重要得多。
7. hombre：(西班牙文)男人，老兄。
8. nada：(西班牙文)不存在，没有，虚无。
9. y：(西班牙文)和，所以，那么。
10. pues：(西班牙文)既然，那么。
11. Our nada who art… nothing is with thee.：这是一段模仿祷告词，其中的名词和动词等实词被"虚无"取代，表明一切事物和行为都是虚无。
12. Otro loco mas：(西班牙文)又一个疯子。这句话表明以世人的标准来看，年长侍者的行为是"不正常"的。
13. copita：西班牙等地所产浅黄或深褐色葡萄酒。

主题探究（Themes）

(扫码阅读)

价值引领（Value Guidance）

人生是虚无吗？

每个人在一生中都会有空虚、迷茫、疲乏的时候，都会有意义感缺失的时刻。人们会思考人生的意义这个问题，最根本的原因其实在于，现在的他无法从生活中体会到意义感和满足感。很多人都知道"人生意义是自己创造出来的，是自己赋予的"这句话，这句话的本意是指当你去做自己喜欢的、自己认为有意义的事情时，你自然而然就会感觉到充足的意义感和满足感。还可以指走出自己的舒适区，多去做一些曾经没做过、不敢做、逃避去做的事情，尝试着建立更多的人际关系，试着去全力完成一个过去被你屡次放弃的目标。

让我们从下面的名言中思考人生的意义吧：

那些为大多数人带来幸福的人是最幸福的人。（马克思）

生活的价值在于创造。（高尔基）

生命跟时代的崇高责任联系在一起就会永垂不朽。（车尔尼雪夫斯基）

你若要喜爱自己的价值，你就得给世界创造价值。（歌德）

内容充实的生命就是长久的生命，我们要以此而不是以时间来衡量生命。（塞涅卡）

生活是一种绵延不绝的渴望，渴望不断上升，变得更伟大而高贵。（杜·伽尔）

做好事的乐趣乃是人生唯一可靠的幸福。（列夫·托尔斯泰）

无论一个人的天赋如何优异，外表或内心如何美好，也必须在他的德性的光辉照耀到他人身上发生了热力，再由感受他的热力的人把那热力反射到自己身上的时候，才能体会到他本身的价值。（莎士比亚）

问题讨论（Questions for Discussion）

1. Do you think the younger waiter will always be so self-satisfied and confident?

2. What do you think the older waiter means when he says "It was all a nothing and a man was a nothing too"?

3. Why does the old man have to be drunk all the time?

4. What does the younger waiter understand about old age?

5. What is the significance of "insomnia" at the end of the story? Why might the older waiter dismiss his dissatisfaction as such?

6. "A clean, well-lighted place", preferably a clean, well-lighted café. The image of the café is central to the story. So, what does it symbolize?

7. Who is the narrator, can she or he read minds, and, more importantly, can we trust her or him?

（请扫码观看视频"A Clean, Well-lighted Place"）

Hills like White Elephants

作品简介 (Introduction to the Work)

"Hills like White Elephants" is a short story by Ernest Hemingway. It was first published in August 1927, in the literary magazine transition, then later in the 1927 short story collection *Men Without Women*. The story focuses on a conversation between an American man and a young woman, described as a "girl", at a Spanish train station while waiting for a train to Madrid. The girl compares the nearby hills to white elephants. The pair indirectly discuss an "operation" that the man wants the girl to have, which is implied to be an abortion.

作品选文 (Selected Reading)

Hills like White Elephants

The hills across the valley of the Ebro[1] were long and white. On this side there was no shade and no trees and the station was between two lines of rails in the sun. Close against the side of the station there was the warm shadow of the building and a curtain, made of strings of bamboo beads, hung across the open door into the bar, to keep out flies. The American and the girl with him sat at a table in the shade, outside the building. It was very hot and the express from Barcelona would come in forty minutes. It stopped at this junction for two minutes and went on to Madrid.

"What should we drink?" the girl asked. She had taken off her hat and put it on the table.

"It's pretty hot," the man said.

"Let's drink beer."

"Dos cervezas[2]," the man said into the curtain.

"Big ones?" a woman asked from the doorway.

"Yes. Two big ones."

The woman brought two glasses of beer and two felt pads. She put the felt pads and the beer glasses on the table and looked at the man and the girl. The girl was looking off at the line of hills. They were white in the sun and the country was brown and dry.

"They look like white elephants," she said.

"I've never seen one," the man drank his beer.

"No, you wouldn't have."

"I might have," the man said. "Just because you say I wouldn't have doesn't prove anything."

The girl looked at the bead curtain. "They've painted something on it," she said. "What does it say?"

"Anis del Toro[3]. It's a drink."

"Could we try it?"

The man called "Listen" through the curtain. The woman came out from the bar.

"Four reales[4]."

"We want two Anis del Toro."

"With water?"

"Do you want it with water?"

"I don't know," the girl said. "Is it good with water?"

"It's all right."

"You want them with water?" asked the woman.

"Yes, with water."

"It tastes like licorice[5]," the girl said and put the glass down.

"That's the way with everything."

"Yes," said the girl. "Everything tastes of licorice. Especially all the things you've waited so long for, like absinthe."

"Oh, cut it out."

"You started it," the girl said. "I was being amused. I was having a fine time."

"Well, let's try and have a fine time."

"All right. I was trying. I said the mountains looked like white elephants. Wasn't that bright?"

"That was bright."

"I wanted to try this new drink. That's all we do, isn't it—look at things and try new drinks?"

"I guess so."

The girl looked across at the hills.

"They're lovely hills," she said. "They don't really look like white elephants. I just meant the coloring of their skin through the trees."

"Should we have another drink?"

"All right."

The warm wind blew the bead curtain against the table.

"The beer's nice and cool," the man said.

"It's lovely," the girl said.

"It's really an awfully simple operation, Jig," the man said. "It's not really an operation at all."

The girl looked at the ground the table legs rested on.

"I know you wouldn't mind it, Jig. It's really not anything. It's just to let the air in."

The girl did not say anything.

"I'll go with you and I'll stay with you all the time. They just let the air in and then it's all perfectly natural."

"Then what will we do afterward?"

"We'll be fine afterward. Just like we were before."

"What makes you think so?"

"That's the only thing that bothers us. It's the only thing that's made us unhappy."

The girl looked at the bead curtain, put her hand out and took hold of two of the strings of beads.

"And you think then we'll be all right and be happy."

"I know we will. You don't have to be afraid. I've known lots of people that have done it."

"So have I," said the girl. "And afterward they were all so happy."

"Well," the man said, "if you don't want to you don't have to. I wouldn't have you do it if you didn't want to. But I know it's perfectly simple."

"And you really want to?"

"I think it's the best thing to do. But I don't want you to do it if you don't really want to."

"And if I do it you'll be happy and things will be like they were and you'll love me?"

"I love you now. You know I love you."

"I know. But if I do it, then it will be nice again if I say things are like white elephants, and you'll like it?"

"I'll love it. I love it now but I just can't think about it. You know how I get when I worry."

"If I do it you won't ever worry?"

"I won't worry about that because it's perfectly simple."

"Then I'll do it. Because I don't care about me."

"What do you mean?"

"I don't care about me."

"Well, I care about you."

"Oh, yes. But I don't care about me. And I'll do it and then everything will be fine."

"I don't want you to do it if you feel that way."

The girl stood up and walked to the end of the station. Across, on the other side, were fields of grain and trees along the banks of the Ebro. Far away, beyond the river, were mountains. The shadow of a cloud moved across the field of grain and she saw the river through the trees.

"And we could have all this," she said. "And we could have everything and every day we make it more impossible."

"What did you say?"

"I said we could have everything."

"We can have everything."

"No, we can't."

"We can have the whole world."

"No, we can't."

"We can go everywhere."

"No, we can't. It isn't ours any more."

"It's ours."

"No, it isn't. And once they take it away, you never get it back."

"But they haven't taken it away."

"We'll wait and see."

"Come on back in the shade," he said. "You mustn't feel that way."

"I don't feel any way," the girl said. "I just know things."

"I don't want you to do anything that you don't want to do—"

"Nor that isn't good for me," she said. "I know. Could we have another beer?"

"All right. But you've got to realize—"

"I realize," the girl said. "Can't we maybe stop talking?"

They sat down at the table and the girl looked across at the hills on the dry side of the valley and the man looked at her and at the table.

"You've got to realize," he said, "that I don't want you to do it if you don't want to. I'm perfectly willing to go through with it if it means anything to you."

"Doesn't it mean anything to you? We could get along."

"Of course it does. But I don't want anybody but you. I don't want any one else. And I know it's perfectly simple."

"Yes, you know it's perfectly simple."

"It's all right for you to say that, but I do know it."

"Would you do something for me now?"

"I'd do anything for you."

"Would you please please please please please please please stop talking?"

He did not say anything but looked at the bags against the wall of the station. There were labels on them from all the hotels where they had spent nights.

"But I don't want you to," he said, "I don't care anything about it."

"I'll scream," the girl said.

The woman came out through the curtains with two glasses of beer and put them down on the damp felt pads. "The train comes in five minutes," she said.

"What did she say?" asked the girl.

"That the train is coming in five minutes."

The girl smiled brightly at the woman, to thank her.

"I'd better take the bags over to the other side of the station," the man said. She smiled at him.

"All right. Then come back and we'll finish the beer."

He picked up the two heavy bags and carried them around the station to the other tracks. He looked up the tracks but could not see the train. Coming back, he walked through the barroom, where people waiting for the train were drinking. He drank an Anis at the bar and looked at the people. They were all waiting reasonably for the train. He went out through the bead curtain⁶. She was sitting at the table and smiled at him.

"Do you feel better?" he asked.

"I feel fine," she said. "There's nothing wrong with me. I feel fine."

注释（Notes）

1. Ebro：埃布罗河位于西班牙东北部，是西班牙最长的河流。
2. Dos cervezas：西班牙语，意为"两杯啤酒"。
3. Anis del Toro：西班牙语，托罗茴香酒。
4. reales：雷阿尔，西班牙的货币单位。
5. licorice：甘草。
6. the bead curtain：珠帘。

主题探究（Themes）

（扫码阅读）

问题讨论（Questions for Discussion）

1. Why does the author choose the title as it is?
2. What's the significance of the setting?

3. Who is the narrator?

4. Has the quarrel been resolved when the story ends? Why did she smile?

5. Why is Jig's nationality not given, while the man's is given? Does she sound American to you? Why or why not? Where might she be from?

6. Would you feel different about the story if the roles of Jig and the man were reversed, that is, if Jig wanted the abortion and the man wanted her to marry him and keep the baby?

7. Is this story relevant today? We know that the story is set in Spain, but if you didn't know it was written in 1927, could you place it in a period of history? If so, when?

（请扫码观看视频"Hills like White Elephants"）

Unit 28
Modern Fiction (Ⅲ)

William Faulkner: "A Rose for Emily"
▽

作者简介 (Introduction to the Author)

William Faulkner (1897—1962), one of the most influential writers in the history of American literature, is a representative figure of stream of consciousness literature in the United States. Faulkner was born in a declining manor family in New Albany, Mississippi. He was fond of reading since childhood, but he did not receive much formal education. He only stayed at the University of Mississippi for more than one year. Faulkner joined the Royal Air Force in his youth, and then briefly traveled to Europe. In the late 1920s, he began to write. Though his work was published as early as 1919, and largely during the 1920s and 1930s, Faulkner was relatively unknown. At first, his works had little influence in the United States and often could not be sold. However, in Europe, some young writers paid attention to his works. In the 1930s, he wrote screenplays for Hollywood to seek greater economic success. In 1946, Malcolm Cowley's *The Portable Faulkner* was published, and Faulkner was widely recognized by the critics. In 1949, Faulkner won the Nobel Prize in Literature "for his powerful and artistically unique contribution to the modern American novel". In his life, he wrote 19 novels and more than 120 short stories, of which 15 novels and most short stories took place in Yoknapatawpha County, which is called "Yoknapatawpha lineage". His most representative work is *The Sound and the Fury*. In a word, Faulkner is undoubtedly the greatest writer of American Southern literature.

作品简介 (Introduction to the Work)

"A Rose for Emily" is a short story by William Faulkner, originally published in *The Forum* in 1930 before being collected in Faulkner's collection, *These Thirteen*, the following year. The story begins at the huge funeral for Miss Emily Grierson. Nobody has been to her house in ten years, except for her servant, so everyone is pretty thrilled to get a peek inside. Spanning approximately 74 years, this short story spins backwards and forwards in time like memory, and shows a southern town torn between the present and the past. The memory in the story skips around back and forth just like our memory work. At the end of it, the story cycles back to where it began, at her funeral. Tobe, miss Emily's servant, lets in townspeople and then leaves by the backdoor. He's never seen again. After the funeral, and after Emily is buried, the townspeople go upstairs to break into the room that they know has been closed for forty years. Inside, they find the corpse of Homer Barron, rotting in the bed. On the dust of the pillow next to Homer they find an indentation of a head, and there, in the indentation, a long, gray hair of Emily.

作品选文 (Selected Reading)

A Rose for Emily

I

When Miss Emily Grierson died, our whole town went to her funeral: the men through a sort of respectful affection for a fallen monument, the women mostly out of curiosity to see the inside of her house, which no one save an old man-servant—a combined gardener and cook—had seen in at least ten years.

It was a big, squarish[1] frame house that had once been white, decorated with cupolas[2] and spires[3] and scrolled[4] balconies in the heavily lightsome style of the seventies[5], set on what had once been our most select street. But garages[6] and cotton gins[7] had encroached[8] and obliterated even the august names of that neighborhood; only Miss Emily's house was left, lifting its stubborn and coquettish[9] decay above the cotton wagons and the gasoline pumps-an eyesore among eyesores. And now Miss Emily had gone to join the representatives of those august names where they lay in the cedar-bemused cemetery among the ranked and anonymous graves of Union and Confederate soldiers who fell at the battle of Jefferson.

Alive, Miss Emily had been a tradition, a duty, and a care; a sort of hereditary obligation upon the town, dating from that day in 1894 when Colonel Sartoris, the mayor—he who fathered the edict that no Negro woman should appear on the streets without an apron-remitted her taxes, the dispensation dating from the death of her father on into perpetuity. Not that Miss Emily would have accepted charity. Colonel Sartoris invented an involved tale to the effect that Miss Emily's father had loaned money to the town, which the town, as a matter of business, preferred this way of repaying. Only a man of Colonel Sartoris' generation and thought could have invented it, and only a woman could have believed it.

When the next generation, with its more modern ideas, became mayors and aldermen[10], this arrangement created some little dissatisfaction. On the first of the year they mailed her a tax notice. February came, and there was no reply. They wrote her a formal letter, asking her to call at the sheriff's office at her convenience. A week later the mayor wrote her himself, offering to call or to send his car for her, and received in reply a note on paper of an archaic shape, in a thin, flowing calligraphy in faded ink, to the effect that she no longer went out at all. The tax notice was also enclosed[11], without comment.

They called a special meeting of the Board of Aldermen. A deputation[12] waited upon her, knocked at the door through which no visitor had passed since she ceased giving china-painting lessons eight or ten years earlier. They were admitted by the old Negro into a dim hall from which a stairway mounted into still more shadow. It smelled of dust and disuse—a close, dank[13] smell. The Negro led them into the parlor. It was furnished in heavy, leather-covered furniture. When the Negro opened the blinds of one window, they could see that the leather was cracked[14]; and when they sat down, a faint dust rose sluggishly about their thighs, spinning with slow motes[15] in the single sun-ray. On a tarnished[16] gilt[17] easel[18] before the fireplace stood a crayon[19] portrait of Miss Emily's father.

They rose when she entered—a small, fat woman in black, with a thin gold chain descending to her waist and vanishing into her belt, leaning on an ebony[20] cane with a tarnished gold head. Her skeleton was small and spare; perhaps that was why what would have been merely plumpness[21] in another was obesity in her. She looked bloated, like a body long submerged in motionless water, and of that pallid hue. Her eyes, lost in the fatty ridges[22] of her face, looked like two small pieces of coal pressed into a lump of dough[23] as they moved from one face to another while the visitors stated their errand.

She did not ask them to sit. She just stood in the door and listened quietly until the spokesman came to a stumbling[24] halt. Then they could hear the invisible watch ticking at the end of the gold chain.

Her voice was dry and cold. "I have no taxes in Jefferson. Colonel Sartoris explained it to me. Perhaps one of you can gain access to the city records and satisfy yourselves."

"But we have. We are the city authorities, Miss Emily. Didn't you get a notice from the sheriff, signed by him?"

"I received a paper, yes," Miss Emily said. "Perhaps he considers himself the sheriff... I have no taxes in Jefferson."

"But there is nothing on the books to show that, you see We must go by the—"

"See Colonel Sartoris. I have no taxes in Jefferson."

"But, Miss Emily—"

"See Colonel Sartoris." (Colonel Sartoris had been dead almost ten years.) "I have no taxes in Jefferson. Tobe!" The Negro appeared. "Show these gentlemen out."

II

Soshe vanquished[25] them, horse and foot, just as she had vanquished their fathers thirty years before about the smell.

That was two years after her father's death and a short time after her sweetheart—the one we believed would marry her—had deserted her. After her father's death she went out very little; after her sweetheart went away, people hardly saw her at all. A few of the ladies had the temerity to call, but were not received, and the only sign of life about the place was the Negro man—a young man then—going in and out with a market basket.

"Just as if a man—any man—could keep a kitchen properly," the ladies said; so they were not surprised when the smell developed. It was another link between the gross, teeming world and the high and mighty Griersons.

A neighbor, a woman, complained to the mayor, Judge Stevens, eighty years old.

"But what will you have me do about it, madam?" he said.

"Why, send her word to stop it," the woman said. "Isn't there a law?"

"I'm sure that won't be necessary," Judge Stevens said. "It's probably just a snake or a rat that nigger of hers killed in the yard. I'll speak to him about it."

The next day he received two more complaints, one from a man who came in diffident[26] deprecation[27]. "We really must do something about it, Judge. I'd be the last one in the world to bother Miss Emily, but we've got to do something." That night the Board of Aldermen met—three graybeards and one younger man, a member of the rising generation.

"It's simple enough," he said. "Send her word to have her place cleaned up. Give her a certain time to do it in, and if she don't..."

"Dammit, sir," Judge Stevens said, "will you accuse a lady to her face of smelling bad?"

So the next night, after midnight, four men crossed Miss Emily's lawn and slunk[28] about the house like burglars, sniffing along the base of the brickwork and at the cellar[29] openings while one of them performed a regular sowing motion with his hand out of a sack slung from his shoulder. They broke open the cellar door and sprinkled[30] lime[31] there, and in all the outbuildings. As they recrossed the lawn, a window that had been dark was lighted and Miss Emily sat in it, the light behind her, and her upright torso motionless as that of an idol. They crept quietly across the lawn and into the shadow of the locusts[32] that lined the street. After a week or two the smell went away.

That was when people had begun to feel really sorry for her. People in our town, remembering how old lady Wyatt, her great-aunt, had gone completely crazy at last, believed that the Griersons held themselves a little too high for what they really were. None of the young men were quite good enough for Miss Emily and such. We had long thought of them as a tableau[33], Miss Emily a slender figure in white in the background, her father a spraddled silhouette[34] in the foreground, his back to her and clutching a horsewhip, the two of them framed by the back-flung front door. So when she got to be thirty and was still single, we were not pleased exactly, but vindicated; even with insanity in the family she wouldn't have turned down all of her chances if they had really materialized.

When her father died, it got about that the house was all that was left to her; and in a way, people were glad. At last they could pity Miss Emily. Being left alone, and a pauper, she had become humanized. Now she too would know the old thrill and the old despair of a penny more or less[35].

The day after his death all the ladies prepared to call at the house and offer condolence and aid, as is our custom Miss Emily met them at the door, dressed as usual and with no trace of grief on her face. She told them that her father was not dead. She did that for three days, with the ministers calling on her, and the doctors, trying to persuade her to let them dispose of the body. Just as they were about to resort to law and force, she broke down, and they buried her father quickly.

We did not say she was crazy then. We believed she had to do that. We remembered all the young men her father had driven away, and we knew that with nothing left, she would have to cling to that which had robbed her, as people will.

III

She was sick for a long time. When we saw her again, her hair was cut short, making her look like a girl, with a vague resemblance to those angels in colored church windows—sort of tragic and serene[36].

The town had just let the contracts for paving the sidewalks, and in the summer after her father's death they began the work. The construction company came with riggers[37] and mules[38] and machinery, and a foreman named Homer Barron, a Yankee—a big, dark, ready man, with a big voice and eyes lighter than his face. The little boys would follow in groups to hear him cuss the riggers, and the riggers singing in time to the rise and fall of picks. Pretty soon he knew everybody in town. Whenever you heard a lot of laughing anywhere about the square, Homer Barron would be in the center of the group. Presently we began to see him and Miss Emily on Sunday afternoons driving in the yellow-wheeled buggy[39] and the matched team of bays from the livery stable.

At first we were glad that Miss Emily would have an interest, because the ladies all said, "Of course a Grierson would not think seriously of a Northerner, a day laborer." But there were still others, older people, who said that even grief could not cause a real lady to forget noblesse oblige—without calling it noblesse oblige. They just said, "Poor Emily. Her kinsfolk should come to her." She had some kin in Alabama; but years ago her father had fallen out with them over the estate of old lady Wyatt, the crazy woman, and there was no communication between the two families. They had not even been represented at the funeral.

And as soon as the old people said, "Poor Emily," the whispering began. "Do you suppose it's really so?" they said to one another. "Of course it is. What else could..." This behind their hands; rustling of craned silk and satin behind jalousies closed upon the sun of Sunday afternoon as the thin, swift clop-clop-clop of the matched team passed: "Poor Emily."

She carried her head high enough—even when we believed that she was fallen. It was as if she demanded more than ever the recognition of her dignity as the last Grierson; as if it had wanted that touch of earthiness to reaffirm her imperviousness[40]. Like when she bought the rat poison, the arsenic. That was over a year after they had begun to say "Poor Emily," and while the two female cousins were visiting her.

"I want some poison," she said to the druggist. She was over thirty then, still a slight woman, though thinner than usual, with cold, haughty black eyes in a face the flesh of which was strained across the temples and about the eyesockets[41] as you imagine a lighthouse-keeper's face ought to look. "I want some poison," she said.

"Yes, Miss Emily. What kind? For rats and such? I'd recom—"

"I want the best you have. I don't care what kind."

The druggist named several. "They'll kill anything up to an elephant. But what you want is—"

"Arsenic," Miss Emily said. "Is that a good one?"

"Is... arsenic? Yes, ma'am. But what you want—"

"I want arsenic."

The druggist looked down at her. She looked back at him, erect, her face like a strained flag. "Why, of course," the druggist said. "If that's what you want. But the law requires you to tell what you are going to use it for."

Miss Emily just stared at him, her head tilted back in order to look him eye for eye, until he looked away and went and got the arsenic and wrapped it up. The Negro delivery boy brought her the package; the druggist didn't come back. When she opened the package at home there was written on the box, under the skull and bones: "For rats."

IV

So the next day we all said, "She will kill herself"; and we said it would be the best thing. When she had first begun to be seen with Homer Barron, we had said, "She will marry him." Then we said, "She will persuade him yet," because Homer himself had remarked—he liked men, and it was known that he drank with the younger men in the

Elks' Club—that he was not a marrying man. Later we said, "Poor Emily" behind the jalousies[42] as they passed on Sunday afternoon in the glittering buggy, Miss Emily with her head high and Homer Barron with his hat cocked and a cigar in his teeth, reins and whip in a yellow glove.

Then some of the ladies began to say that it was a disgrace to the town and a bad example to the young people. The men did not want to interfere, but at last the ladies forced the Baptist minister—Miss Emily's people were Episcopal[43]—to call upon her. He would never divulge what happened during that interview, but he refused to go back again. The next Sunday they again drove about the streets, and the following day the minister's wife wrote to Miss Emily's relations in Alabama.

So she had blood-kin under her roof again and we sat back to watch developments. At first nothing happened. Then we were sure that they were to be married. We learned that Miss Emily had been to the jeweler's and ordered a man's toilet set in silver, with the letters H. B.[44] on each piece. Two days later we learned that she had bought a complete outfit of men's clothing, including a nightshirt, and we said, "They are married." We were really glad. We were glad because the two female cousins were even more Grierson than Miss Emily had ever been.

So we were not surprised when Homer Barron—the streets had been finished some time since—was gone. We were a little disappointed that there was not a public blowing-off, but we believed that he had gone on to prepare for Miss Emily's coming, or to give her a chance to get rid of the cousins. (By that time it was a cabal[45], and we were all Miss Emily's allies to help circumvent[46] the cousins.) Sure enough, after another week they departed. And, as we had expected all along, within three days Homer Barron was back in town. A neighbor saw the Negro man admit him at the kitchen door at dusk one evening.

And that was the last we saw of Homer Barron. And of Miss Emily for some time. The Negro man went in and out with the market basket, but the front door remained closed. Now and then we would see her at a window for a moment, as the men did that night when they sprinkled the lime, but for almost six months she did not appear on the streets. Then we knew that this was to be expected too; as if that quality of her father which had thwarted her woman's life so many times had been too virulent[47] and too furious to die.

When we next saw Miss Emily, she had grown fat and her hair was turning gray. During the next few years it grew grayer and grayer until it attained an even pepper-and-salt iron-gray, when it ceased turning. Up to the day of her death at seventy-four it was still that vigorous iron-gray, like the hair of an active man.

From that time on her front door remained closed, save for a period of six or seven years, when she was about forty, during which she gave lessons in china-painting. She fitted up a studio in one of the downstairs rooms, where the daughters and granddaughters of Colonel Sartoris' contemporaries were sent to her with the same regularity and in the same spirit that they were sent to church on Sundays with a twenty-five-cent piece for the collection plate. Meanwhile her taxes had been remitted.

Then the newer generation became the backbone and the spirit of the town, and the painting pupils grew up and fell away and did not send their children to her with boxes of color and tedious brushes and pictures cut from the ladies' magazines. The front door closed upon the last one and remained closed for good. When the town got free postal delivery, Miss Emily alone refused to let them fasten the metal numbers above her door and attach a mailbox to it. She would not listen to them.

Daily, monthly, yearly we watched the Negro grow grayer and more stooped, going in and out with the market basket. Each December we sent her a tax notice, which would be returned by the post office a week later, unclaimed. Now and then we would see her in one of the downstairs windows—she had evidently shut up the top floor of the house—like the carven torso of an idol in a niche, looking or not looking at us, we could never tell which. Thus she passed from generation to generation—dear, inescapable, impervious, tranquil, and perverse.

And so she died. Fell ill in the house filled with dust and shadows, with only a doddering[48] Negro man to wait on her. We did not even know she was sick; we had long since given up trying to get any information from the Negro

He talked to no one, probably not even to her, for his voice had grown harsh and rusty, as if from disuse.

She died in one of the downstairs rooms, in a heavy walnut bed with a curtain, her gray head propped on a pillow yellow and moldy with age and lack of sunlight.

V

The negro met the first of the ladies at the front door and let them in, with their hushed, sibilant[49] voices and their quick, curious glances, and then he disappeared. He walked right through the house and out the back and was not seen again.

The two female cousins came at once. They held the funeral on the second day, with the town coming to look at Miss Emily beneath a mass of bought flowers, with the crayon face of her father musing profoundly above the bier[50] and the ladies sibilant and macabre[51]; and the very old men—some in their brushed Confederate uniforms—on the porch and the lawn, talking of Miss Emily as if she had been a contemporary of theirs, believing that they had danced with her and courted her perhaps, confusing time with its mathematical progression, as the old do, to whom all the past is not a diminishing road but, instead, a huge meadow which no winter ever quite touches, divided from them now by the narrow bottle-neck of the most recent decade of years.

Already we knew that there was one room in that region above stairs which no one had seen in forty years, and which would have to be forced. They waited until Miss Emily was decently in the ground before they opened it.

The violence of breaking down the door seemed to fill this room with pervading dust. A thin, acrid pall as of the tomb seemed to lie everywhere upon this room decked and furnished as for a bridal: upon the valance curtains of faded rose color, upon the rose-shaded lights, upon the dressing table, upon the delicate array of crystal and the man's toilet things backed with tarnished silver, silver so tarnished that the monogram[52] was obscured. Among them lay a collar and tie, as if they had just been removed, which, lifted, left upon the surface a pale crescent[53] in the dust. Upon a chair hung the suit, carefully folded; beneath it the two mute shoes and the discarded socks.

The man himself lay in the bed.

For a long while we just stood there, looking down at the profound and fleshless grin. The body had apparently once lain in the attitude of an embrace, but now the long sleep that outlasts love, that conquers even the grimace[54] of love, had cuckolded[55] him. What was left of him, rotted beneath what was left of the nightshirt, had become inextricable from the bed in which he lay; and upon him and upon the pillow beside him lay that even coating of the patient and biding dust.

Then we noticed that in the second pillow was the indentation[56] of a head. One of us lifted something from it, and leaning forward, that faint and invisible dust dry and acrid in the nostrils, we saw a long strand of iron-gray hair.

注释（Notes）

1. squarish：有点方的,近似方形的。
2. cupolas：圆屋顶,穹顶。
3. spires：尖塔,尖顶。
4. scrolled：具有涡卷装饰的。
5. the seventies：指 19 世纪 70 年代。
6. garages：汽车修理厂。
7. cotton gins：轧棉机。
8. encroached：侵占。
9. coquettish：卖弄风情的。
10. aldermen：(美国和加拿大部分地区的)市政委员会委员。
11. enclosed：把……封入信封,随函附上。
12. deputation：代表团。
13. dank：阴湿的。

14. cracked：破裂的,有裂纹的。
15. motes：尘埃。
16. tarnished：(使)失去光泽。
17. gilt：镀金的。
18. easel：画架。
19. crayon：彩色炭笔。
20. ebony：乌木。
21. plumpness：丰满,丰腴。
22. ridges：(平面上的)隆起,脊,垄。
23. dough：生面团。
24. stumbling：结结巴巴说话,一再出错地说话。
25. vanquished：征服,击败。
26. diffident：谦卑的,害羞的,缺乏自信的。
27. deprecation：反对,不赞成。
28. slunk：偷偷摸摸地走。
29. cellar：地窖,地下室。
30. sprinkled：洒(水),撒(粉末)。
31. lime：石灰。
32. locusts：洋槐。
33. tableau：(由一群模特或静止不动的人扮演的故事或历史中的)画面,场景,活人造型。
34. silhouette：暗色轮廓,剪影。
35. the old thrill and the old despair of a penny more or less：这里指由古至今,"多一分钱喜极、少一分钱悲绝"的心情。
36. serene：平静的,安详的。
37. riggers：装配工,脚手架工,吊运工。
38. mules：骡,马骡。
39. buggy：小型车,轻便车。
40. imperviousness：不能渗透的,透不过的。
41. eyesockets：眼窝,眼眶。
42. jalousies：固定百叶窗。
43. Episcopal：(苏格兰和美国的)圣公会。
44. H. B.：即荷马·巴伦(Homer Barron)英文首字母。
45. cabal：秘密政治派系,秘密小集团。
46. circumvent：克服(问题,困难)(尤指暗中智取)。
47. virulent：恶毒的,充满敌意的。
48. doddering：(尤指因年迈)衰弱而步履蹒跚的。

49. sibilant：发咝咝声的。
50. bier：棺材架，停尸架。
51. macabre：恐怖的，令人毛骨悚然的。
52. monogram：交织字母，花押字（由两个或多个字母，尤指姓名首字母交织组成的图案，用以标明物属或用作标识）。
53. crescent：月牙形，新月形。
54. grimace：怪相，鬼脸。
55. cuckolded：给……戴绿帽子，与……的妻子（或丈夫）通奸。
56. indentation：压痕。

主题探究（Themes）

（扫码阅读）

问题讨论（Questions for Discussion）

1. In the short story, Emily is introduced as "a fallen monument", "a tradition", "a duty". What does the writer mean by this?

2. Why did Emily murder her lover? Did he deserve any compassion?

3. Who is the narrator of the story? What's the chronology of the narrative? What effects does it have?

4. Please interpret the symbols in the short story, such as the "rose" in the title, the big house, the pocket watch, the stationary and the hair, etc.

5. "A Rose for Emily" is a story about the extremes of isolation—by physical and emotional. Which character is more isolated, Tobe or Miss Emily? Does the town play a role in Miss Emily's isolation? If not, why not? If so, what are some of the things the town does to isolate her?

6. Is Emily trapped by the past? If so, which elements of the past trap her? Does she try to escape the trap?

（请扫码观看视频"A Rose for Emily"）

Unit 29
Contemporary Poets

Wallace Stevens: "The Emperor of Ice-Cream"
Robert Frost: "The Road Not Taken"

▽

作者简介 (Introduction to the Authors)

Wallace Stevens (1879—1955), a famous American modern poet, was born in Reading, Pennsylvania. He is considered to be one of the most respected American poets in the 20th century. He studied at Harvard University and later received his Bachelor of Laws from New York Law School. After graduating from New York Law School he became the Bar in New York in 1904. And also in this year he met Elsie Rachela, a young woman from Reading whom he married in 1909. They had a daughter, Holly, who was born in 1924 and later edited her father's letters and a collection of his poems. In 1916 Stevens joined the Hartford Accident and Indemnity Company, an insurance firm in Hartford, Connecticut, and he became a vice president of the firm in 1934. He worked there despite his increasing success as a poet until his death. Although he is now recognized as one of the major American poets in the twentieth century, Stevens was not able to publish his *Collection of Poems* until the year before his death, after which he was widely recognized. His main works are: *Ideas of Order* (1935), *The Man with the Blue Guitar* (1937), *Notes Toward a Supreme Fiction* (1942), and *The Auroras of Autumn*. In 1955, Wallace Stevens died in Hartford, the capital of Connecticut. Many poets such as James Merrill and Donald Justice had acknowledged Stevens as a major influence on their works, and his impact may also be seen in John Ashbery, Mark Strand, Jorie Graham, John Hollander and others. In a word, Wallace Stevens is no doubt one of the greatest American poets in the 20th century.

Robert Frost (1874—1963), a four-time Pulitzer Prize winner, is one of the most popular American poets of the 20th century. Frost was born in San Francisco. His father died when he was 11 so his mother moved him to New England. Frost started writing poetry at the age of 16 and published his first poem at 20. In 1897, he was admitted to Harvard University, but he dropped out due to tuberculosis. Three years later, his eldest son died. In 1912, his family moved to England because his poetry could not impress American newspaper editors and publishers. There, he not only wrote a great deal of poetry, but gradually perfected his unique poetic skills. During this period, he met the American exiled poet including the modernist literary master Ezra Pound and the British poet Edward Thomas. In 1913, Frost finally published his first collection of poems, *A Boy's Will*, which was well received by critics. Frost then compiled and published his second collection of poems, *North of Boston*. In February 1915, the Frost family moved back to Franconia, New Hampshire, USA. By this time, Frost's first two collections of poetry had been published in the United States and were widely praised by poetry critics. He subsequently published four collections of poetry, *New Hampshire*, *Collected Poems*, *A Further Range* and *A Witness Tree*, which won four Pulitzer Prizes in 1924, 1931, 1937 and 1943 respectively. During his lifetime, Frost received honorary degrees from 44 universities around the world, including honorary doctorates of letters from Oxford and Cambridge in 1957. As a poet, Frost deserves the title of Poet Laureate of the United States.

The Emperor of Ice-Cream

作品简介 (Introduction to the Work)

Ice-cream is so tasty and wonderful, there should be an emperor of it, right? This is sort of what Wallace Stevens is getting at in his poem, "The Emperor of Ice-Cream", first published in 1923. He is suggesting that we take a moment to appreciate all of the delicious and fun things that life has to offer without worrying about all of the technical stuff. The technical and serious stuff, according to Stevens, is often silly and not worth fussing over. Hence, we get a title like "The Emperor of Ice-Cream". The interesting thing about this poem is that all of the delightful language we get occurs during a funeral. Why fret about the fleeting, superficial conditions of existence? We should take a moment to appreciate things for what they are rather than what they seem. The main point of this poem seems to be that we need to start living more in the here and now. After all, one day we'll all end up like the dead woman at the funeral, with our feet sticking out of the sheets. The question is, how would you like to spend all the time you have between now and then? Worrying about appearances, or indulging your sweet tooth? We knew you and Stevens would hit it off.

作品选文 (Selected Reading)

The Emperor of Ice-Cream

Call the roller of big cigars,

The muscular one, and bid[1] him whip[2]
In kitchen cups concupiscent[3] curds[4].
Let the wenches[5] dawdle[6] in such dress
As they are used to wear, and let the boys
Bring flowers in last month's newspapers.
Let be be finale of seem.
The only emperor is the emperor of ice-cream.

Take from the dresser of deal[7],
Lacking the three glass knobs[8], that sheet
On which she embroidered[9] fantails[10] once
And spread it so as to cover her face.
If her horny feet protrude, they come
To show how cold she is, and dumb.
Let the lamp affix[11] its beam.
The only emperor is the emperor of ice-cream.

作品译文(扫码阅读)

注释 (Notes)

1. bid：命令，吩咐。
2. whip：搅打(奶油或鸡蛋)等。
3. concupiscent：好色的，贪欲的。
4. curds：凝乳(牛奶变酸后形成的白色黏稠物质)。
5. wenches：(古或幽默)少女；妓女。
6. dawdle：闲逛。
7. deal：pine(松木)或者其他便宜的木材。
8. knobs：把手。
9. embroidered：刺绣，装饰。
10. fantails：扇尾鸽。
11. affix：使附于，可固定。

主题探究（Themes）

（扫码阅读）

问题讨论（Questions for Discussion）

1. What's up with the title? What is an "emperor of ice cream"?
2. Wherever we see the emperor, we see "ice-cream". What does "ice cream" symbolize?
3. Why is "emperor of ice-cream" is "the only emperor"? What's Stevens saying about power in this refrain?
4. How does the speaker of the poem, as an authoritative director, participate in this theme of power?
5. How about the form and meter of the poem?
6. What's the importance of the last two lines of each stanza?

The Road Not Taken

作品简介（Introduction to the Work）

First published in Robert Frost's collection *Mountain Interval* in 1916, almost a century later "The Road Not Taken" is still quoted left and right by inspirational speakers, writers, commercials, and everyday people. Most people have been faced with a fork in an actual road or path, and not been sure which path to go down. Of course, today, we can whip out a GPS or cell phone and figure out which is the correct path. But if we're beyond the reach of satellites, we just make a choice, unaided by technology. We might pick the road that gets us where we want to go, or one that takes us somewhere new, but either way, the road we choose takes us to where we are. Just like trying to pick a path when we're driving or walking, we've all had to choose from different paths in life: which job to take, which college to go to, which girl or boy to ask to homecoming—the list of life's choices is endless. And for every metaphorical road we take in life, there is a road not taken. One of the big questions we face is whether or not to take the well-beaten, typical path. Is that the best choice, or should we be non-conformists and take the less-traveled route? Years into the future, after making our decision, how will we feel about the path we've chosen? Robert Frost's "The Road Not Taken" is about these quandaries, present in every person's life. A lot of people think this poem is encouraging us to take the road that's less traveled. And while it's easy to fall into that well-beaten path of analysis, it's not exactly accurate. So make sure that when you read this poem, you take your own road, whether it's the road less traveled or not.

作品选文 (Selected Reading)

The Road Not Taken

Two roads diverged[1] in a yellow wood,
And sorry I could not travel both
And be one traveler, long I stood
And looked down one as far as I could
To where it bent in the undergrowth[2];

Then took the other, as just as fair[3],
And having perhaps the better claim,
Because it was grassy and wanted wear[4];
Though as for that the passing there
Had worn them really about the same,

And both that morning equally lay
In leaves no step had trodden black.
Oh, I kept the first for another day!
Yet knowing how way leads on to way,
I doubted if I should ever come back.

I shall be telling this with a sigh
Somewhere ages and ages hence[5]:
Two roads diverged in a wood, and I—
I took the one less traveled by,
And that has made all the difference.

作品译文(扫码阅读)

注释 (Notes)

1. diverged：分岔，岔开。
2. undergrowth：下层灌木丛。
3. as just as fair：同样公平地。
4. wanted wear：踩踏的较少，want 在这里作 lack 解。
5. hence：从此后，从今后。

主题探究 (Themes)

(扫码阅读)

问题讨论 (Questions for Discussion)

1. Do you think the road the speaker took was really the less traveled one? Why?
2. What do you think the chances are that the speaker will get to come back and try the other path?
3. Do you think the speaker regrets his choice, or is happy about it? Why?
4. What type of choices do you think this fork in the road represents for the speaker?
5. What personal choices does this poem remind you of?

Unit 30
American Drama

Tennessee Williams: *A Streetcar Named Desire*

▽

作者简介 (Introduction to the Author)

Thomas Lanier Williams (1911—1983), known by his pen name Tennessee Williams, is considered as one of the most outstanding American playwrights in the 20th century. He was born in Columbus, Mississippi, which is in the middle of the United States. Williams was the second of Cornelius and Edwina Williams' three children. Raised predominantly by his mother, Williams had a complicated relationship with his father, a demanding salesman who preferred work instead of parenting. The relationship between his parents was also very tense. This depressing family atmosphere also provided motivation and material for Williams's later creation. In 1929, Williams entered the University of Missouri to study journalism, but under the pressure of his father, he dropped out of school and went home to find a job as a salesman. However, he did not like this job and often wrote poems and stories after work. In 1937, Williams returned to the University of Iowa to study. At the age of 28, Williams moved to New Orleans, where he changed his name and his way of life. In New Orleans, Williams wrote many plays, which brought him great success. In his later years, Williams was addicted to alcohol and drugs because of the poor evaluation of his works. In 1975, he wrote several new plays and memoirs, telling the story of his life and pain. Tennessee Williams won the Pulitzer Prize twice for his *A Streetcar Named Desire* and *Cat on a Hot Tin Roof*. Many of Williams's most acclaimed works have been adapted for the cinema. He also wrote short stories, poetry, essays, and a volume of memoirs. In 1979, four years before his death, Williams was inducted into the American Theater Hall of Fame. Along with contemporaries Eugene O'Neill and Arthur Miller, he is considered among the three foremost playwrights of 20th-century American drama.

作品简介 (Introduction to the Work)

A Streetcar Named Desire, a play in three acts by Tennessee Williams, first produced and published in 1947 and winner of the Pulitzer Prize for drama for that year. One of the most admired plays of its time, it concerns the mental and moral disintegration and ultimate ruin of Blanche DuBois, a former Southern belle. After encountering a series of personal losses, she leaves her once-prosperous situation to move into a shabby apartment in New Orleans rented by her younger sister and brother-in-law. Her neurotic, genteel pretensions are no match for the harsh realities symbolized by her brutish brother-in-law, Stanley Kowalski. In the last scene of the drama, at another poker game at the Kowalski apartment, Stella and her neighbor, Eunice, are packing Blanche's belongings while Blanche takes a bath in a catatonic state, having suffered a mental breakdown. Although Blanche has told Stella about Stanley's assault, Stella cannot bring herself to believe her sister's story. When a doctor and a matron arrive to take Blanche to the hospital, she initially resists them and collapses on the floor in confusion. Mitch, present at the poker game, breaks down in tears. When the doctor helps Blanche up, she goes willingly with him, saying: "Whoever you are—I have always depended on the kindness of strangers." The play ends with Stanley continuing to comfort a crying Stella, while the poker game continues uninterrupted.

作品选文 (Selected Reading)

A Streetcar Named Desire
(Excerpt)
Scene Eleven

It is some weeks later. Stella is packing Blanche's things. Sound of water can be heard running in the bathroom. The portieres[1] are partly open on the poker players—Stanley, Steve, Mitch and Pablo—who sit around the table in the kitchen. The atmosphere of the kitchen is now the same raw, lurid one of the disastrous poker night. The building is framed by the sky of turquoise[2]. Stella has been crying as she arranges the flowery dresses in the open trunk. Eunice comes down the steps from her flat above and enters the kitchen. There is an outburst from the poker table.

STANLEY:
Drew to an inside straight and made it, by God.
PABLO:
Maldita sea tu suerto[3]!
STANLEY:
Put it in English, greaseball[4].
PABLO:
I am cursing your rutting[5] luck.

STANLEY[prodigiously elated]:

You know what luck is? Luck is believing you're lucky. Take at Salerno[6]. I believed I was lucky. I figured that 4 out of 5 would not come through but I would... and I did. I put that down as a rule. To hold front position in this rat-race you've got to believe you are lucky.

MITCH:

You... you... you.... Brag... brag... bull... bull.

[Stella goes into the bedroom and starts folding a dress.]

STANLEY:

What's the matter with him?

EUNICE[walking past the table]:

I always did say that men are callous things with no feelings, but this does beat anything. Making pigs of yourselves. [She comes through the portieres into the bedroom.]

STANLEY:

What's the matter with her?

STELLA:

How is my baby?

EUNICE:

Sleeping like a little angel. Brought you some grapes. [She puts them on a stool[7] and lowers her voice.] Blanche?

STELLA:

Bathing.

EUNICE:

How is she?

STELLA:

She wouldn't eat anything but asked for a drink.

EUNICE:

What did you tell her?

STELLA:

I—just told her that—we'd made arrangements for her to rest in the country. She's got it mixed in her mind with Shep Huntleigh.

[Blanche opens the bathroom door slightly.]

BLANCHE:

Stella.

STELLA:

Yes, Blanche?

BLANCHE:

If anyone calls while I'm bathing take the number and tell them I'll call right back.

STELLA:

Yes.

BLANCHE:

That cool yellow silk—the bouclé[8]. See if it's crushed. If it's not too crushed I'll wear it and on the lapel that silver and turquoise pin in the shape of a seahorse. You will find them in the heart-shaped box I keep my accessories in. And Stella… Try and locate a bunch of artificial violets in that box, too, to pin with the seahorse on the lapel of the jacket.

[She closes the door. Stella turns to Eunice.]

STELLA:

I don't know if I did the right thing.

EUNICE:

What else could you do?

STELLA:

I couldn't believe her story and go on living with Stanley.

EUNICE:

Don't ever believe it. Life has got to go on. No matter what happens, you've got to keep on going.

[The bathroom door opens a little.]

BLANCHE [looking out]:

Is the coast clear?

STELLA:

Yes, Blanche. [To Eunice] Tell her how well she's looking.

BLANCHE:

Please close the curtains before I come out.

STELLA:

They're closed.

STANLEY:

—How many for you?

PABLO:

—Two.

STEVE:

—Three.

[Blanche appears in the amber⁹ light of the door. She has a tragic radiance in her red satin robe following the sculptural lines of her body. The "Varsouviana"¹⁰ rises audibly as Blanche enters the bedroom.]

BLANCHE[with faintly hysterical vivacity¹¹]:

I have just washed my hair.

STELLA:

Did you?

BLANCHE:

I'm not sure I got the soap out.

EUNICE:

Such fine hair!

BLANCHE[accepting the compliment]:

It's a problem. Didn't I get a call?

STELLA:

Who from, Blanche?

BLANCHE:

Shep Huntleigh…

STELLA:

Why, not yet, honey!

BLANCHE:

How strange! I—

[At the sound of Blanche's voice Mitch's arm supporting his cards has sagged and his gaze is dissolved into space. Stanley slaps him on the shoulder.]

STANLEY:

Hey, Mitch, come to!

[The sound of this new voice shocks Blanche. She makes a shocked gesture, forming his name with her lips. Stella nods and looks quickly away. Blanche stands quite still for some moments—the silverbacked mirror in her hand and a look of sorrowful perplexity as though all human experience shows on her face. Blanche finally speaks but with sudden hysteria.]

BLANCHE:

What's going on here?

[She turns from Stella to Eunice and back, to Stella. Her rising voice penetrates the concentration of the game. Mitch ducks his head lower but Stanley shoves back his chair as if about to rise. Steve places a restraining hand on his arm.]

BLANCHE[continuing]:

What's happened here? I want an explanation of what's happened here.

STELLA [agonizingly]:

Hush! Hush!

EUNICE:

Hush! Hush! Honey.

STELLA:

Please, Blanche.

BLANCHE:

Why are you looking at me like that? Is something wrong with me?

EUNICE:

You look wonderful, Blanche. Don't she look wonderful?

STELLA:

Yes.

EUNICE:

I understand you are going on a trip.

STELLA:

Yes, Blanche is. She's going on a vacation.

EUNICE:

I'm green with envy.

BLANCHE:

Help me, help me get dressed!

STELLA [handing her dress]:

Is this what you—

BLANCHE:

Yes, it will do! I'm anxious to get out of here—this place is a trap!

EUNICE:

What a pretty blue jacket.

STELLA:

It's lilac colored.

BLANCHE:

You're both mistaken. It's Della Robbia blue[12]. The blue of the robe in the old Madonna pictures. Are these grapes washed?

[She fingers the bunch of grapes which Eunice had brought in.]

EUNICE:

Huh?

BLANCHE:

Washed, I said. Are they washed?

EUNICE:

They're from the French Market.

BLANCHE:

That doesn't mean they've been washed. [The cathedral bells chime] Those cathedral bells—they're the only clean thing in the Quarter. Well, I'm going now. I'm ready to go.

EUNICE[whispering]:

She's going to walk out before they get here.

STELLA:

Wait, Blanche.

BLANCHE:

I don't want to pass in front of those men.

EUNICE:

Then wait'll the game breaks up.

STELLA:

Sit down and…

[Blanche turns weakly, hesitantly about. She lets them push her into a chair.]

BLANCHE:

I can smell the sea air. The rest of my time I'm going to spend on the sea. And when I die, I'm going to die on the sea. You know what I shall die of? [She plucks a grape] I shall die of eating an unwashed grape one day out on the ocean. I will die—with my hand in the hand of some nice-looking ship's doctor, a very young one with a small blond mustache and a big silver watch. "Poor lady," they'll say, "the quinine[12] did her no good. That unwashed grape has transported her soul to heaven." [The cathedral chimes are heard] And I'll be buried at sea sewn up in a clean white sack and dropped overboard—at noon—in the blaze of summer—and into an ocean as blue as [Chimes again] my first lover's eyes!

[A Doctor and a Matron have appeared around the corner of the building and climbed the steps to the porch. The gravity of their profession is exaggerated—the unmistakable aura of the state institution with its cynical detachment. The Doctor rings the doorbell. The murmur of the game is interrupted.]

EUNICE[whispering to Stella]:

That must be them.

[Stella presses her fists to her lips.]

BLANCHE[rising slowly]:

What is it?

EUNICE [affectedly casual]:

Excuse me while I see who's at the door.

STELLA:

Yes.

[Eunice goes into the kitchen.]

BLANCHE [tensely]:

I wonder if it's for me.

[A whispered colloquy takes place at the door.]

EUNICE [returning, brightly]:

Someone is calling for Blanche.

BLANCHE:

It is for me, then! [She looks fearfully from one to the other and then to the portieres. The "Varsouviana" faintly plays] Is it the gentleman I was expecting from Dallas?

EUNICE:

I think it is, Blanche.

BLANCHE:

I'm not quite ready.

STELLA:

Ask him to wait outside.

BLANCHE:

I...

[Eunice goes back to the portieres. Drums sound very softly.]

STELLA:

Everything packed?

BLANCHE:

My silver toilet articles are still out.

STELLA:

Ah!

EUNICE [returning]:

They're waiting in front of the house.

BLANCHE:

They! Who's "they"?

EUNICE:

There's a lady with him.

BLANCHE:

I cannot imagine who this "lady" could be! How is she dressed?

EUNICE:

Just—just a sort of a—plain-tailored outfit.

BLANCHE:

Possibly she's—[Her voice dies out nervously.]

STELLA:

Shall we go, Blanche?

BLANCHE:

Must we go through that room?

STELLA:

I will go with you.

BLANCHE:

How do I look?

STELLA:

Lovely.

EUNICE[echoing]:

Lovely.

[Blanche moves fearfully to the portieres. Eunice draws them open for her. Blanche goes into the kitchen.]

BLANCHE[to the men]:

Please don't get up. I'm only passing through.

[She crosses quickly to outside door. Stella and Eunice follow. The poker players stand awkwardly at the table—all except Mitch, who remains seated, looking down at the table. Blanche steps out on a small porch at the side of the door. She stops short and catches her breath.]

DOCTOR:

How do you do?

BLANCHE:

You are not the gentleman I was expecting. [She suddenly gasps and starts back up the steps. She stops by Stella, who stands just outside the door, and speaks in a frightening whisper] That man isn't Shep Huntleigh.

[The "Varsouviana" is playing distantly.

[Stella stares back at Blanche. Eunice is holding Stella's arm. There is a moment of silence—no sound but that of Stanley steadily shuffling the cards.]

[Blanche catches her breath again and slips back into the flat. She enters the flat with a peculiar smile, her eyes wide and brilliant. As soon as her sister goes past her, Stella closes her eyes and clenches her hands. Eunice throws her arms comfortably about her. Then she starts up to her flat. Blanche stops just inside the door. Mitch keeps staring down at his hands on the table, but the other men look, at her curiously. At last she starts around the table toward the bedroom. As she does, Stanley suddenly pushes back his chair and rises as if to block, her way. The Matron[14] follows her into the flat.]

STANLEY:

Did you forget something?

BLANCHE[shrilly]:

Yes! Yes, I forgot something!

[She rushes past him into the bedroom. Lurid reflections appear on the walls in odd, sinuous[15] shapes. The "Varsouviana" is filtered into a weird distortion, accompanied by the cries and noises of the jungle. Blanche seizes the back of a chair as if to defend herself.]

STANLEY[sotto voce[16]]:

Doc, you better go in.

DOCTOR[sotto voce, motioning to the Matron]:

Nurse, bring her out.

[The Matron advances on one side, Stanley on the other. Divested of all the softer properties of womanhood, the Matron is a peculiarly sinister[17] figure in her severe[18] dress. Her voice is bold and toneless as a fire-bell.]

MATRON:

Hello, Blanche.

[The greeting is echoed and re-echoed by other mysterious voices behind the walls, as if reverberated[19] through a canyon of rock.]

STANLEY:

She says that she forgot something.

[The echo sounds in threatening whispers.]

MATRON:

That's all right.

STANLEY:

What did you forget, Blanche?

BLANCHE:

I—I—

MATRON:

It don't matter. We can pick it up later.

STANLEY:

Sure. We can send it along with the trunk.

BLANCHE [retreating in panic]:

I don't know you—I don't know you. I want to be—left alone—please!

MATRON:

Now, Blanche!

ECHOES [rising and falling]:

Now, Blanche—now, Blanche—now, Blanche!

STANLEY:

You left nothing here but spilt talcum[20] and old empty perfume bottles—unless it's the paper lantern you want to take with you. You want the lantern?

[He crosses to dressing table and seizes the paper lantern, tearing it off the light bulb, and extends it toward her. She cries out as if the lantern was herself. The Matron steps boldly toward her. She screams and tries to break past the Matron. All the men spring to their feet. Stella runs out to the porch, with Eunice following to comfort her, simultaneously with the confused voices of the men in the kitchen. Stella rushes into Eunice's embrace on the porch.]

STELLA:

Oh, my God, Eunice help me! Don't let them do that to her, don't let them hurt her! Oh, God, oh, please God, don't hurt her! What are they doing to her? What are they doing? [She tries to break from Eunice's arms.]

EUNICE:

No, honey, no, no, honey. Stay here. Don't go back in there. Stay with me and don't look.

STELLA:

What have I done to my sister? Oh, God, what have I done to my sister?

EUNICE:

You done the right thing, the only thing you could do.

She couldn't stay here; there wasn't no other place for her to go.

[While Stella and Eunice are speaking on the porch the voices of the men in the kitchen overlap them. Mitch has started toward the bedroom. Stanley crosses to block him. Stanley pushes him aside. Mitch lunges[21] and strikes at Stanley. Stanley pushes Mitch back. Mitch collapses at the table, sobbing.

[During the preceding scenes, the Matron catches hold of Blanche's arm and prevents her flight. Blanche turns wildly and scratches at the Matron. The heavy woman pinions her arms. Blanche cries out hoarsely and slips to her knees.]

MATRON:

These fingernails have to be trimmed. [The Doctor comes into the room and she looks at him.] Jacket, Doctor?

DOCTOR:

Not unless necessary.

[He takes off his hat and now he becomes personalized. The unhuman quality goes. His voice is gentle and reassuring as he crosses to Blanche and crouches[22] in front of her. As he speaks her name, her terror subsides a little. The lurid reflections fade from the walls, the inhuman cries and noises die out and her own hoarse crying is calmed.]

DOCTOR:

Miss DuBois.

[She turns her face to him and stares at him with desperate pleading. He smiles; then he speaks to the Matron.]

It won't be necessary.

BLANCHE [faintly]:

Ask her to let go of me.

DOCTOR [to the Matron]:

Let go.

[The Matron releases her. Blanche extends her hands toward the Doctor. He draws her up gently and supports her with his arm and leads her through the portieres.]

BLANCHE [holding tight to his arm]:

Whoever you are—I have always depended on the kindness of strangers.

[The poker players stand back as Blanche and the Doctor cross the kitchen to the front door. She allows him to lead her as if she were blind. As they go out on the porch, Stella cries out her sister's name from where she iscrouched a few steps up on the stairs.]

STELLA:

Blanche! Blanche, Blanche!

[Blanche walks on without turning, followed by the Doctor and the Matron. They go around the corner of the building.]

[Eunice descends to Stella and places the child in her arms. It is wrapped in a pale blue blanket. Stella accepts the child, sobbingly. Eunice continues downstairs and enters the kitchen where the men, except for Stanley, are returning silently to their places about the table. Stanley has gone out on the porch and stands at the foot of the steps looking at Stella.]

STANLEY [a bit uncertainly]:

Stella?

[She sobs with inhuman abandon. There is something luxurious in her complete surrender to crying now that her sister is gone.]

STANLEY[voluptuously[23], soothingly]:

Now, honey. Now, love. Now, now, love. [He kneels beside her and his fingers find the opening of her blouse] Now, now, love. Now, love....

[The luxurious sobbing, the sensual murmur fade away under the swelling[24] music of the "blue piano" and the muted[25] trumpet.]

STEVE:

This game is seven-card stud[26].

注释（Notes）

1. portieres：门帘,门帷。
2. turquoise：绿松石色,青绿色。
3. Maldita sea tu suertol：西班牙语,你这该死的运气!（这句话是西班牙语,是一种比较情绪化、带有懊恼或埋怨意味的表达）
4. greaseball：外国佬。
5. rutting：处于发情期的。
6. Salerno：萨勒诺是意大利西南部港市,1943年9月8—18日盟国登陆部队和德军曾在该市沿岸激战。
7. stool：凳子。
8. bouclé：法语,绉纱衣服。
9. amber：琥珀色,黄褐色,蜜黄色。
10. Varsouviana：瓦索维亚纳舞曲。（瓦索维亚纳舞起源于19世纪,是模仿玛祖卡、波尔卡和雷多瓦等几种舞的一种舞蹈。）
11. vivacity：活力。
12. Della Robbia blue：所谓的"德拉·罗比亚蓝"是指意大利佛罗伦萨文艺复兴风格的先驱者之一,雕塑与制陶大师卢卡·德拉·罗比亚（1400—1482）制作的加釉赤陶浮雕和器皿所特有的颜色。他的代表作有佛罗伦萨大教堂的《耶稣复活》弧面窗及《耶稣升天》浮雕等,以他为开创者的德拉·罗比亚家族出过众多浮雕与彩陶大师。
13. quinine：奎宁,金鸡纳霜（过去用于治疗疟疾）。
14. Matron：（养老院及旧时医院中的）女护士长。
15. sinuous：摇曳生姿的,动作柔软的。
16. sotto voce：音乐术语,指小声地演奏或表演。
17. sinister：邪恶的,有害的,不祥的。
18. severe：简朴的,朴素的,不加修饰的。

19. reverberate:发出回声,回响,回荡。
20. talcum:爽身粉。
21. lunge:冲,扑,突然向前的动作。
22. crouch:蹲,蹲伏。
23. voluptuously:满足感官地,激起性欲地。
24. swelling:(声音)增强,变响亮。
25. muted:(声音,说话声)轻柔的。
26. seven-card stud:七牌戏(扑克),一种纸牌游戏。

主题探究(Themes)

(扫码阅读)

问题讨论(Questions for Discussion)

1. Does the play condemn or condone Stanley's type of masculinity? What or whom does *A Streetcar Named Desire* hold up as an ideal form of masculinity?

2. Is the Kowalski marriage a healthy one?

3. What is the play's view of the old South and its ideals—as something romantic to be admired, or as something archaic and no longer applicable?

4. Blanche says the only way to deal with a man like Stanley is to sleep with him. Is sex a means or an end for Blanche? For Stanley?

5. How is Blanche's drinking different from Stanley's drinking?

6. At the end of the play, has Blanche really lost touch with reality? Does she belong at a mental institution?

7. How is Blanche's tragedy related with the old South?

Unit 31
Black American Literature

Toni Morrison: *Beloved*
▽

作者简介 (Introduction to the Author)

Toni Morrison (1931—2019) is an important African American writer in contemporary American literature. Morrison was born and raised in Lorraine, Ohio. She was born in an extremely ordinary black family. Her mother worked as a maid in a white family and her father was a blue-collar worker. Even though she was born in such a common family, Morrison still studied hard and embarked on the road of black female literature. She graduated from Howard University with a bachelor's degree in English in 1953. In 1955, she received a master's degree in American literature from Cornell University. In 1957, she returned to Howard University, got married and had two children but she got divorced in 1964. Morrison became the first black female novel editor of Random House in New York City in the late 1960s. She established her reputation as a writer in the 1970s and 1980s. Morrison's works are praised for addressing the serious consequences of American racism and the experiences of American blacks. Her first novel, *The Bluest Eye*, was published in 1970. The critically acclaimed *Song of Solomon* (1977) brought her national attention and won the National Book Critics Circle Award. In 1988, Morrison won the Pulitzer Prize for *Beloved* (1987); she was awarded the Nobel Prize in Literature in 1993. She is the eighth woman who has won the Nobel Prize for literature since it was awarded in 1901, and the first black among the ten American writers who have won the prize. On the night of August 5, 2019, Toni Morrison died at the age of 88. People will always remember that Toni Morrison is the most famous and significant African-American woman writer.

作品简介 (Introduction to the Work)

A mother slits her baby girl's throat because she has this deranged idea that she's saving her daughter from a fate worse than death. Sounds like one of those crazy mothers who ends up on the evening news, but it's actually a true story: back in 1856, a runaway slave named Margaret Garner killed one of her kids—a two-year-old girl—with a butcher knife, in order to keep her away from slave catchers. She would have killed her other children and herself, too, but she was caught before she could complete the deed. And there you have the starting point for *Beloved*. This is one of those "based on a true story" books. But since the author is none other than the esteemed, Nobel Prize-winning Toni Morrison, you better believe that the book is way more than that story. The book is about a slave woman, Sethe, who—before the book even begins—kills her baby girl in order to keep her away from slave catchers. That baby girl, called Beloved, ends up haunting the house in which Sethe and her youngest child Denver live. But *Beloved* is more like a Great American Novel. It is a story about America's relationship with slavery, but it's also a story about rebirth and redemption for those who seem irredeemable. In the following chapter, schoolteacher showed up at the house with one of his nephews, the sheriff, and a slave catcher. In the woodshed, they found Sethe's sons, Howard and Buglar, lying in the sawdust, bleeding. Sethe was holding her bleeding daughter, whose throat she had cut with a saw. Stamp Paid rushed in and grabbed Denver before Sethe could dash her brains out against the wall. Because none of the children could ever be of any use as a slave, schoolteacher concluded that there was nothing worth claiming at 124 and left in disgust. Sethe's older daughter was dead, but Baby Suggs bound the boys' wounds and struggled with Sethe over Denver. Denver nursed at Sethe's breast, ingesting her dead sister's blood along with her mother's milk. The sheriff took Sethe, with Denver in her arms, to jail.

作品选文 (Selected Reading)

Beloved[1]
(Excerpt)
Part 1 Chapter 16

When the four horsemen came—schoolteacher[2], one nephew, one slave catcher[3] and a sheriff[4]—the house on Bluestone Road was so quiet they thought they were too late. Three of them dismounted[5], one stayed in the saddle[6], his rifle ready, his eyes trained away from the house to the left and to the right, because likely as not the fugitive would make a dash for[7] it. Although sometimes, you could never tell, you'd find them folded up tight somewhere: beneath floorboards, in a pantry[8]—once in a chimney. Even then care was taken, because the quietest ones, the ones you pulled from a press, a hayloft[9], or, that once, from a chimney, would go along nicely for two or three seconds. Caught redhanded, so to speak, they would seem to recognize the futility of outsmarting a whiteman and the hopelessness of outrunning a rifle. Smile even, like a child caught dead with his hand in the jelly jar[10], and when you reached for the rope to tie him, well, even then you couldn't tell. The very nigger with his head hanging and a little jelly-jar smile on his face could all of a sudden roar, like a bull or some such, and commence to do disbelievable things. Grab the rifle at its mouth; throw himself at the one holding it—anything. So you had to keep back a pace, leave the tying to another. Otherwise you ended up killing what you were paid to bring back alive. Unlike a snake or a bear, a dead nigger could not be skinned for profit and was not worth his own dead weight in coin.

Six or seven Negroes were walking up the road toward the house: two boys from the slave catcher's left and some women from his right. He motioned them still with his rifle and they stood where they were. The nephew came back from peeping inside the house, and after touching his lips for silence, pointed his thumb to say that what they were looking for was round back. The slave catcher dismounted then and joined the others. Schoolteacher and the nephew moved to the left of the house; himself and the sheriff to the right. A crazy old nigger was standing in the woodpile with an ax[11]. You could tell he was crazy right off because he was grunting—making low, cat noises like. About twelve yards beyond that nigger was another one—a woman with a flower in her hat. Crazy too, probably, because she too was standing stock-still[12]—but fanning her hands as though pushing cobwebs out of her way. Both, however, were staring at the same place—a shed. Nephew walked over to the old nigger boy and took the ax from him. Then all four started toward the shed.

Inside, two boys bled in the sawdust[13] and dirt at the feet of a nigger woman holding a blood-soaked child to her chest with one hand and an infant by the heels in the other. She did not look at them; she simply swung the baby toward the wall planks[14], missed and tried to connect a second time, when out of nowhere—in the ticking time the men spent staring at what there was to stare at—the old nigger boy, still mewing, ran through the door behind them and snatched[15] the baby from the arc[16] of its mother's swing.

Right off it was clear, to schoolteacher especially, that there was nothing there to claim. The three (now four—because she'd had the one coming when she cut) pickaninnies[17] they had hoped were alive and well enough to take back to Kentucky, take back and raise properly to do the work Sweet Home[18] desperately needed, were not. Two were lying open-eyed in sawdust; a third pumped blood down the dress of the main one— the woman schoolteacher bragged about, the one he said made fine ink, damn good soup, pressed his collars the way he liked besides having at least ten breeding years left. But now she'd gone wild, due to the mishandling of the nephew who'd overbeat her and made her cut and run. Schoolteacher had chastised[19] that nephew, telling him to think—just think—what would his own horse do if you beat it beyond the point of education. Or Chipper, or Samson. Suppose you beat the hounds past that point that away. Never again could you trust them in the woods or anywhere else. You'd be feeding them maybe, holding out a piece of rabbit in your hand, and the animal would revert—bite your hand clean off. So he punished that nephew by not letting him come on the hunt. Made him stay there, feed stock, feed himself, feed Lillian, tend crops. See how he liked it; see what happened when you overbeat creatures God had given you the responsibility of—the trouble it was, and the loss. The whole lot was lost now. Five. He could claim the baby struggling in the arms of the mewing old man, but who'd tend her? Because the woman—something was wrong with her. She was looking at him now, and if his other nephew could see that look he would learn the lesson for sure: you just can't mishandle creatures and expect success.

The nephew, the one who had nursed her while his brother held her down, didn't know he was shaking. His uncle had warned him against that kind of confusion, but the warning didn't seem to be taking. What she go and do that for? On account of a beating? Hell, he'd been beat a million times and he was white. Once it hurt so bad and made him so mad he'd smashed the well bucket. Another time he took it out on Samson—a few tossed rocks was all. But no beating ever made him… I mean no way he could have… What she go and do that for? And that is what he asked the sheriff, who was standing there amazed like the rest of them, but not shaking. He was swallowing hard, over and over again. "What she want to go and do that for?"

The sheriff turned, then said to the other three, "You all better go on. Look like your business is over. Mine's started now."

Schoolteacher beat his hat against his thigh and spit before leaving the woodshed. Nephew and the catcher backed out with him. They didn't look at the woman in the pepper plants with the flower in her hat. And they didn't look at the seven or so faces that had edged closer in spite of the catcher's rifle warning. Enough nigger eyes for now. Little nigger-boy eyes open in sawdust; little nigger-girl eyes staring between the wet fingers that held her face so her head wouldn't fall off; little nigger-baby eyes crinkling up to cry in the arms of the old nigger whose own eyes were nothing but slivers looking down at his feet. But the worst ones were those of the nigger woman who looked like she didn't have any. Since the whites in them had disappeared and since they were as black as her skin, she looked blind.

They unhitched[20] from schoolteacher's horse the borrowed mule that was to carry the fugitive woman back to where she belonged, and tied it to the fence. Then, with the sun straight up over their heads, they trotted off, leaving the sheriff behind among the damnedest bunch of coons they'd ever seen. All testimony to the results of a little so-called freedom imposed on people who needed every care and guidance in the world to keep them from the cannibal life they preferred.

The sheriff wanted to back out too. To stand in the sunlight outside of that place meant for housing wood, coal, kerosene—fuel for cold Ohio winters, which he thought of now, while resisting the urge to run into the August sunlight. Not because he was afraid. Not at all. He was just cold. And he didn't want to touch anything. The baby in the old man's arms was crying, and the woman's eyes with no whites were gazing straight ahead. They all might have remained that way, frozen till Thursday, except one of the boys on the floor sighed. As if he were sunk in the pleasure of a deep sweet sleep, he sighed the sigh that flung the sheriff into action.

"I'll have to take you in. No trouble now. You've done enough to last you. Come on now."

She did not move.

"You come quiet, hear, and I won't have to tie you up."

She stayed still and he had made up his mind to go near her and some kind of way bind her wet red hands when a shadow behind him in the doorway made him turn. The nigger with the flower in her hat entered.

Baby Suggs noticed who breathed and who did not and went straight to the boys lying in the dirt. The old man moved to the woman gazing and said, "Sethe. You take my armload and gimme[21] yours."

She turned to him, and glancing at the baby he was holding, made a low sound in her throat as though she'd made a mistake, left the salt out of the bread or something.

"I'm going out here and send for a wagon[22]," the sheriff said and got into the sunlight at last.

But neither Stamp Paid nor Baby Suggs could make her put her crawling-already? girl down. Out of the shed, back in the house, she held on. Baby Suggs had got the boys inside and was bathing their heads, rubbing their hands, lifting their lids, whispering, "Beg your pardon, I beg your pardon," the whole time. She bound their wounds and made them breathe camphor before turning her attention to Sethe. She took the crying baby from Stamp Paid and carried it on her shoulder for a full two minutes, then stood in front of its mother.

"It's time to nurse your youngest," she said.

Sethe reached up for the baby without letting the dead one go.

Baby Suggs shook her head. "One at a time," she said and traded the living for the dead, which she carried into the keeping room. When she came back, Sethe was aiming a bloody nipple into the baby's mouth. Baby Suggs slammed her fist on the table and shouted, "Clean up! Clean yourself up!"

They fought then. Like rivals over the heart of the loved, they fought. Each struggling for the nursing child. Baby Suggs lost when she slipped in a red puddle and fell. So Denver took her mother's milk right along with the blood of her sister. And that's the way they were when the sheriff returned, having commandeered[23] a neighbor's cart, and ordered Stamp to drive it.

Outside a throng, now, of black faces stopped murmuring. Holding the living child, Sethe walked past them in their silence and hers. She climbed into the cart, her profile knife-clean[24] against a cheery blue sky. A profile that shocked them with its clarity. Was her head a bit too high? Her back a little too straight? Probably. Otherwise the singing would have begun at once, the moment she appeared in the doorway of the house on Bluestone Road. Some cape of sound would have quickly been wrapped around her, like arms to hold and steady her on the way. As it was, they waited till the cart turned about, headed west to town. And then no words. Humming. No words at all.

Baby Suggs meant to run, skip down the porch steps after the cart, screaming, No. No. Don't let her take that last one too. She meant to. Had started to, but when she got up from the floor and reached the yard the cart was gone and a wagon was rolling up[25]. A red-haired boy and a yellow-haired girl jumped down and ran through the crowd beloved toward her. The boy had a half-eaten sweet pepper in one hand and a pair of shoes in the other.

"Mama says Wednesday." He held them together by their tongues[26]. "She says you got to have these fixed by Wednesday."

Baby Suggs looked at him, and then at the woman holding a twitching[27] lead horse to the road.

"She says Wednesday, you hear? Baby? Baby?"

She took the shoes from him—high-topped and muddy—saying, "I beg your pardon. Lord, I beg your pardon. I sure do."

Out of sight, the cart creaked[28] on down Bluestone Road. Nobody in it spoke. The wagon rock had put the baby to sleep. The hot sun dried Sethe's dress, stiff, like rigor mortis[29].

注释（Notes）

1. Beloved：心爱的人，本书译作"宠儿"，系塞丝亲手杀死的女儿的名字。
2. schoolteacher：农庄主，加纳先生的妹夫。
3. slave catcher：猎奴者。
4. sheriff：（美国的）县治安官。
5. dismounted：下马，下车。
6. saddle：鞍，马鞍。

7. make a dash for：向……猛冲。

8. pantry：餐具室,食品储藏室。

9. hayloft：干草堆。

10. the jelly jar：果酱罐。

11. ax：斧头。

12. stock-still：静止地。

13. sawdust：锯末,木屑。

14. planks：木板,板材。

15. snatched：一把抓起(某物),夺。

16. arc：弧,弧状物体。

17. pickaninnies：(常冒犯)小黑崽子。

18. Sweet Home：甜蜜之家,塞丝十八年前逃离的农庄名。

19. chastised：厉声训斥,严厉谴责。

20. unhitched：解下(或解开)(套绳等);解下(套住的东西)。

21. gimme：give me。

22. wagon：(运)货车。

23. commandeered：征用。

24. knife-clean：刀锋般光洁的。

25. rolling up：到达。

26. their tongues：这里指鞋舌头。

27. twitching：抽动。

28. creaked：嘎吱嘎吱作响。

29. rigor mortis：一个源自拉丁语的医学术语,在英语中翻译为"stiffness of death",即死亡的僵硬。

主题探究（Themes）

(扫码阅读)

问题讨论（Questions for Discussion）

1. Was Sethe justified in killing Beloved? Why or why not?

2. Is Beloved a ghost? Is she a dead person come back to life? Or is she a random

girl who's been possessed by the spirit of Beloved?

3. Why is the book separated into three parts?

4. If you were to pick one narrative perspective for the book (instead of the several that make up the book), whose perspective would you pick? Why?

5. The end of the book makes it so that we're not entirely sure what happened to Beloved. Do you think Beloved is gone by the end of the book, or do you think she's still around?

6. How would you feel about Sethe if Sethe were a man—a father who killed his child?

7. What would this story be like if Sethe and her kids weren't African American? Could the story even exist?

Unit 32
Chinese American literature

Amy Tan: *The Joy Luck Club*
▽

作者简介 (Introduction to the Author)

Amy Tan (1952—), a famous Chinese American female writer, was born in Oakland, California. She grew up there and attended primary and secondary school. In 1966, her father and older brother both died from brain tumors. Shortly after these sad passings, Tan's mother moved her and her younger brother to Switzerland. She and her mother didn't get along well when she was in high school. Many of the challenges between them stem from Amy Tan's rejection of Chinese culture. In 1969, the family returned to San Francisco, where Tan could go to college. She majored in English after deciding that pre-medicine was not suitable for her (this decision, together with Tan's decision to move with her boyfriend, led to a greater rift between mother and daughter). The rich heritage and raw struggles of Tan's family inspired her to start writing. Amy Tan's mother told her a secret in her later years: Tan has three more half-sisters in Chinese Mainland. The secret deeply shocked Amy Tan and then it became the theme of her creation. In 1987, Amy Tan wrote *The Joy Luck Club* based on the experiences of her grandmother and mother, and published the book in 1989. This book was a great success as soon as it was published. This book has won a series of literary awards such as the "American Book Award". As one of the most popular Chinese American writers, Amy Tan occupies a special position in American literature. The themes of cultural conflict, generation gap and the emotional confusion of the protagonist reflected in her works attract a large number of readers.

作品简介 (Introduction to the Work)

The Joy Luck Club is a 1989 novel written by Amy Tan. It focuses on four Chinese immigrant families in San Francisco who start a club known as the Joy Luck Club, playing the Chinese game of mahjong for money while feasting on a variety of foods. The book is structured similarly to a mahjong game, with four parts divided into four sections to create sixteen chapters. Each part is preceded by a parable relating to the themes within that section. The three mothers and four daughters (one mother, Suyuan Woo, dies before the novel opens) share stories about their lives in the form of short vignettes. Meet Suyuan,

An-mei, Lindo, and Ying-ying. These mothers all left China in the middle of the 20th Century for America, where they all hoped they could forge a better life and raise happy families. They're all deeply informed by their cultural heritage: their views on child-rearing, education, marriage, and careers are all based in Chinese custom and philosophy. These moms know they know what's best. Now meet their daughters: Jing-mei, Waverly, Lena, and Rose. These women have been raised in San Francisco and, while they all have a vested interest in their cultural heritage, they also have a vested interest in becoming "American". These daughters are interested in become empowered women of the 1980's, with the jobs, the power suits, and the hairstyles that entails. These daughters know they know what's best. In a twist that's actually no twist at all, these moms and daughters don't always see eye-to-eye. We get a glimpse into all of these women's worldviews and histories, moving between character perspectives in order to understand the complications that plague all family relationships and the special complications that arise from a generational clash and a cultural clash all at once. In the excerpt, Jing-mei opens her narrative by explaining that after her mother, Suyuan, died two months ago, her father, Canning, asked her to take her mother's place at the Joy Luck Club. Suyuan and Canning Woo have been attending the meetings of the Joy Luck Club since 1949, shortly after they emigrated from China to San Francisco. In fact, the San Francisco version of the club is a revival of the club Suyuan founded earlier, while she was still in China. Jing-mei tells her mother's story about the club's beginning.

作品选文 (Selected Reading)

The Joy Luck Club
(Excerpt)
Jing-Mei Woo: The Joy Luck Club

My father has asked me to be the fourth corner at the Joy Luck Club. I am to replace my mother, whose seat at the mah jong table has been empty since she died two months ago. My father thinks she was killed by her own thoughts.

"She had a new idea inside her head," said my father. "But before it could come out of her mouth, the thought grew too big and burst. It must have been a very bad idea."

The doctor said she died of a cerebral aneurysm[1]. And her friends at the Joy Luck Club said she died just like a rabbit: quickly and with unfinished business left behind. My mother was supposed to host the next meeting of the Joy Luck Club.

The week before she died, she called me, full of pride, full of life: "Auntie Lin cooked red bean soup for Joy Luck. I'm going to cook black sesame-seed soup."

"Don't show off," I said.

"It's not showoff." She said the two soups were almost the same, chabudwo[2]. Or maybe she said butong[3], not the same thing at all. It was one of those Chinese expressions that means the better half of mixed intentions. I can never remember things I didn't understand in the first place.

My mother started the San Francisco version of the Joy Luck Club in 1949, two years before I was born. This was the year my mother and father left China with one stiff leather trunk[4] filled only with fancy silk dresses. There was no time to pack anything else, my mother had explained to my father after they boarded the boat. Still his hands swam frantically between the slippery silks, looking for his cotton shirts and wool pants.

When they arrived in San Francisco, my father made her hide those shiny clothes. She wore the same brown-checked Chinese dress until the Refugee Welcome Society gave her two hand-me-down dresses, all too large in sizes for American women. The society was composed of a group of white-haired American missionary ladies from the First Chinese Baptist Church[5]. And because of their gifts, my parents could not refuse their invitation to join the church. Nor could they ignore the old ladies' practical advice to improve their English through Bible study class on Wednesday nights and, later, through choir[6] practice on Saturday mornings. This was how my parents met the Hsus, the Jongs, and the St. Clairs. My mother could sense that the women of these families also had unspeakable tragedies they had left behind in China and hopes they couldn't begin to express in their fragile English. Or at least, my mother recognized the numbness in these women's faces. And she saw how quickly their eyes moved when she told them her idea for the Joy Luck Club.

Joy Luck was an idea my mother remembered from the days of her first marriage in Kweilin[7], before the Japanese came. That's why I think of Joy Luck as her Kweilin story. It was the story she would always tell me when she was bored, when there was nothing to do, when every bowl had been washed and the Formica table had been wiped down twice, when my father sat reading the newspaper and smoking one Pall Mall cigarette[8] after another, a warning not to disturb him. This is when my mother would take out a box of old ski sweaters sent to us by unseen relatives from Vancouver. She would snip[9] the bottom of a sweater and pull out a kinky[10] thread of yarn, anchoring[11] it to a piece of cardboard. And as she began to roll with one sweeping rhythm, she would start her story. Over the years, she told me the same story, except for the ending, which grew darker, casting long shadows into her life, and eventually into mine.

"I dreamed about Kweilin before I ever saw it," my mother began, speaking Chinese. "I dreamed of jagged[12] peaks lining a curving river, with magic moss greening the banks.

At the tops of these peaks were white mists. And if you could float down this river and eat the moss for food, you would be strong enough to climb the peak. If you slipped, you would only fall into a bed of soft moss and laugh. And once you reached the top, you would be able to see everything and feel such happiness it would be enough to never have worries in your life ever again."

In China, everybody dreamed about Kweilin. And when I arrived, I realized how shabby my dreams were, how poor my thoughts. When I saw the hills, I laughed and shuddered at the same time. The peaks looked like giant fried fish heads trying to jump out of a vat of oil. Behind each hill, I could see shadows of another fish, and then another and another. And then the clouds would move just a little and the hills would suddenly become monstrous elephants marching slowly toward me! Can you see this? And at the root of the hill were secret caves. Inside grew hanging rock[13] gardens in the shapes and colors of cabbage, winter melons[14], turnips[15], and onions. These were things so strange and beautiful you can't ever imagine them.

"But I didn't come to Kweilin to see how beautiful it was. The man who was my husband brought me and our two babies to Kweilin because he thought we would be safe. He was an officer with the Kuomintang[16], and after he put us down in a small room in a two-story house, he went off to the northwest, to Chungking[17]."

"We knew the Japanese were winning, even when the newspapers said they were not. Every day, every hour, thousands of people poured into the city, crowding the sidewalks, looking for places to live. They came from the East, West, North, and South. They were rich and poor, Shanghainese[18], Cantonese[19], northerners[20], and not just Chinese, but foreigners and missionaries of every religion. And there was, of course, the Kuomintang and their army officers who thought they were top level to everyone else."

We were a city of leftovers mixed together. If it hadn't been for the Japanese, there would have been plenty of reason for fighting to break out among these different people. Can you see it? Shanghai people with north-water peasants, bankers with barbers, rickshaw pullers[21] with Burma[22] refugees. Everybody looked down on someone else. It didn't matter that everybody shared the same sidewalk to spit on and suffered the same fast-moving diarrhea. We all had the same stink[23], but everybody complained someone else smelled the worst. Me? Oh, I hated the American air force officers who said habba-habba sounds to make my face turn red. But the worst were the northern peasants who emptied their noses into their hands and pushed people around and gave everybody their dirty diseases.

"So you can see how quickly Kweilin lost its beauty for me. I no longer climbed the peaks to say, How lovely are these hills! I only wondered which hills the Japanese had reached. I sat in the dark corners of my house with a baby under each arm, waiting with nervous feet. When the sirens cried out to warn us of bombers, my neighbors and I jumped to our feet[24] and scurried[25] to the deep caves to hide like wild animals. But you can't stay in the dark for so long. Something inside of you starts to fade and you become like a starving person, crazy-hungry for light. Outside I could hear the bombing. Boom! Boom! And then the sound of raining rocks. And inside I was no longer hungry for the cabbage or the turnips of the hanging rock garden. I could only see the dripping bowels of an ancient hill that might collapse on top of me. Can you imagine how it is, to want to be neither inside nor outside, to want to be nowhere and disappear?"

So when the bombing sounds grew farther away, we would come back out like newborn kittens scratching our way back to the city. And always, I would be amazed to find the hills against the burning sky had not been torn apart.

"I thought up Joy Luck on a summer night that was so hot even the moths fainted to the ground, their wings were so heavy with the damp heat. Every place was so crowded there was no room for fresh air. Unbearable smells from the sewers[26] rose up to my second-story window and the stink had nowhere else to go but into my nose. At all hours of the night and day, I heard screaming sounds. I didn't know if it was a peasant slitting the throat of a runaway pig or an officer beating a half-dead peasant for lying in his way on the sidewalk. I didn't go to the window to find out. What use would it have been? And that's when I thought I needed something to do to help me move."

My idea was to have a gathering of four women, one for each corner of my mah jong table. I knew which women I wanted to ask. They were all young like me, with wishful faces. One was an army officer's wife, like myself. Another was a girl with very fine manners from a rich family in Shanghai. She had escaped with only a little money. And there was a girl from Nanking[27] who had the blackest hair I have ever seen. She came from a low-class family, but she was pretty and pleasant and had married well, to an old man who died and left her with a better life.

"Each week one of us would host a party to raise money and to raise our spirits. The hostess had to serve special dyansyinfoods[28] to bring good fortune of all kinds—dumplings shaped like silver money ingots[29], long rice noodles for long life, boiled peanuts for conceiving sons, and of course, many good-luck oranges for a plentiful, sweet life."

What fine food we treated ourselves to with our meager allowances! We didn't notice that the dumplings were stuffed mostly with stringy[30] squash and that the oranges were spotted with wormy holes. We ate sparingly, not as if we didn't have enough, but to protest how we could not eat another bite, we had already bloated ourselves from earlier in the day. We knew we had luxuries few people could afford. We were the lucky ones.

"After filling our stomachs, we would then fill a bowl with money and put it where everyone could see. Then we would sit down at the mah jong table. My table was from my family and was of a very fragrant red wood, not what you call rosewood[31], but hong mu[32], which is so fine there's no English word for it. The table had a very thick pad, so that when the mah jong paiwere spilled onto the table the only sound was of ivory tiles washing against one another."

Once we started to play, nobody could speak, except to say 'Pung[33]!' or 'Chr[34]!' when taking a tile. We had to play with seriousness and think of nothing else but adding to our happiness through winning. But after sixteen rounds, we would again feast, this time to celebrate our good fortune. And then we would talk into the night until the morning, saying stories about good times in the past and good times yet to come.

"Oh, what good stories! Stories spilling out all over the place! We almost laughed to death. A rooster that ran into the house screeching on top of dinner bowls, the same bowls that held him quietly in pieces the next day! And one about a girl who wrote love letters for two friends who loved the same man. And a silly foreign lady who fainted on a toilet when firecrackers went off next to her."

People thought we were wrong to serve banquets every week while many people in the city were starving, eating rats and, later, the garbage that the poorest rats used to feed on. Others thought we were possessed by demons—to celebrate when even within our own families we had lost generations, had lost homes and fortunes, and were separated, husband from wife, brother from sister, daughter from mother. Hnnnh! How could we laugh, people asked.

It's not that we had no heart or eyes for pain. We were all afraid. We all had our miseries. But to despair was to wish back for something already lost. Or to prolong what was already unbearable. How much can you wish for a favorite warm coat that hangs in the closet of a house that burned down with your mother and father inside of it? How long can you see in your mind arms and legs hanging from telephone wires and starving dogs running down the streets with half-chewed hands dangling from their jaws? What was worse, we asked among ourselves, to sit and wait for our own deaths with proper somber faces? Or to choose our own happiness?

"So we decided to hold parties and pretend each week had become the new year. Each week we could forget past wrongs done to us. We weren't allowed to think a bad thought. We feasted, we laughed, we played games, lost and won, we told the best stories. And each week, we could hope to be lucky. That hope was our only joy. And that's how we came to call our little parties Joy Luck."

注释(Notes)

1. cerebral aneurysm：脑动脉瘤。
2. chabudwo：差不多。
3. butong：不同。
4. trunk：(放衣物的)大箱子,旅行箱。
5. the First Chinese Baptist Church：第一中国浸礼会。
6. choir：合唱团,(教堂)唱诗班。
7. Kweilin：桂林。
8. Pall Mall cigarette：Pall Mall 系英美烟草 British American Tobacco Group (BAT)生产的香烟品牌,音译为"波迈",也称"长红"。
9. snip：(多指用剪刀迅速地)剪。
10. kinky：卷曲的。
11. anchoring：把……系住,使稳住,使固定。
12. jagged：凹凸不平的。
13. rock：这里指的是钟乳石。
14. winter melons：冬瓜。
15. turnips：萝卜。
16. Kuomintang：国民党。
17. Chungking：重庆。
18. Shanghainese：上海人。
19. Cantonese：广东人。
20. northerners：北方人。
21. rickshaw pullers：黄包车夫。
22. Burma：缅甸。
23. stink：恶臭,异味。
24. jumped to our feet：一跃而起,"腾"地一下蹦起来。
25. scurried：(人,小动物)小步快跑。
26. sewers：下水道,阴沟。
27. Nanking：南京。
28. dyansyinfoods：点心小吃。
29. ingots：锭,铸块。
30. stringy：(食物)多纤维的,有筋的。
31. rosewood：黄檀木。
32. hong mu：红木。
33. Pung：碰。
34. Chr：吃。

主题探究 (Themes)

(扫码阅读)

问题讨论 (Questions for Discussion)

1. Who transforms in this novel? In what ways do they change?

2. Do you agree that friendship is significantly less important than motherhood in *The Joy Luck Club* and blood trumps every other type of relationship in this novel?

3. How does the older generation of women view America? Is it positive overall?

4. Do you agree that the older generation of women in *The Joy Luck Club* remain foreign in the U.S. despite living in America for many, many years?

5. The first parable includes a woman who hopes that in America her daughter's worth won't be "measured by the loudness of her husband's belch." In America how is the worth of the women of this book judged?

6. There are four different mother-daughter stories presented here. What kinds of universal truths about mothers and daughters, if any, can you draw out of these stories? That is, what are the similarities in all the mother-daughter stories?

7. Suyuan seems to think that being Chinese is in your DNA and therefore her daughter is Chinese. Lindo, on the other hand, seems pretty sure that Waverly is not at all Chinese. Why the difference of opinions? Do you agree with either Suyuan or Lindo?

(请扫码观看视频 *The Joy Luck Club*)